CHILDREN OF MU

Daniele Azara

*To my father: without your collection of books and comics
this book would not exist.*

*To my mother: you taught me what a mother is willing to do
for her children.*

*To Ilaria: because everything makes sense
and we both know it.*

And finally to Aaron: through your eyes, I understand.

Contents

北極
北
北洲
INTERIOR UPPER INTERREGNUM
MEDIUM SMALL INTERREGNUM
西洲
中洲
海
食人国
西洋
MEDIUM LOWER INTERREGNUM
VII REIGN
II REIGN
天空
IX REIGN
MU
THE JUDGES CHAMBER OF TIME

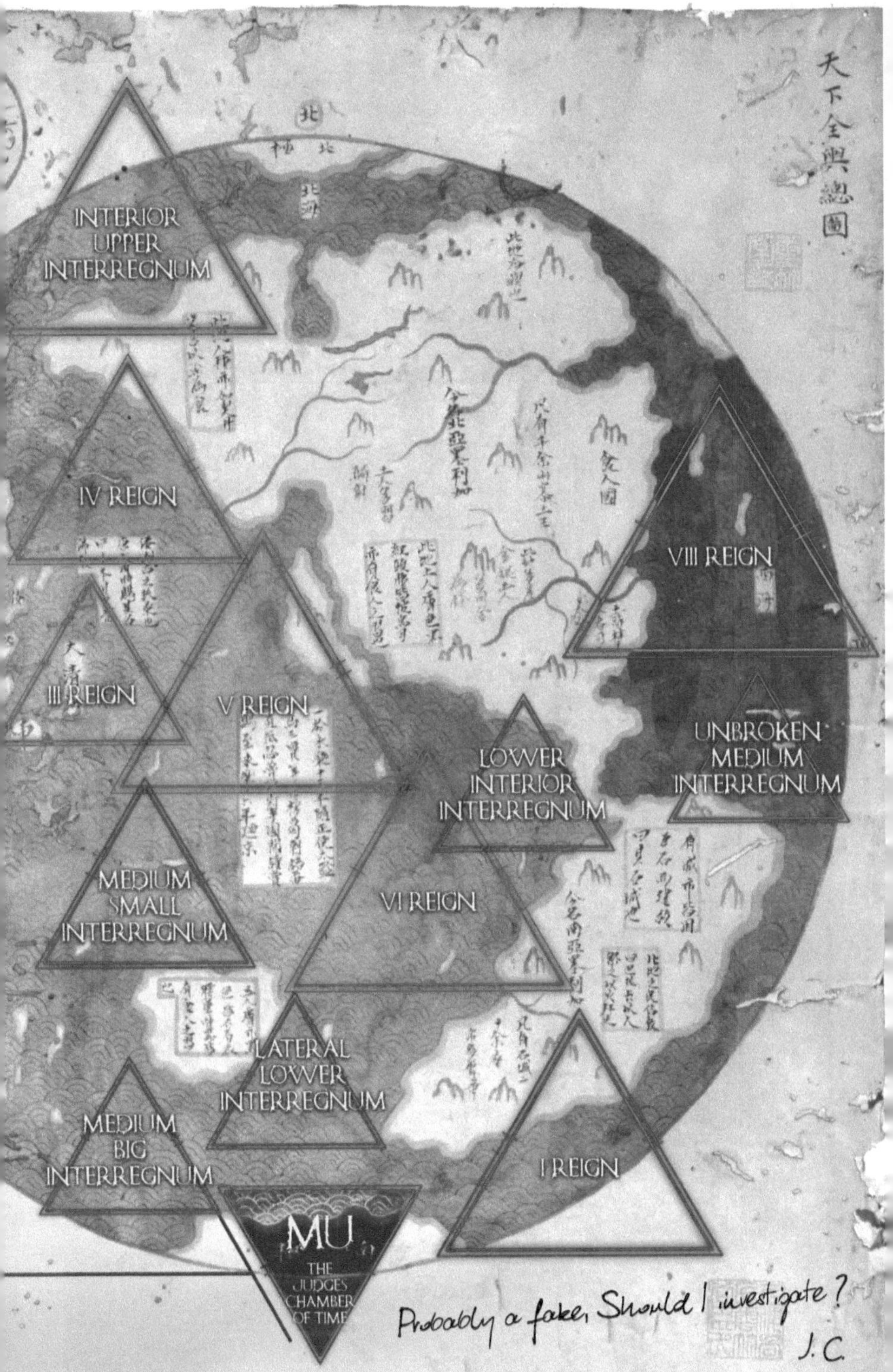

天下全輿總圖

INTERIOR
UPPER
INTERREGNUM

IV REIGN

III REIGN

V REIGN

VIII REIGN

LOWER
INTERIOR
INTERREGNUM

UNBROKEN
MEDIUM
INTERREGNUM

MEDIUM
SMALL
INTERREGNUM

VI REIGN

LATERAL
LOWER
INTERREGNUM

MEDIUM
BIG
INTERREGNUM

I REIGN

MU
THE
JUDGES
CHAMBER
OF TIME

Probably a fake, Should I investigate?

J.C.

Prologue

Being fourteen is difficult, and it sucks. So young Adam Uyan thought. Not for the thousands of neuronal connections that bloom like mushrooms in a wood in the head of a teenager at every single heartbeat, nor for the hormones, bulky chemical substances that can put the body and mind through catastrophic and uncontrollable mutations.

For Adam, it was reality to be difficult and to suck. It made him feel inadequate. Too many questions without any answers.

How do you express your thoughts when they're marked by uncertainty? How do you turn into music such delicate arrangements, forcing them to be played by empty cans of canned beans?

Of course, Adam did not ask these questions – he lacked the vocabulary – but, like every fourteen-year-old, he wanted to have the power to express himself or, better still, to be heard. All his concentration was aimed at widening the passage, to find the right way to refine the instruments he had been given. Yet somewhere within himself, Adam ended up confronting the overwhelming feeling, oppressing and stifling, that there was not enough time to walk such a long and inscrutable road. Watching life from his fourteen years of experience made it look short, a repetitive cliché of duties toward parents, teachers, or bosses; towards a woman he would one day marry and then look at with boredom and resentment until his nineties, or towards his unborn child. And although Adam had a clear idea of how he had come to the world, he couldn't understand what kind of folly took hold of people to make them want to relive that infernal cycle.

When his feet touched the rough and smooth stones of the shores of the great lake, Adam shivered. He was an active boy, robust and used to swimming. But that day in late July, the water appeared dark and felt cold, despite the already blazing sun.

The southern part of the lake was reserved for tourists and was crowded by people who had reached the renowned summer resort since the early hours of the morning, winning the crazy lottery of a dusty parking lot on that sweltering Saturday. Like every year, Adam's family had rented a bungalow in the exclusive part of the resort, well away from the public areas and from which they could access a private, clean, quiet beach.

On the public side, sunshades and colourful loungers tinted the volcanic sand. The drumming music of the kiosks created an indistinct carpet of sounds that mingled with voices, penetrating the still waters of the lake, where hundreds of people cackled euphorically. They also rented small yellow pedal craft, from which improvised divers performed a hundred metres from the shore. It was all business as usual; Adam knew it after ten years of regular summer attendance.

So he threw away his thoughts, braced himself and held up the plastic and aluminium paddle, but only after he had put on his red lifejacket. Ever since Maggie Ryan had told him that the red of his jacket looked mighty fine against his jet-black hair, Adam wore it all the time, making his parents happy as well, busy as they often were discussing politics with their umbrella neighbours, the Farrells.

Fortunately, Adam had the canoe to keep him busy during the long morning hours. His friends must have had a late night and were likely still under the sheets in their air-conditioned refurbished bungalows' rooms.

With a firm grip, the boy caught the canoe from the shore and pulled it into the water. Splashing it to avoid salt scaling, since the lake was once connected to the sea, he was scrupulous in wetting first his wrists, then his face and neck.

With a last glance to his parents, he wondered if that sense of inadequacy in expressing one's thoughts did not affect adults as well. Their movements and tone of voice didn't show any uncertainty. But perhaps, Adam thought, it was all confidence betraying an intimate, shaky truth that had not abandoned them since they were kids.

Sophie, his mother, looked for a moment in his direction and, holding her hat by the broad brim, waved at him. Adam greeted her back before taking his seat, tucking his legs in the belly of the small boat.

With a few well-balanced paddle strokes, the canoe speeded up swiftly, leaving the noises to fade behind. As the tranquillity of the lake allowed his mind to get rid of the world, Adam began to appreciate the heat of the sun on his tanned skin. He kept a quiet and soft rhythm so that the canoe seemed to go by itself, slipping silently on the liquid fabric of the lake. Small red buoys bobbed a hundred meters away. Loud chattering attracted Adam's attention. Some of the older boys had begun to dive from their pedal boats, laughing.

They went further out than usual, he thought as he rowed with more determination.

Maggie. It was there that his mind headed every time it was possible to free it. That thought was his secret place, his hidden star. Even just thinking about her made everything sweet and intimate. A feeling of peace that, though broad, he didn't have to explain to anyone or translate into any language. When he thought of Maggie, he imagined situations where she was charming and affectionate.

In these travels of the heart and mind, they went out together hand in hand, to the theme park or the cinema, ending the evening on the beach with a long, passionate kiss. Adam didn't dare to go beyond the kiss in his fantasy. With other girls, his mind wandered in more or less feasible situations, but even the mere thought of combining Maggie with sex revolted him, as if she were something to defend from that strange and somewhat brutal world.

The red buoys. Where had they gone? Adam looked around and realised he had gone far beyond the bathing waters. Turning, he noticed that he had passed the small safety nets. Not that the lake was dangerous, but often in the summer, because of the fires, tanker aircraft came gathering water to be thrown on the frequent blazes on the hills, so it wasn't smart to stay too long so far out.

With a peek to the cloudless sky, it was quite easy to see that there was no fire in the vicinity, or even yellow and red twin-engined planes gliding over the lake with their low, deafening rumble. In fact, in the shadowy part of the lake, the one on which the tallest hill stood reflected, it seemed to him that the sounds had gone as well as the light. He could see the rowdy boys on their pedalos pushing each other and ending up in the water, but almost no longer heard their voices.

It's so peaceful, he thought.

Relaxing backwards, Adam sighed. The water was dark, almost black from the shade and depth – over 100 meters. But it was a placid, brilliant and clean water.

"Maggie," he whispered, tasting every letter.

When he was alone, and sure he could not be heard, Adam succeeded to overcome any kind of barrier pronouncing that name. Although Maggie was as cheeky to him as to anyone else, he knew she had a big heart. He had known that before the summer holidays when, on the subway away from the people of Saint Paul, she had handed him one of the iPod's headphones, allowing them to listen to *Umbrella* together.

She hadn't said anything.

At the end of the song, she had smiled before joining her stupid friends. How he hated them and how much he hated that school. No one could feel normal going to a school like that, full of kids with behavioural needs. Saint Paul could have changed a Pokemon, Adam thought, halfway between irony and bitterness. Luckily there was Maggie every day.

Realising how much time had passed, and fearing his parents would have a nervous breakdown, Adam decided to return to the red buoy line and slipped the paddle into the water.

He didn't immediately realise what had happened.

One hand was bleeding, and the other was sore.

There was no trace of the paddle, except for the water lapping against the base of his swaying canoe. He looked around. His mind had made such a leap from his thoughts on Maggie Ryan to the lost paddle that it took a few seconds to rationalise what had happened. The paddle had been torn off him with such force that its upper part, slipping down, had scratched and burned his hands.

Without the paddle, he couldn't move.

Adam looked around again, a feeling of panic growing. He was sure it wasn't a joke. There was nobody around and no one could remain underwater for so long. No bubbles, no suspicious movements. There were no sharks or big fish in the lake, that was certain. He knew the place very well.

Nothing seemed to make sense.

His hands now bled a lot and were hurting badly. Adam had to find the courage to pull his legs off the canoe, balance on the seat and crouch on the saddle. He was too far out for someone to hear him call, or for swimming back towards the beach. But he could get help from the boys on the pedal boats.

Again, like ten minutes before, he shuddered at the thought of getting into the water, but there was no other way. Taking a deep breath, he filled his lungs, preparing to swim with all his strength and without stopping, all the way to the red buoys. With his muscles warmed up from all the activity and the adrenaline, Adam got set to tackle the heavy water of the lake on his way to safety.

He was ready. Relaxing his legs, he dived into a three metre long arc, flying stretched from the boat. Immediately before entering the water, he seemed to glimpse not its own reflection, but the darting of large, brilliant eyes and a huge, frightening grin. Adam ended his dive with an excellent dip, slipping into the water almost without raising any sprays.

And he never came back to the surface.

PART ONE

INTO A PERFECT WORLD

*"What we see depends on how we look;
the structures of matter reflect the structures of the mind."*

Fritjof Capra

1

The clock, tall and grey, ticked in the headmaster's office. The long moments of silence between Mrs Fawcett and Mr Richardson were marked by that sound, familiar and disturbing at once. Every movement of the second hand seemed to last an eternity, its sound sudden, angry and powerful like a hammer blow on a nail. The same nail that Andrew Fawcett had felt planted in his head from the moment he had opened his eyes that morning.

"Headmaster Richardson," Emily continued, repeating for the umpteenth time the name of the old, but still good-looking man seated behind the huge desk, "I'm sure Andy will be happy in this institution and that he will behave very well."

The man looked slightly puzzled at the woman, who was smiling in the same exact way as when she had entered a short while before. "Mrs Fawcett, I read here that your son has never had discipline issues related to violent or antisocial behaviour, which are in fact the daily bread of this institute. Are you sure you want him to join Saint Paul? The government has provided you with several alternatives in the area, and it is my suggestion that you evaluate other places more suited to the needs of the boy."

Emily seemed confused, gave a sideways look at her son and continued, "Mr Richardson, as you know we have only recently moved to the city, and it was by chance that I was able to keep my old job. I have to commute 25 miles every morning to reach my workplace, and this institute is really the only one that would allow me to arrive on time."

"Madam, maybe I did not explain myself properly..."

"No, no," Emily interrupted him, "you've explained yourself very well, Headmaster Richardson. But see here, Andy is a quiet and responsible young man. I'm sure he'll stay out of trouble."

"Mum..." Andrew said, trying to intervene in a dialogue in which he was the silent protagonist.

"My love, trust me," she comforted him, placing a hand on his knee.

The man looked on patiently. "I cannot stop you from enrolling your son at Saint Paul, but I would like him to decide," he concluded. Then he turned to the boy, leaning on his elbows over the desk. "Andy, you look like a bright boy. Do you know why you are here?"

"Because I've had problems in other schools, Mr Richardson." The mother had repeated that name so many times that it felt weird pronouncing it, as if it were a mantra.

"Can you tell me about it?"

"Yes, sir. Non-violent, antisocial behaviours. According to my teachers, I was disinterested in learning and social relationships. I can't deny either."

The headmaster stared at him with some intensity. A thick aftershave reached Andy and for a moment he found himself back to normality, when his Dad was still with his Mum and still wearing his fresh and impressive morning cologne. The man closed the file with the name "Andrew Fawcett" printed on it by the Department of Education.

"You must know that this institute was created roughly eighty years ago by a very generous lord who wanted to provide an education for kids who had trouble getting into national schools. Did you know that?"

"Yes, sir. It means that it gathers all those nasty characters destined to become criminals, rejected by the rest of the world because they are considered unsuitable and that would normally be diluted between the ordinary people in normal schools."

"Andy!" cut in Emily, staring at the ground in his direction. "Do not be rude to Mr Richardson!" she intimated, continuing to look down. She never looked at him when she told him off. Perhaps she felt guilty about not being able to hold on to her husband, thought Andy sometimes. But then he would think again.

Andy was very worried about his Mum's psychological health. Since moving to the new home, her mood had worsened. Often she had a strange and sweet smell of alcohol about her and was unstable. At night she wept and had become even more protective of her son, so much so that on a few occasions Andy had felt like the roles had been reversed and that he had become the parent.

"It wasn't rude," said the headmaster. "It is perfectly fine to express an opinion, and Andy did it with manners," he declared. "However, I do hope you don't think what you said. Nobody here is refusing you, Mr Fawcett, and Saint Paul is a normal school, albeit with its own rules."

This man is either crazy, or lying, or is an idealist, Andy thought.

"In any case," Richardson was saying, "if you decide to join us, I will not be preventing you. It would be a pleasure to have a gifted student like you." He stretched out a hand towards him. Even if he did not smile, it was clear that he loved his job and that he was sincere, at least in the way he spoke.

Andy turned briefly towards his mother. Emily smiled at him proudly, as if to invite him to shake hands with that stranger who had just tried to lecture him. He felt guilty. She was bending over backwards, and he could not even convince his own Dad to remain with them. He didn't feel like creating more problems over the choice of a school – to him, it didn't matter where he went. It was not the first time he had enrolled and probably would not be the last.

He had to admit he had no choice. He smiled courteously and stretched over the table. He really hoped with all his heart that entering this school did not equate to his death sentence. Saint Paul – the school for young people unsuitable to society…

2

Tonos was an unusual name. Anyone in the world could think that; however, it was odd even among the members of his own large family.

The names of his nearest relatives were, in fact, softer and less suspicious, like Aminion, his father, Nermala, his mother or Cunion, his brother. Tonos thought that his name concealed a hint of isolation and loneliness. Often, as a child, he had felt neglected and over time he had diluted the relationship with his closest loved ones, perhaps for fear of suffering or perhaps because of his soul was colder than that of his kin. His introverted side had made him a stranger with his own people, who had been known since time immemorial as Fir Bolg.

Tonos had been raised according to the customs of his people. He had not tarried and, thirty years before, while the world was busy with the Cold War, believing in being in charge of his own destiny, he had taken the typical bags that gave his people their name and left. Travelling the world, at times on the surface but mainly via the Great Roads hidden in the Mother's womb and forgotten by men millennia ago, he had sought, met and eventually married the cause of those who call themselves the followers of Belial, but who many of their enemies call "slaves". At their disposal, and at that of his own solitude, he had offered his skills. The same skills just used to kill Adam Uyan.

Pulling his head out of the water just enough, hidden beneath the shaded rushes, the Fir Bolg kept an eye out for every possible sign of danger. His eyes, accustomed as they were to the perennial darkness of the highways, hurt even if he kept them shut, so he had to rely on his keen hearing. Only when he was convinced it was safe did Tonos begin to catch his breath.

Short of air, almost on the verge of fainting, he allowed his lungs to refill with control. For a moment his sight clouded over, leaving optical hallucinations to crawl on the retina. He had strained his body to the limit. Fir Bolg had a bad relationship with water and that mission had required him to stay in it for too long – something which would have discouraged his more audacious clansmen. Tonos, however, was famous for having survived the flooded caves, eating what he found in the water. He was the best candidate, and such courageous attitude would surely reach the ears of a female eager to mate. It was a good motivation, the best when it came to engaging in the mission entrusted to him.

The Fir Bolg took a second, deep and silent breath to clear his sight. The vast area of high and dense reeds from which he had emerged had turned out to be a strategically excellent choice, difficult to reach from the ground, surrounded by swamps and unmanageable even with a small boat. The giant belched. All that noise of trees and animals disgusted him. He could not wait to return to Mother's belly and forget that there was such a world as this on the surface. He wanted to return underground immediately and tell his kinfolk about his mission.

The lungs filled up a third time, deeper still. His red, coarse, thick hair slipped back into the water. A simple circular wave, breaking against the rushes, was all that remained of a being modern men, strange to say, ignored the existence of.

Even though Tonos was convinced to have acted in secrecy, the figure which emerged from behind the tall pines, confirmed the exact opposite.

He was a tall, well-built man with symmetrical features and a long half-moon scar on his right cheek. He wore a pair of simple raw jute trousers, a white t-shirt and a hiking backpack on his shoulders, looking empty.

The man leaned into the rough bark of the tree and sighed, annoyed and worried. "Idiot of a Fir Bolg," he whispered. "Now they will know that we are looking for him."

3

"Andy, you're not upset with me, are you?" asked Emily before turning on the car engine.

"Of course not, why should I be?" he smiled.

"Good. It's important for me to know that I have your support. I could never forgive myself for having betrayed the trust of my little darling." Her eyes were already shining.

"Mum, look," Andy said soothingly, pointing to the twentieth-century structure beyond the wrought iron barriers, "The school is beautiful. It's a great old building. There are sports fields and everything else. What are you apologising for? There's nothing to forgive."

A boy appeared behind the gate, with broad shoulders and a gloomy and ominous look. He wore a shellsuit, black as his eyes. He seemed to be looking straight in Andrew's direction.

"Also," Andy continued, pulling away from his silent observer, "Mr Richardson seems a decent guy."

"Isn't he? I think so too. You know, I've always known when a school wasn't right for you, because you're too smart. But this time I have a good feeling, love. I'm sure that you'll make lots of friends here, and they will know what a wonderful boy you are. It's exciting! Summer is almost over and in less than a month you'll begin in a new school. I'm so proud of you."

When they slipped into the dense lunchtime traffic, the mysterious young man had his gaze still fixed on Andrew until he disappeared from view, hidden behind a bin lorry.

"You know that you are my little genius, don't you, love?"

Andrew felt relieved to be away from that strange observer. "Yes, Mum. But please don't say things like that in front of my mates like you did at Northern High. OK?"

"I swear."

They broke out laughing.

"Did I really do that?" Emily asked, jokingly.

"Mum…"

"Okay, Okay. I promise I will avoid any kind of nickname in front of your schoolmates, if…"

"If?"

"If you promise me we can catch up in the evening, when we are at home alone!"

"You're wicked."

"Promise?"

"Promise," Andy surrendered. "Now, can we get ice cream?"

Emily looked at her son. She was so proud of him. The world did not seem to understand him, just reject him, as if there was a poison, a drug in other people that prevented them from realising how precious he was, with his messy curls and straight nose. From the moment he was born, she had been certain that one day Andrew would show everyone just how amazing he was. A mother knows these things.

The search had begun soon after Adam had failed to return home and was reported missing by his parents to the local law enforcement. The maritime unit had a few boats, small and fast, but could also count on the aid of the city police, which provided four shifts of agents during the most intense tourist seasons. Within an hour, the rescue team had covered much of the lake surface.

Agent Helena Dowson, assigned that morning to lake patrol to reflect on the punch she had landed on a colleague the night before, had just reached the spot where the Fir Bolg Tonos had disappeared for the last time.

Thick rushes stood three feet high on the water surface and there was no way to proceed closer to the shore. As well as her impulsive side, Helena possessed a great investigative instinct and just had to take a look at the reeds to rule out the possibility that the missing boy might have attempted the obstacle course through the plants.

It was while watching the shore that she noticed the man with the backpack and jute pants.

Amin Akenre, of the fallen Paneb Akenre dynasty, was still there, sitting on the stump of a dead Scots pine. He was so wrapped in his own thoughts that he was startled when the woman spoke to him.

"Good morning," she called out authoritatively to overcome the boat engine noise.

Exploiting the residual inertia of the boat in approaching the bamboo rushes that separated the water from the beach of rocks and grass, the two found themselves at an acceptable distance to avoid shouting.

Sleeper guards, people's containment tools, defenders of social order, summed up the man in his mind to establish the most appropriate line of behaviour.

"Hi, I'm talking to you. Hello," the woman added. "I'm Agent Helena Dowson."

The woman was wearing a light white and blue uniform, covering a body honed by training, not too slender, but endowed with graceful proportions. She kept the start-up button pressed for a couple of seconds and the engine died with a low rumble. She was no longer in her youth. The hair tucked neatly into the hat, the trained and tanned arms which poke out of her short linen sleeves, betrayed a propensity for the understated.

"We're looking for a kid, fourteen, black hair," she continued. "He's on a red canoe with a white paddle and is wearing a red lifejacket. You didn't happen to see him around here, did you?"

Amin wiped his forehead with a cloth. "A boy, you said? No, I haven't seen anyone."

"Have you been here long?"

The man snorted. "No."

"Okay, thank you anyway," she said, puzzled and a little taken aback by the apparent lack of interest shown towards an officer. Where did courtesy and manners go? The boy might have met a girl and gone to some deserted beach, forgetting the world. In truth, she expected to receive such a call within the next few minutes. *By God*, she thought, *this wouldn't justify such indifference.*

A "Mph" came out of her mouth, unexpected.

Perhaps the man heard it, because he said something Helena didn't catch. With the outboard engine cord in her hand, she turned just enough to answer.

When she felt the sudden and unpleasant feeling of nausea, her first thought went to that morning's milk. Despite being lactose intolerant, sometimes she enjoyed the pleasure of a cappuccino at the bar by the lake, accepting the consequences of it, if only for the pleasure she felt when the foam slid softly down her throat.

No, the feeling she was experiencing was different, not physical. It felt a lot like when her ex had left with five minutes notice. It was a feeling of confusion, adrenaline and fear. It was panic.

"We have found his canoe, beached," she said, trying to look calm and professional. She would never let anyone see her struggling, so she waved and pulled the engine line. The small boat grumbled to life, engulfed in the usual puff of white smoke, but didn't have time to rev further before it emitted an asthmatic cough and shut down. The woman immediately made a second attempt.

Silence. The engine was no longer showing any signs of life.

Unfounded panic was growing steadily in her, taking her heartbeat through the wringer. The hyperventilation made her head spin, but she used her remaining strength to pull the engine line one more time.

"Come on..." she growled between her teeth, glancing at the shore. Amin sat there, motionless, staring at her with a penetrating and indecipherable look.

He had received a fair amount of training on the so-called contemporary world, that of the people of the One, and he had spent a lot of time with those who, sometimes, are called Sleepers by the commander of the world. He had known some of the societies defined as democratic or industrial; he had lived in big cities and had been on missions with his other brothers in places where the faded memory of the truth was still kept.

He had been wary of the languid and deaf nature of the modern world. But the memory of his origin, the perception of his own legacy, torn away from him by an unjustified accusation, made him incapable of interfering with these strange individuals, convinced of their freedom and free will. *Bricks in the Temple of the Great Intention*, thought Amin, without realising that his innate and strong wish for domination, in him since birth, was already taking over the woman.

When the engine refused to start for the third time, Helena did something so impulsive that she couldn't really justify. As if facing an ancestral and irrational danger, she sought a defence. Breaking police regulations, she brought her hand to the holster secured to her belt and loosened the safety.

Exposed to a threat she could not understand, she began searching for the source of that terrible discomfort. Her eyes wandered over the possible threats society believed to exist in a place such as a lake, like the dark water, the trees, captured in a still fight and anchored by the stones and mud of the shore, or the menacing hill which hung over her. That troubled search ended the moment her eyes fell on the only other human being in the vicinity.

Amin stood up slowly, using his surroundings as a distraction in a bid to conceal the disgust he sometimes felt when interacting with Sleepers. He didn't hate them. Quite the contrary; he felt a deep pity for their precarious existence. Sometimes he wondered how they could endure life when they were so far from Awareness. Any other lower people would act according to the limits imposed by the Mother and would spend their lives without questioning or accessing any answers.

But humans were different, and the constant confrontation with those lost and naive eyes,caused Amin to regret every minute spent outside the Kingdoms.

He had to interact, find some kind of contact with the Sleeper. This he had been taught and this he did. "Do you think he's dead?" he asked, feigning interest in the woman's search.

It was too late though; the officer didn't react well. The sensibility of her Sleeper essence was such to resonate with that of Amin, feeling it deeply.

With irregular movements, Helena grabbed the walkie-talkie hooked to her left shoulder. She heard her own voice, from far away, calling the station by the lake, but the microphone returned grating sounds of metallic crackles and electric snaps.

"We don't think anything, sir," she mumbled, unsure. "We are just looking for a little boy who got lost at the moment."

Dead? Why should he be dead? she asked herself.

When he realised that the situation was deteriorating fast, Amin recalled its essence, pushing it into the abyss of his own being. It was no longer the time of domination. It was the time of obedience to the servants. And of decadence.

"I'd be happy to be able to help in your search, but since being here, I have not met anyone. You're wasting your time, in my opinion," he said, slipping a red cap over his head. "Can I go?" he added, with a friendly smile.

The man's question was enough for Helena to regain self-control. She rubbed her eyes, feeling like she was returning to see the world for what it was. She swallowed and sat on the rubber seat. "Yes, sure. Thanks, you can go," she said.

The man stood there looking at her for a few more seconds. Then he walked away, stepping over the trunk on which he had sat, with slow, careful movements, disappearing between the shrubberies.

He had more important things to do than stay there philosophising about the condition of the Sleepers. The Fir Bolg were the problem now. He couldn't know what was going through Tonos' mind, but he was certain that his action, committed in broad daylight and in such a crowded place, was not his idea or his leader's. No giant of that race enjoyed leaving the highways and much less being exposed to the danger of being seen by the Sleepers. There was someone else behind that act, someone who knew the plans of identification and removal that Amin was supposed to carry out. Someone who was trying to sabotage those plans by exploiting these dull creatures. He needed to talk with Tonos' chief right away and there was only one place where a Fir Bolg of two and a half metres and a quarter of a ton in weight could have taken refuge.

Underground.

*

"Helena, are you there?" crackled the walkie-talkie on her shoulder.

Dowson replied, still distracted. The engine started on the first attempt. Still stunned, she pointed the nose of the small boat in the direction of her colleagues.

As soon as her face felt the sunlight, the heat removed the last dregs of anxiety she had experienced and, strangely, even the memory of Amin – his features and voice – turned into details that did not need to be remembered.

Oblivion's power had been imposed on that luminous dot that shone somewhere inside her, almost extinguishing it. All that remained was the aftertaste of sadness for those who have lost something, mixed with the optimism of those who ignore everything.

Fate would give Helena a long and serene life. She would have a large family, a fine house and a good pension. What she would never know is how close to death she came on that day.

5

Emily Fawcett didn't like many things. Among these things was botany. Although her taste in plants was something left to be desired, she couldn't help but notice that she was staring at the most horrible, scruffy and disgusting garden she had ever seen in her life. Not that she had seen many, given that she had always lived in the city, but the image of all those intermingling plants and crumpled grass left no room for alternative judgment.

True, there were flowers. But they were so messy, randomly scattered and with such mismatched colours to be a visual nuisance rather than a pleasure. One could even hear a muddy rivulet running somewhere, emanating a pungent wet smell of algae. Maybe there were frogs, or even toads. At worst, mice. And there was no escaping that situation. It was not a shabby public park and, unfortunately, not even her own. That stagnant and smelly jungle began where rusty partition nets separated her back garden from that of her neighbours opposite. Indeed, Emily noticed that the climbers had already taken over the nets. Maybe one day she'd even find them inside the house, with toads, mice and who knows what other disgusting creatures.

Andrew came out through the French door of his room and stood beside his mother, with a pipe in his hand. "The bathroom drain doesn't work," he simply said.

Emily had her hair tied back, her fists planted on her hips and a look between the resigned and the perplexed. "Yes, honey. I'll call the plumber tomorrow," she replied, absently.

Andrew looked closer at the neighbours' garden. It was a dark green patch, dirtied in places by more or less bright colours. It had a decadent air about it, but he felt that this decadence was due more to the position in which the two small back gardens were placed within the dark, central cloister of a twelve-storey building rather than to their composition. Andrew's was no larger than thirty square meters, with a trimmed lawn and some shabby flowerbeds. In essence, it appeared neater, but no less decadent. The problem was the building. Actually, to think about it, the whole neighbourhood.

"Well," Emily said, refocusing. "If nothing else, you have your own private access to the back."

Andrew turned to look at the crates still stacked in every corner of their small apartment. "It's great, Mom."

She picked up the rake from the ground and sighed. "I need to tidy the place up this weekend. I'll go back to work on Monday, and I don't want to leave you in a messy house. Especially the garden. If you want to help, see if you can get those climbers over there off our net, darling," she glanced towards the neighbour's yard.

He realised that his mother was not kidding and, without much enthusiasm, he headed towards the green and thorny wall that had taken over their rusty net.

He walked all along the fence, noticing how hard it was to see beyond it. There were just a couple of less dense areas, through which it was possible to spy curiously shaped plants, tall grass, and a small pitch of soil with large stones perhaps used as chairs. He noticed a stream and tried to figure out where it came from and where it got to, but couldn't.

Of the apartment itself there was very little to see. It opened at the bottom of the high and dark cloister, which had no balconies on the upper floors, but only small windows, perhaps bathrooms – it made him think of a hive. Andrew glimpsed two French doors, similar to those of his own home, thanks to the creativity of eighties architecture. If that was the case, then that flat would also have a small corridor opening on a lounge with open plan kitchen to the left and a corridor with two bedrooms on the opposite side. The living room and the small room should look over the garden.

"Andy? Are you removing those green monsters off our net?"

"Huh? Er, yes, Mum. I think I'll need scissors. I'm going to get them from the car."

Emily mumbled her agreement, still bent over the grass, under the big floral hat she wore as sun protection – the sun only hit the internal shaft of the building for forty-four minutes a day, between 12:30 and 13:14, and it was now late afternoon.

Andrew went back in, crossed the small foyer to the front of the building, with its drab silvery elevator, and went out from the main entrance. He walked along the pavement and crossed the road. He reached the grey parking lot, half empty at that time, and found the rust-coloured Fawcett-mobile. That particular tint came with a 15% discount on the price tag, and a self-explanatory reason for the generosity of the car's dealer.

Perhaps precisely because of its chromatic contrast, Andrew's attention was projected, almost bounced, beyond the car. Beyond all cars, for that matter.

Right behind the parking lot, a large green hill lifted toward the sky, hiding from sight various amenities such as the railway, some unfinished yards and, much further down, the lumbering overpass that led to the city centre.

The jagged perimeter of that grass and earth giant was surrounded by a net on which a string of tedious signposts hang, informing on the next set of works for the construction of a new mall. A few dozen metres up, on the broad summit, the bulldozers had eradicated many of the tall trees, which were now lying abandoned and alone, stacked without order against each other, like corpses without a proper burial. Andrew could not avoid the similarity between that chaotic and somewhat depressing picture and his own garden. This reasoning took little more than a second to form and the thought of the garden had already created another association of ideas. *If the apartments are the same, maybe there is a family opposite us. Maybe there's someone my age.*

Cheered up, he got into the car, pulled the scissors out of the case from the glove compartment and went back running. But instead of going home, Andrew stopped right in front of the back entrance of the building, which looked exactly like his own. He tried to peek inside, but the reflection on the glass just allowed him to guess what the foyer looked like. So he began to check the names, surnames and firms' acronyms on the intercom until he thought he had identified the corresponding buzzer to his own: 1B. Through the cracked plastic cover he couldn't see anything but a faded piece of paper, half slipped inside.

No names.

Andrew re-checked both buzzer's columns and realised that there were many slots without details. He was a bit disappointed and short of ideas.

"Need anything, boy?" asked a hoarse male voice behind him, making him jump on the spot.

A black man in his sixties towered over him, his bulk almost entirely concentrated in a prominent belly. His arms and legs were slim and his posture was crooked.

"No, sir. Yes, sir..." he stammered.

The man looked at him suspiciously.

"I'm looking for a person. People! " he said. *I'm not doing anything wrong!* he thought as he tried to justify himself. But, in the cities, people were wary even if they lived opposite each other.

"Who?" the man asked him even more suspiciously.

"No one in particular. I just wanted to... I..."

"Better go, kid. This is not the place for intercom games." He turned his back on him as he opened the main door with a key stuck in a bundle of many labelled others. The door closed slowly, slamming with a final metallic slap that made the glass rattle.

Andrew was disappointed for the second time. *For Goodness' sake, that giant must be the janitor. Of course, who else can he be?*

"Andyyy!" Emily's voice echoed between the buildings, barely softened by the concrete structures. Andrew found her standing like a stockfish in front of their door.

"Where did you end up, darling?"

"The car key got stuck, Mom," he lied, without even knowing why.

"Again? Tomorrow I'll leave it at the garage while I go to work. Did I tell you there's one right in front of the hospital?"

"Great. By the way, do you have any idea who lives opposite us? "

Emily stopped to think about it, the key in the keyhole. "I don't know, love. I think it's an old couple."

"Old? As in… *decrepit?*" Andrew felt the third disappointment in less than five minutes dawning on him.

Record.

He could not really say he had started well in the new home. The neighbourhood was a sad dormitory, hosting only a few dogs and some cats as day residents. The garden was a disaster that would make her mother go bonkers one day and the day after too. And the janitor thought he was probably a thief, a rogue, a bully or who knows what else.

Even though he couldn't change the neighbourhood or the garden, he would need to do something to better impress the man.

Everyone knew that befriending the janitor was the smart thing to do.

And Andrew knew that. He knew the words he should have said to the man would come to him, sharp and effective, with a delay of about twenty-four hours. More or less at four in the morning. As always.

6

In the black and deep gloom of the cave, Tonos' companions waited silently for his return, surrounded by tree roots and dripped on by the incessant drops of moisture exuded from the clay walls forming the enormous lake. Gaps in the ceiling created bizarre and feeble games of light on their tough skin, but the darkness did not represent an obstacle for the three Fir Bolg.

Even though they were a race used to surviving in the belly of Mother Earth for countless millennia, relying on the absolute secrecy of its hidden highways, they were wary by nature. Their instincts pushed the three giants to a nervous wait consisting of the grinding of sharp teeth, broken gasps and darting eyes. Long spears of wood and stone, tightly clenched by thin bony fingers covered by intricate nets of veins, sought invisible enemies. The smell of wet ground blended with the acrid smell of sweat, saturating the grotto. Kile was the name of deru, the head of the small clan of four, identifiable because he wore a *Choiddenain*, a helm-weapon forged before the Oblivion by the ancestors of the Fir Bolg, the wise giants Thuata de Danann. Because of their violent nature, the Fir Bolg had been denied access to the Ancient Knowledge necessary to create such artefacts, so a Fir Bolg wearing a *Choiddenain* did so with arrogant pride. In fact, the mere view of such object was sufficient to discourage the most decisive contender to command.

So, when the sensitive younger ears perceived footsteps in that dark underworld, the first thing they did was to evaluate the response of their deru.

With a click of the glottis, he ordered them to get ready for a possible threat. Then, with effort, Kile let his living essence vibrate. The helmet became entangled with energy, and the symbols engraved on it began to respond to that supreme call, uncaring for the identity of the caller. The symbols ordered atoms of nitrogen, oxygen and argon, known as "air", to merge with solid microparticles and prepare to vibrate at such speed as to transform into plasma gas if requested to. The hole in the right temple of the *Choiddenain* released a hiss, an interlude to pure destructive power.

The footsteps came very close, then stopped.

"Tonos," croak a deep voice from behind the corner closest to Kile.

"Nun," answered one of the clan.

"Doime," said another.

"Kile," concluded the deru. "Come forth, brother, show yourself." As soon as Kile relaxed, the hissing died down and the ancient weapon of the Thuata de Danann became inert once more, a magnificent helmet of red gold.

Tonos took a few steps towards his comrades and, for a while, they stood squaring up to each other suspiciously, as required by the Reunion ritual of the Fir Bolg.

This may have seemed strange considering that the clan had been separated for only a few hours, but it would not be so if one understood the distrustful nature of these giants, the vile deeds they were responsible for and the extreme slowness of their mental processes.

Suddenly, they all fell sitting on the ground, in unison.

"I broke the life of that little Sleeper, deru Kile,"Tonos said.

The others responded with a grunt of approval while Kile's face was awash with a wide, satisfied, giggling grin. The clan exchanged pats on the back and congratulations.

"Are you sure he's dead?" asked Nun, who was just over two feet high and was the smallest and the most pessimistic of the group.

Tonos nodded, staring at his clan leader. "There are only two of them left now."

"Only two, yes. Two isn't many," said Doime, who was nearly two-and-a-half feet and with a spherical belly of red hair.

"Don't try to count in my presence," Kile warned him.

"We should tell the Translator of Light, shouldn't we?" continued Tonos, who always needed to know what to do next.

"We'll tell him when I decide," he snarled, then smiled, satisfied.

But the toothless grin suddenly turned into alertness, readjusting the ungainly traits of his sharp face. He jumped up, sniffing the air like a hunting dog. At the click of his glottis, the other Fir Bolg rose silently to form a circle. In the absence of a real weapon, Tonos grabbed a huge boulder of over fifty pounds.

"A Translator of Light. Obviously. Riffraff like you can't even get food to feed on," said a voice from the thickest shadow. "It is unthinkable that you can conceive any initiative."

"Who are you?" asked Kile, his voice threatening.

"I'm the shadow. Why, can you not see me? Fir Bolg have good sight in the dark," he added sarcastically.

The giants' white faces turned from corner to corner of the cave, unable to locate the source of the sound.

"Your breed is said to have been on the verge of extinction, and let me tell you… the choice to side with a Translator of Light, standing between a Prince of the One and his goals, does not look brilliant in terms of survival."

"Prince?" Kile grinned as he searched. "Fir Bolg have no princes. We are followers of the true destroyer of the World, Belial!"

"Belial! Belial!" the other screamed.

"Your prince is nothing to us," said the deru, smug.

"Don't get nervous, *ghigantes*. Precisely because they are aware of the weaknesses of some races, each Pure sends their messengers with the task of making sure that each of you remembers being subjected to the Great Intention, and is obliged to live according to the teachings of the One. No alternatives are contemplated. There are no alternatives."

Kile was not stupid. He knew he had broken laws to which, whether he liked it or not, he was bound like any other living creature, Woken or Sleeper, conscious or unconscious, Roused or destined to Oblivion. However, a doubt came to mind, one that a Fir Bolg could not ignore. "Are you a messenger of the judges?" he asked the darkness, while such an eventuality was already frightening the simple minds of his clan mates.

The voice sounded closer, just behind the head of the deru, becoming almost a whisper. Kile tightened his jaw while a drop of sweat slid over his wrinkled, and rough temple.

"You have already broken the Code of the One, and Belial's followers do not have the rights of citizens," was the answer. "If I was a messenger of the judges, you would not be alive, Fir Bolg. Now, tell your clan to lay down their weapons and lay to rest that ancient helmet you're not worthy to wear. "

A large vein on Kile's forehead seemed ready to burst, then the deru snorted and the clan lowered their weapons.

Right at the centre of the circle formed by the giants, a shadow began to swell, intertwining with and summoning smaller and jagged shadows. From it emerged a man dressed in jute pants, a white t-shirt and a backpack on his shoulders. It was Amin.

The Fir Bolg looked like massive waves ready to crush him, but for the time being they were only tightening that circle made of a ton of mighty bones, nervous muscles and huge weapons.

"We didn't break any law," Tonos said, defying the man not tall enough to come to his chest.

"Oh yes you did," Amin said. "The fourth precept of the Code of the One says that Purity must rule mankind. Purity shows us the way to perfection and prevents those like you from making decisions only princes can make. You Belial followers knew that the Brotherhood of Shadow was looking for the boy on behalf of His Perfection, Prince

Here Paneb Akenre LXVI. You break the Code by denying me the information I now order you to give me. Tell me now which Translator of Light you speak of and which court he is assigned to. If you do this, I will spare your life, as long as you return forever in the deep galleries from whence you came. The world does not need the folly of Belial's followers, but order and laws. So it was decided by the only authority, the nine secrets, the judges of the One."

The Fir Bolg were not experts in history or Atlantean tradition, but like all conscious beings they were well aware of the forces that dominated the world. The fear flowing in their veins was far from irrational. Yet, at the bottom of their huge heart, they hunted blindly against the world, compromising their survival instinct.

"We kill him too," said Doime, a big Fir Bolg. "He's just a Shadow Hound, a renegade, a fallen noble."

"Yes, kill him," Nun said with a trembling voice. "Exiled by his own people, he moves alone. No one will know that we have met him."

The Fir Bolg took a step forward.

Stupid, dull giants. How is it that a lineage of such animals may have descended from those noble predecessors, the Thuata De Danann, so magnificent as to create the Ancient Knowledge? Amin sighed but did not move. "Listen to me, Kile. I will kill one of your comrades. When I'm done, you'll tell me who told you about the boy. If you do not, I'll wipe out your clan one by one. Then I will kill you."

Kile did not answer, but it was as if a silent order had crossed the cave. The Fir Bolg jumped forward. Doime twirled the long wooden spear, sweeping the air with the engraved stone blade. A grim note split the darkness without finding its target. Amin had disappeared in the shadows.

His voice was echoing again in the underground's thick drizzle. "I knew that there would be no way to reason with you."

Nun took a swing at the spot where the voice seemed to come from, but found nothing, raising only dusty ground and roots.

Amin had reappeared behind the Fir Bolg group. He looked serious and focused, his sarcasm gone.

"Kile, the Great Intention has forged superior individuals for 130 centuries, ever closer to perfection, ever nobler. That I have been removed from that perfection does not make me a being less close to it. I have within me the strength of those people, and since embracing the Shadow I have been able to abandon all diplomacy. I can use any means to achieve my purpose, Fir Bolg! Even those denied to the Pure. Now you will find out what it means to oppose the Great Intention."

Doime charged Amin, his spear stretched forth like the shaft of a small tree.

Kile didn't even have time to register the exact words of the Shadow Hound. Doime had already fallen to the ground, gurgling helplessly. Amin had not touched the Fir Bolg, but his eyes had changed, resembling doors open onto the universe, coloured by millions of bright stars as deep as eternity. In the centre of his forehead, skin and bone had become almost transparent, so strong was the light that seemed to stem from an undefined point in the Hound's head, shaping an inverted triangle whose low extremity touched the nasal septum.

"Doime!" Tonos yelled.

Amin kept staring at the Fir Bolg with those infinite, lost eyes. A low sound vibrated in the air, almost imperceptible.

"He's consulting one of the Seven Orders!" Kile said, backing away.

"What?" Nun followed in turn. "He can't do it; he's a Pure Atlantean. Pures are forbidden to draw on the Four Forces. It's impossible!"

"No Nun," said Kile, "he is no longer a Pure. He's no longer subject to the rules of Atlantean nobility. "

Nun shook his thin, grim head with a grunt of disgust. "Then you are like one of our enemies, you are like a son of Mu! We have to destroy you," he shouted hysterically.

Amin stepped forward. "The First Order of creation, "Death", says that everything that has a beginning must have an end. I asked and received from the Four Forces that time had its effect on Doime's heart. His body is young, but his heart is ageing and will soon stop beating," he replied, as Doime's agony ceased.

"You're crazy, exiled! Do you want to unleash the Nemesis even against yourself?" Tonos thundered.

"Those like me have nothing to lose, Fir Bolg. I am just an instrument. All I can aspire to is to serve Purity so that it becomes even stronger after I'm gone," he said, and there was an imperceptible veil of sadness in his voice. Then he thundered, "Now, Kile, answer!"

"Giants' word, I don't know anything about the Translator of Light."

Amin approached again. "The giants' word is credible only in the Milesians' mouth, as it was for your brothers Thuata De Danann. It is not so in the mouth of a Fir Bolg. You lie."

Nun gave a start and brought his hands to his throat, emitting a series of guttural noises that echoed in the cave. He fell, kneeling in the mud. Amin was motionless, soaked by the water falling from the low vault. His hand held a long rod made of horn, dark and smooth, stuck deeply into Nun's throat, more than four feet away. It was made of a soft material, with reddish reflections.

Orichalcum, the living metal of Atlantis, thought Tonos with a shiver. *A toxic material. But only Translators of Light can control it...*

"I don't know the Translator. I've always talked to his herald," Kile insisted, his voice beginning to shrink.

Nun had fallen forward and from his mouth came a smoke-like condensation. His body was shaken by convulsions.

Tonos was unable to act. Panicky, he turned to Kile. He knew that he would be the next target and he did not want to die. No Fir Bolg was able to establish a dialogue with the Four Forces. On the other hand, Amin seemed well gifted for a Pure Atlantean and had enough courage to challenge the Orders of creation that could have destroyed him in a single instant. At the same time, he was equipped with Atlantean pseudo-technology, that which the people of Mu called gorann.

"Answer my question," Amin thundered.

Kile put his hand on Tonos' shoulder. "Attack him," he said.

The eyes of the giants crossed for a moment, and Tonos perceived a vacuous expression in his leader's eyes – way too calm. But he could not refuse a deru order. Thus, with a frightening cry, he threw himself on Amin.

The Hound did not expect such a move, risky even for a Fir Bolg, and was overwhelmed by the physical power of the giant, making him fall to the ground. Tonos continued to scream with his white eyes opened wide, slamming his opponent against the rocky wall. Amin was incapable of generating the vibration that allowed him to dialogue with the Four Forces and was now at the mercy of that frightening force. Another crash and semi-liquid fragments of Orichalcum flew everywhere. Luckily the soft ground had dampened the blow.

Tonos hurled himself at the man who was trying to get up, stunned. Amin knew that he had no chance against a fierce Fir Bolg, fighting for his own life. He sprang back up, still very agile despite the previous impact undoubtedly damaging his ribs. Gritting his teeth, he faced his enemy, who in three steps had already covered six or seven feet. Tonos was afraid and his transfigured face was a mask of wicked wrath.

The Fir Bolg had been a cruel and bloody race since the time before what the books of Sleepers had called the "Ice Age", until the extermination of their wise ancestors, the Thuata de Danann. For the Fir Bolg they were all enemies, including the children of Mother Earth or people of Mu, beings unworthy of life who talked to the Four Forces of which they were slave. Even the Hound, then, was like those people.

In an instant, Tonos was on him, but this time the exiled shifted to the side, using a large root as a spindle to move away faster. He landed with balance, but immediately perceived a well-known feeling, a counter-vibration he had learned to recognise during his long training in the citadel of the Brotherhood of Shadow.

A powerful and calm keh, he thought. Ancient Knowledge!

The *Choiddenain* snorted with a hiss like a loud cry. The gases compressed by the forces of physics formed a cone of white, almost luminous powders. With a deafening roar, the beam of the ancient weapon struck the ground, creating a glowing hole, while Amin jumped out of the way to avoid a frightening death, being corroded alive.

Tonos also stepped back while Kile directed his head and helmet to follow the Shadow Hound.

Some particles of corrosive dust reached Tonos' face, burning him. He looked at his deru, upset, pleading for pity. Kile looked cold and absent. His movements were mechanical and uncoordinated, like those of a marionette. He was no longer the leader and protector of the little clan of Fir Bolg.

Amin moved quickly to avoid the deadly beam of the *Choiddenain* by interposing Tonos between him and the ancient weapon, gaining just enough time to let the *Orichalcum* in his blood act as a mantle, causing him to disappear in the shadows.

At that moment the jet invested the terrified giant in full. When the horrible screams of the Fir Bolg exploded in the cave, the Hound was already in the sunlight of the surface, panting while trying to stop the haemorrhage of his Essence the Atlantean metal was eating.

He stood up, gazing at the placid lake. Another act of a 13,000-year long war had just been completed.

7

Okay, it was not actually 04:00 am, but it was close enough. "You must be responsible for the building. Very pleased to meet you; my name is Andrew Fawcett and I live on stairwell A, ground floor. Luckily I met you, would you be able to help me?" There, something like that. A serious, composed, polite young man.

Not the stammering fool, half blinded by the sun, yob-like, of the other day.

Andrew switched on the lamp next to his bed. A faint blue glow seeped through the French door.

He looked around, losing his gaze on the still half-filled boxes spread out in the room. Some of his most prized possessions had been immediately sorted, especially the most important collections of comics, such as "Blade of the Immortal" and "Neon Genesis Evangelion"; then he had found the perfect anti-mother-dusting-action placement for his "Lost" and "Battlestar Galactica" DVDs. Andrew was very fond of the latter, because it reminded him of a clumsy father and a surreal dialogue in which his Dad had tried to convince him that the one created in the 70s was a far superior series to the modern one, full of special effects and beach types. It had been one of the few fun discussions they'd ever had and also one of the last before he and Mum had split up.

The old and very slow Dell computer was still cocooned in bubble wrap, and he knew it would stay like that for a long time to come. Andrew was not a fan of those machines and for the time being there was no money for an Internet connection anyway. He found the games repetitive and boring. Perhaps the move would convince him to let it go altogether.

He had pulled out some essential clothing, shoving overflowing boxes in the cupboard willy-nilly.

Sleep, on the other hand, had completely given up on him, probably gone for a ride up the hill behind his building, on that sad, dark green mound half eaten by the bulldozers.

He slipped on the flip-flops Mum had bought him, claiming they would improve his posture, and took a slow, lazy tour of the flat.

Emily had done a colossal job to give a semblance of order to the apartment and was now asleep, probably with the help of a few pills, crooked sleeping mask on her face and half-open mouth – a funny sight indeed.

Without making any noise, Andy approached the bed and covered her, adjusting the mask with careful movements and putting the pillows back together. He watched his mother for a few minutes, yawning, as if to make sure nothing would happen to her. Then he went into the kitchen to get some fruit juice. He grabbed the entire bottle and decided to go to the garden to drink it, like a scene of some edgy movie, but with peach juice instead of rum. As he returned to his room, he seemed to feel a vibration in the air, deep, almost imperceptible. He thought it was the old refrigerator, but when he turned that way, the sound had already vanished.

When the French door opened with a squeak, Andrew felt a pleasant gust of warm air on his face; it had been channelled into the cloister of the building and had managed to descend thirty meters in that concrete pipe of red bricks, right up to his face. He breathed deeply. Dropping onto the step, half asleep, he took a long sip of juice. He glanced distractedly upward. Much higher, the sky could be glimpsed through the handkerchiefs left hanging on the last floor. The sound of a toilet flushing and the light of a window going out took away any poetry from the night atmosphere in an instant.

With the average age in this building, the flushing will sing all night long, he mused.

He took another sip of the peach and started to get up, but when he turned around to reenter, he stopped in his tracks. The DVD box set of "Battlestar Galactica" had disappeared from the bookcase.

Dazed, he tried to visualise his room from a few moments before and to convince himself that the box set had to be there. He reached Emily's bedroom, but his Mum was still asleep.

The front door was closed and there were no noises to be heard.

Wary, he returned to his room searching into the chaos of the boxes. And right there, at the base of the bookshelf, behind a large box of winter sweaters, he found the set, with some of the disks out of the case, as if it had fallen off the shelf. Andrew couldn't really explain how it could have happened. He passed his hand over the shelf to make sure there were no obstructions or other objects before putting the box set back in its place. For a few seconds he sat there, thinking about it, but not much came up, as often happens when dealing with strange, simple and after all harmless events. If human beings paid more attention to details, they would learn to recognise extraordinary things. But that night Andrew was not yet ready, and soon he was overwhelmed by sleep and much more concrete thoughts on the following day: his first day at Saint Paul.

As he slipped into bed, he knew that this time he would have to do the impossible: to be accepted in the school of Headmaster Richardson. He reviewed all the behaviours that could be defined as wrong in a school context and all those that could get him in trouble, promising to keep away from them and to endure, endure everything at any cost. He didn't want to give his mother any more pain. He couldn't bear it and, after all, he was the man of the house. He had to take his responsibilities.

Immersed in anti-trouble tactics that would have made the formidable Chinese general Sun Tzu envious, Andrew fell asleep. When his eyes closed, on the opposite side of the garden, just beyond the thin rusty net, another pair of eyes were staring at him through the open French door. They were large, curious and intelligent eyes, but also full of suspicion. And lethal.

8

The man was striding along. The heels of his modest but elegant shoes echoed decisively on the ruined marble floor. The long corridor, typical of apartments of the beginning of the previous century, gave access to all the rooms, but the man was heading towards the last one, the one with the door closed. He stopped and stood for half a minute in reverent silence, then drew a short breath and knocked.

There was no answer, so he did what he knew was allowed to him. He lowered the handle and barely opened the door. With his lips to the dark gap, he said, "Lord, allow me to disturb you."

"Say what you have to say," answered a low, deep voice from the darkness.

"Your servant must go away."

"And why do you disturb me for this?"

The man bit his lip. "I just wanted to make sure you didn't need anything," he added in a trembling voice. "You have not eaten, or left the room, for three days."

There was no answer. Through the glimmer of light that penetrated from the corridor, it was possible to glimpse a few details of the furnishings, the carpets and little more.

"We do not fear for your health," the man added quickly. "We know there is nothing that can defeat you. We were just wondering…"

"I do not need anything. Go now, " the voice cut short.

"As you wish. Isabel is next door, at your service."

The man took a half step back, made a slight bow and closed the door carefully. The noise of his heels faded away. Amin sighed. Sitting on the bed in a dim light, he tried to breathe in slowly. A grimace of pain appeared on his face as the ribs, which had been slammed against the walls of the cave, were forced to expand under the lungs' pressure. That was not what made him so weak though. The last few hours had passed quickly and the damage was less severe than he had believed. He even managed to sleep.

The two previous nights, on the other hand, had been passed prey to the terrible and excruciating spasms caused by the *Orichalcum*. The deepest and most volatile part of the Shadow Hound's mind had wavered without guidance in a sort of delusional state, multiplied to infinity. The feeling he had experienced was linked to the risk of seeing his own essence split from the physical body, torn away by the metal.

The *Orichalcum* used the essence to stabilise its own molecular structure and, thanks to this renewable source of energy, it became changeable, allowing its host to shape it at will. Until it was activated the metal was inert, even if toxic. As soon as the host overcame the influence of the metal, it gave way to an uncontrollable reaction. The *Orichalcum* would take over and begin to drain essence like a leech drained blood. If the process was not interrupted by a perfect control of mind and body, the host could suffer serious damage or even death. And since its essence could not return to the Source of everything, it remained imprisoned in the metal, destined to dissolve forever into nothing.

Amin had succeeded in preventing the *Orichalcum* from taking over. He found himself staring at the dark copper ring on his middle left finger. It was a simple and ruined ring, as if it had been at the bottom of the sea for a thousand years. This pseudo-interface had protected him.

But he felt a deep sense of shame, like he had betrayed the nobles and his prince. Shame for having lost all that time recovering, for not being able to defeat the followers of Belial. Shame for not having prevented the useless death of a Sleeper, for not being able to identify the conspiracy of a Translator of Light. But at least there was a remedy to this, and the games were not yet done. They had killed the wrong boy and would try again, maybe this time choosing the right one.

He got up with difficulty and stood still for a few minutes, perceiving every limb, every muscle, every tendon, every cell of his perfect body.

He had to act with caution and find a strategy; otherwise his mission would fail dishonourably. A Translator of Light was a fearsome adversary, powerful and with many supporters. Especially if he acted in darkness, without leaving a trace.

The Translators of Light had often been prosecuted for infractions of the Code of the One because of their craving for power, unhealthy and unstoppable. Halfway between priests and engineers, they lived pseudo-technology as a form of sacred art and venerated the results as the miracles of Father Gorann, the divine incarnation of that ancient and forgotten war that had thrown the world into Oblivion, the great war in which they had been able to exploit pseudo-technology and all its power. This distorted and disturbing view of the world had often led them into open conflict with the Atlantean principles, so much so that it was common practice to have them monitored by surveillance guards.

Unfortunately, there could be no pseudo-technology without Translators of Light. Thus, enveloped in their impenetrable cloud of unspeakable mysteries and secrets, the "lucifers", as they were sometimes called by their enemies, were a lesser evil which the Lords of Matter had to tolerate.

But all these were futile reflections. It was time to act.

Naked, Amin came out of the room slowly, trying to accustom his eyes to the morning light.

"Onagros," he called softly.

From one of the other doors a woman in her mid-thirties, with thick dark hair and big green eyes, came out immediately. She approached him with small steps, her eyes on the floor.

"Here is your servant, sir. How can I satisfy you?"

Amin had a small cough, to which Isabel seemed to react with a start, almost scared.

The Shadow Hound noticed the woman's reaction. "I'm fine, Onagros. Do not be afraid for me. Now bring me something to eat," he continued, matter-of-fact.

Isabel disappeared without ever taking her eyes off the floor and a few minutes later she joined Amin in a room with heavy red curtains, full of animal skins on the floor and a large, luxurious and comfortable looking bed.

She laid out a tray on a low table in front of the bed, smelling of sweet and sour fragrances and embellished with flowers and quartz powder. She quickly tasted the food before handing it to her master, then stepped aside, without leaving the room.

Amin wrapped himself in a warm cloak and ate in silence, ignoring her.

After breakfast, he was led into a large bathroom and Isabel helped him to wash, using only very soft sponges and never daring to touch him with her bare hands, as she had been taught. Her movements were delicate and precise, as she had always performed them. Wiping him off with a soft and fragrant cloth, she helped him to dress comfortably, wearing clothes suitable for a man in his thirties who lived in the city.

"Any news for me?" Amin broke the silence.

"No, sir. Nobody has contacted us," the woman replied. "I can provide you with a means of communication, if you wish."

"No, nothing *gorann*, Sleeper. I'll do it myself."

"As you wish, sir," she replied softly.

Amin headed for the front door, slipping on his jacket with a pause of pain. "If I still need you, I'll come back," he said as he left.

The woman gave a small bow as the door closed. She was full of pride – bursting with it. Her life made perfect sense. She had been blessed by the rare honour of being able to host and serve a king-god, a human and divine being. A creature she had learned to know from his grandfather's words, who in turn had heard them from his grandfather and the countless generations who had served them. A luminous and powerful creature to whom Isabel felt she belonged completely. The Pures, as Amin had been before he became a Shadow Hound, called subjects such as her "Onagros", and their absolute loyalty was taken for granted. The Onagros were Sleepers, like most of the human beings in the world. The only difference was that, although they could not understand the extraordinary abilities of the king-gods, in a very remote past they had sworn to serve them everywhere and at any cost, partly out of fear of their destructive force and partly for the admiration of the miracles they could accomplish. In truth, the Onagros had made this choice at the time when the One, Evenor, guided the thought and actions of Atlantis. Now everything was different. The struggles for power in the courts were incessant, and the enemies were multiplying inside and outside the Kingdoms. Yet the Onagros didn't care: they would follow their gods forever, in every condition and without sparing themselves, such was the obedience that they had for them.

Filled with an inexpressible joy, Isabel went to the kitchen, where she made a long, bitter coffee. She sipped half of it and prepared to call her boss to justify her being late for work.

On the other side of the house, Amin's thoughts were quite different. He was worried. The silence received in response to his attempts at contacting the court was perhaps an indication that the link between them had broken and his message had not reached its destination. Despite the importance of his mission, or perhaps precisely for this reason, he could not reach directly the court of prince Ananaki Mneommon XXXIX and from there, safely, get in touch with his prince, Here XLVI. He could not trust anyone, and the two were had been on bad terms since the generation of their Pure fathers. If his message had been intercepted and his messenger destroyed, it meant that someone, or something, was now also looking for Amin to finish the job. He had to get the intelligence to its destination without moving too far and in the shortest possible time. There was a way to get the attention of the right people, but it was neither a wise nor a safe way. Furthermore, it could attract unwanted attention for several miles.

Still, Amin saw no other effective move in a situation that was increasingly turning into a big and dangerous affair. He would recall an eon, the messenger of the judges, the living sentence. And he wasn't sure whether to hope that it would listen to him or not.

He looked around. The road was busy downtown, perhaps also because of the black curling clouds that angered modern human beings, as they did their predecessors. *We do it for you, even if you don't know it*, he thought.

To fulfil his plan, he would need only two things. A broken mobile and an athletic policewoman named Helena Dowson.

9

The Fawcett-mobile's radiator breathed in the exhaust pipe fumes of the SUV crawling in front of them. The road was partially flooded due to the night rains and, despite the traffic caused by it, there were still several bicycles darting on the slippery sidewalks. Bikes were always a good compromise for short journeys, even in the rain.

In the polished cockpit of her car, filled with the mysterious and chemical fragrance "Iris Blue", Emily had just put on a Frank Sinatra CD, now resurrected for a live performance at Madison Square Garden of *My Way*.

Andrew recognised the undisputed value of the artist, but his mind, at 07:30 in the morning, couldn't put together even the most modest of mental processes. How long had that guy in a tuxedo been dead for? A thousand years before, perhaps shortly after Dante Alighieri.

"So, how do you feel about your first day at the new school?" Emily managed to ask, after preparing the question since breakfast.

"Good," he tried to answer, talking over Frank. "Mum, I thought that maybe I could use the public transport to go to school."

Emily started. "But love," she said, trying not to betray her concerns, "we live miles from the centre. Who knows how long it would take you… and then the public transport is full of strange people."

"I've already checked. There's a bus that stops in front of the house, just across the road, and that ends at the subway station."

"Subway?" Emily stammered.

"Yes, I don't remember the name of the stop. Anyway, from there I make fifteen stops and get out…" Andrew paused, as if waiting for something. "… right there!" He pointed to two tall poles with the white "M" on a red background. "Saint Paul is a little further. I could get off here, now, to tell you the truth."

Emily tried to keep calm, but she felt the ground beneath her feet slipping away.

Andrew knew in his heart that it was a big ask for his mother, who was always so apprehensive.

"It seems so complicated, and anyway, I drive by this road. It really doesn't bother me taking you." She sought understanding in her son's eyes.

"If you didn't have to drive through the centre, you could sleep an hour longer – we could both do it. And why waste your break to come back here and take me home? Did they take you to school at fourteen?"

"Those were other times, honey…" she said, feeling stupid.

"Sure," he gave up. "Don't worry. I didn't really want to take bus and metro every day back and forth. Yes, you're right."

Silence.

A man in his early thirties crossed the street right in front of the Hyundai's bonnet. He was a tall, athletic guy, covered in a long jacket with a fur collar. Andrew followed him with his eyes, fascinated by something he could not explain, unable to stop himself.

Emily was silent, though she wanted to say something at all costs. But the words didn't come, and she feared to say the wrong ones, as often happened. She had promised herself not to do it again. The truth was that she didn't feel like it. She couldn't bear throwing her son into the world, a world that had shown so often it didn't want him and had rejected him as an unwanted guest. Or maybe she didn't want him to suffer new disappointments. At the same time, however, she knew she couldn't protect him forever, and that tortured her. She took a long silent breath, covered by good old Frank in the background. When the SUV covered the umpteenth foot forward and then stopped, she moistened her lips, glanced at her son and unlocked the doors, which she always kept closed.

"Listen love, why don't you do this last bit on foot?" she said, offhandedly. "We are standing still here and I don't want you to be late on the very first day."

Andrew was puzzled for a moment. Then he clicked, unfastened his seatbelt without saying anything, grabbed the rucksack and put on an *Appleseed* cap, with Motoko Kusanagi on the front and the inscription, *Terrorist, if you hate this world so much, don't come back.*

"Love you, Mom," he said, pecking her on the cheek before running out of the car.

I love you too, Emily thought as she watched her son walk off the sidewalk, barely dodged by a pair of bicycles that had passed him at full speed.

"You stupid… pay attention!" She shouted at the cyclists. But they didn't seem to hear.

On that day Mrs Fawcett, who continued to use her maiden name, began a new bad habit, one of the few she had missed, and bit the nail of her left thumb like a dog in search of fleas.

PART TWO

IGNORE, LEARN, FORGET

"With knowledge comes doubt."

Wolfgang Goethe

10

The entrance of Saint Paul was not like Andrew remembered it. The wrought iron gate was the same, as was the courtyard that stretched along the nineteenth-century facade of the building.

But that day there were people. A river of backpacks, books, hairstyles, sweatshirts, jackets, piercings, tattoos, portable consoles, mobiles and, perhaps, even knives was pouring into the prodigious front doors of black wood surrounded by carved marble. Andrew advanced in awe, shoved by strangers passing him by as if he did not exist.

"Move!" people shouted.

"Come on! Get the fuck out of my way!" someone else said.

Like a salmon in the stream, he was forced to follow the flow towards the front door, which on that day reminded him of enormous jaws, insatiable for the young lives about to dive into it. From the windows of the building, the heads of the first arrivals appeared, some of whom were throwing toilet paper on the latecomers before disappearing, surprised by the janitors. The general climate was chaotic, to say the least, if not downright hellish. The entrance hall was mayhem. Some of the pupils were jumping from class to class looking for mates from previous years or friends from other groups, while others were already gathered in small cliques, pointing out the newcomers, the ones predestined to be teased.

Right, thought Andrew, looking for his Northern Star in that chaos, *let's avoid ending up among their targets.*

"Are you Andrew Foquet?" asked a voice behind him.

Andrew turned puzzled and a little surprised. "Fawcett," he corrected, rhetorically.

A thin, wavy-haired boy, much taller than he was, stared at him above deep, under eye bags and a vague charming smile. "Yes, you're French, then?"

"No, not at all."

"I'm Carlyle, Carlyle Ferguson. Nice meeting you. I'll be your guide for the next few days," he said, extending his hand.

Andrew was about to grab it when Carlyle was shoved against him – they almost crashed to the ground.

"Look, how nice," said an unpleasant voice that Andrew could not immediately identify. "The king of the queers has already found a new boyfriend!"

A chorus of laughter erupted in the general hubbub.

Andy withdrew from the unwanted embrace. He saw a group of three boys, about sixteen, walking away laughing. A blond guy turned to him, showing his middle finger.

Great start, he thought.

"Let's make one thing clear," Carlyle said quickly, picking up his books. "I'm not one of those... like he said, so keep your distance. Clear?"

"Very," Andrew answered.

"And I hate French people..."

"I'm not French."

"Even better. You'll have to stay with me for the next fifteen days. You're not going anywhere without me, not even to the toilet. During PE you will stand next to me and if you need anything, well, don't break my balls and do it yourself. All right?"

"Yes, fine."

Carlyle started to walk away, and Andrew followed him to the centre of the large atrium, which was emptying of the students. The clamour was still unbearable and the screeching of rubber shoes on the newly polished marble sharpened the noise pollution.

"OK," continued Carlyle, "since you look like a smart guy, let's start by saying that things here don't work like in other schools. Don't be fooled though – there is supervision. Only it's hidden," he explained, leaning against a column. He used his chin to point at the column next to them, as if to show him something. They looked at each other. "Well? Can't you see it?"

"Actually no."

"Oh my God. Are you blind?"

Andrew still couldn't get it.

"The column – a part of is not plaster, it's white glass. There's a video camera behind it. The building is full of them. That's how Richardson keeps order here."

"Cameras? They must be well hidden because I don't—"

"You're not as smart as I thought," Carlyle cut him short. "Follow me, but be careful what you do."

From the entrance hall, two large flights of stairs went up to long sided balustrades; at their base, in the middle, were four wooden display cases with neatly ordered sheets, pinned behind plastic panels. A large number of students had stopped in front of them and, compared to the general atmosphere, seemed to speak little and in low voices. Andrew noticed a girl burst into tears, immediately consoled by her friends. She had long red hair, light skin and slender hands cupping her sobbing face.

He stood back and watched the scene.

"Ah, yes. There are still people who don't know yet," said Carlyle.

"About what?"

"Adam Uyan's accident. He came to school here. He's dead."

The group of friends escorted the red-haired girl to the stairs, passing near them. She seemed desperate, immersed in a deep pain, expressed only by barely restrained sobs. The voices of the others overlapped in competing to find the most useless words of comfort. Andrew had seen those kinds of tears only once before, his mother's at his Granny's funeral. At that time Dad had been there too, but he remembered him quiet and distant, a grey spot on a sad day.

"How did he die?" Andy asked, as they started climbing the stairs.

"Drowned in one of the lakes outside the city. The canoe overturned and got trapped below."

Andrew felt sorry. He didn't know the guy, but he could read the pain of loss from every movement, gesture and posture of the girl who was now moving away.

"Were you friends?" he asked.

"Actually no. He was in another class. But it's not that. Uyan was a rich kid who thought himself better than the others because of it. If you're here though, your money counts for nothing. For your parents you're still a public liability, right? Still, he felt like he was above us all and had no friends. Anyway, he was here less than a year."

My mother doesn't think I'm a public liability, Andrew tried to convince himself. "And who was the one crying?" he asked.

"Which one? Girls cry for anything."

"The one with the red hair."

"Ah, that's Magdalene Ryan, Maggie. Another rich kid."

"Were they..."

"Huh? You mean, going out?" Carlyle asked with a grin.

"Something like that."

"Not that I know. How... but you're a monster!"

"What? Why?"

"You want to get it on with the ex of a dead guy still warm in his coffin!" he laughed.

"No, I..."

"Young Foquet has just arrived and already wants to put his hands inside some bra! Diabolical!'

"I'm not that kind of guy. Only, I was sorry, she was crying and..." *And then the right words will come to mind at the usual time*, he said to himself.

Carlyle kept laughing. "You're funny, Foquet."

"Fawcett," he replied.

On the upper floor, the institute was divided into two great wings: the lower and upper school. There were different classes for each group, divided by letter. Carlyle stopped in front of a door labelled "9-C". The bell announced the first call.

"Well, Mr… Well, Andrew, this is your class. The first bell is a call, the next is the beginning of the lessons. If they find you wandering after the second you're in serious trouble, understood?"

"Understood."

"Enjoy yourself," Carlyle greeted, "see you at break, unfortunately."

"Thanks."

Notwithstanding his turbulent scholastic career, the fourteen-year-old enrolled in the register with the name of Andrew Parker Fawcett had not lost a year until now. Or rather, he had lost the previous one, but having been registered by his father, a year in advance, back in Year One, meant that he now found himself with others of his own age. René Fawcett, who actually had French origins from his grandfather side, had always been very strict about his son's education, at least at the beginning. The moment he started travelling for work, however, he had begun to lose interest in his son's family and school life. Still, Andrew had not given up. He was convinced that if he worked hard he would regain his father's attention. His grades went up, and the teachers were all enthusiastic about him. They were already talking about a great future and the best universities.

Then, suddenly, Andrew stopped looking at his books, let alone listening to the lessons. One day he turned distracted towards a window and stopped altogether, without turning back. Without explanations to anyone.

The school's reaction had not been the best; the headmaster's even less so since the promising Fawcett had also ceased any exchange with the teachers, treating them with disinterest and boredom. Everything could be tolerated, but not this behaviour. The results were not long in coming.

The famous institute in which Renè had enrolled him soon told them that the boy's presence was no longer appreciated, inviting them to take him to a more suitable place. And so it was done. But Andrew's behaviour didn't change. Within six months, he had tried four new schools.

Despite how many times Emily asked him what was wrong and René's attempts to have him talk to a psychologist, Andrew kept to himself. He had realised that his father would no longer be interested in him, no matter what he did.

A year later, his parents invited him to sit on the white leather sofa and announced that they were separating. It took a further year of atrocious cohabitation with a father he barely saw, except for a couple of days a month. Then Andrew was called into the study and was told that René would never return from one of his business trips. He would stay in another city with a woman who was not his mother and a little brother on the way. Yes, a little brother…

What happened next, for Andy, was a blurred memory. He remembered a bustle of suitcases and clothes; car rides in the rain for hundreds of miles and his grandmother's house smelling of incense and roast chicken. And his Mum's endless tears mingling with steamed up autumn windows.

This happened a year before, the year in which Andrew skipped most of the school year, and that was spent with dramatic ups and downs from which he and his mother came out stronger and closer. Everything seemed to want to change and he felt happy. New job for Emily, a new city far from the bad memories, new school. Even the hair on Andrew's chin was new, a deeper voice and the height that now allowed him to notice the regrowth on his Mum's head.

Enough with these childish thoughts, he had told himself many times. *Enough with tears. Enough with pain.* Everything seemed to want to change, and change was what the crippled Fawcett family needed. Andrew wanted to embrace it without looking back, fighting himself, if necessary, to let it come uncontested by fear and childish attitudes.

Thus he stepped firmly into class 9-C, which greeted him with the smell of damp, wet jackets, a tropical temperature and blinding neon lights in contrast with the dull frame of the windows. Inside, about twenty boys and girls were chatting, while somewhere still walking to their seats looking uncomfortable.

Andrew had a sheet of Dean Richardson's secretary reading: "Close up, scale A, Class 9-C, desk D". He found it immediately, followed by the distracted and curious looks from the first row on the right. Without saying anything, he put down his bag and took off his jacket, looking for a free coat rack. He noticed that the class was made up mostly of males, and he lingered on a face that was familiar to him, but he could not remember from where. Without further ado, the object of his scrupulous analysis stood up to meet him.

He was at least a foot taller than Andrew and had very deep dark eyes and black hair. His face was pale, but he had a sturdy body for one so young. When their noses were less than two inches away, Andy recognised him. He had seen him right here at the school, after his conversation with Richardson, staring at him through the front gate of the institute. The look was the same, cold and disturbing. Alien.

"Are you one of them?" he asked in a low voice.

Hot breath hit Andrew's eyes. He swallowed, not knowing what to say. "Who?"

The boy moved even closer; in the class an unsettling silence began to fall.

"You are nothing. Do you understand? And you know nothing."

He said it with such loathing and anger that Andy was amazed. It seemed to harbour an age-old hatred of him and of all his relatives, both near and far, simply because they existed. This made no sense. And then, who were *them*?

Andrew knew he had no choice but to humble himself in the very first minute of high school, and although he had already taken it into account, now that he was in the situation he felt he could not bow to the usurper so easily.

"Repeat what I said," ordered the boy, contracting his lips to emphasize every single consonant and splashing saliva like a rabid dog.

Andy swallowed again. Perhaps at the Saint Paul, they welcomed even crazy murderers with a smile and no one had told him.

"Kyle! Bercut is coming!" warned a voice from somewhere.

For a never-ending moment, their eyes were fixed on each other. Andrew couldn't stop, more out of fear than because he was trying to understand the meaning of that hate; Kyle, on the other hand, looked amused with a sort of mad grin on his face. When the door opened with a metallic snap, the boy shifted slightly, dodging it smoothly before heading towards his seat. Andrew realised he was the only one left standing when Professor Bercut appeared behind him.

"Good morning Mr...?"

"Fawcett," he replied in a whisper.

"Ah, Mr Fawcett. One of the new arrivals. Good. Come along," said the man, pointing to the empty desk. "And remember, I'm Professor Bercut, and when I ask you something you'll be kind enough to answer by adding my name at the end of the sentence." He placed his briefcase down without even turning.

"Yes, Professor Bercut."

The man gave him a brief look before putting on a pair of round glasses. The second bell announced the beginning of the lessons.

"Ladies and Gentlemen, well met. I hope you have had some restful holidays. A new era begins for you, whether you are repeating the year or not, and it will be a very hard journey; Saint Paul has an excellent reputation for the quality of its teaching. A reputation that, it goes without saying, it wants to keep." He turned to the whiteboard and with a black marker he wrote his name down. "My name is Benjamin Bercut and I'm the Deputy Head of Saint Paul. I teach Languages and

History, so you will spend a good part of your time with me. You can call me Mr Bercut or Professor Bercut. Other appellations are not contemplated. Understood?"

The class response was nothing short of timid.

"Very well, I'm sure your vocal cords will soon overcome the trauma of the first day. In the classroom, electronic devices of any kind are not allowed, including mobile phones and so on. If found, they will be confiscated and donated to the school fund. Last year, thanks to the inability of your colleagues to follow the rules, we made 4,800 pounds. Can't complain, really. Now, without wasting any more time, let's open our textbooks on page fifteen. We will begin with a brief summary of prehistoric eras, then move on to the appearance of the first civilizations in 5,000 BC."

There was a rustle of pages being turned, and Bercut began his lesson.

Andrew turned slightly to the left, peering in the direction of Kyle with bated breath. The boy was staring back at him with defiance. He still wore that disquieting grin. The strangest thing for Andy was that it was not clear whether he was doing it to resume the conversation interrupted by Professor Bercut or, rather, to comment on the contents of the lesson..

11

When the bell rung, Bercut finally concluded. Almost three hours had passed.

"Before you go for your break, Headmaster Richardson would like to make a short speech to mark the beginning of the year," he said, stopping the general rise from the desks.

After a few seconds, in perfect synchrony, the intercoms of the class croaked to life. "Dear boys and girls, this is Headmaster William Richardson, and I would like to give you my personal welcome to Saint Paul for another year. A welcome to our new students too. A year full of commitment and hard work awaits us, as well as great experiences to share together. We have planned two long trips and numerous excursions to museums and other cultural places inside and outside the city. I remind everyone that for any problem or enquiry you can contact Miss Faltermayer on the first floor, next to the school office."

Kyle had already started towards the door, under the stern gaze of Bercut, stopping in front of it with the doorknob in his hand. Two other kids followed him closely.

"*Omnia munda mundis*, said St. Paul. Everything is pure for the pure," the principal continued. "The benevolent founder of this institute believed in the purity of the young and in their importance in the world as saviours of the future. And so we also believe in each of you, and we hope to see you improve the world."

The silent clash of looks between Kyle and Bercut kept up. Both appeared calm as if they were old enemies who knew each other's moves well.

"Tomorrow morning at 09:00, a mass will be held in memory of our friend, Adam Uyan, who died last month in a canoe accident. Everyone is welcome. If someone wants to leave a message to the family, please contact Miss Faltermayer. Thank you for your attention."

The intercom had barely crackled its closure that Kyle's foot was already over the threshold. Andrew was certain that his overbearing classmate would be waiting for him in the corridor to finish the unreadable speech he had begun, but when he looked out it was Carlyle's face he saw.

"Do you want to give me a heart attack?"

"Come on, Foquet, don't be so tense. Relax, come with me."

The two joined the crowd that was coming down the stairs. They came out of the large rear glass door, on which was printed the Saint Paul logo, a shield with a book in the middle, and they found themselves in the great inner cloister. The structure of the school was really very beautiful and austere and the courtyard was not far off those standards. Surrounded by a colonnade with access to offices, indoor gyms and social rooms, its open area was decorated with fountains and low walls, including a small agora that recalled a Greek theatre.

"Have you had any problems in class?" Carlyle asked, sitting next to other students on one of the walls, and unwrapping a sandwich.

"No, why? Was I supposed to?"

The other shrugged, a resigned expression on his face.

"Let's say a bully wanted to off me for no reason, but I guess it's normal here."

"Nah. Saint Paul isn't as bad as you think. It'll all be because of Richardson's control systems."

"Don't tell me that you believe there are really cameras in the columns?"

"Yeah. And not just in the columns. Take a closer look at the dolphin in the central fountain," he added mysteriously.

Andrew did not even turn around. "Come on, Carlyle. Is this a prank you've created especially for the newbies?"

"Why would you say that, oh untrustworthy one?" he answered, laughing.

"I'm right, am I not?"

"Clearly. Is it so obvious?"

"And this is your idea of fun?"

"To tell the truth, not really. It was an idea of Martin Grayson, third year. Him and his friends love it."

"I don't. It's bullshit."

Carlyle bit into the sandwich. "So, what were you saying about your close encounter?"

Andrew sighed, also unwrapping a tuna sandwich. "You know when you look at someone for a while and they take offence? Like, what the fuck are you looking at?"

The other nodded in understanding.

"That. What kind of question is it, anyway? If I look at you it's because God gave me eyes."

"Flawless reasoning. But were you staring at him?"

"He reminded me of someone."

"Are you gay?"

Andrew turned to his companion. "No, but what's that got to do with it?"

"Nothing. But since you were staring at a man who reminded you of someone, it could have seemed like an 'approach' excuse."

"You are mental. Anyway, he immediately goes off on one and runs towards me, spit flying in my face and telling me a series of incoherent sentences, which I still don't get."

"What did you do?" asked Carlyle, genuinely curious.

Andy realised that he no longer remembered Kyle's words. "Nothing, Bercut came in and he was gone."

"I can imagine who you're talking about, young Fosset. Let's say that Kyle has very defined principles, even if nobody understands them. Sometimes he's very quiet and thoughtful; you see him sitting by himself, sad, thinking, eyes lost in space. Sometimes he gets mad about nothing. But there's always a reason. He has no friends, except those who follow him out of fear. For some in the school, he's a kind of paladin. On several occasions he's also defended losers like us from the older kids, risking a lot. No sympathy for him in the upper classes and some seventeen-year-old would do him out, if they could."

"And why don't they?"

Carlyle smiled. "Because Kyle is a demon. You should see him in a fight. Nobody can stop him when he uses his fists. Once, last year, he faced four older boys alone."

"What happened?"

"It was in the gym, when it was deserted. Nobody knows exactly. We only know that two ended up in hospital, one was still sleeping by the end of the day and the other changed school. From that moment, everyone respected him way more."

Andrew followed the story, fascinated.

"Of course, he came out battered too, but he never complained about his attackers with the headmaster. As if to say: *Careful, I can hold my own, and I don't need anyone's help!*"

"Tough guy, the way you describe him."

Carlyle put the last piece of sandwich in his mouth. "Yes, but don't be fooled. He's a weirdo."

"I noticed. Why do you say that? "

"There's a rumour going around that he's not quite right in the head. His fixations, for example. Like, almost always when he goes out into the yard, the first thing he does is to look at the sky for something. Looks and looks again. Then he stops, smiles and returns among the others."

"How odd."

"Not as much as when he tortures animals. Lizards, frogs and insects. He comes up with the weirdest way to kill them. His friends enjoy watching him and say that he talks to the animals while he kills them!"

"This sounds even stranger. Tell me more."

"What else can I say? He particularly has it in for a certain loser."

"Who?"

"Don't you live near the subway, down after the railway, in the red high-rises?"

"Yes, why?"

"Then you should know him. It's your neighbour. I had to read your card and I'm sure he lives near you."

"I only have old geezers for neighbours. Unless… wait, but who? The one from the Amazonian garden? I doubt even that they are alive. I've never seen them before – imagine if there's a kid in there."

"I assure you he's there. And you want to know something really weird?" Carlyle looked at him with a conspiratorial look.

Andrew nodded.

"Seen anything strange on the intercom?"

"No, it's almost empty of names. There are only acronyms. Want to keep me on tenterhooks for much longer?"

"He's named just like the one that drowned in the lake. Adam Uyan."

"The name's the same?"

"Yeah," Carlyle took a theatrical pause. "Spooky, huh?"

Andrew was almost convinced it was another of his mate's jokes, but let it go. "And Kyle has it in for this Uyan?"

"It seems so. He's always breathing down his neck, even out of school. Nobody knows why, but you know, Kyle is an out-of-the-ordinary guy, and nobody cares for him apart from poor Uyan."

"Does he come to school here?"

"Adam? Yes, 4-A."

Andrew looked around, as if to identify a familiar face that he remembered seeing around his house.

Carlyle finished his Coke. "Come on; maybe today you did Uyan a favour and you just don't know. Perhaps you've convinced the strange Kyle to divert a bit of his attention from him to you," he burst out laughing.

"But I didn't do anything to him…" Andy protested, then the bell announced the end of the break.

12

Faith would have given Helena Dowson a long and peaceful life, even if she were only a Sleeper. She would have a large family, a house of her own and a pension.

Or at least that's how it should have been. This course of events, from the moment she opened her eyes to the sound of the alarm clock that Tuesday in October, had become uncertain and out of focus. A powerful and determined will stood between Helena and her quiet future. A will in the total control of a man named Amin, former heir of the Herèpen Aptan dynasty.

She got up slowly, passing from the bed to the couch, still traumatised by sleep. After a coffee and some cereal with milk, she took a quick shower and got ready to leave. She took the gun, checked the safety, and went out the door twenty-nine minutes exactly from when she woke up, as per the strict times that marked her day.

That morning traffic and bad weather dominated the city. That's why Helena had recently bought a new electric bicycle that allowed her to reach the police station in twenty minutes. Despite it being a rather chilly day, she appreciated the cold wind that helped her along and, when she reached the foot of the hills, she triggered the electrical system, left the lever and climbed effortlessly next to the tram.

*

At that precise moment, Amin knocked on the glass door of the bookshop "Davies', since 1870". He didn't perceive any movement from the inside. When he knocked again, a stocky figure appeared, gestured to the timetable with the opening times and disappeared again. He was a short man of about sixty with a square face and small eyes. He wore large rectangular glasses of black onyx, linked together by a brass chain, and wore a faded brown fustian suit. Amin waited, patiently.

The central square was full of autumnal scents. The anachronistic carriages that led the tourists around the most characteristic areas of the city were still all lined up in the middle. The horses were dozing and, from time to time, they caught glimpses of the passersby or their drivers in the miserable little piece of the world they could see. Further on, a famous white marble fountain waited for someone to throw a coin, like a vain pledge. The shutters of the shops were still lowered, while the excited shouting from the cafes indicated the morning activities had started. Finally, a street police car made slow turns around the square.

The great machine created for the Sleepers was coming to life, like every other day, since millennia. It took different forms in the world, but the substance didn't change; it remained as it had been imagined by the Lords of Matter. A precise, magnificent and perfect machine.

Atlantis.

Amin inhaled such infallible greatness and filled himself with it. All around him was the overwhelming proof of the superiority of man on Mother Earth that announced the ineluctability of the fulfilment of the Great Intention. He felt proud, the only feeling that was not yet rare in his emotional sphere.

The door behind him opened with a plaintive creak of wood. "Good morning. Excuse me, I was tidying up. After all, it's not quite opening time," said Shaun the librarian with a friendly smile. "Come in, please. It's still cold out there."

Amin passed him without saying anything and entered the library.

The room was cosy and the walls were covered with ancient reddish wood panels, emanating a strong smell of resin. There were shelves everywhere and several tall bookcases occupied the whole room. In the back, a narrow spiral staircase led to a low and dark loft.

"Were you looking for something in particular?" the old man asked as he cleaned his glasses, which he then put on, wrinkling his nose.

Amin snorted, carefully choosing his words. "Tales. Do you have any?"

"This is a historical bookstore, sir," the man chuckled. "We have many ancient books, especially non-fiction books. Since my grandfather opened it, we have always treated only antiquities, medieval manuscripts, rare works. The kind of books that people put on a lectern in their home. We don't deal in children's books, I'm sorry."

"Are you sure?" Amin took a few steps, looking formal, sniffing the smell of the room. "And yet it seems to me that you are well supplied."

Shaun approached the shelves, amazed and confused. "How is it possible? Let me see, where? Well, I can't understand how can it be..." he said, hurrying to check.

"Are you not the owner? Don't you take care of cataloguing all this? Your library is full of tales."

The man was trying to follow the client, examining all the titles he could see on the shelves around them. Then he shrugged, defeated. "I don't understand, sir. I don't see any fairy tales. Here are the shelves of ancient translations of apocryphal and mythological texts. And more in here, as you can see, our speciality, the sacred texts."

Amin turned away from the old man and smiled. "Exactly. Tales."

Shaun stared at the man, twisting his jaw to one side, impatiently. *The day has started with a tough customer, I see! Let us give a lesson to this arrogant young man*, he thought. "Well, I don't consider sacred texts fairy tales. In some, limited I'd add, views, such works could be considered legends, myths or, why not, stories. The dimension of a text like those found here has its roots in the very heart of the human existential experience. But their importance in contributing to the evolution of thought is such that it doesn't allow me to consider them as simple suggestions with a final moral, such as fables. If you want to buy something, please tell me what you are looking for and I will try to help you. If not, can I recommend the main street bookshop?" he concluded, thinking, *Now the ball is in your court, ignoramus!*

Amin opened an old book with a restored cover, a copy of Giordano Bruno's *Shadow of Ideas*. Leafing through it, he said only: "Good. I'm looking for a history book."

The old man smiled triumphantly. "See? You're in the right place after all. Are you looking for a particular title?"

"Not exactly. But the Great Gorann is the subject that interests me."

The lead of Shaun's pencil broke on the sheet of paper, where it was resting ready to scribble the title. The man looked up at Amin, who stared at him impassively.

"Do you prefer a more precise description, perhaps? I would like to investigate the war between Mu and Atlantis, the fall of the first moon and the long Oblivion. Don't tell me that you have nothing about it in your old bookshop?" he emphasised the word "old" with contempt.

"But this is a historical bookstore, sir. These things of which you speaks are..."

"Tales?" asked Amin, approaching.

Shaun stepped back slightly, bumping into a couple of ancient manuscripts on a nearby reading table. "Yes, of course, fairy tales," he said, picking the items up. "Not that I really know much about it. It's the result of various legends from different historical periods, different sources and for different reasons."

"Tell me what you know, old man. Bestow your culture on me. Is this not your job?"

"Sure. Well, I'm not a teacher, but... The myth of Atlantis was born with the Greek philosopher Plato, who spoke about it in two of his works, the *Timaeus* and the *Crizia*. The city of Atlantis is the representation of a powerful civilization that sins with *ubris*, pride, and therefore it's punished, destroyed by flames and swallowed by water because of a cataclysm triggered by the angry gods. It is one of the most famous myths of antiquity," the bookseller finished, clearing his throat.

Amin stared at him with an indecipherable expression. "Charming. Go on."

"Mu is the lost continent where man was said to be born, the cradle of life, whose tradition should be contained in the stories of priests and shamans of the so-called primitive societies. At least, this is what the British Colonel James Churchward claims in his books, written while serving in India, at the time a British colony. The legend of Mu was the basis for the ruminations of some secret European esoteric societies in the early twentieth century, then linked to the rise of Nazi power." Shaun, who was tidying up as he spoke, put the last book on the shelf and took a deep breath. "More than this, I can not tell you. Try the Internet, maybe. That's the best place for myths and inventions."

"Myths and inventions," the strange customer repeated. "Shame."

"I can't help you further, I'm sorry," the old man cut short, accompanying him to the exit. "I hope to see you again here if you need books like the ones we sell."

Amin held out his hand to the man, who wavered as he held it.

"Thank you. So if it's okay with you, I'll be back in two lunar cycles, when you'll have managed to get me a pact between giants with a Milesian."

"What?" the man stammered.

Amin moved closer, illuminated by the cold light of the morning on one side of the face and the warm one of the shop on the other. "And tell your friends of the *Arkanum* to stay put in their hovels, whatever they might perceive in the Essence. I'm not here for you, old man, but give me the slightest annoyance and I promise I'll unleash against you a whole horde of Scavengers," he threatened him with a petrifying serenity.

"Who are you?" asked the bookseller through clenched teeth, while a low menacing vibration was spreading across the room.

"Listen to my words, Shaun, son of Saul. If you have survived so far, it has been thanks to your privacy and to the merit of mine. Your destiny is linked to the whims of my boredom. Your name may be reported to court as a reactionary. Now quench your *keh* and let's talk. This is not a place for confrontation."

The old man kept staring at the ice-eyed young man with a stony look, but the vibration was fading. "We live in peace here. It is not our war, brother. Don't hold grudges against those who are innocent."

"You have made your choices. Now don't regret them."

"But don't you see that Mother Earth is on its last legs? You risked destroying it once before. And now you want to condemn the whole community, including yourself, descendants of Evenor?"

"Neither me nor you are called to make any decisions about the fate of the world. It's up to others," Amin cut him short.

"What do you want from me?"

"I told you, I want a pact of giants with a Milesian, a pact of non-aggression."

"I can't. I don't have this power. As you can see from my stature, I am not a giant!"

"No, but you're a man of Asperia. And where there is Asperia there is always a Milesian."

Shaun tried to reason with him. "In any case, I can't do it in such a short time. Even if I could find a giant, the *Arkanum* will never grant it. We both know it. And, even if it did, I cannot guarantee that it would respect the pact."

"It's your problem, old man. If you cannot keep a muzzle on your warmongering brothers, it will be all the worse for you and your descendants. But tell them to be very careful about the choices they make. This time it is not about skirmishes. The princes will react against any act perpetrated against me or the mission I am carrying out," Amin lied.

Shaun looked around confused.

"Do what I told you," the Hound continued, "and I give you my word that you will be spared. The word of an enemy like myself is a hundred times better than that of the friends you have chosen."

"May I know your name, since you know mine?" asked the old man, still looking him straight in the eyes.

"I am the one who has many names. But none of them reveals who I am." With that, he left the bookshop.

When the door closed in a tinkling of bells, Shaun leaned against the wooden counter, his eyes welling up with rage, fear, and helplessness. He thought about all the possibilities, but none was feasible. Perhaps the nameless man was bluffing, but he could not risk it. He had to warn his brothers, and look for one who possessed a wisdom superior to his own.

He wiped his face – it was not the time to commiserate. He closed the shop quietly, greeted his neighbour, who waved at him through his own designer windows, and walked towards the large marble staircase where some boys were sitting playing guitars and smoking.

A blue-orange patch had emerged in the palm of his hand, with which he had squeezed Amin's hand, and the small trace of *Orichalcum* that had settled there began to ache; a reminder of what fate awaited the traitors of the mighty Lords of Matter, just as the princes of Atlantis had long since been called.

Shaun had to reach someone who was only about five hundred yards away from his bookshop, but it would take him the entire morning. With the Milesians, there was no hurry, and rituals had to be respected. Although they lived in a world foreign to them, they had never renounced rituals. Indeed, not happy with those they always had, which had seen the rise and fall of endless kings, they had invented another in an attempt to adapt to the passage of time, in the ages and habits of the Sleepers.

So Shaun set off on what the giants called the "mountain path", the only way to find, recognise and be accepted by a representative of the First People.

*

"Soldier of Atlantis!" called Amin in a clear and powerful voice, so that a very chic lady, wearing an expensive fur coat, turned. One of the carriage horses pricked up its ears and began to neigh, retreating with the utter puzzlement of the coach driver.

Daniel stared at the face of the man who had called him. He had the feeling that the world, in the personal meaning he gave to the word, had gone out of focus. All of a sudden he could no longer give importance to what, until a moment before, had been the crucial problems of his existence. They had volatilized by virtue of a monumental event that he recognised, but which he would not have been able to explain to anyone, perhaps not even to himself.

A man, perhaps younger than he was, faced him, but he was unable to tell his age. He was tall and dressed in a casual way. What attracted him the most was the harmony of the forms and his extraordinary and brilliant face. The nose and eyebrows were regular; the eyes were marked by light dark circles and appeared black. They expressed such decisiveness, such violent will, that it would be enough to order a mountain to move. The skin was brownish, almost golden, every hair bright and full. This perfect face stood out even more when one noticed a flat scar stretching from the ear to the middle of the right jaw. Still, the scarring could not weaken the strength of that figure.

Daniel had forgotten the question he had been asked. But he felt he would have consented to any of the man's requests.

Amin approached him with a smile, studying the traits of his new soldier. "I need you to do a service for your lord."

"Order and it will be done," Daniel heard himself say.

"See that man who is climbing the stairs? The old man in the velvet jacket."

"I see him."

"His name is Shaun. He is a conscript of Atlantis. He belongs to the Third People and maintains contact between the people of Mu who live in this region and the ruling Prince ".

"Yes, my Lord."

"Follow him. He will stop and talk to a strange man dressed in a long robe, with hands in his pockets and a foolish smile on his face. When this happens," Amin said, taking Daniel's hand, "I will know and you will be free."

"Your will is mine."

Daniel did not know what he was doing or why. But he didn't care. The main thought that occupied his mind was to carry out that task; he felt that for the first time his life made sense and that his fate was in his hands, finally. This was enough to bid his lord's will, even if it brought him to the extreme sacrifice. Wife, children, parents, work: everything had passed into the background. The very meaning of the word "world" had changed, replaced by something of which he could only perceive power and urgency, something of which he was a part: the Great Intention.

13

"How did it go, honey?" Emily asked as soon as her son got into the car.

"Hi Mum, great, yeah. I met the Deputy Head, Lord Bercut. Seems nice enough."

"Glad to hear it. And your classmates?" she rolled on.

"All good, more or less. I'll tell you more in the next few days. Can we go now? I'm starving!"

Emily started the engine, but she had not even shifted into gear when someone knocked on the passenger window. It was Carlyle.

Andrew lowered the window and the boy stuck his head into the car.

"Hey," he winked. "Is this your mum?" he asked, morbidly.

Mrs Fawcett reached out with a friendly smile. "I'm Andrew's mum. Emily."

"Pleased to meet you, ma'am. I'm Carlyle Ferguson. But you can call me Carly."

"Carly?" Andrew snapped. "Did you need something, *Carlyle?*" he asked, annoyed.

The other seemed to snap back to reality. "There's PE tomorrow. Remember your tracksuit and a change of clothing."

"I'll remember, sure."

"You know, ma'am," Carlyle leaned over Andrew, "I was assigned to be your son's guide for his first days at Saint Paul," he added, pleased with himself.

"That's great. Well, thank you for your help then, Carly. "

Andrew was getting annoyed now. "Yes, thanks."

"Of course, a boy like you doesn't need help," he said absently and sarcastically. "But it's my job to protect you and make sure you don't forget anything, as you know." He gave him a backhanded pat on the front of his shoulder that tasted a lot like *What a pretty Mummy you have.*

"Yes, thank you again. See you tomorrow." Andy cut him short and began to close the window. Carlyle stepped back with that moronic smile still on his face.

"See you soon, Mrs Foquet!" His voice faded out behind the window.

"It's pronounced Fawcett," Emily waved and put the car into gear.

"Nice chap. I'm sure you'll become friends," she said in a matter-of-fact tone.

Andrew didn't add anything, eager to get away from there.

Carlyle was strange, but nothing compared to Kyle. After the unjustified attack of the morning, he had completely ignored him. He had spent most of his day looking out the window, putting on the broody stranger act. At the end of the day, he had disappeared in the chaotic river of students, swallowed by the jumble of second-row parked cars, horns and shouting.

Are you one of them? Andrew thought of Kyle's words.

"Mum, did you move my DVDs off the shelf?" he asked, caught by a sudden intuition.

"No, honey, I don't touch your movies. I know how much you care." Emily protested. "Why?"

"Nothing. It's just that last night a strange thing happened. I thought I'd left a box set in the bookcase, but when I came back from the kitchen I found it on the floor."

Emily went pale and shivered. "My god, I hope there are no rats in the house!"

The neighbours' garden was so tangled that perhaps during the night some animal had made it through the net and entered the house. Or maybe it was a pet from a nearby flat. He had to do something about it, if only to protect his precious DVD collection. And, perhaps, he could also learn more about his young neighbour, Adam Uyan.

The simplest explanations were never the first to appear in Andrew's mind. The previous night he had gone to sleep concocting who knows what kind of dark explanation for the box set falling. He always had to have an unfathomable mystery behind any event. He wasn't to know that this time he was right. The significance of this would only become apparent two weeks down the line. For now though, he snorted and relaxed in his seat, looking forward to his dinner.

14

The mountain path worked a bit like the mechanism of a safe. The numbers were represented by the amount of minutes a person had to stop in a series of places, waiting to move on. And these transition places, in a way, represented the various rotations that the safe's knob must complete to unlock the door.

Every Milesian had a sort of personal combination, like a phone number, which made it possible to trace it. This combination changed every day and every hour due to very complex calculations. Yet any giant would have said that it was simply an intuitive method.

For the giant Trummugan, the mountain path was a little more complex than for his peers. He and Shaun had known each other since the latter was born. At that time, the Milesian was already considered an adult. They had shared many joyful events, but also sad and mournful ones. Shaun's last sixty years of life had seen powerful forces colliding, which had caused great suffering both for the Sleepers and the Roused ones.

The man and the giant had gone through the end of the century together, united in protecting their community by mediating, where possible, between the extreme fringes of what remained of the people of Mu and the Lords of Matter, with their ambitious and bloodthirsty surrogates.

Human beings, the Third People, lived in such a state of amnesia that their hidden memories had sunk more and more in the deep well of the unconscious and didn't even remember the reason for their existence. The more this distance became unbridgeable, the more the powers that had caused it influenced the mind and the decisions of the Sleepers, so much so that the events of the real world had taken the form of creeping nightmares, manifested through thoughts and actions unworthy of creatures born awaken.

Breaking the diktats of Atlantis, Trummugan had initiated Shaun's four sons in the ancient arts in order to perpetuate the traditions of Mu. The two were friends, but the man was still obliged to walk the mountain path like anyone else. And not just out of respect for tradition, but because otherwise, disguised through Ancient Knowledge as he was, Shaun would not have recognised his friend even if he crashed into him.

As for the giants and their relationship with the cities of the Sleepers, they seldom chose them as dwellings, though some, like Trummugan, were attracted to these locations and ran the risk of being noticed, not so much from the lazy and short-sighted eyes of men, but from the more careful ones interested in finding dissidents and reporting their presence at court for a profit.

Trummugan couldn't help but immerse himself in that environment, artificial and forced, chaotic and senseless, lost and frightened. A world made up of ghosts that spent their lives wondering what the reason was for their existence, when in fact it was the first, simple answer with which they came into the world. The giant was fascinated by so much astonishing beauty fretting towards daily nothingness, forgetful of the power of every single individual, their extraordinary nature and blind to the light that shone around them at every moment. Vacuous eyes, distracted by a game of mirrors that would not deceive a child, looking for a mutual consolation to fill only for a few moments. A waste so huge to leave a giant speechless.

Shaun approached the man sitting on the park bench opposite the majestic villa built by a dictator now forgotten. A few joggers overtook him, headphones in place, uncaring of the unstable weather.

He sat down and waited a moment before speaking. "You should avoid coming into town."

A hand rose to greet him. Only the hand. Not a word.

"It has become a very dangerous place, this, Trum," he continued. "There are many who would be happy to report your presence at the Atlantean court." He glanced at his friend, who did likewise.

Daniel spied on the couple through the pouring water of a large nineteenth-century fountain. It was just as his master had described. The man he had followed was sitting next to a strange guy, dressed in an oversized, brown trench coat of heavy fabric, a thick, colourful woollen scarf around the neck, wide dark glasses and a wide-brimmed hat – a model which was coming back into fashion. He had a broad but rigid smile on his face which created an endless network of wrinkles on his skin. The man spoke to him, but it didn't seem to cause any change in that great and singular smile.

"This morning a man came to the bookstore, Trum," continued Shaun. "He says he knows everything about us and has threatened to report us at court if we don't procure him a pact between giants."

Trummugan turned his smiling face towards his friend and began to speak without moving a single muscle of his mouth, as if he were a ventriloquist. The voice, sharp and shrill, seemed to come from an unspecified point, high up behind him. "Good morning to you too, my friend. Did this unexpected visit made you forget your manners?"

Shaun tried to reply but was cut short.

"A pact between giants can only exist between giants, as the definition says. Unless, of course, it's about something special. Who was this man you described? What position does he occupy in the bigger picture of Atlantis? Above all, does he belong to the descendants of Evenor or the brutal followers of his twin, Belial?"

"I don't know much, Trum. I tried to find out, but he noticed that. There was something noble about him – he spoke like a nobleman, at least. At first he made fun of me, then he said he has many names. But now, all I can think of are our boys, especially one of them."

"Mmm…" Trummugan grumbled. "If he hides his true name, it must be important."

"What do you mean, my friend?"

The giant kept smiling, caught up in his reasoning. He raised a hand, the only gesture he seemed capable of doing. "A man with such a secret identity, who acts without asking and has no need to threaten unless his actions are his own and as unknown as his true first name."

"What are you thinking about?"

"I think maybe he is a Shadow Hound on a one-way mission."

Shaun looked at the giant in disbelief. "I thought they were all gone!"

"No, they have not disappeared. Lackeys that run without asking are always useful to rulers. With the speech about his name, our friend gave us a clue, maybe voluntarily. Maybe he's not so stupid not to understand he needs allies. And us."

"I can't tell why, but since last month's lake accident, not a day has passed when I don't fear unwanted attention on us. The Shadow Hounds act on behalf of the court. I don't feel like underestimating his threats, however much you may consider them unfounded."

Trummugan seemed to go on with his own line of reasoning. "For any other court, for sure. But we don't know that he works for that of Prince Here-whatever, who reigns on this part of Mother Earth. If this man has to move with so much circumspection, it's because he is not acting on his home turf, so to speak."

"He's shown to know who we are and that we have a giant with us."

The other paused for a long time, playing with his gloved thumbs. Their rubbing deformed the fabric, as if there was nothing solid there.

"He's a man with nothing to lose," Trummugan reasoned aloud. "He has lost all reasons for living, except for the one linked to the Atlantean concept of being bricks and not human beings. First he is a king-god, then something happens; maybe he makes a mistake or is tricked by other pretenders. A sentence is issued against him by the highest legislative body, the judges. And suddenly he's no longer a noble nor a citizen, which according to Atlantean law means no longer human." The giant made a short pause. "Therefore, he loses his name and more basic rights recognised to a living creature by the Lords of Matter. The other hounds become his only judges, beings full of hatred for what they are no more. If he survives, our fallen is transformed. His only mission becomes the ransom of a death that saves the honour of his name and returns to his family their lost dignity. Thus he is sent on a mission to the world of the dormant ones. An unknown world that he has only studied in books, but whose dynamics he ignores. As with regards to the missions they carry on, you know what I'm talking about."

"Murders," Shaun concluded. "This is their main job. I tremble at the thought of what he could do if he found the boy."

Trummugan turned to follow a lady who was pushing a pram. "The sentence which condemned a Pure to exile can only derive by betrayal or by the murder of another Pure. These are inconceivable acts in the minds of the nobles. To destroy a pure bloodline can jeopardise the whole Great Intention. It's similar to the reactions the Sleepers have towards religions. Without control."

Meanwhile, the woman had sat on the bench opposite them and was fumbling with a milk bottle and a silver thermos.

"In any case," the giant went on, "the man without a name, who perhaps has sent someone to spy on us while we speak, has never been forgiven and his guilt has not been forgotten. I don't think his mission is murder, otherwise he would have acted. He's preparing something loud, part of a much greater plan. That's why he doesn't want interference."

"Do you think he's being followed?"

"More or less. I'm thinking of a shadow far deeper than the one that lodges in the heart of our nameless friend. If he's looking for help on this part, he expects to find none on the other."

The woman stared at him for a moment, returning the smile. She had not realised that it was the only possible expression for that puppet that somehow hid a giant.

"I share your fears. But perhaps this situation may not be completely negative," Trummugan continued.

"What do you mean?"

"I wonder at the need for so much aggression if what this man seeks is… a pact of non-aggression, that is, the certainty not to enter into conflict."

Shaun thought for a moment, absorbed. "It's strange, it's true. But

I still wouldn't underestimate him."

Even with that smile on his face, the tone of the giant became serious. "No. It is undoubtedly a real threat, but we must figure out the circumstances around this man without a name before we can act."

"What are you going to do?"

"What is necessary. It is time to convene the *Collegium*." He stood up with his hands in his pockets.

Shaun followed him. "Calling the *Collegium* is always a risk, as you well know. A risk which at the moment is based on reasoning of which, forgive me, we have no confirmation."

The giant laughed and bowed to his friend. "You think? But don't you know that the Milesians are the direct descendants of the noble Thuata De Danann, the wisest creatures that ever existed?"

"I didn't mean to offend you, Trum. I apologise."

"I am not offended in the least. Your fear would be founded if it was based only on my words. But in recent days some brothers shivak told me they had heard of the arrival of a Shadow Hound in their area of the Sleepers' city. Other friends have also informed me that the Onagros were excited, as if they knew they had to host someone of importance. And I am convinced that it is the same person in all these cases. You have your proof," he finally grinned.

Shaun removed his glasses to clean them, irritated. "Why did you not say this before?"

The man began to move away. "I wanted to hear your version without compromising it."

"Where are you going?"

"For a walk! The lenticular fluid is drying out and needs air to recover. I will wait for the call."

Shaun sat back down, looking at his friend shambling away. A small group of joggers ran to meet him. Everyone avoided him, except one, distracted by the form of a jogging companion. When the man hit Trummugan, it seemed that a car had hooked him with a rope and pulled away at full throttle. He bounced back with a thud, landing two yards away, tumbling into the lower ditch that skirted the fence. The others didn't notice, leaving the poor man to climb back towards the road half soaked.

The giant disappeared among the small crowd by the rides. A careful eye would have noticed the leaves and the branches of the great oaks move, as if blown by wind, almost four yards above the children playing.

Shaun witnessed the scene, amused. For a few minutes, the man of Mu stood still, breathing the scent of trees and earth. He felt full as a reassuring presence cocooned around him. The huge and powerful breath was a hoarse panting, tired and slow, a vibration that went right across him. "Mother," he whispered with infinite and compassionate love. He would have loved to do more for her, but he knew he could not win the war alone. And he let himself be lulled, immersed in the tired, but still sweet embrace, the embrace of the only mother of every living being.

Daniel had watched the conversation without hearing the words. When both figures had gone, he was left with doubt. What to do? Should he go back or stay there and wait for the arrival of his lord?

When even the last drop of *Orichalcum* slipped into the fountain through his nails, Daniel regained himself. Cursing for the unplanned walk in the park, he slipped away quickly, puffing and combing his hair with his hands.

Amin brushed against the water surface of the fountain. The pseudo-technological metal immediately recognised its interface and penetrated in an instant into what appeared to be a normal silver ring, rising from the transparent liquid. Watching carefully, it would have been obvious to all that the ring was not around the finger of the Shadow Hound, but grafted into it.

The Hound closed his eyes. And knew.

15

“Raise your head, Valkyrie,” ordered the man in a gentle but firm tone.

Athena raised her face, beautiful, with sculpted cheekbones and deep black eyes. Her hair, shiny and smooth, fell like silk off her shoulders. “Prince,” she greeted him steadily.

The large room was empty. A bright, intense shaft of light descended from an opening in the ceiling, bouncing off the dark fur the woman wore around her neck and off her pale face and black painted lips.

The floor was carved with three shallow concentric rings of water, joined in a single point by small bridges inlaid with archaic motifs linked to the Atlantean tradition. Each ring represented a different degree of purity and indicated how close to the Prince a person could stand. Athena was allowed to enter the second ring. As a Valkyrie, she could have accessed the first, but after the events involving Amin, heavy repercussions had trickled down to her as well.

At the centre of the three rings of water, elevated by a throne of circular stairs, stood a wide and ancient metal column of green-blue hues, carved neatly with the primordial symbol of Atlantis – three concentric rings, from whose middle extended a downward line, which in turn was cut by three further horizontal wavy lines. That forged metal pillar, cast in pure *Orichalcum* fifteen centuries before, protected the prince from impure eyes, should they enter the hall.

The prince was the column in an imaginary temple on which the struggle of man to free himself from the slavery imposed by nature was fought; his physical appearance was voided, to be fused with the symbol of Atlantis. Whoever spoke to the prince spoke to the column and, therefore, not to a person but to the very project of human revolution imagined by a young man called Evenor, thousands of years before.

At the base of the spiral staircase, two figures stood several yards away, lit up by shafts of light identical to those which hit Athena. On the left was a white-haired man, dressed in a white and red tunic. His face was radiant, though hidden behind the indecipherable composure of old age. He wore no ornament but a large bright ring on the index finger of the left hand. His posture was steady and serene.

On the right, there was another, much more obscure figure. Bent within a purple and bronze coat, he seemed crushed by an invisible weight. The shadows created by the light grew thicker with each fold of the clothing, and at each corner of the twisted body, as if uncomfortable near that creature. The shaky hand held a long stick of metal, straight and uncarved; sometimes he switched hand as if he tired by just leaning on that perch. The head was covered by a curious bicorn mitre, inlaid with golden symbols. His breathing was heavy and could be heard even from a distance.

The voice emerged again from the column. "We need to talk about Amin, Athena."

Her hand tightened around the ritual spear. She looked at the ancient Nephilim Cornelius, advisor to the prince, and Fidias, the disgusting Translator of Light who had persecuted Amin with so much ferocity in his darkest moment.

Cornelius' voice interrupted the tense silence which filled the hall. It was a strong and reassuring voice. His oratory skills and his charisma were incomparable. "The prince has reason to believe that Amin has turned the mission assigned to him from the Court in a sort of strange personal initiative. The Shadow Hound had been sent to pick up a young man, a Roused one, of whom great things are said among the people of Mu. It seems that in his research, Amin has instead killed a Sleeper, believing it the one we were looking for."

Athena swallowed the information as if it were resin. But she didn't speak.

"Unfortunately, it does not end here. Amin also turned against some Fir Bolg who had tried to defend the Sleeper. He killed them all."

Since when are Fir Bolg interested in Sleepers' kids, or in something that is not self-pity? Since when does an Atlantean court sully itself with such contemptible creatures? thought the Valkyrie. Then she replied, "Prince, I hear with sorrow your just words. Amin is a fallen one, it's true. But this does not make him insane. He is a valiant warrior and has always been faithful to the Great Intention, to the prince past, our father, and now to you. His deeds were inscribed on the walls of Avalon and long poems were sung in sadness when he was condemned. Amin has paid for his mistakes with his head held high, as it should be with a Pure Atlantean. I am certain that he continues to act with righteousness even in his life as an exile."

"Do you believe that this court does not speak true?" asked Cornelius, calmly.

"The words, the thoughts and the actions of the prince are the truth. But I was not simply summoned to listen."

"Of course not, Athena. Speak."

"The facts recounted to me are true. But perhaps the reason why they happened reached the Prince distorted somewhat?"

"The prince is listening."

She played her card. "I did not know that the descendants of Evenor had made alliances with Belial's followers."

An irritated whisper shot out at that.

Fidias. Athena continued on. "The magnificence of the prince and his wisdom are one with the millennial power of Atlantis. I do not understand the presence of dirty Fir Bolg in the business of the Pure court of Here XLVI. I ask forgiveness for my ignorance."

She waited.

"Amin is a fallen one and his position is already compromised. I hope these rumours prove groundless," was the cold reply of the Prince.

At that point, Fidias intervened. His voice was a whisper, as if nourished not by breath but by a continuous uninterrupted emission, a mechanical hiss. "But if they were confirmed, Amin would embarrass our court before the Nine Kingdoms and should be stopped immediately."

"The prince is grateful to you for bringing your words and your mind. He will carefully evaluate your thoughts," hastened to add Cornelius.

The Valkyrie withdrew a few steps, looking at the polished stone floor.

"I can trust you, Athena, can I not?"

The Prince's question came to her like a poisoned dart, but she didn't flinch. She swung the tip of the spear against the centre of her own chest. She felt the sharp blade wedging beneath the breastbone and her diaphragm contracted. "I am a Valkyrie, Widow to the emperor. My name is what I am. On my blood and my purity, I swore the oath of loyalty to the only emperor, that you represent in the world. On my blood and my purity, I renew it this very moment. Command me to kill myself and I'll do it right away."

Cornelius looked worriedly at the column, then back to her, adding, "You can return to your pupils, Athena."

The woman repositioned the spear by her side and left the room, walking over the third ring of water and slipping through the two rows of Valkyries that made up the prince's personal guard.

What was Fidias planning? Were the accusations and suspicions on Amin true? Turning the spear against itself, Athena had hoped to receive from the prince the order to use it. But she suspected that the idea of what she once called brother and that of the scheming Fidias were quite different. Whatever was happening, it was the prince's will to conclude the matter of Amin within the court, without appealing to the judges. It was his right. From the moment Amin had fallen, his life depended solely on the sovereign.

The sage Cornelius, who had always sided in defence of his pupil, was at a disadvantage, and mainly reduced to silence. Inside of herself, the brave and sad Athena knew that there could be a worse alternative to death. That they sent her out of Avalon, into the world of the Sleepers, to look for Amin. The man she had always loved, her spouse. To kill him.

*

"She does not have the strength to face the mission, my lord," whispered Fidias, wiping his lips wet from *Orichalcum*.
"But she's the only person Amin would listen to in the event he was not involved in the Sleeper's murder," said Cornelius. "Something we cannot currently be certain of, except for the fragmented information reported by the Translator of Light, whose provenance is unknown."

Fidias clenched his shiny teeth violently.

Prince Here sighed. "Placing our trust in Fir Bolg has not been a good choice. Athena is right. If it became known, it would be a source of great embarrassment for this court."

Fidias intervened. "We must use all the means necessary to track down the young man who lives in the world of the Sleepers, lead him here and find out if he is who we think. All means!"

"Prince," said Cornelius, "for over four millennia we have abandoned direct interference in the life of the Sleepers to guide them better, protecting them from the risks of the conflict between Atlantis and Mu. Unwise actions could awaken the kind of attentions that we do not want. Atlantis has many enemies, my Lord. The dissidents of Mu gathered in the *Arkanum*, launching continuous attacks on our outposts in the world of the Sleepers. The lists of conscripts diminish; multitudes await only a signal to unite and unleash the mystical forces that sleep in the belly of Mother Earth. Among the Sleepers, those who love calling themselves Enlightened are becoming more audacious and dangerous. Their arts and technology have reached unprecedented levels. Their two empires, the Sword and the Compass, which unite the Twelve houses in which they gather, are strong and organised. We cannot even keep them all under control. And never mind our brothers, the followers of Belial, who bring chaos in the world of the Sleepers."

"Enlightened?" Fidias croaked. "You are ancient and wise,

Nephilim, but in exalting the skills of our adversaries you forget the power of pseudo-technology. There is no *Arkanum*, mystical force or Enlightened that can compete with the Atlantean armies. The princes, in their infinite goodness, tolerate these annoying presences for the love of the human race, but could annihilate them with the help of the *kaisers* and pseudo-technology!" shouted the Translator of Light, spitting purple metal from his nostrils.

Cornelius continued to speak to the column, ignoring Fidias' monologue. "It would scare even the most loyal supporter of the Great Intention to see how little awareness the Sleepers have achieved. They are disbanded and their actions empty, lacking any motivation. The very consciousness of humanity falters. I am afraid that at this moment even the smallest distraction from our part could lead to a catastrophe."

"What must the prince hear?" The Translator of Light was enraged. "Atlantis holds full control of the world, from its own dirty old roots to the highest building of its cities, from the depth of the Essence of the Sleepers to the most rebellious and despicable son of Mu who still walks the soil of our Kingdoms. What are you insinuating, ancient one? That there is someone who can overthrow Atlantis and the Great Gorann? This is blasphemy!"

For the first time, the advisor turned to look at Fidias. "Is it not to avoid this possibility that we are looking for the boy?" he asked coldly.

The other fell silent, retreating into the darkness with a metallic rumble.

"What do you suggest, then, wise Nephilim?" asked the prince.

"I suggest taking time. We already have someone following Amin's moves. If he's not guilty of what Fidias accuses him of, I'm sure he'll find out who we're really looking for."

"So be it," he sanctioned. "But in the meantime, let the Avalon be brought near the borders of the Kingdom, that this movement may be proclaimed to the other rulers and the judges. Let's get closer to the Sleepers. I want to be able to intervene at any time."

Cornelius made a slow bow. "Your word is perfect, prince."

In the darkness in which he was holed up, Fidias grinned. He had obtained what he wanted.

A few moments later, less than two hundred nautical miles to the north of the frozen Amery platform, a vast, titanic and invisible mass rippled the placid blue table of the Antarctic sea. Above it, a whirlwind of clouds began to gather, bringing bad weather and thunder.

More or less at the same time, in about fifty places in the world, meteorologists, captains of cargo ships, military managers, thousands of employees and billions of technological tools, created the conditions for the safe and invisible passage across the Atlantic of Prince Here XLVI. The Avalon. The greatest pseudo-technological machine in the world. One of the nine fragments left of the original and mythical city of Atlantis.

16

For the first time in a long while, Andrew really felt at home. In the soft lights created by *abat-jour* that Emily had so protected during the many house moves, the dated vanilla carpet gave the living room a smooth and relaxing velvety appearance. From the open plan kitchen, a reassuring scent of roast beef, mixed with the just-right TV noise, gave the house a touch of life that instilled optimism. At the end of the day, they were both coming home – their home.

Andy sighed, satisfied, and began to clear the table. Emily was busy in the bathroom, and soon she would lie on the couch with the excuse to look for some movie to watch before ending up on yet another reality TV show, pretending not to care. Even of this, she would enjoy very little, collapsing under the effect of her pills. Andy didn't like that his mother took that crap, but in his heart, he knew that she would soon stop – as soon as she recovered from her past, as he was recovering.

He couldn't know that adults are much slower to react to the defeats of life, and that sometimes they even stopped doing that. Had he suspected it, he still wouldn't have wanted to break that moment of inner optimism.

Three-quarters of an hour later, the dishwasher announced the end of its cycle and he helped his mum move from the couch to the bed. After tucking her covers up, he finished tidying up. It was past ten when Andrew dropped onto the sofa with a satisfied air about him. The house was still a mess, but in his eyes, it seemed more than acceptable.

At that time the channels available did not offer many attractive possibilities. After jumping from one to the other for a few minutes, he noted with regret that he had missed the first episode of a new SF series. Fruit juice in hand, he put the DVD of *Twelve Monkeys* into the reader, a film that he had never been able to see from start to finish. After covering his legs with a blanket, he leaned back.

"Well, Mr Fincher. Shall we?" he said aloud.

Play.

When he woke up, his right arm was asleep and tingling. On the TV, the main menu screen of the DVD told him that yet again, David Fincher had not managed to convince him to watch one of his movies.

Taken between the desire to get more comfortable in his bed and the inertia of the first sleep, he reached out to turn off the light, and the living room plunged into darkness.

He dreamed of the red-haired girl, in tears and dressed in mourning with black lace over her face, throwing red roses on poor Adam Uyan's grave. The image was not only sad, but disturbing. The leaden sky, full of rain and cold wind that swept the autumn leaves, was just the beginning of something that waited somewhere, beyond the walls of the dream, entangled in the earth and in the wood of the trees, in the varnish of the coffin and in the girl's clothes. Andrew felt compelled to approach to look at the epitaph engraved on marble.

It said: "Help me."

The boy winced in his sleep. Anxious, he tried to get out of the nightmare, but right then the lid of the coffin was blown away and a large bony hand grabbed him by the leg, dragging him into the depths of the earth. Andrew tried to fight, to oppose that indomitable force, but he was yielding. He looked up and a glow reached him, enveloping him. The hand lost its strength and he was free. Then the light hit him in the eyes and he woke up.

Staring at the ceiling, Andy felt very calm in his confusion. He still felt that steady, clean light in his eyes. The feeling soon disappeared.

He sat on the sofa, looking around. Then, tucking his feet in the slippers, he staggered to his room, with the promise to avoid Fincher before going to sleep in the future. Walking next to the kitchen counter, he stepped on something that shattered immediately under his soft shoes. There were cereals scattered everywhere. The family size box, just bought, was lying on the floor next to the counter.

Andrew was forced to wake up at the thought that there could be a huge animal running around the house. The French door of the living room was closed, but previous tenants had installed a low pet hatch. And coincidentally, a trail of cereals ended right under the counter, where the plastic bag in which they came in lay empty. Trying to be quiet, he grabbed a broom and approached the French door. He moved the curtain aside enough to see the garden. He looked around, scouting every corner.

And he saw it.

A reddish-brown creature, slightly bigger than a hand, was climbing the net by the right wall. It had a large round head, with protruding ears, and used all four limbs nimbly. It turned and stared at the boy, as if it had noticed she had been caught. Its eyes were wide and round, surrounded by hair lighter than that of the body.

He wasn't sure, but Andrew thought it was some kind of monkey. He had envisioned everything else, but not a monkey. He remembered reading somewhere that they could be very aggressive, especially the small ones. A bit like Chihuahuas.

The little monkey kept staring at him, motionless. So he decided to implement the cat tactic. He opened the window and went outside, still armed with the broom. Closing the window behind him to keep the cold out, he saw that the little creature was still there, munching on something. It wasn't difficult to guess it was his breakfast. Andy took a few steps forward, brandishing the broom as if it were Excalibur. He took a deep breath in preparation to scream the animal away, forcing it not to return – that was the tactic of the cat – and raised Excalibur to the sky. He was about to make the scariest sound possible when the monkey anticipated him, baring two rows of very white teeth and emitting a screeching so high that Andrew jumped back, stumbled on the rake he had left in the middle of the garden and fell with a thud. The monkey looked at him with an air that Andrew would have defined as satisfied.

The ears of the animal pricked up suddenly, as though it heard something, and it disappeared through an opening between the net and the wall.

Andrew started to get up, defeated. If Emily found out that a monkey walked back and forth in her kitchen, she would faint, then call the army.

Storing the rake in its cupboard was the first part of an operation that would also include cleaning the kitchen from the snack remains of the neighbours' pet, fixing the net and repairing the latch to the French door. A total cover-up. He took the garden tool to put it back on its hook. Perhaps it was because his soft slippers did not make any noise on the grass that Andrew heard the sound. A soft voice, like someone whispering. Intrigued, trying to remain silent, he approached the net, looking through that intricate tangle of plants. At first, he saw nothing, then he noticed the long tail of the little monkey twisted around what he recognised as being the sleeve of a sweatshirt.

The creature was sitting docile on a boy's arm, almost invisible in the darkness. He seemed to be seated on one of those blocks of marble buried by moss that were scattered everywhere in the garden of the Fawcett's neighbours, and he was caressing what was supposed to be his strange pet.

A little excited about finally finding out his neighbour was his age, Andrew decided to introduce himself.

"Hey! Are you Adam?" he said softly.

His neighbour's reaction was none too enthusiastic, let alone that of the monkey. Both jumped on the spot, as if someone had woken them up with a fanfare in the middle of the night. The boy called Adam looked around, trying to understand from where the voice came, while the little monkey vanished quickly into the branches.

"I'm here, do you see me?" Andy continued, waving his hand. "I'm sorry to have frightened you. I found your monkey in my kitchen. I followed it out here and saw you."

Adam spotted him, but kept looking around as if scared of something.

"You go to Saint Paul too, don't you?" Andrew pressed him.

The sound of the neighbour's French door was heard opening, and a kneaded voice, old but strong, uttered a few words in an unknown language which sounded like a reproach or a threat.

Adam stared at Andrew for a few moments, then ran into the house, closing the door behind him.

It was their first meeting.

17

Amin had enjoyed the satisfaction of the fortuitous start of his plan for only a few seconds. He had savoured it and immediately dismissed it, so as not to lose focus. He couldn't have hoped for a better situation. Not only had the conscript Shaun quickly made contact with a Milesian, but he had also let slip to be worried about a particular boy. Could he be the one he was looking for?

When he reached the road, he identified the maritime police building right away, lit by powerful spotlights; to either side of those hung the country's flags. A handful of identical cars were parked out front, and only a few noises could be heard coming from the windows of adjacent houses. The moon was full, spreading a cyanotic nuance to the sky, its stars made invisible by the luminous Sleepers' city. The Hound shivered. This world was such a foreign reality, he doubted he could ever get used to it. And he didn't understand how the Woken ones could live there. Of course, some of them had no choice, but for the others it was a conscious decision.

Sometimes, in the depth of his soul, he let himself be infected by the sense of loneliness that assailed him in front of that sheer quantity, so massive and so empty. Quantity of space and numbers. Quantity of different occupations, most often ridiculous and puny. Quantity of words wasted in many ways and for very trivial reasons. Quantity of light, which, however, did not serve to remove from the heart of the Sleepers the suspicion that there was something observing them beyond the reassuring glow of the fire. To change everything to always find oneself back at the starting point. This was the fate of the Sleepers.

After his second rebirth as a Shadow Hound, and the more frequent contacts with that world, he sometimes felt contrasting feelings of pity for the humans, so like him, yet so different. So ignorant and scared. And alone.

A man and a woman came down the short staircase that led to the entrance of the building and Amin recognised her immediately. *Helena Dowson, defender and protector of other Sleepers.*

The two stopped to talk and the Hound walked towards them. Just before reaching them, the man seemed to notice him, before focusing on the words of his colleague once again. A few yards away, Amin recognised Helena's voice; her tone was relaxed and friendly, very different from the one she had used with him a few weeks earlier on the lake's shores.

He was now near the sidewalk when he sensed something. Without outward reaction, he continued on, turning the corner of the building. There, with his back to the wall, he looked around. The alleys were silent, and the noise of the little traffic that flowed in the main street seemed far away. The roofs of the surrounding edifices were dark, while the street was flooded by tall lamps. A high level of humidity was already covering the road.

Helena's voice turned to laughter.

But there was something wrong. A dangerous will had focused its attention on him, without manifesting itself, perhaps because of the presence of the Sleepers, or perhaps because it was unsure of what the Hound was.

With a rattling and irritating noise, a scooter darted on the road, its driver singing loudly, headphones on under the helmet. When both sounds melted in the night, even the strange presence seemed to have vanished.

Amin considered whether or not to use his Essence, the living *keh*, to understand what was happening, but to do so would reveal him as a Woken one. He desisted from the idea and did something very odd for a noble, no matter how disgraced.

He bluffed.

Performing a gesture he had seen many Sleepers do, he fumbled in his pocket and grabbed the mobile phone that had been "donated" to him by a passerby, that afternoon; he placed it against his ear and pretended to listen. The phone had neither SIM card nor battery, but as soon as Amin moved it closer to him, it lit up immediately, fulfilling its purpose in the presence of a Lord of Matter. A welcome song and a vibration came out of the device.

The Hound took a few steps on the sidewalk, waiting for the situation to develop, but nothing happened. When he put the phone back in his pocket, he realised he could no longer hear Helena or the man. He immediately turned the corner and noticed that he had gone. The young policewoman, on the other hand, was bent over fiddling with a sizeable water-repellent fabric that she was trying hard to put over her uniform trousers.

She noticed his presence and turned with a smile, perhaps hoping the man she was talking to had come back. Her enthusiasm subsided almost immediately, however, when she saw it wasn't him.

"Good evening, Helena," said Amin.

"Look, I'm off duty now. I've been working for twelve hours straight, and I must go home. If you need help, you can ask my colleagues in there," she replied, glancing at him just enough to check that it was nothing serious or urgent.

"I do not need your colleagues. I need you."

That voice! Helena gave a start and all the events of a strange morning, some time ago, came back to her. "I know you," she said softly. "You're the guy I met at the lake while we were looking for the missing boy."

"It's me," the Hound confirmed.

Helena had associated that morning with a feeling of anguish and discomfort, though she couldn't explain why. The man seemed like a regular person. She was confused. "How do you know my name and where I work?"

"You told me your name. And it's easy to find you even without asking the Onagros."

"I'm afraid I don't understand…"

"I need you," Amin cut short. "I need you to listen to what I have to tell you about the boy who died in the lake."

The policewoman winced. At the station, all they did was talk about murder in the Uyan case. The police had leaked the hypothesis of an accident, but no one believed that. According to the coroner, the signs of struggle on the young man's body were unequivocal. Someone had held him underwater. Someone with great strength and great resistance. An athletic man, just like the one standing before her.

Her experience took control of the nerves. "Very well, Mr… ?"

"I will tell you my name at the right time."

Helena expected such an answer. "In that case, I won't be able to help you. If you think you have something important to share, you can do so by entering the building to your right and knocking on the third door – Missing Person Department. Alejandro Consom will be glad to assist you."

Amin regarded her, as if looking at a child, but the woman managed to keep her eyes on him, albeit with difficulty in the dazzling spotlights.

"I doubt, or rather, I'm sure you cannot understand what I want to reveal to you. But I'm equally certain that, if you listen to me, you will not be disappointed. You're the right person."

Helena thought it best to accompany him inside if only to ensure her colleagues' support in case the man decided to misbehave.

The worst are those who appear calm, she thought. "All right, sir. Come with me." She pointed to the building with the large white and blue police sign.

Not caring for the other Sleepers, the Hound walked inside and across the atrium. "We have to talk in a room with a mirror. Do you have any?"

The policewoman didn't answer. She motioned for him to continue on and at the same time gave a very clear look to his colleague, Dee Martins, a tall, broad-shouldered young man of Colombian descent. He understood her on the fly and followed them to one of the interrogation rooms. Before entering, Amin merely said, "You are enough."

"All right," she replied, and before closing the door, she whispered to Martins, "Uyan."

He widened his eyes and nodded. At that time of night, there was almost no one left in the office, and he would need to take care of the recording alone.

The interrogation room was rather small. The floor was covered with dark carpeting, partly unglued, while the ceiling was lowered with the typical shingled plastic of the public administration offices. One of the long walls had low windows with bars, something the thick Havana curtains could not hide completely. On one of the shorter walls, however, a long, dim mirror extended from one corner to the other, covering it completely.

At the centre of the room was a short, metal table perhaps as old as the building itself, with some chairs around it and a microphone emerging from its centre. The flashing red light of a CCTV camera pulsed in a dark corner of the room, untouched by the vibrant neon light.

Amin paused for a moment to look at the mirror. "That will do."

"Take a seat," invited him, Helena.

"Yes. It will take some time."

On the opposite side of the glass, Dee Martins turned on the monitor labelled "Room 2" and pressed the record button.

"Do we have permission to record this conversation, Mr... ? Can you tell me your name now?"

"Record? As you wish. You can call me Amin."

What kind of name is Amin? wondered Martins.

"Amin... what else?"

"Amin is enough, for now. Let's see what happens."

Helena gave in. "Sure. Very well. So, Mr Amin, you came to our office to ratify your position on the Uyan case. Is this correct?"

The man snorted.

"We need to hear your confirmation, sir," she said, pointing to the microphone.

"I do not know who this Uyan is, but if he's the boy killed in the lake last month, then yes, your words are true."

Killed! Helena and Dee had the same reaction.

"As you know, the case is about an accident, not a murder," she said, trying hard to appear impassive.

Amin moved his chair sideways. Helena realised that he was looking for an optimal position to look at the mirror while talking to her. Everyone knew that those mirrors were transparent and were used to observe the interrogations from the outside, but she had the feeling that this man was not interested in that. He seemed to be interested in the mirror *itself*, not what was behind it.

Two good minutes of patient silence passed by. Dee Martins waited, with the intermittent rustling of hard disks in the background.

"It does not matter what your investigations say," began Amin. "The young man who died in the lake was killed."

"By whom? "

"By a Fir Bolg named Tonos. He held him under water until his Essence abandoned the body. I believe a Translator of Light is trying to find the boy before me. But they have killed the wrong one."

Dee Martins laughed. *Another crazy one.*

Helena didn't know what to think. She barely got half of the words spoken by the man, but it seemed strange to her that, for some reason, she felt he was not lying. He really believed what he had told her. "So they killed young Uyan by mistake, confusing him with someone by the same name? And you, Mr Amin, do you also want to kill this boy?"

"No. I have been ordered to take him to my prince's Avalon."

"Good. Who are these Fir Bolg?" the woman asked seriously, jotting comments on a piece of paper.

Dee almost fell from the chair. *What are you doing, Helly?*

"They are descendants of the First People, giants, the only survivors of the lineage of the Fir, which also included, before their extinction, the Fir Domnan and the Fir Gaileon. For millennia, they have been living in the vastness of the ancient Great Roads and hardly ever came out, since they were forbidden to do so. But they are stupid and dangerous beings, ready to sell themselves to anyone who can give them a more destructive power." He paused, as if remembering something. "All this is not important for our purposes since you'll never see one."

"I see. And where are these… Fir Bolg?"

"They are dead. You cannot deal with them."

"Who killed them?"

Amin stared at her and Helena felt a jolt in her heart. Not emotional, but physical. She was sure the man had killed someone, those giants maybe. The earpiece she had worn before entering the room, crackled.

It was Dee Martins. "Helena, I'll call you a 666."

It was the code with which her office referred to the psychiatrists. She moved her head slightly, indicating No.

"Helly, we can't carry on an interrogation like this, without a lawyer or a shrink. It's illegal. And what makes you think he's not a mythomaniac?" Martins insisted.

"You can't expect me to believe in stories of giant murderers," she continued, regaining control of the situation.

"Not at all," said Amin, distracted again by the mirror. "But it's irrelevant if you believe me. This is not the purpose of our meeting."

"No? What would it be then? Care to tell us?"

"It's a waste of words, believe me."

"Try me."

"They've cut me off. The messages I sent to the court have never arrived, and I cannot run the risk of reaching Avalon, losing the information I acquired if I were killed. What we are doing here, right now, is to evoke an observer through the mirror, which is acting as a window. What I say is the truth, and therefore I am breaking the sixth precept of the Code of the One. It says: "Nothing of what was or is can be revealed by a Woken one to a Sleeper." If a Pure like me were to break the Code, it is an even more serious offence, and an observer is sent to ascertain the breach so that the judges can be notified. It's a trick to enable me to talk to them. That is what we are doing here."

Helena turned to the mirror. "You want me to believe that there's something observing us from the mirror?"

"It's not here yet, but it's moving. Soon, the great Hall of Time will be synchronized with this room, and I will be able to reveal the conspiracy of the Translator of Light to those who need to know, jumping with a single step over all the levels of Purity that are precluded to me – I do not know yet whether for their direct involvement or not. You, Helena, are helping me. Your very nature, unknown to you as a Sleeper, is suitable for my purpose. Like many women, what you hear and see is perceived at a greater depth than it does in men, a depth much closer to your Essence and, therefore, to your potential state of Roused one. The moment you absorb my words, you are sending them through the mirror to the observer, who goes back, through what you call space and time, to their source. You."

Dee Martins had never come across such a fantastic scenario. He was almost captivated by it. Never mind Harry Potter!

"We're not here to talk about me," Helena wavered, feeling lightheaded. "You came here to tell us of your involvement in the murder of Adam Uyan. Leave giants, mirror monsters and judges out of it!"

"An observer is not a monster. It is what human beings become when they choose to serve the Great Intention beyond the limits of the *lumina*. Or death, if you prefer."

The woman leaned forward on the table. "Enough of this nonsense! Who are you, really?"

"Now you are ready to listen," replied the Hound, leaning back. "You are ready to repay the observer for his constant labour."

Dee Martins wrote two sentences on a piece of paper: "Split personality disorder and self-referential language." It could be useful to the psychiatrist.

"The name chosen for me since ancient times is Amin Setiana Akenre. I am a direct descendant of Evenor and I was born in the Avalon of the most Pure prince Aken Paneb Akenre LIII, blood brother of my most Pure father, Seti Setiana Akenre, seventy-nine years ago."

Helena looked at him, puzzled.

"With human beings like us, time is kind," said Amin.

At least he's not an alien from Krypton, thought Dee, sipping a soft drink.

"And what kind of human being would you be?" asked the woman.

The Hound glanced in the mirror and smiled oddly, as if to underline his patience in the face of the obviousness of the answer. "We are the descendants of Evenor, the only emperor of the world, founder of the Great Intention and saviours of humanity. We are the heirs of the most powerful and great civilisation that has existed for over fourteen thousand years on this Earth. We are Atlanteans, Helena. Citizens of Atlantis, the beacon of humanity and sovereign of the world."

Something happened in the mirror. For a moment, its reflection twisted, but Amin immediately caught the change, his expression becoming triumphant.

Helena Dowson was still baffled, however. Not for the fantastic answer, but because she seemed to have already witnessed that scene. She was experiencing an intense *déjà-vu* feeling.

Amin looked at her, tilting his head to the side. "What's happening, Helena? Can you feel its arrival?"

The woman tried to answer, but couldn't find the right words; she muttered something meaningless, looking for Dee beyond the mirror.

"It is useless to seek solace in your friend. Whatever will happen, for one reason or another, his physical senses will be diverted and distracted by what he cannot accept to see. His Essence will refuse to perceive the incomprehensible and will drive him away from it. You are the ones who want to spend your existence as Sleepers, which is why you cannot understand." He became very serious. "Silence now. It's coming."

Helena seemed to perceive her surroundings in slow motion. The window through which she had witnessed dozens of interrogations was darkening. But not in its reflection, rather in depth. It was becoming three-dimensional. Like the surface of a placid lake swept by the wind, the mirror rippled; a long sound, almost imperceptible, escaped from it, akin to that of a didgeridoo.

It was at that moment that the hard disks went out. With a dying whisper similar to the *shhh* of those who demand silence, Dee realised that the system was no longer recording. As the glass rippled, he turned to check the USB ports. Then, with some difficulty, he slipped under the desk to control the plugs. In doing so, he bumped his head and cursed.

In the interrogation room, the reflections in the mirror split into a thousand fragments and everything became still. The CCTV, the vibration of the neon lights, the clocks. The noises disappeared, and only that sound remained, increasing steadily. Helena listened to her breathing, full and slow, the mind dilating just like when she was underwater, motionless on the shallow seabed.

Amin rose from his chair and stepped forward. He pulled out the mobile and threw it in the mirror. On contact, instead of bouncing back, the object remained entangled in some sort of dense material which began to absorb it.

"I'm Amin Setiana Akenre. I request an audience in the great hall of the emperor of Atlantis and to the nine ancient ones, so they can listen to me and judge my actions. I request an audience at the council of judges of the Code of the One. I ask permission to access the Hall of Time, from where they fulfil the Great Intention! I bring truth in my hands and my Purity to testify that I am your legitimate and worthy son. Atlantis, rise!" the Hound screamed. The murmuring died out. Amin's eyes widened.

The ticking sound of the analogue clock broke into the room, and at that moment Dee bumped his head for the second time, scared by the sudden recovery of the hard drives. When he sat down again, the first thing he saw was Amin in front of the mirror, wearing a horrified expression, staring at him. Helena was on the ground. He rushed out the door, holding the gun, and crashed into the interrogation room with the weapon pointed at the suspect.

"Stop!" he cried at Amin. He bent over Helena to check her neck pulse. She was alive, and he urged her to recover with small flicks on her cheeks. "What did you do to her?" He was furious. Not only with that madman, but with himself for having committed the more trivial of errors in underestimating him.

Helena recovered immediately. But as she opened her eyes, she snapped backwards, crawling on the floor until her shoulders found the wall; she was sobbing and breathing with difficulty.

"It's all right, Helly!" Dee tried to reassure here, still targeting Amin.

"I don't understand," murmured the Hound, turning around. "What has happened?"

"Don't move or I'll kill you!" shouted the policeman. "I swear I'll kill you like a dog. You're crazy!"

As if he had not even heard it, Amin headed for the open door. Dee Martins, who had never fired at anyone in his life, pointed at the man's heart and pulled the trigger. The gun didn't shoot. He checked the safety, but it was off. He tried again and failed. Excited voices were heard in the corridor. Someone must have heard the commotion.

Amin stopped to look at Helena. "It will pass soon enough, do not worry. The tears come from your captive Essence trying to tell you that what you've seen is all real. Sleepers with a strong Essence cry more. Unfortunately, from now on, you will live with knowledge you should not have received and that nobody will ever believe. Maybe one day you'll want to kill yourself. Don't do it."

Dee pressed the trigger, again and again, trying to shield a convulsing Helena with his own body.

"We are all bricks in a temple, Helena. In this, you and I are the same," concluded the Hound with cold sincerity, partly distracted by impenetrable thoughts.

Dee watched him go away. Many years later he would still not be able to explain why the gun had not fired or even why he did not square up to the man. He had never been a coward and would not be again.

But that day went like this. And the strangest thing he would discover a few hours later, when he realised that the CCTV had recorded nothing.

Some agents entered the room. Only then did Dee recover, pretending to know why they had not stopped the man that had just come out of the room.

Nobody had seen him.

Reemerging from the shadows of one of the rooftops, Amin sat down on the edge of the building, perplexed. The judges had refused to listen to him, and, at the same time, they had punished him for his action. And this made no sense. What was happening? Were the very foundations of Atlantis involved in a dark plan? It was not possible. Of one thing the Shadow Hound was sure. The boy called Adam Uyan had to be much more important than what he had been told. What did he represent for Mu? And for the prince?

He had to understand the meaning of what was happening, and the only way to do it was to find the young man before anyone else did.

18

When, during break time, Andrew searched for his odd neighbour in the schoolyard, to apologise for disturbing him, he was told the boy was absent. The same happened for the next three days. At the weekend, the windows of the house remained closed, and not a trace of movement could be seen, as if the whole family had packed up and vanished into thin air.

The following Monday, however, glass of milk in tow, Andrew went to check the cereal he had left as bait on the wall by the net. Their absence confirmed that the monkey had struck again. He certainly didn't believe they could have left the animal alone for so long. In fact, even the French door, now that he looked properly, was not closed. Rather, it was merely propped, swaying lazily to that little wind that swirl on the floor of the cloister.

Andrew finished the milk, dressed quickly, then told his mother that he would wait for her outside. He went around the building and waited. It was about 07:00.

Not two minutes had passed before the door swung opened.

The same black man he had met before looked at Andrew head to toe. "Still here?" asked the janitor.

Andy had his answer ready but was immediately interrupted.

"I know who you are, boy, don't worry. I met your mother the other day. Tell her the tart was delicious and thank her from me."

"Ah, great," he managed to reply awkwardly, caught off balance again.

The man held out his hand, and when Andy took it, he squeezed it hard. "My name is Gerald. I'm the janitor of these buildings. Sorry if I seemed brusque last time, but you can't be too careful in this neighbourhood."

"It seems an OK place to me," he replied, with a grin.

"You are Andrew, right? Well, new areas such as this one are left a bit to themselves by the police. And since they've opened that building site, the hill has become a refuge for small groups of stragglers, especially at night."

"I haven't seen anyone."

"That's because good boys sleep at night, don't you think? In any case, stay away from there. It's not safe. Loads of dangerous machinery and holes."

Andrew glanced at the hill surrounded by the red plastic fence of the construction site. It did look dodgy. "I will do, thank you. Can I ask you something, Gerald?"

The man's face lit up with a white-toothed grin. With ease, he retrieved a half-smoked cigar from his woollen vest breast pocket and brought it to his mouth. "Shoot."

"You know where I live, right? What can you tell me about the people who stay across from me?"

Gerald eyed Andrew with curiosity. He had the look of a homicide detective, more than a janitor. Humane and stubborn at the same time. "Quiet old people. They live with their grandson, Adam. The boy has lost his parents, and his grandparents take care of him."

"Oh, I see."

Gerald passed his cigar from one side of his mouth to the other. "But?"

"It's nothing, only… I was wondering if you saw them recently. See, I go to school with Adam, but I haven't seen him at break time lately."

The man began to scour through the accumulated mail in the communal mailbox, mechanically throwing away advertisements.

"Andrew, living with old folks is not easy for a young man. Adam's grandparents are good people, but they are also very apprehensive. They don't allow much personal freedom to your classmate. And considering how bad things are around here, I don't feel like blaming them. Fortunately, my daughter lives in another city. You're lucky to have such a young and smart mother, son."

"It's just that it doesn't seem normal, even for old people, to spend the weekend at home with all the windows shut."

Gerald gave a booming laugh. "And why would you think that? The Uyans often go away for the weekend — in the countryside, I think — to visit relatives, the last ones that Adam has."

"That makes sense," said the boy, although it did not explain the monkey. He decided not to mention it.

"They are very discreet people. I don't even have a copy of their keys in case of an emergency. It's a different generation," concluded Gerald, finishing with the mail. "And this morning, Adam has already left. Ten minutes ago."

"Already? But it's seven o'clock!"

The man shrugged.

Emily emerged from around the corner loaded up with bags and parcels, out of breath. She greeted the janitor, who returned the wave, and headed for the car.

Andrew rushed to help her.

"What were you talking about with Mr Gerald?" she asked him.

"Our neighbours."

Emily interpreted her son's attempt to find a bridge to his neighbour as a desperate search for a friend. She prayed every night for this to happen. She had also tried to establish a relationship with them, but without success.

"Did you talk to them?" Andy asked, curious.

"Not exactly. At first, I thought there was nobody home. Then, as I walked away, I heard the door opening, and I noticed old lady Uyan on the threshold, in the shadow."

"Right, like Granny, who couldn't see so well and kept the lights off saying that it made no difference anyway!" he said, trying to play down the absence of his grandmother while remembering her. They both laughed, though with a vein of sadness.

"She stood there quietly, on the doorstep," Emily continued. "So I approached her, introducing myself. Then I showed her the cake, and she accepted it gladly. At least I think so. She wore a scarf that covered her head and the sides of her face, but it was clear that she was happy about the cake and thanked me with a thousand bows. Very nice."

"What did she say to you?"

"She said, thank you. Or, rather, thankeeuu... I think they are foreigners. Mrs Uyan is sick, though. I think she suffers from emphysema, poor thing."

"And did you also meet the other members of the family?"

"Unfortunately no. She seemed uncomfortable, behind that half-closed door, and with her sickly appearance I didn't want to disturb her. There'll be another opportunity, you'll see," she added with a smile. "I'll make another cake and we'll bring it there together!"

Andrew nodded, even if something didn't quite fit.

19

When Isabel looked through the bronze peephole and saw Amin, she winced. Almost trembling, she opened the door with deference, bowing her head as a sign of respect. "It is an honour you have considered us again, sir."

The Hound proceeded through to the living room full of tapestries and Sleepers' artefacts of great value. Against the walls, three high bookcases stood empty. Even the draperies had been wrapped in thick cardboard cloths, and there were boxes stacked everywhere. "You are leaving, Onagros?" he asked.

"I can explain, sir," answered the woman in a trembling voice.

Steps on the marble floor heralded the arrival of her companion, the man who had assisted Amin in his hard days of recovery from the *Orichalcum* poisoning. The Atlantean noted that the steps were determined, firm. Unusual, given where he was, and charged with a peremptoriness that was perceptibly discharged to the ground, of someone who already has in mind what the next action will be. There was no slowdown in the approach, no hint of stopping.

"Do not force me to kill you." Amin had barely time to finish the sentence before the man entered through the archway into the living room, holding something stretched forward. There was a dull, liquid sound. The long, thin purple needle kneaded itself to the shield of *Orichalcum* that had appeared on Amin's forearm.

The Hound stared at the sharp point as it melted, liquefying in the shield. "A *Tooth of Shadow!*" he muttered, but he had no time to think.

The man renewed his assault, unsheathing a long dagger, also purple and iridescent. It was glistening. Between the two men began a circular dance. From the corner of his eye, Amin watched Isabel, backed against the wall, her hands covering her mouth. She didn't seem to share the same confidence as her traitorous companion.

"Onagros!" he turned to the man. "I hope you have more courage than that which you employed to use that poisoned dart against me. You will need it."

The man rushed forward, drawing a suddenly arched trajectory with his dagger, but he was too slow. Amin dodged his opponent's attack, at the same time evaluating his techniques. He had learned not to underestimate anyone, but the Onagros could not hide his limited combat abilities.

"Don't you see that they've sent you to die? The purpose of your betrayal is to have you killed. Come! Tell me who hired you and I promise I will spare your life."

"You are nothing but a fallen now. Your promises are worth nothing. You're a traitor to the Code of the Great Intention!" replied the other, throwing himself forward. He swung vehemently two, three times, but he only struck the void and an old painting hanging on the wall.

"You're wrong, servant. Whoever hired you lied to you," said the Hound, avoiding the umpteenth blow, which this time broke the wooden column of the entrance arch. "If you die, you will only make those who plot behind the Code of the Great Intention stronger. Give up your weapons!"

"The poison contained in the *Tooth of Shadow* will soon have its effect. Whether I die or not, you will follow me!" the Onagros replied through gritted teeth.

Poor, foolish Sleeper, thought Amin. In one movement, at the latest thrust of his opponent, he slipped along the blade with the palm of his hand to divert it from him and found himself face to face with the man. He grabbed him by the neck and, using his weight, he lifted him off the floor, pushing him against the bookcase. The blow shook the large piece of furniture, and a twisted breath came out of the Onagros' mouth, who slumped to the ground. He tried to move, but excruciating pain prevented him. Amin stepped aside. The *Orichalcum* blade withdrew, disappearing into the Hound's skin. Isabel had slipped to the floor, her hands cupped over her face.

"The *Tooth of Shadow* takes its name from the brotherhood to which I belong and that created it millennia ago. The hounds spend a long time in contact with poisons, especially with those of pseudo-technological nature. Much of this training focuses on how to bear them, to fight them and cancel them." While speaking these words, Amin began to sweat. Purple sweat beads covered his temples and cheekbones, pouring out along his facial features. His eyes transformed, like in the cave when he fought against the Fir Bolg, and a faint golden light made the centre of his forehead glow. A light vibration hung in the air.

The Onagros realised he had failed. He tried to grab his dagger and get up, but the Atlantean shook his head to dissuade him. Still, with pain, he hauled himself upright, knife in his trembling hand. He tried to lunge but fell into the Hound's arms. Amin's blade had perforated his lungs, destroying every layer of tissue it encountered. He could hear every gasp of air turning into a whistling sound with each inhalation. The man's face was becoming pale, his lips blue, but in spite of his extreme condition, the Onagros tried to raise his dagger again to hit Amin.

Isabel sobbed.

The Hound blocked his wrist and the dagger fell to the ground.

"Your death is not in vain. You have served the Great Intention well. Know it." Amin stared into his eyes as they slipped into darkness. "Now go, back to the Source, Onagros. Where everyone is equal." When he laid the man's body on the ground, the breathing had stopped.

Isabel gripped the door handle in terror and fumbled to open it. In a panic, she managed to pull it free, and when it flung open, she stood facing a woman with tied back hair, a firm gaze and a .357 Magnum pointed at the Hound. The woman motioned for Isabel to leave and she entered the house without losing her target.

"Now you'll tell me everything," she ordered the Hound, nervously.

Amin stood up with a sigh. "You should not be here. The situation is deteriorating."

"You will tell me everything!" Helena cried.

The Hound needed allies. He was isolated, and the only contacts he had left were a giant of Mu, a conscripted bookseller and a Sleeper. Bad combination. "So be it," he said. "But know that this is a journey from which you do not return."

"Who are you really?"

"I told you. I'm an Atlantean."

"And I?" she asked, wavering, gun outstretched. "Who am I?"

Amin stared at her. "You are a Sleeper, a human being to whom your true nature has been hidden to contribute to the Great Intention, the millennial plan to free human beings from the grip of a cruel nature and defeat its worshippers, the people of Mu." He approached the weapon that was aimed at him and lowered it, continuing to stare at the woman in the eyes. "Against me, this does not work," he added.

"You want to kill that boy, don't you? Adam Uyan?"

"No, but I have to find him before someone else does, to save him."

"How do I know you're not lying to me?"

"I am of noble blood. I never lie."

"All I know is that you're a killer."

"Help me find the boy. He can help you understand too."

The woman was dazzled by a ray of sunshine coming through the windows, from which a brief glimpse of the city could be seen. She leaned against the door, exhausted.

Amin followed her gaze, beyond the glass. "Welcome to the real world, Helena."

PART THREE

THE MEANING OFTHINGS

*"A person's life almost always consists
of a series of events of which the last
could also change the sense of the whole."*

Italo Calvino

20

“Nice tits, pretty face, nice thighs and a really big mou—”

"Hi Carlyle," Andrew walked in, interrupting his mate in the middle of his brief to the Biel brothers. The other stopped, blushing, and stammered a greeting. There were a few seconds of silence. Jacob and Ron Biel looked around embarrassed.

"How's it going?" Andy asked.

The sound of the bell generated a general stampede and Carlyle dodged his friend to get to class. Andrew had the inkling that the discussion had concerned him, somehow, but decided he could find out later that day.

Before break time, the most disparate rumours about Mrs Fawcett had already made the rounds of Saint Paul five times. The comments could be summarised as such: Andrew had a very charming mother, who was also available to educate the younger boys. And from that moment, Andrew's reputation increased a little, which had its benefits, including the end of some jokes related to the mysterious "control systems" of the school. On the other hand, Andy had other things to do during recess, and he soon forgot about Carlyle's gossip. Once in the schoolyard, he immediately spotted his neighbour sitting on the wall, on the sidelines. He had the posture of someone who felt besieged, and in fact, two older girls were all over him, thrilling with a thousand brace-laden smiles and little affectations.

Andrew walked up towards him.

"Is it true that you play the guitar?" asked one of the two girls.

The other one nudged her. "Wasn't it the piano?"

Adam was holding a book, its title hidden from view. He didn't seem distracted from his reading and merely nodded.

"See? He plays them both," the first one rejoiced.

"How cute!" the second cooed.

It was at that point that Kyle got between Andrew and Adam. "What are you looking for?" His tone was serious but calm.

Andrew was speechless.

"You look like someone who's looking for something," Kyle added, slightly more threatening.

"No. I…"

They stared at each other for a second or two, then Andrew looked away, trying to think fast as the tension rose.

"It's very dangerous to look for something, Fawcett. Mind your own business."

Andrew didn't understand, but nodded; by now he had decided that the only form of dialogue with that energumen was to say, "yes", as you did with madmen. Maybe he really was crazy.

"You are not like the people here, I know, but keep it in mind and you'll go far."

Andrew couldn't refrain himself any longer. "I don't understand anything when you speak. I don't want problems, and I'm not doing anything wrong. If something's the matter, just tell me." He was amazed at his own determination, a strange sense of euphoria sweeping over him.

Kyle smiled and approached him, whispering in his ear, "You're lucky. With all that is going on, I've got bigger fish to fry than wasting my time on you. Just for the way you spoke to me, I should have broken your rib. If you insist, though, I promise I will not think twice about giving you a lesson. You got it?"

Andy felt his euphoria waning. Kyle backed away, staring at him and, before turning, making a curious gesture, drawing a slow line with his finger from the base of his left eye downward, as if drawing a tear. Andrew took a couple of seconds to shake his head of his tormentor and only then did he realise that Adam had disappeared.

Soon after, Carlyle joined him, as if nothing had happened. "So, did you do English?"

"What?"

"Surprise assessment, don't you remember?"

"But if it's a surprise, how can I know?"

"Uh, right. Come on, though! I told you yesterday to call me. I got the info from Derish, who's going out with Mrs Sullivan's daughter — you know her, right?"

"I forgot. I was busy."

"With your mum?" Carlyle asked, disinterestedly, winking at the nearby Biel brothers.

"None of your business. In any case, I'm ready," remarked Andrew, looking around. The business with his neighbour was starting to get on his nerves. He wondered why he was so keen to know him when the boy was so clearly not.

"Are you sure? Have you read chapters five and six?" his mate pressed on.

"Huh? No, Carlyle, I was thinking about something else." It was at that point that Andy realised that perhaps he wasn't ready at all. "Thanks for telling me. I'm going to revise."

"And don't say that Carly doesn't love you. Also, I am always willing to come to your place… for tutoring lessons."

"You? You're failing in all your subjects!" Andrew commented as he climbed the stairs.

"Yes, but in Sex Ed I am king," he announced, wiggling his hips out of Fawcett's eyeline. And he took a slap upside the head from Grayson, the brawny PE teacher.

*

Professor Sullivan was a woman as tender and maternal as she was inflexible. It was in the middle of the surprise assignment that Andrew was summoned on the intercom to the school office to take a call. Surprisingly, despite being upset, she gave him permission to leave.

In the office, the sixty-year-old Miss Faltermayer was waiting for him with the receiver in her hand. "Andrew Fascet?" she extruded between her voice and her chewing gum.

The boy smiled and grabbed the phone. "Hello?"

"It's me, love."

"Mum? Is everything OK?"

"Fine, darling. We had a bit of trouble here at the hospital – I can't talk now. I don't think I can come and fetch you. I'll send a cab."

"Are you crazy? Do you know how much it will cost us? We really can't afford it," he said, trying to avoid Faltermayer's insistent attention.

"Then I will ask the office to let you stay with them until I'm done, all right?"

"Mum, they don't do after-school. And in any case, I don't want to stay here after the end of the lessons. I'll take a bus or something." Silence. "Trust me, Mum. I'll call you as soon as I get home."

"Do you have your keys?" Emily asked, faintly.

"Sure. Don't worry though. Promise me?"

"I'll try. You're my precious darling. Be careful, for heaven's sake!"

"Will do. I'll call you at four."

Andrew returned the handset to Miss Faltermayer, who looked at him with sincere disinterest. He climbed the stairs back to his surprise test, feeling seriously unprepared. But everything just washed over him – he felt a great responsibility and was excited by the inebriating freedom waiting for him at the end of the school day, like a white horse outside the gates of Saint Paul.

When he stepped outside the building, aware that he didn't have to run to his mother waiting in the car, Andrew moved toward the gate and crossed it as if it was a real ritual. The Biels and Carlyle approached him. "Where's your mum?" asked the latter.

"She's not coming today. I'm getting home by myself."

It seemed to him that the boys looked disappointed for some reason. But Andrew didn't care and began to walk on the sidewalk, planning his route. He bought a ticket for the tube, got into the station at rush hour, among school and university students and those leaving work. He used the wrong set of turnstiles and got a lecture from the guard.

For some of the stops, he was squeezed in a human sea that smelled of sweat and mildew, but when the train passed the central station, he found himself in the carriage with a group of students singing a One Direction song.

It was at that moment that he saw Maggie, the girl who he had met on his first day of school, crying for the death of Adam Uyan. Hesitantly, he sat in front of her, trying to cross her gaze. She was looking down, bored or sad perhaps, absorbed in the music streaming through a pair of white headphones.

Boy, was she pretty.

Her hair was wild, but graceful and long, her fingers slender, just like he remembered from the first time he saw her. She wore a colourful scarf over a dark jacket, which suited her school uniform and thick white socks, slipping into black waxy shoes. She seemed much older than he was – Andrew wondered why there was such a difference between boys and girls. Then he realised that Maggie was watching him. Embarrassed, he immediately looked away, cursing himself for having lingered on her body for so long. But he didn't mean to offend her – he would have to apologise.

"Don't you go to St. Paul?" she asked, catching him by surprise.

"Yes," he answered suddenly. "I'm the new kid," he added, feeling that a monosyllabic answer was not suitable for the situation.

Maggie just tilted her head to the side, as if to study him.

"How come you go home alone?" was the first thing that came to his mind.

She snorted. "I'm almost fifteen. Who would I go back with? My mother?"

Andrew began to sweat. He was generally pretty good at talking to girls, but with Maggie, so cheeky and beautiful, he had difficulties even thinking. "My name is Andrew Fawcett," he announced, in an avoidable tone of voice too reminiscent of a James Bond movie.

He was supposed to get off at the next stop, but he thought about continuing the journey, at the cost of getting lost, for the chance of spending more time in her company. Still, the girl didn't react. When the doors opened with a puff of compressed air, he put the rucksack on his shoulder and started to leave. "Well, bye then, Maggie," he said, stepping onto the platform.

She looked at him, possibly astonished that he knew her name, but immediately recovered, showing a very unpleasant and sarcastic smile. However, Andrew found it charming just the same.

The train moved on with a rumbling, metallic noise and disappeared into the tunnel. His fourteen-year-old heart was still pounding hard. He'd never felt this way before. He might not have made the best impression with Maggie, but he was still enveloped in a feeling of excitement, discovery and euphoria. He left the tube and walked along an avenue of low houses and well-tended gardens. He knew the road by heart, given the amount of time he had dreamt about the day he would walk home by himself. A hundred yards more and he would arrive at the bus stop that would take him home. He had also taken less time than expected and was already wondering how to suggest to his Mum that definitive solution. He didn't want to look bad with Maggie anymore… *I'm almost fifteen. Who would I go back with? My mother?*

He crossed the street and slowed down to enjoy the walk. He was in a residential neighbourhood, quiet at that time. A few cars passed him by and a couple of people walked their dogs along the tree-lined avenue. Shortly before reaching the intersection on which he would need to turn, he was distracted by some laughter. It came from a side road, cut off by a semi-hidden parking lot a few dozens yards away, positioned between the only two buildings of the street. He peered in that direction. And he immediately recognised one of the voices.

Some guys were standing on the ramp leading down to the garage. In the midst of them, leaning against a sunlit wall, was Kyle. In one hand he held a magnifying glass. With the other, he had a large, shining green lizard pinned against the wall. Laughing sadistically, he was bringing the lens back and forth from the body of the reptile, burning it. The silent and primitive creature struggled to escape that torture, but without hope.

"What are you doing?" Andy shouted before he could think about it.

His voice distracted the thugs' attention away from the reptile. Kyle stepped forward, handing the lizard over to his accomplice. The guy lost his grip, letting the animal ran away and slip into a hole in the wall.

"Idiot!" Kyle scolded the boy who had let the animal escape. "Scram!" he ordered. The boy did, running past Andrew with his head low.

It dawned on Andy that he had become the new lizard.

"Once again, the annoying and curious Fawcett is beneath my

feet." The bully looked at him while the others smirked, approaching menacingly.

If Andrew had tried to escape or react, they would have reached him and overwhelmed him. He could not compete against Kyle alone, let alone against the other five bullies. He just hardened, unable to think of a better plan. He took a deep breath. "It's not cool to hurt animals," he muttered.

"Is that so?" Kyle replied. "Does it bother you that we're having fun torching a lizard?"

Andrew began to step back, just long enough to keep the distance between him and his toughs as they approached, surrounding him.

"Come on now, guys…" he hesitated.

The first push came from behind, and the punch that Kyle gave him felt like a baseball launched by a pro straight to his breastbone. At first, he couldn't expand his ribcage, then the pain hit him. Andrew collapsed, barely leaning against the wall of the garage ramp.

"You've never fought, and you don't know pain," the voice in his ear told him. "You don't know what it means to react to those who want you to succumb and determine your destiny." He hit him again. Andrew's face flared in a tingling that soon began to burn. The world slowed down.

"Sometimes it's necessary to push those who are weak, so they can rise. Push them by any means, even if this could cost them their life," Kyle declared militarily to his cronies.

Andy was grabbed by the scruff and raised. His rucksack was ripped from his shoulders and thrown to the bottom of the ramp.

"You're so weak," Kyle whispered again. "I'm doing it for you, believe me." He hit him in the stomach. Andrew fell backwards, rolling near his bag.

"There is no mercy in this world," he heard Kyle saying, as the tears mixed with his sweat. "We must not show any with those who don't have the strength necessary to live. Living means being in danger." His voice was serious and sad. It seemed that he carried the burden of all the woes of the world on his shoulders.

Andrew forced himself to get up, sending back his tears. He staggered as he used his backpack as support and a water pipe as a lever. He felt nauseous and in pain everywhere, but couldn't stay down. If he could survive without a father, he could also take a few punches.

Kyle raised the sleeve of his blue jacket, his fist clenched. He grabbed Andrew by the neck, crushing him against the wall.

"Kyle! What are you doing?" someone shouted.

The boy stopped. "There's no peace today."

A figure stood at the top of the ramp.

Andrew thought of Gandalf in *The Lord of the Rings*, a book he had begun a thousand times and a thousand times abandoned at the arrival of the protagonists in Rivendell.

"Why are you doing this? Why do you keep doing this?" the figure continued, exhausted as if it were the thousandth time he had asked that question.

Kyle climbed back to the top of the ramp. Passing by his misfits, he shoved right and left, insulting them. Nobody reacted.

"Do you also find it unfair to punish the weak?" he growled, pushing Andrew's saviour to the ground.

"Please stop it. There's no need for this."

"Aren't there enough weaklings walking the earth?" turning to his crew, he shouted, "Scum! You are all weak and useless scum. What am I going to do with you? You're only meat." They all listened in religious silence, not only as if they were expecting that speech, but as if they wished to listen to it. "What, I ask you?" he shouted to the boy by his feet. "To hell with it!" he said with a gesture of disgust, moving away. After a few moments of uncertainty, the group ran after him.

Andrew leaned carefully against the wall, checking for broken bones. He seemed to be whole, but in pain. The skin of his left cheekbone ached like hell, as if it had been torn away. When he hit, Kyle was methodical and cold as well as violent. He looked up the ramp in search of his saviour, who was still lying, his eyes open and bright, staring at the clouds.

"You okay, Adam?" he asked.

The boy came back from who knows what thoughts. "Yes. Kyle wasn't as heavy as other times."

Andrew held out his hand and helped him get up.

"Thanks," he said. "I only returned the favour."

"But I've done nothing for you."

"You saved that lizard from a horrible and senseless death."

"And is it good enough to get beaten up by a thug?"

Adam stopped, serious. "It should be enough for anyone. I am sure that if it had the chance to be heard, the lizard you saved would convince you of its immense gratitude."

The chance? Andy thought.

They took a few steps, in silence.

"My name is Andrew Fawcett. I'm your neighbour. Remember? We met the other night in the garden."

"I remember. And from today I'll call you Andrew kind-heart, saviour of the lizard," he joked. His smile was contagious and bright. It gave out a sense of peace.

"Then you will be Adam the brave, saviour of Andrew!"

The two laughed heartily and walked home, leaving the bus stop behind.

21

"This is absurd. Absurd!" Helena paced to and fro in her living room. That house had cost her too much, and it was hard to maintain on a police worker's salary – when she got it with her ex-boyfriend, she certainly didn't think she'd have to pay for it by herself. On top of that, the plumber had done a horrible job and many of the pipe joints in the wall were leaking, soaking the walls and lifting the wooden floor in the corners. The air conditioners never worked, and she had recently been notified that the facade of the building had to be renovated and she would have to pay even more money. Money she'd had to loan from her parents, who would no doubt start with the usual criticism against her dangerous lifestyle. Her father would then insist on exploiting people he knew to make her return to the city where she was born, working in a more convenient place, like an office. But Helena was not keen on an office job – she loved the action too much. In those moments, any frustration that went through her head reassured her. It made her feel normal in a world of normal problems. She was exhausted, though.

Amin watched through the shutters down to the street, looking worried. It was about 22:00, the weather had settled, but there was not a soul to be seen; the woman had been mumbling all day, going from attempts at rationalising the situation to total desperation. He knew that Helena was in a difficult position; her whole being, her vitality, screamed for freedom, as if they were in a vigilant coma, trying to be heard by those in charge of pulling the plug.

"Helena, try to relax. I know it is hard, but your fretting does not help."

She glared at him. "Who the hell are you? I don't even know why I brought you to my house. All this is absurd. And you don't know shit. Nothing. There must be an explanation. This isn't life, this isn't reality! Or maybe I'm going crazy. What do you know about how it feels? You come from your world of toys, of giants and various monsters, of comic superpowers. You're a fucking superhero. I'm talking to a superhero!" She began to cry again. "I always hated comics!"

"There is only one world and one reality. The perception we have of these is different."

"Can you hear yourself? I would love for you to disappear now. But if you do, what happens to me? And what will happen to that kid? You speak like a Buddhist philosopher, but you kill giants underground when you're pissed off. These *Atlanteans*," she charged this word with a contempt that came straight from the heart, "are they all philosophers? Do you attend lessons on hermetic in the morning, and remedial terrorism at night?"

"I was not raised to explain reality to a Sleeper and would not be able to, so I do not try. But I can tell you to focus on what we have to do. I assure you that the boy we are looking for is able to free you from the nightmare you are currently experiencing."

"Good. A little boy will give me serenity. What can he tell me that you can't?"

"His talent is not in speeches, nor could all the words in the world save you."

"So to the list of weirdness, we also want to add a child with magical powers?" she whispered approaching him with reddened eyes.

Amin smiled, a gesture that would once have been replaced by a death sentence.

Helena continued: "And what should we do to find this kid? Any brilliant ideas, Pure prince?"

"You should tell me. You know the rules of the Sleepers' world better than I do. It should not be hard for a policewoman to find a person in the city."

She turned and collapsed into a chair, switching on her laptop. The machine, however, didn't respond. "What's the matter now?" Helena muttered.

"It is my fault," Amin replied, approaching. "I do not know all the extensions of the *gorann* you use."

"The computer is dead because you're here?"

"No, it is its nature to become inhibited before a Lord of Matter. Its pseudo-technological essence prevents it from functioning if it does not receive my permission."

"But it's just a damn computer!"

"All that you call technology derives from the father spirit of the *gorann* — it's an extension of it. Mankind underestimates the intention with which it is manufactured, which is the imprint of thought that generated it. Turn it on."

Helena was about to retort, but gave up and pushed the button. The fan of the PC went on, and the OS displayed the startup screen. She withdrew her hands from the keyboard but, immediately afterwards, fascinated, she gently touched it, as if it were a house cat rather than an electric appliance bought at a discount store.

"What do you want to do?" he asked.

"You don't need to be a policeman to find a person today. We've got Internet." She opened the browser and did a quick search which didn't last too long. "He's not here."

"Did you not say you could find him?"

"It was a possibility, but without some more information I can't."

"I have nothing more to give you, unfortunately. The boy is well protected by his people."

"Then we need to look in the registry list. And I can do it alone, from the district." Dealing with normal things, such as bureaucratic problems, diminished the anguish that tightened her chest.

"Will it take long?"

"At least a couple of days."

"Inexcusable!" cried the Hound. "The boy risks his life every moment – we may not have two days."

"Why are you looking for Adam Uyan? What's so special about him?"

Amin took a few steps back, returning to the window. "I do not know."

"Look, if you need my help you must tell me everything, otherwise you can go fuck yourself."

"Helena, I am tired of your coarse language and I need you focused. The boy is important for several reasons, but I do not know why various factions are so interested in him. I was only told what is necessary and I assure you that no part of it would be useful right now. All I know is that my people have been waiting a long time for the birth of a very special person and someone believes that this boy may be that person."

"Is that all? A religious thing?"

The man smiled. "You could not be further from the truth. What Atlantis is interested in is much more concrete than religions ever were."

"I need to eat," Helena cut in. "I feel nauseous." She went over to the fridge, opened it and pulled out some cold chicken.

"You are a strong woman and I appreciate this."

Helena was full of anger, but not immune to that compliment. Her emotions were so conflicting that she was ashamed to feel pleasure in hearing those words. Was that another trick of that mysterious man who, in a moment, had swept away her existence? "What are these factions you mentioned – governments? Secret services or thereabout?" she asked.

"Your governments only serve to control and organise the human masses."

"Nothing wrong with it, but you haven't answered my question."

"A human being, by definition, does not need to be governed —
think about it."

"I have no time for a Sociology class. Get to the point."

"Very well. The factions have been in a state of dispute for many
millennia, a real war. A silent war, but also a bloody one. Often the
Sleepers pay its price with their own life, without even knowing it."

"This war… what's its purpose?"

"Dominion. Whoever wins can choose the destiny of mankind in
All That It Is."

"You mean the Universe?"

"As well."

Helena became dubious and took a box of ice cream out of the
refrigerator.

Amin went on. "Our definitions of things are different from yours,
but in some senses they match. As you can imagine the stakes are very
high."

"You still haven't answered. Who are these forces or factions in
conflict?"

"The war is between Atlantis and Mu."

"Mu? Never heard of it."

"It is the name of a land that no longer exists. Mu is where
everything began, where mankind was born and made slave to the
same nature who had given birth to it. One day a young man was
born, destined to change everything. His name was Evenor, and he
was the one to imagine humanity free from the whims of nature, able
to transform itself into what was intended from the beginning and
becoming the last species to be awakened, the point of arrival of an
infinite cycle flowing from the Source."

"Go on. What happens then? Actually, hold on. What period are
you referring to? There is no trace of this in history."

"12,837 years, nine days and seven hours from Evenor's date of
birth, the only emperor of Atlantis."

Helena tried to get her thoughts in order, but the first event she
remembered from her History lessons was that the pyramids in Egypt
dated from around 4,500 BC. "And what happened next?"

"Mu did not agree with Evenor's vision. He had a twin named
Belial, very different from his brother. He was stronger, impetuous
and more violent. For a long time he constituted an important defence
for Evenor."

"Was Evenor a sort of prophet?"

"For a part of his life he travelled to bring his own thought to the
Gentiles and often extended his help to the sages of Mu. His followers
grew, but so did the distrust of the people of Mu."

"Why were they bothered? Did they not have freedom of expression at that time?"

"The world was very different, Helena. The Sleepers did not exist, and mankind was awake. There was no war, and there were no deceptions, only life."

"It sounds idyllic. The Garden of Eden."

"It was not. Mu refused to place the Third People, human beings, in their rightful place. Evenor dared to support this truth."

Helena took a big spoon of ice cream, its familiar taste and sweetness reassuring her a little. "What caused the war?" she asked.

"One day Evenor wounded himself trying to save a child left behind to die during a storm. He lost his senses for many cycles. Belial used this period to prepare an attack against the land of Mu. At first, they were only skirmishes. Then, when the pseudo-technology, the means by which men would break away from the umbilical cord with the Earth, began to be used to produce weapons, everything precipitated and the conflict widened. When Evenor woke up, it was too late. He tried to reconcile everyone, but it was not possible. The violence unleashed by Belial was uncontrollable, and when Mu reacted, the forces of the world took over and the destructive spiral became a giant, unstoppable wave. And today we still fight."

"You said that Atlantis is the sovereign of the world. You lied, then."

"No. Atlantis reigns over the world, but has not yet succeeded in fulfilling its great purpose, the Great Intention – to free humankind from its link with nature."

"Man is an animal like any other."

"You only say this because you're a Sleeper."

"You mean we're not animals? We act the same: we are born, we eat, we reproduce and we die."

"The lower creatures do not ask questions and cannot receive answers."

"Questions like who are we or where are we going? We ask them because our brain is more developed, but we still can't get the answers!"

"This is where you are wrong. Each Woken one is born with the answer to these and many other questions. Every human being is born awake. No lower creature follows the same path."

Helena felt drained. The sense of exhaustion was overwhelming. She emptied the ice cream container and tossed it into the bin. Was it possible that all the answers that every being human wanted to know were there, ready to be discovered?

"That's enough for now," Amin interrupted. "We are losing time on futile matters."

"One more thing. How many Woken ones are there?"

"Nobody knows the exact number. The population of Atlantis amounts to twenty thousand inhabitants and it never varies. The smallest part is composed of Pure beings."

"So few?"

"They are enough to rule the world. If the boy we are looking for is really who Atlantis thinks he is, he would be enough to change the fate of everyone. We are perhaps on the verge of a radical change, the beginning of a new era of splendour for humanity."

Helena smiled sarcastically. "When I joined the police I thought I was helping people in my own piece of world, not that I'd take part in a global revolution."

"The Sleepers have always taken part in the Great Intention, unaware. Help me, and I will do all I can to make everything clear to you. Your reward will be knowledge."

"For now, I just need to know that I'm doing the right thing, though I'm still not sure who the good or the bad guys are in this story," she pointed out, sitting back down at her computer. She picked up her own notes on the murder of Adam Uyan and began to sift through the witness accounts and data concerning the victim. "How do you think the killers found Uyan?" she asked the Atlantean.

"Someone in the Sleepers' world must have provided some information."

"And what did you know? Why were you at the scene of the crime?"

"My information concerned this area of the city and the name of the boy."

"But how did you know that the murdered boy was not the person you were looking for?"

"The Adam I'm looking for lives with two old people. The one at the lake was there with his parents. It was enough to understand he was the wrong person. Unfortunately, Fir Bolg are not so clever. They are executors."

"So our Adam lives with his grandparents."

"They are not his relatives, but his guardians. Though I am sure that those who live around him will think that they are his grandparents, yes."

"An old couple defending a special kid? The oddities never end in this story."

"Nothing is as it seems, Helena. Those two are very dangerous, and it is better to meet young Adam when he is alone."

The woman resumed her reading and after a few minutes raised her head with a vacant look. She got up, took the phone book and searched it for a moment. Then she closed it, absorbed. "Can it be?" she wondered aloud.

"What?" Said Amin.

Helena didn't answer but plunged back into her notes. She pulled out one file and returned to type on the PC. She examined a few web pages, read and wrote some more. Then she drew back on the seat, satisfied.

The Hound was intrigued by her behaviour.

"I got it! Maybe it's him. We often use secondary sources in the police, their inclinations and habits, to get more information on the victims."

"I see…"

"You said the Fir Bolg are pretty stupid, dull and think little, right?"

"Yes, they are quite the opposite of their Milesian relatives."

"Whoever gave them the information had to know where the boy would be at that moment. And to do it, he needed to also know where he came from, what area of the city."

"Go on."

"I crossed the data on the area in which he lived and the habits of his family. I found the place where he went to school. It was something that struck me, because despite being of excellent family, the victim was registered with a school program for young people with insertion problems – Saint Paul."

Amin frowned, motioning for her to continue.

"All those enrolled in schools like Saint Paul are registered by the police at the request of the institute itself, for safety reasons. All I had to do was to look in the files of the department, where I can log in, to find a list. And bingo!" She turned the screen of the PC in the direction of the Hound. He did not turn around, though, and Helena felt a stab of disappointment. "There's another Adam Uyan at the Saint Paul! In the file it says that he lives with his grandparents. Curious, right?"

Amin did not change expression.

"Are you listening to me? I don't need a round of applause, but at least one drop of enthusiasm!"

Amin turned now, very serious. "They've found us."

22

Yanosh 236 realised that Amin had felt him. Although very young, he had ten years of experience in the field, but it was the first time he found himself in front of a second-class demon, perhaps top-level, according to Jaffe's Tabula, and a chill ran down his spine. He put his hand to the earpiece. "They know we're here. Make the call. From now on we speak only via VIB."

"Roger that," said a voice from the other side.

Helena's phone vibrated and then rang. She started to answer, then looked at Amin. "Are they Fir Bolg?" she asked, frightened.

"No. Answer the phone."

She did. "Hello?"

"Good evening, Agent Dowson. This is Patrick Miller from Scotland Yard. I apologise for the late hour. Have I disturbed you?"

Helena was taken aback. She watched Amin taking a quick tour of her house. "Not at all. How can I help you?"

"We are investigating the murder of Adam Uyan on behalf of the superintendent. We heard that you were busy questioning a suspect."

Helena instinctively knew that lying would be the wrong move. Maybe they were trying to figure out if she was involved as an accomplice. "That's correct. I was just preparing a report on it."

"Great. We also learned that the suspect fled during the interrogation."

"You should ask my colleagues. I was unconscious at the time."

"May we could ask you a few more questions before you finish your report? We're getting a lot of heat around here on this case."

"Of course, I can stop by tomorrow if you give me an address."

"Actually, we could stop by just now, if it's not too much trouble."

"Now?" Helena was not keen on this unusual procedure.

"Yes, we are on duty for an operation with the Environmental Reclamation Department. We're dealing with the trash," he said, laughing.

She didn't feel like joining in.

"It's not going to take us long, and we could be there very soon."

Helena looked at Amin, who shook his head as if he had listened to the conversation.

"Agent Miller, it's quite late, and I'm very tired. I'll stop by tomorrow if it's all the same to you."

A few moments of silence followed her answer.

"Of course, no problem. We tried," he said, laughing once again. "Goodnight, Agent Dowson."

Amin approached her. "I do not think he was your colleague, but it does not matter. Take what you need and let us get out of this trap."

Helena understood from his gaze that the Atlantean was not joking. She felt the nausea and pain rising again, but she said nothing. She ran to her room, opened her suitcase and threw in some comfy clothes, a few mementoes, photos and several rounds of bullets for the .357 Magnum. In two minutes exact, she had returned to Amin.

*

Yanosh 236 was still there, standing at the corner of the road, about 300 meters from the brick-coloured building. He continued to monitor the situation with his mind, trying to stay focused. The tablets he had taken prevented him from passing out, but he would not hold up for much longer. The demon had created a barrier which interfered with his extrasensory faculties – there was no doubt that the clash was unequal. No human being, even a powerful Enlightened like him, could have competed with a demon of that level. Then he saw the first movements on the side of the building and on the roof. He could relax for a moment and take a deep breath.

The unit of Karman warriors approaching the policewoman's apartment moved in silence. They were trained to coordinate themselves through the powers that arose from enlightenment: what one saw, everyone saw, while maintaining complete individuality. The Karman warriors did not have a hierarchy, since there were no orders to follow or any strategies other than immediate adaptation. They relied on those who had more experience, and it was always the same warriors who kept communications with the psychic or magical reconnaissance units. Marcus, the leader of the group, had chosen a C.A.T.I.L.I.N.A. support unit for the operation, a psionic soldier able to use special powers in battle, and he had been offered Yanosh 236. It was enough for him that the young man belonged to the Elmuth family – the rest did not matter. The Karman warriors didn't ask questions, they simply acted.

Marcus used the low vibration coming from his chest to warn his five-strong team of his position. He immediately got the answer he expected. He activated his dermo-adaptive power propulsion suit. The thin wetsuit that he wore under his clothes thickened with an almost imperceptible hiss and he knew that the others had done the same thing. He turned the corner and jumped no less than five yards to the roof of Helena's building, rolling with an aikido move; he reached the parapet and flattened himself against the wall.

Now that the C.A.T.I.L.I.N.A. unit and his extrasensory abilities had been left behind, the Karmans needed some sort of passive support to identify the demon, otherwise they would not be able to recognise him. Marcus wore a dark glove with five rubber buttons on his palm and, as he tightened it with Velcro, the gizmo came to life, providing general information on the environment and the electrodynamic perturbations that were unleashed in the presence of dark beings. He tried to interpret the signals by pressing the buttons on the palm of his hand. There was something there; it registered as a peak and, soon after, nothing.

"He's simulating," he told the other warriors through the voice. "Let's go in now." He coordinated with the positions of his companions and spun on the wall, landing on the service ladder, leaping with a single movement inside the corridor window that had been opened by one of his comrades, Sebastian, of the Lockmead family. On the other side of the corridor, two more from his team appeared: one remained on the stairs, the other came out of the window with a sudden move that went against every law of gravity. Two other warriors checked for movements in the immediate exterior of the building, ready to stop anyone coming close. The information provided by Yanosh restricted the field of play to the second upper floor, where there were only two doors. Marcus ordered the second warrior to reach the furthest opening, while he and Sebastian approached the one on his left.

The gizmo's reading was still uncertain. There were humans in the area, but the glove was not a radar, so the number of people and their position were hard to spot. Marcus trusted his reading skills and tried to focus on his senses. He did not have much time and had to act fast. These kinds of operations were very dangerous. If someone saw them, he would have to kill them. *The sacrifice of the few for the salvation of all*, he thought.

He modified the reading of the gizmo and activated the Shield of Perseus. He sensed a psychic wavering motion. This could indicate a person under intense emotional stress. But even a demon could feel like that if hunted. He doubted that these dark beings could have feelings, but he had learned that the gizmo read that kind of mental activity. He decided to move. He made a dry sound with his throat, felt the pressure rise on his face, his eyes seeming to pop out of their sockets. He tightened his right hand and then brought his left closer, as if to hold an invisible object.

"O fathers, lead our spirits to victory over darkness," he whispered softly. All the Karman did the same thing.

He made a quick gesture, a semicircle in the air, focusing on the mechanism of the door and touching it with his hands. The metal made a dry sound and splinters came out of the lock in pieces. Sebastian shouldered the door open, which gave as if it had been hit by a car, and entered a room lit only by a few lamps.

Helena fired and hit Sebastian in the chest. The powerful bump from the armoured .357 bullet stopped the race of the Karman warrior by lifting him and causing him to crash to the ground. Marcus rolled to the side, behind the short wall of the open kitchen. As she followed him with the gun, Helena approached the column in the middle of the living room. Hers was a quiet neighbourhood, filled with good people. Now that she had fired, they would immediately call the police.

Marcus understood who this woman was, and it was not the demon they were hunting. "Agent Dowson," he said from behind the door, "we don't want to hurt you. Tell us where the person who was with you is and I promise nothing will happen to you. "

Just like Amin had told her.

Helena leaned over, enough to look in the direction of the kitchen, when she felt a vibration coming from the wooden floor, which rose and creaked. She turned abruptly, but too late. Sebastian was on her. She tried to shoot but found her hands blocked. She rotated her elbows and hit him with her knee. The impact was absorbed without the man perceiving any pain. On the contrary, he grabbed her with an unstoppable force, lifted her up and threw her against the sofa, overturning it. Helena got up right away, gun in her hand. Never give up the gun. She aimed for his face and fired, striking the column. Sebastian moved around her, using the furniture as cover. He was too fast and didn't give her enough time to aim properly. She tried again when she saw him emerge from one side and jump against a wall. Maybe she had hit him, but in any case the man didn't stop and threw himself on her, crushing her with his weight.

In the meantime, a commotion had ensued outside the apartment. The Karman had used a camouflage procedure, taking the neighbours off guard and ordering them to remain indoors because it was a police operation.

Well done, Marcus thought as he approached Helena, immobilised by Sebastian.

The two men wore common clothes but also dark gloves, military amphibians consisting of one piece; their foreheads were covered by what appeared to be a thick black rubber band on which smooth ear covers and mono-lens glasses were hooked. Their skin looked darkened, as if they had applied some sort of camouflage product.

"Sons of bitches!" Helena cried, crushed by Sebastian's weight.

"Be quiet, woman," the man told her, unable to hide his disgust.

"Where is he?" Marcus asked again.

"I'm a police officer. Let me go or you'll be in big trouble," she threatened them.

Marcus made a slow tour of the living room. "You're in danger. We can help you. You only need to tell us where he went. He's still around here, is he not?"

"I don't know what you're talking about. Let me go!"

It was then that the head of the Karman understood.

Yanosh 236 was sitting in the backseat of the Voyager, trying to relax his mind. The blood had stopped leaking from his nose and ears and he would soon be able to resume his monitoring. When he felt the cold blade against his throat, he opened his eyes and gave a sob, but did not move. The power of the demon overwhelmed him without even having to activate his extrasensory abilities. He was seized by an atavistic terror and fought hard not to scream or react. He had no way out, he knew that right away.

"Pitiful beings," Amin whispered, wrapped in an unnatural shadow. Yanosh tried to erect a mental barrier, but the blade began to burn his skin. He desisted.

"Order your men to let go of the woman."

"*And one after the other, the legions of darkness fall, vanquished by the true Light…*" began to recite Yanosh, while a tear ran down his face.

"You do not need the woman."

"*The Dukes of evil retreat towards the darkness of visceral caves, the assault is irrepressible, as deadly as it is pure. There is no hatred, but only faith…*" he continued, as he was praying.

"Fool."

"*And the monsters of the black abyssal forges drown in the whirlpool of water and before the kings, the lion, they flee overwhelmed by terror…*"

"Your death is useless."

"*And all past ages now return to his eyes, from dawn to dawn, they run in a vortex, in peace, forever,*" concluded Yanosh, closing his eyes.

A thousand needles of Orichalcum, each thin as a hair, pierced his brain, creating a multitude of ischemia that killed him instantly. The C.A.T.I.L.I.N.A. collapsed without making a sound.

"Yanosh!" Amin could hear through the corpse's earpiece.

Marcus was staring at the half-hidden car below, through the window. All the Karman warriors knew what had happened. Without a tactical support unit, even the valiant Enlightened warriors were in grave danger. A high-level demon was able to do anything, altering their perceptions or even reality itself. Attacking him without any psychic defence could lead the whole team to destruction.

"*Iashtannalusis, lariah eyne dolvar*," Marcus said in the *mirror-tongue* through the molecular communication system. No known technological device could have intercepted those words, though demons were capable of everything. The secret language of the Enlightened, the *mirror*, granted a further level of crypto.

Sebastian lifted Helena effortlessly, took the gun out of her hand, almost dislocating her wrist, and dragged her with him, staring at her with disdain. "If you peep, I'll cut your throat."

She was a well-trained woman, who had disarmed many men even larger than the one who now dragged her helplessly across the floor, but she had never seen a force of that nature, so unstoppable.

They gathered on the roof, using the service stairs. Helena counted four of those prodigious and silent individuals. They acted without speaking, yet they were coordinated. She wondered where Amin was. She was sure he was in the neighbourhood, and maybe he was watching them. Even the Karman warriors were cautious, as if waiting for something.

Marcus looked around, accepting the perceptions of others. "I know you're here, monster," he said without raising his tone of voice. "We have the woman. Show yourself."

"Many that move like one," a voice was heard in the darkness. It was Amin's, deeper than normal, as if filtered by a wall of water. "Karman combat unit, I presume."

"Come out where we can see you."

One of the men turned abruptly, slicing the air with his fist. There was a creeping noise, as if that empty hand held an invisible sword.

"You have no chance, but maybe I'll spare your lives if you free Helena."

Sebastian passed the woman to a younger companion, who had the same extraordinary strength, and approached Marcus.

"Demon, what you did against the defenceless Yanosh is repulsive. For each of us who falls, a thousand come together to bring about your defeat. Even if you kill us all, you will not get anything. Armageddon is your destiny. Now, dictate your conditions and maybe you'll save your life. "

The Hound appeared on the ledge of the next building, which was a few yards above them. His figure was amalgamated with shadows, as if he were two-dimensional. Only the eyes shone with a faint blue glow. The contours of his body were unclear, enveloped in a sort of black, motionless smoke. Seeing him like that, he really looked like a hell demon. Helena felt fear and wondered if those people, who after all were actual humans like her, could not be her salvation.

"Finally you show yourself," Sebastian commented.

"Go away, Enlightened, and leave the woman here. These are my conditions. You are of no interest to me."

Marcus just turned his gaze to his right and Helena realised he was staring at a faraway spot just above her shoulder. Taking advantage of the distraction, she called Amin's name.

A taut, blue line materialised in the air, emitting a sharp hiss that came only after a few moments. It remained there for a couple of seconds, then disappeared as if it had been nothing more than an after image. The dogs near the building began to bark. Alarms from houses and cars nearby went off in a deafening melody of uneven sounds.

Everything happened very quickly.

What was supposed to have been the shot fired from an unknown weapon had missed Amin, who had returned to the shadows. In that cacophony of sounds, a shock wave threw Helena to the ground and it seemed to her that the light had dimmed only on the roof of her house. The yellow lanterns that had seen her on so many romantic evenings with her former partner seemed to lose energy.

It is its nature to inhibit himself in the presence of a Lord of Matter, she recalled him saying.

The Karman warriors prepared to receive their enemy, hands clenched around non-existent hilts. Then something happened which Helena could only define as a liquid cloud of black vapours and a very strong wind that did not affect her. At the centre of it, enveloped in coils of flames of metal fluids, she saw Amin, illuminated by a powerful glow that shone on his forehead and behind his head. For a moment, she thought of the representations of Jesus or of Christian saints with their flaming haloes, or those of the Indian gods.

The warriors snapped quickly to attack the Hound on all fronts, coordinated as one.

"On your knees!" ordered Amin in a devastating voice. The second wave of pressure that exploded made her ears whistle and Helena was thrown off the parapet. She barely managed to grab an old TV aerial, which bent but did not break, leaving her suspended almost nine yards above the pavement.

Marcus was on his knees, like the rest of his team. He had hoped that the sniper armed with the E.R. Gun could catch the demon by surprise, killing him with an ionised bullet fired at seven miles per second. Instead, the woman had saved him, demonstrating incomprehensible behaviour in the eyes of those who had been fighting darkness for six millennia.

The talismanic protections performed by the exorcists on their weaponry had not served much against that monster, and the magical seals had split at the second attack of the demon. The control of the enemy over technology was still far beyond their understanding, even for the more efficient Smithsonian of the Crotonei family. Now every Karman warrior was immobilised in that humiliating position, and the sniper would not be able to fire before the two minutes needed by the gun to cool down. Marcus evaluated the situation. It was over. Amin approached him, but he faced him with the firmness of those who do not intend to surrender and do not fear death.

"They will hunt you down and find you. We have your profile and we know your face."

"I hope so," said the Hound, and added with contempt: "*Sleeper*."

"Do what you must do, that I can reach my fathers. Once with them, do not worry, my will can make those who hunt you even stronger."

"I do not want to kill you. I'm saving your life so that you can remember me. Follow me and you will find many other demons for your cause." Amin whirled around and ran to the ledge, where he jumped.

Helena saw him throw himself into the void above her head and she seemed to fall into a thick, oily liquid. She found herself in a vacant, dark apartment on the ground floor of a house that had been emptied the day before. The Atlantean pointed to the French door that looked out on the garden, beckoning her to follow him. But she could not walk. A cramp hit her and she gave a strangled moan.

"A part of *Orichalcum* has penetrated your body," Amin explained, raising her in his arms. "Your Sleeper world is a real hell."

Helena caught his witty remark. Then everything became dark, the sounds muffled and she fell into an artificial, deep sleep.

*

When Marcus regained control of his armour, he rose to his feet and struggled to reach his companions. But they were all dead, though without visible wounds. The only survivor, who had not been involved in the fight, jumped on the roof, approaching the scene frantically.

"Have you checked?" asked Marcus, bending over Sebastian, who seemed asleep.

"They're looking for a boy," answered the other, staring at the bodies.

Police sirens were getting closer and closer.

"Evacuation?" asked a voice in the earpiece.

"There's no time," Marcus replied. "We'll use the nullifying devices."

"Can we not take them with us for a proper burial?"

"We have no other choice, unfortunately. We will glorify them by telling their story. One day we will be one in the imperishable Light, sure in its triumph over the darkest darkness. That day we will look at the mountain in flames and we will know that all the suffering and pain for the lost ones will have been consecrated to the blood of the last enemy fallen on the battlefield," Marcus said moving away, followed by the surviving Karman warrior.

When the police patrol got on the roof, they found nothing. On the grey floor some smoky halos indicated the result of a physical force of which they knew nothing, so they didn't notice it, thinking it was moisture or pollution, and they looked elsewhere for evidence of a crime they would never find. The dogs were barking again.

23

“What did they do to you?” Emily asked her son, bewildered. She was pointing at the red cheekbone.

“Nothing, Mum. I got hit by a ball during PE, that’s all.”

She approached him suspiciously, feeling guilty for allowing Andy to come back alone.

He took his mother’s face in her hands. “It was just a ball that rebounded off the crossbar of the goal. I did everything myself.”

Emily still wasn’t convinced, though it didn’t look like a fist or a kick bruise.

Andrew avoided more questions by starting to clear up the table. “Today I met our neighbour, you know?” he told her cheerfully.

Mrs Fawcett was taken aback.

“We walk back together from school. He’s a good guy. We were thinking of going to and returning from school together. The road seems longer than it looks, actually. Is that okay with you?” he continued, flooding his mother with words.

“Andy, I don’t know. Yes, maybe so. I can take you in the morning and perhaps when I can’t...”

“Everything went fine. There are a lot of guys who make the journey with us, and from the metro to here you can walk it in a quarter of an hour.”

Andrew’s tone did not leave her much choice. “Let’s try for a few days, then,” she bargained.

“A month,” he bartered back.

They looked at each other and laughed. It was an important moment, a rite of passage to independence. And they were both aware of it. Andrew was on trial and would do well to stay out of trouble, but he knew that his mother’s surrender was unconditional. If everything went smoothly and he managed to avoid Kyle, a new life would start for him. And they both knew this too.

Emily, proud of her son, felt that the request also marked the beginning of an inexorable departure. The thing that frightened her most was realising that it was she who needed him now.

“Let’s finish cleaning, I’m exhausted,” Mrs Fawcett said, putting on her fluorescent orange rubber gloves. “So, what about our neighbour, then?” she added, yawning.

Andrew thought his Mum had already taken her sleeping pills. However, he grabbed a cloth and began to dry the dishes Emily passed to him, telling her about his walk home with Adam, omitting the bit with Kyle and his henchmen. "Well, he's kinda quiet," he said without revealing too much. "He likes animals, and his grades at school are among the highest. He really likes music too."

"Why is he enrolled at Saint Paul?"

The question took him off guard, but he tried to hide his disappointment. "I don't know. But I can't understand why you're asking me something like that. You don't need to be a criminal to attend Saint Paul, right?"

Emily knew she had said something wrong, but she felt tired, too tired. "I'm sorry, love. I don't feel too good. Maybe I have the flu. I didn't mean anything bad. I just want you to find honest friends who won't disappoint you."

"I think I can handle judging a person," Andrew snapped, though quietly.

Something had broken in their conversation. Emily tried to retaliate, but her son didn't leave her much space and, as soon as they had finished tidying up, she left. In her room, she went to bed in her dressing gown.

Andrew couldn't explain the reason for the oppressive feeling that had seized him for the first time, showing him his mother as a vampire thirsty for his presence at all costs. It had been a very complicated and emotional day, but he felt that it wasn't the only explanation. He was troubled and wished to taste that sensation of freedom he had felt at the school's exit, outside the gate, for the rest of his life. He wanted freedom to be and to own, to have his personal spaces, to fulfil his drives and even his insecurities. He didn't want to feel obliged to tell her everything. Being the man of the house meant being an adult. He didn't want to exclude her from his life, but he needed room. It was the first time he had felt like this and could not say whether it pleased him or anguished him more.

He went out into the garden with a bottle of apple juice in his hand and sat down on an overturned vase they had not yet managed to arrange. The air was cooling, but it was still pleasant. The dwarf monkey stared at him with its round, questioning eyes, the half-open mouth showing small, sharp teeth. It was anchored to the garden's dividing net, hung with all its paws and its tail wrapped around a rusty metal peg.

"Hi Mamuk," Andrew greeted her. Adam had told him its name. "Want some juice?" he joked. The little monkey disappeared quickly among the leaves.

Maybe it wasn't his night, he thought.

"Hi," he heard immediately after, beyond the intricate plants of the front garden.

Andrew identified the spot where the voice was coming from and shortly after, Adam appeared by the net with Mamuk on his shoulders.

"Oh hi!"

"Mamuk says that the saviour of the lizards is sad. Is it because of Kyle?" asked the boy with his peaceful expression.

Andy stood up immediately. "Are you crazy? Don't let her hear you. If my Mum finds out I got into a fight, she will not let me go home alone even at ninety!"

Adam nodded. "Sorry."

He subsided. "No, I'm sorry."

"Well, you may not be suffering from the beating, but something is bothering you."

"That obvious?"

The neighbour gave Mamuk a knowing look.

"Right, even the monkey noticed. The truth is I don't know what's wrong with me. And my mother… I love her, but she's always on my case, trying to get what I don't even have. Or maybe it's just me."

"A mother is only capable of being such. It protects us, gives us nourishment, pampers us and accompanies us throughout our lives. But you cannot expect her to know when and how to step aside, don't you think?" Adam said with a slightly sad expression on his face.

"And your parents?"

"I've never met them."

"Are they… dead? The janitor told me. Or at least I understood that."

"I've always lived with my grandparents, but they never talk about it. Now I don't even mention the subject. You know, they're a little bit unusual, and it's hard to understand each other."

"They keep a very tight rein, huh? Still, they let you come and go from school alone."

"Yes," said the other unconvinced.

"Where are they from? My mother told me they seemed foreign. You know, she brought a cake a few days ago and exchanged a few words with your grandmother."

"They were delighted by the cake. They should not eat sweets, but for that of your mother, they made an exception. I didn't even get to try a piece of it!"

Andrew didn't say anything. He motioned for him to wait and disappeared back into the house.

He came back a minute or so later with a big piece of cake on a plastic plate, which he passed to Adam over the net.

"You didn't have to, but thank you," he said, placing it on one of those strange marble benches they had in the garden and breaking a corner off with his fingers.

"It's nothing."

"My grandparents come from Eastern Europe and struggle to speak the language here."

"Russia?"

"No," Adam replied, tasting the cake. "Yum, good! Moldova, from the mountains."

"They were shepherds, then."

"I would say more hunters than shepherds."

"And have you always lived here?"

"Do you mean in this house? Yes, shortly after being born we moved here. I was born in a village not far from the city and they were ready to take me with them."

"Why did they not want you?" he asked, not very tactful. But Adam did not seem to mind.

"They wanted me, but they couldn't keep me with them. They had a dangerous life, though I'm not sure what they did."

"Forget it, I've done enough snooping. After all, we've known each other for half a day!" And they burst out laughing. Even Mamuk laughed, although it didn't understand the reason for so much joy, a feeling only felt when it ate almost to bursting point. But if its master laughed, it was fine.

The husky and incomprehensible voice of Adam's grandfather interrupted that moment.

"I have to go!" the boy said hurriedly.

"Can't you stay and talk here, in the garden? We are surrounded by ten floors of bricks, better than a castle! I know they're apprehensive, but..." then he turned to the figure hidden behind the shutter.

"Good evening. I'm Andrew Fawcett, your neighbour."

There was only an abrupt moaning in response, in some tongue he couldn't understand, and the shutter closed.

Adam smiled. "I told you, you're lucky. See you tomorrow."

"OK. Shall we meet at the bus stop at quarter past seven?"

"Sure. Thanks for the cake."

"Oh, do you like movies? I'm a big fan of TV series."

"We have no television, actually. Perhaps you could lend me a book."

Andrew was puzzled and a bit disoriented. "I should have some in the boxes."

"Good, then do something for me. Choose a book and I will read it. It's a bit like a movie, is it not?"

"All right," the other shrugged. "I'll look for something really cool."

Adam went back into the house with Mamuk in tow and Andrew decided he was a real nice guy. On the other hand, his grandparents were really not; they seemed oppressive and he almost felt a lack of air at the idea of living with them every day, as if it were his problem, not Adam's. All of a sudden, Emily's apprehensions seemed less excessive.

*

In the room, the candlelight made a huge effort to penetrate the darkness, barely lighting the terracotta floor. Here and there, disorder reigned supreme. Dirty clothes, cans of drinks and pizza cartons were piled up with such a chaotic look that almost seemed like modern art. The wallpaper was battered, greasy and often torn; deep gaps opened in the old sofas and armchairs, while most of the knobs or corners of the furniture were eroded, as if they had been chewed. An acrid smell dominated the air.

Unfortunately, kind Mrs Flaherty had not been around to tidy up the house for a few days. Old Shaun had warned them that there had been problems and that it was better to avoid any connection between him and Adam, but he had not specified what problems these were.

"*Ehhh*... Shoult bont not with Sleeperrr," said a raucous, cacophonous voice.

"If the *Collegium* has made us live in a city," replied Adam, "it is unthinkable that they took this decision without realising I would make friends. Andrew is a good person; there are no shadows in his eyes."

The figure slid from the ceiling to the wall, with a smooth and silent movement. Something on his face shone like pure ivory. "*Ahhh*, not be a know-it-all, Atam, son of Iunia. Many tangers lurk in Sleepersss, yes? Hearts ant mints is fickle. Mankint always weak. Since sleep, even more. Not be teceivet by appearancesss."

"Enough, Ahiga." A second figure with an equally peculiar voice, but a more determined and austere tone, appeared, placing long black claws on a leather chair, which creaked and threatened to overturn. "Tees speeches concern boy not, and we no jutges."

"In night of times," Ahiga continued, speaking to Adam, "us Sikal warnet the Thuata Te Tanann on risks of wakening sapiens race. Better if left them in Oblivion."

There was a snarl halfway between a big cat and the hiss of a sea crocodile. "Stop it, Ahiga!"

"*Shhh*, Sorry, boy." Then to the other, "Me try only help, Yzenn."

"Our people have made a lot of mistakes, Ahiga," Adam replied, "but we cannot go on living and thinking as we did before the Great Gorann. It is unfair and our Aeterna guides would not agree. They cannot prevent me from having friends among the Sleepers when we find good in them. Andrew has a big heart and a powerful spark."

"Talk like *Naacal*, boy. Careful, you not one yet," said Ahiga, looking discreetly at Yzenn. Then he grabbed a can of cola, looked inside it and bit the object with a metallic screech, cutting it in two to savour the little remaining content. His big cat eyes dilated when they touched the sugars dissolved in the black liquid.

"Ahiga try protect you, Adam," Yzenn went on. "We not wise as *Naacal*, but *Collegium* gave you to us. When under our protection, you to what we tell you. They agree too."

The young man shrugged. "I always stick to your rules, brothers. But I have overcome the age of childhood and I must interact with living beings in order to fully understand the Mother."

"No your tecision. No ours, young Atam," Yzenn let out an asthmatic whistle. "Bring your intention to *Collegium*, who wants you away from Sleepers. *Collegium* is summon next waning moon for tiscuss your contition. Talk there."

The shivak named Ahiga made an energetic leap that landed him on the opposite wall. His large hands and part of the long, disjointed feet caught on the wallpaper as if they had nails. A picture fell, but the impact had been almost silent. "We tefend you, Atam. Many things that... *hhh...* you not know," he said emphatically.

Adam picked up the two halves of shredded tin and tossed them into a bag. "I'm sure you act in my best interest, shivak brothers. With the same energy you should also avoid any contact with the Sleepers," he said, throwing the cardboard tray on which Emily Fawcett's cake had been placed. "It's not good for you to eat sugars, you know," he scolded them.

Ahiga slipped on the carpet, moving on all fours and rushing to smell the tray, the large head, sprinkled with iridescent colours, extended forward with long nostrils placed on the shaggy skull that dilated and contracted. "*Ehhh*, right," he commented, unconvinced.

"It makes you unfocused," the boy insisted.

Yzenn also slid past them. He stood on his two legs and a long, coloured, elegant crest shot up from his powerful back all the way up to his head. He snatched the tray from Ahiga's hands and handed it to Adam, who finally threw it.

"First watch you, tonight, shivak!" he reproached his kinsman.

Ahiga seemed to be offended by that busk reaction.

Adam put a hand on his neck with a sympathetic gesture of

solidarity. "Everyone has weaknesses," he said.

"Will not to it again, brothers." On all fours, the creature put his chin, decorated by a band that held the small beard back, out of the French door. His big eyes penetrated the darkness like it was daylight. Sure that no one was looking, he began to climb the cloister wall. His body reacted immediately and millions of photosensitive cells changed the colour of his hair into the dull red of the building's bricks. With some graceful vertical leaps, the shivak found itself on the roof, lit only by the silver moonlight. The city of the Sleepers was a carpet of bright, colourful lights, some of which moved at great speed, far away. Similar buildings stood all around and far away, and the adjacent hill had not yet been covered by cement. He reviewed all the possible escape routes and the weak points of that position, as he did every evening, checking for anomalies.

Satisfied, he got up to his feet and took a deep breath before contracting every single muscle in his body. The double rib cage backed up, stealing a little breath; the movable jaw forced itself towards the middle, turning his powerful jaws into a more acceptable profile. The hairs became so compact that they looked like skin and their colour became dark; the claws backed into his knuckles, causing him some pain, and so did the feet, which forced themselves to get stuck in one of the three joints; finally, the broad membrane tail returned to the orifice just below the centre of the spine, disappearing.

He pulled out a pair of trousers, flip-flops, a hat and a wide shirt from a bag hidden in a chimney and wore them with a grimace of disgust. Now he looked like a human being. Only by observing him very closely and in full light could one be aware of being in the presence of a rare example of a shivak, of the Second People of the Sikal, a race of formidable warriors awakened by the Thuata de Danann tens of thousands of years before the humans.

Ahiga sat on an air conditioning duct and relaxed, looking at the moon. From there it was difficult to feel the breath of the Mother, but not for a shivak.

We will keep this young man safe, my Mother. Who knows that one day he cannot give you back a smile, he thought.

He pulled a new cola can from his backpack, the emergency one, and started to bite it. Then he snorted, uncorked it and took a sip. His pupils dilated.

PART FOUR

EVERYTHING CHANGES, NOTHING CHANGES

"Begin by doing what is necessary, then what is possible. And suddenly you will surprise yourself by doing the impossible."

Francesco d'Assisi

24

The next day it rained. The weather was uncertain, alternating moments of apparent tranquillity with violent thunderstorms. Dark clouds made the sky two-dimensional and too close. Emily had to leave very early, even before her son woke up. With more tangled hair than usual and a sleepy walk, Andrew found a note from his mother attached to the refrigerator with a magnet: "I have an emergency in the office. I preferred not to wake you up. Stay at home as it threatens to rain. PS: I'm sorry for yesterday. Mum."

It took him a while to understand what he was reading. He was glad that his Mum had admitted her fault and was sorry she had felt bad enough to apologise. On the other hand, though, he felt annoyed at the rain comment. He grabbed the phone to try and reason with Emily, his fighting spirit overcoming every logic, but as he dialled the number he stopped. He hung up slowly, had breakfast and got dressed, grabbed an umbrella and went to school.

The bus stop was crowded with people lining up to get in. He skipped a couple of runs, but there was no sign of Adam. He waited until he could, then he decided to go alone. Who knows what had happened to his new friend. Did his grandparents take the same decision as his Mum, keeping him home because of the rain? There was so much water coming down that the umbrella was practically useless. His shoes and legs were soaked through and through, and the crazy traffic made it impossible to cross the road without being splashed further.

When he arrived in front of the Saint Paul, Andrew found himself lining up with a multitude of students, standing in front of the entrance.

"What's up?" he asked a senior.

The boy answered, barely turning around to look at him. "There seems to have been flooding last night. They are trying to figure out if we can enter or not. We're hoping for the best. That is, we're hoping not."

He waited a few minutes, huddled to the others as if they were all in line for a concert. The people behind pushed, the ones ahead complained, all this under the seriously heavy rain, umbrellas at eye level and backpacks being flung from one side to the other. Then a shout of triumph was heard, and the pressure of the people in front turned against him. The rumours about the closure of the school for that day followed one another quickly. Some classrooms were inaccessible, and the old cellars were flooded; even the heaters didn't work. The crowd disappeared in all directions, while the parents, those with the cars still parked in front of the institute, swore at Head Teacher Richardson, or at the weather, or at bad luck.

Andrew went for shelter under the balcony of a building nearby just before a new squall broke. He had no choice but return home. Adam had spared himself the trip, at least. Two people caught his attention. They seemed out of context, perhaps because they appeared calm. They were watching the school, or maybe the students – he couldn't say.

The woman was younger than his mother. She had blonde hair of medium length, held back in a ponytail by a clip or a rubber band. Her skin was red from the cold, and she wore black teardrop glasses, despite the rain. A dark coat, in which she kept her hands, stood out over her beige trousers. She had a slender figure, not very tall. A transparent plastic head wrap protected her from the water.

The man next to her didn't seem affected by the rain. He was very tall, athletic; he looked like an actor. He stood there, motionless, dressed in a heavy coat that reached over his knees, looking around. When his gaze met Andrew's, the boy sensed something unpleasant and felt the need to leave. He didn't want to walk by them, so he took the opposite direction to the subway, thinking of catching it at the next stop. He walked towards the square less than half an hour from there.

The rain began to fall thick. A long colonnade allowed him to stay dry for part of the route, passing by the many students who had sought its shelter to smoke.

It was then that he noticed Kyle. He was walking with a fast, nervous step, stomping away. He was following someone, roughly fifty yards ahead. It was Adam. After a moment of uncertainty, he crossed the street, trying not to get noticed. There was something going on and he didn't like it.

Kyle walked under a shorter colonnade, then turned, stepping down some stairs. Andrew stopped and noticed that the bully had taken an alleyway that ran behind a structure full of large air vents. Going down, a little further on, a portion of transparent Plexiglas housed an ambulance. The sign indicating the entrance to the A&E was legible in transparency, although overturned. With extreme caution, Andy approached the alley and looked on.

Some large garbage bins were surrounded by plastic parts and paper soaked in rain. One of these even had a red cross painted on its side and Andrew's imagination wondered if it contained human remains. He was excited, though he felt that fear could take over any moment. What would Emily do if she knew that he was going around in the rain, chasing sociopaths like Kyle? But there was no trace of the bully, or of Adam.

So he gathered his courage and entered the alley. The rain thundering on the sheds that protected the rubbish covered the sound of his footsteps but also prevented him from noticing the presence of possible attackers.

Some cloths, wrapped in plastic, were dyed dark red. One of these bags had opened letting a red liquid seep into the puddles – it did not leave much doubt as to its nature. Andrew wondered how it was possible that such things could be kept like that, and he jumped away, disgusted, so as not to sully his shoes. If there was one thing he could not stand, it was blood.

He heard a metallic thud and noticed that it came from around the corner, where another covered alley slipped to the left, behind the bins. He approached, swallowing, and leaned forward slightly.

It was a blind lane and it ended no more than a dozen yards away from him. Towards the back, some steps led to an emergency door, from which a white light emerged. There was a metal intercom equipped with a camera. It looked like a service entrance. There was no sign of Adam, while Kyle was there, looking nervous, going back and forth in front of the stairs, occasionally kicking or pushing some stacked metal buckets.

A loud crash of thunder ripped through the sky and Andrew winced. Maybe he had been wrong in following Kyle, but he was afraid he would take revenge on Adam for helping him the day before and finish what he had started. He thought about going around and entering from the A&E to warn his friend, but to be honest, he didn't even know why Adam had entered through a back door. Perhaps he would cause even more troubles by telling the hospital of his presence. So he didn't move and waited for something to happen, even if he really didn't know what he would do if things went south.

At least a hundred years went by before the emergency door opened and Adam appeared. When he and Kyle saw each other, they stood there for a few seconds, so that Andrew thought to intervene before the worst happened.

Instead, nothing happened.

Adam went downstairs and faced Kyle, who was eight inches taller than him. They started talking, but the rain prevented Andy from hearing what they were saying. Then Adam put a hand on Kyle's shoulder and he lowered his head, bringing a hand to his face. He was crying. Sobbing.

Andrew was shocked, astounded.

Suddenly, the bully pushed Adam away and threw a terrible punch against the wall. It seemed to Andrew that the bricks were crumbling in a cloud of fragments, but the noise of the water prevented him from seeing well. It was then that it stopped raining and he could finally hear their conversation.

"Adam, this is useless, do you understand that? Helping these people is useless. Their lives begin and end without any reason! They are an insult to Mother Earth; they are an obstacle, a waste of time! What do you expect to get by giving them a moment of Awareness before dying?"

"That in that moment, they know what it means to be alive. That they feel 'All that is'."

"And for what purpose? If we lose the war there will be nothing left. It will be the end of our Mother, do you understand?" he tugged at Adam's sleeve.

"What should I do then, Kyle?"

"What should you do? Fight, Adam!"

"I'm not a warrior, you know that."

"Fight with the tools Mother gave you. Use the gifts you have received! Find the warriors that will help us overthrow Atlantis!"

There was another loud crack of thunder.

Adam stared at his interlocutor severely. "I will never endorse the *Arkanum*, Kyle. Provided I am worthy of the gifts given to me, I will use them only to fulfil Mother's will."

"But She's dying!" cried Kyle desperately. It struck Andrew so deeply he felt tears welling in his eyes.

"Yes, my brother. But I assure you that never once has Her will been destructive towards those who are killing Her. It only takes time. She is strong enough to resist as much as needed."

Kyle wiped his tears. "The day will come when you'll have to decide who to side with, Adam. Maybe before it does, you'll have change your mind." He took a few steps, staring at the sheds above him. "I have decided. At the next crescent moon I will accept the sacred *Hirshammag*."

"You don't have to do it. Not now. Listen to Abriaros and the *Collegium*. Then you will decide, calmly, whether to follow in your father's footsteps."

"You have your talent, I have mine. I am ready to do anything to save Her. Also to do what others don't have the courage to do. Be strong, brother. And if She'd refuse me and send me back to the

Source, remember how much love I have in me for Her."

Andrew realised too late that the conversation was over and rushed back from where he had come. In the heat, did not see an old bum rummaging through hospital waste and fell into the puddles, apologising, out of breath and agitated. He snapped back to his feet and continued to run, hoping he had not been seen.

Kyle walked out of the alley, crossing the old man too.

"I did not touch him, shivak," he told him.

The bum covered with rags followed him with his eyes. "*Shhh, goot,* Kyle of Ghion. *Goot for you,*" Yzenn replied over his asthma, exposing his face to the abundant rain.

25

Andrew turned the key in the door until it could go no further. An inexplicable agitation pervaded him, his heart was beating loudly without giving signs of stopping and it throbbed in his temples. He didn't understand what was happening. His mind tried to prevent a terrifying and irrational presage, of understanding something he didn't see, but which he felt the urge to control.

He sat on the bathtub, drying his wet hair, and cried. And he couldn't stop. He slid down into a corner, under the sink, unable to drive the tears back.

What is happening to me? he wondered, in anguish.

He breathed deeply, placing his head in his hands, and began to calm down. What did Adam and Kyle say? Strange, disconnected, nonsensical phrases. Who was this Mother whose death they feared? Andrew couldn't tell, but as soon as his mind even touched the idea, desperation assailed him.

He wanted to deny hearing the whole conversation. He tried to believe it had never taken place, and only then did everything seem to return to normal. He got up and walked around the house, concentrating on anything else but that: his homework, his troubles with his mother, even Maggie Ryan. Exhausted, he lay down on the sofa and drifted away.

The whole house was shrouded in darkness. The rain was beating heavily inside the faded red brick cloister.

The sudden ringing of the phone woke him up. Andrew looked at the clock; it was almost noon. "Hello?"

"Hi honey, how are you? You sound strange."

He wouldn't have even been able to explain what had happened. He felt dizzy, but the events of the morning now seemed far away. "All good, Mum. I just fell asleep."

"You did well not to go to school. I was convinced you would go anyway. Did you see that dreadful rain?"

Andy didn't really want to talk. "Yes, that's why I didn't feel like going," he lied.

"There's dinner in the fridge. I'll be late tonight too, honey. I'm so sorry. It's chaos here and I can't leave."

Still excuses.

"Don't worry, Mum. I'll eat in a while, then do my homework. See you later."

"All right. Kiss!"

Andrew fell back on the couch. The sound of the intercom made him jerk. He approached and, hesitantly, picked up the handset without talking.

"Hi, It's Gerald. Is Mrs Fawcett home?"

It was the janitor. "It's Andrew. Mum's still at work."

"I knew someone was back," he said, but Andy had a feeling he wasn't talking to him.

"There's a person who would like to talk to you here. I'll let her in."

The boy still felt uncomfortable. Who could it be?

There was no peephole in the door so he couldn't check who was coming. On the other hand, he had answered, declaring his presence, and could not avoid the meeting. The doorbell rang.

Andrew opened the door, not without difficulty, given the number of key turns he had given when he got in. Gerald was smiling, his cigar between his white teeth. Behind him was the woman dressed in black whom he had seen some time earlier in front of Saint Paul. There was no trace of the man. Andrew winced.

The janitor leaned over the boy. "She's from the police. I have already checked the documents. But don't worry, she's not here for you," he whispered. Then he turned to the woman. "Agent, this is Andrew Fawcett."

The policewoman took off her glasses. She had a hard expression and deep, tired blue eyes. The eyebrows tilted at the ends, giving her a helpless look. The voice, however, was strong and very firm. "Hi, Andrew. I'm Agent Helena Dowson. You can call me Helena if you want. Is your mother there?"

The boy was unable to react and simply answered her. "No, Miss. She's at work."

"I see. We're investigating a case and we believe some kids your age may have seen something. Can I come in?"

Andrew didn't know why, but he was convinced that the woman was lying. "I haven't seen anything, Miss."

"I'd like to ask you some questions. Do you mind if we sit down? It will only take a few minutes."

Judging by the look on his face, Gerald seemed to appreciate Agent Dowson very much. And he made a grimace of disapproval at Andrew's resistance. "Come on, Andrew. Agent Dowson is doing an important job for our safety. Do your duty."

The boy gave up and let the policewoman enter.

"Thanks, Gerald. Very kind of you," she said, dismissing him.

The janitor made to close the door. "At your service. If you need anything else, you know where to find me."

Andrew and Helena sat down on the sofa. The woman looked around. "You have a very nice house."

"Thank you, Miss."

"Your mother – what's her job?"

"She's a nurse."

"And you do everything alone? You must be very mature for your age."

Andrew noticed that the policewoman had not mentioned his father. She must have guessed that the man of the house was missing. "I should do my homework," he cut short.

"Sure, I'm coming to the point. I'm investigating a crime that took place during the summer and we think there are some people in danger, living in this area."

"I don't know how to help you."

"Have you seen anything… strange, recently?"

Andrew swallowed. He was not used to lying to the police. "Strange? I don't understand," he mumbled.

"Something out of the ordinary. That has intrigued or frightened you."

Helena was playing the part of the behavioural analyst. It was evident that the boy knew something, but she had to be very careful not to shut him up. Amin had suggested that she move alone; he would watch her from a distance. He had told her that his presence could alert Adam's guardians, so she was doing her job, using rationality and training to get information.

"Andrew, there's no need to be nervous. If you don't know, it's not a problem," she said softly. "Only, tell me the truth, please. The life of one of your peers is in danger. This is serious."

Andrew nodded. He had a great wish to let off steam, but he didn't know whom to trust. And above all, he didn't know what to say.

Helena changed strategy, unveiling her hand to study the boy's reaction. "You don't want anything bad happening to Adam, do you?"

He snapped to his feet. "I don't know anyone by that name," he said, staring elsewhere, nervous. "I haven't offered you a drink. How rude of me."

The policewoman remained seated, calm. "Fruit juice?" she asked, conciliatory.

Andrew headed for the kitchen. He glanced through the window to Adam's apartment. He could not think of anything but the homonymy between the dead boy at the lake and his friend. That strange friend of his, who spoke with a royal bully and had the power to make him cry.

Helena's hand stopped his from trembling as he poured the juice. "Andrew, trust me," she said, then took the glass and sipped the juice, looking at the garden too.

"I saw you this morning at school," the boy revealed. "You were with a strange man."

The policewoman was struck by the definition that Andrew had given of Amin. "He's a colleague of mine," she said, smiling, "and I recognise that he's a very strange man. The investigations we are carrying out start right from Saint Paul. We went to take a look. It was Head Master Richardson who gave us your name, along with that of another dozen students."

"If you fear for this Adam, why don't you go to him?"

"Things aren't so easy, Andrew. We must first investigate." Helena put the glass down. "Adam lives right there, does he not?" she said, pointing to the opposite garden. "Come on, I can't believe you don't know a boy your age who attends your school and with whom you share a garden."

Andrew felt crushed. He leaned against the fridge. "I can't help you," he said dejectedly.

Helena looked at him with her intense blue eyes. She took the jacket from the sofa and left a business card on the coffee table. "All right. Here is my number."

Andrew nodded and led her to the door. Once alone, he heard Gerald's compliments to the policewoman, then the voices stopped and the silence returned. He took her card and was tempted to tear it, but he slipped it into his pocket instead.

He stood there thinking, then thought some more. There were too many pieces that didn't make a sensible image. Suddenly, he was surrounded by monkeys, dissociated adolescents, his refusal of his mother and of a friend he had the feeling of knowing forever. Did he need to talk to Adam about what he had seen? Maybe he should. Yes, and he also had to tell him about the policewoman who was looking for him, and at the same time demand an explanation. There was no other way.

He took his jacket, then heard a clinking noise at the living room French door. He retraced his steps and realised that Mamuk was scratching at a corner of the glass. It had something in its hands. Andrew opened the window and leaned over to the little monkey, who climbed up his arm to his shoulder, tickling him.

"Hi, Mamuk."

The monkey stared at him from close range. Its amber eyes looked human at that distance. It handed out a piece of wrinkled paper to

Andrew and stared back at him. In a moment it had already reached the lawn and in a couple of jumps, it had climbed over the net.

He opened up the piece of paper, which was folded in four. There were no words, just a drawing, perhaps done with a fountain pen. It depicted a parallelepiped. Next to it, a comma of ink. Above, a moon and a star. As Andrew tried to understand its meaning, he had the feeling that fresh air was invading his mind, while an interpretation of the drawings overwhelmed all other thoughts, evident and without doubt of any sort. He turned the piece of paper in his hands, but there was nothing else. It didn't matter. He was sure he knew what the message meant.

26

When Emily came home, she was even more exhausted than the night before. She made sure her son was OK, skipped dinner and lay down on the couch with her sleeping pills. She didn't need them. By 21:00, she had collapsed in front of the ad for a new amazing abdominal toning machine.

Andy waited a while longer, then convinced her to go to bed. His Mum mumbled something about brushing her teeth and fell asleep twenty seconds after her face touched the pillow. He left her, put on his jacket and waited for ten o'clock. He turned off the lights, grabbed the keys and closed the door behind him, putting the key in the lock to prevent it from producing suspicious clicks or other noises. Emily rarely woke up during the night, but without sleeping pills, she might have a lighter sleep.

The parking lot behind the building was lit by yellow street lamps that laid their soft light on the parked cars, making them all look like cabs. Where the light ended, the hill began. Andrew searched for a passage through the fence and had no difficulty finding it. The hill was almost completely bare of living trees, but the carcasses of the ones which had been cut down were numerous and the mud produced by the incessant rains made the climb tiring. Andrew turned on a small LED flashlight, one of those given away at service stations, and made his way through the branches and the cut logs, trampling over what should have been radiant green branches slanting toward the sky. The noises of the motorway were far away and a nocturnal quiet reigned in the area, so that the steps on the wood and the branches turned into rackets. Andy had a precise idea of where to go.

From the top of the hill, one could enjoy the panorama of lights and colours of the city. There were few stars in the sky, but it did not look like it would be raining again. He approached a stack of logs fallen one on top of the other, whose fronds intertwined to create foliage even more impressive than that of a single tree.

He stepped in it, making his way through the branches. "Adam, are you here?" he called softly.

In the centre, the branches opened to create a small space. Dozens of fireflies twirled around, illuminating the boy sitting on one of the felled trunks. Adam caressed the wood. "Do you know that a tree stays alive for a long time after it has been cut?"

Andrew sat down at a distance. "Adam, you're in serious danger."

"Oh yes?"

"Look, I can't tell you why, but you're in danger. They are looking for you."

"I know."

"Where are your grandparents?"

"At home. They are distracted at the moment. I gave them two packets of snacks and now they are recovering from eating."

Andrew came up. "What is happening?"

"It's not easy to explain."

"If you brought me here, there has to be a reason. I don't understand."

"All in good time. Why did you follow me this morning?"

Andy blushed. "I… I wasn't following you. I saw that Kyle was and I was afraid he wanted to hurt you. But…" he searched for the right words. "I heard your conversation. Then the police arrived and asked me a lot of questions. And you sent me that piece of paper with the drawing. I don't even know how I managed to find you."

"The fact that you have understood the meaning of the drawing speaks volumes about you, saviour of the lizards."

"Adam, don't joke. The police are involved here. What the hell did you do?"

"Listen, Andrew, you can trust me. I haven't done anything. I knew this day would come and that I could not stay here forever. I'm just sorry to have to go now that I had found a special person like you."

"Go? Where do you have to go?"

The boy didn't answer. He bent to the ground, touching it with the palm of his hand and inhaled.

"Adam, whose mother is dying? And why does the thought alone destroy me?"

The other sat on the ground and smiled. "You suffer because inside you there is something special. You know it. Even if it isn't expressed, this gift that binds you to Her speaks to you. And you feel moved if you think She's in danger."

"Who are you talking about?" he asked with a lump in his throat.

"You know."

Andrew shook his head in disbelief. There was something inside him that stirred, but it made no sense, it was just a ball of emotion and disbelief. "No, I don't know. I don't understand."

"We're talking about your Mother."

"Is my mother in danger? What do you mean? What do you know? Why?"

"Not Emily, but your Mother, who is also mine and hers too. The Mother of all."

Andrew kept shaking his head. It was a strong concept, and he couldn't get it out of his mind.

"Many would not agree that I tell you all this. It is very dangerous for both of us."

"Don't make fun of me, Adam," Andy defended himself, increasingly agitated.

"You know I'm not."

"Stop it!"

"She doesn't want you to get dispersed in the Oblivion of men. You are strong. The *keh* that animates you is so powerful, and so close to the surface, that it would be a huge waste if you did. She told me since the moment you moved near our house."

The boy tried to block those words with all his might, but there was something, a deep flow within his soul that prevented him.

"You must allow the Four Forces to act on you and through you."

Andrew climbed over the trunk to leave and run away. Get away from those fantastic stories, away from the nonsense. Instead he stopped. In the hand that he had placed on the tree trunk he felt a delicate warmth spreading. He was overwhelmed by the feeling that a river of resin was running from his eyes to his feet, which had become heavy. He felt the flow slipping away from the plants, draining him.

It was impossible for him to feel their suffering, and yet...

He retraced his steps and touched the trunk properly. The feeling came back even louder. He heard a sound, a roar. But not with his ears. The sound ran from his feet to his forehead and he seemed to shatter, that his being was expanding while still retaining a definite shape. The rumble became a breath and the breath became water. He seemed to inhale the water, without suffering.

Then everything went quiet.

Adam was still sitting on the ground, staring at him. "Did you hear it?" he asked as Mamuk jumped on his shoulder.

Andy looked at his hands. "Yes," he admitted, without knowing what. Adam motioned for him to come closer. "Why do I feel like I've met you before?" he asked.

"We've always known each other," Adam replied, as Mamuk nodded. "We are brothers because we are children of the same Mother."

"Are you... human?"

The other smiled, placing a hand on his shoulder. "Neither more nor less than you."

"Who is looking for you? Where will you go? What should I do?"

"Be calm. We don't abandon brothers, ever. My brothers will not abandon me and I will not abandon you."

Saying this, Adam lifted a hand to his friend's head, then brushed against his forehead. "I cannot wake you, brother. Forgive me. But I can make sure that wherever I go, you will know how to find me. This is my gift to you. This is the will of the Mother. She knows." He put his palm on Andrew's forehead.

A golden glow lit Adam's forehead and nape, and long, shining filaments evaporated from his skin to form incomprehensible patterns on his neck, arms and hands. His pupils became one with the iris and his eyes opened like doors to iridescent stars.

Emptiness.

Andrew did not hear and could not see.

For a moment he seemed to understand everything, beyond his age, his gender, his body, his mind.

For a moment he no longer feared.

For a moment he no longer needed.

For a moment, only one moment, he was at peace.

For a moment he grasped the infinite, and he thought it trivial.

Distances and time lost their meaning, while life was revealed to him in the most basic of definitions. Then an innumerable fragmentation of faces, places and events exploded within him, without any need for bond or coherence between them, without the need for knowledge.

When he began to feel the pressure crushing him, he felt suffocated, enveloped in a fluid fog, shocked by a beat that shook him like a twig at every stroke. He felt a sharp pain in his arms and legs before his limited senses regained the upper hand.

Silence.

Fireflies reappeared before his eyes. It was hard to breathe and every breath of air felt like fire. His throat was parched, and like never before he realised how hard it was to be alive.

Adam helped him to sit down. And Andrew, who after the abandonment of his father had promised himself not to do it anymore, cried for the second time that day. The sobs shook him. His friend hugged him and he vented all the anger, suffering and joy he had inside. When it subsided, there were no words to say and the two listened together to the noises of the branches moved by the wind.

"What changed in me?" Andrew asked.

"Nothing. Something has started, but I cannot know where it will take you. She will decide for you, She will show you the way. In the end, you'll know. And whatever you find, you will be free."

"I feel… different. But also the same." He seemed to see everything for the first time. Every little detail excited him; it was a rediscovery that took place not so much with the senses, but with something that had a direct connection with reality in the depths of his chest. The most sublime instruments could finally play his score.

"Now you can enjoy the joy of living, brother. But be careful. One cannot know life without knowing death. You must also face darkness and pain, because everything is part of Being."

Andrew paused on Adam. "Your forehead is shining," he remarked, watching the light emanating from his friend's face. "And your arms… your body is full of these luminous drawings. You're not just Adam. You're something more."

The boy's smile went out. The glow faded in a moment and everything turned dark. Even the fireflies had disappeared. "Listen," he said, taking Andy's face in his hands, "everyone in your condition needs a guide to help him. You will recognize yours when you see them. Do you understand? Without a guide, you will not survive."

Andrew felt something was wrong. Anxiety invaded him and he felt an intense acrid smell that reminded him of a petrol station, but a thousand times more intense, and his eyes began to burn. A misshapen note exploded in the air, first very low, so as to make the earth tremble, then high enough to make the ears ring.

The boys threw themselves on the ground, seeking shelter behind the trunks. Andrew stared at his friend, trying to figure out what was happening, questioning him with his eyes. He saw that those of Adam were wide open in fear. Terror also took over him.

A sound of steps. Very close.

Something walked right past their shelter, emitting grunts similar to those of a pig crossed with a cat. Another note exploded and the boys covered their ears with their hands, pushing as much as possible to prevent the grinding sound from driving them mad.

A dull thud. First on a branch, then on the trunk just above their head.

The smell was unbearable.

Andrew could now hear a slow breath, a whistle followed by a metallic trail accompanied by a rattling clink. A faint voice, perhaps that of an old woman, or a child, was panting and making his skin crawl.

What was that creature? In what world could something so insane be able to live? Not in the real world, this was certain. But what was happening was real; it was not a dream.

Andrew analyzed all the possibilities that his science-fiction culture suggested to him. But, hell, there was a great difference between saying that you believe the Star Trek warp engine could work and be hunted down by a monster after your blood.

He looked at Adam, trembling, tucked under the furthest trunk. He felt a courage within him that he didn't understand. Not that he wasn't afraid – he was almost paralysed by terror, but he understood that his duty was to protect his friend. It was his job.

He closed his eyes for a moment. He thought of his father and mother, Head Teacher Richardson, and Maggie. Then he snapped back up to the side of the creature, trying to run fast, jumping logs and trampling branches. Behind him, there was a scream and Andrew realized that the creature had started to chase him, performing leaps that generated thuds just a few yards from him.

He aimed for the ridge of the hill in an attempt to put as much distance as possible between the monster and Adam, slipping between the felled trees and jumping over the stumps of trunks until he reached a level pitch on which stood a low white prefab, perhaps the office of the site manager. He tried to open the door, but it was closed. He circled the little house and hid behind the digger. There was no trace of the creature.

The noise of the traffic became stronger down there. From his position, Andrew could see his building, just over a hundred meters away. It wasn't far, but the ground was rough. He would need to move with caution.

The other Adam Uyan came to mind, the one who had died in the lake. The belief that he had been killed became a certainty in his mind.

He leaned over the excavator and moved toward the white prefab. Halfway there, he realised he was being observed. Perched on top of the excavator's blade was a small figure in long strips of red fabric. The creature jumped on the ground, remaining hunched. Seeing it so closely, it was the size of a seven or eight-year-old child. It was very thin, and its skin had a hue that, in the halogen lights around him, looked an anaemic burnished green. The creature was bald and the features of its face were minute, though almost imperceptible: it seemed to want to hide them from the boy's sight.

It approached a couple of steps, rubbing the red robes to the ground. It stank and seemed to smell the air with that mixture of disturbing whistles and rattles. At times it rotated the head, like a dog listening to a curious sound.

Andrew took a few steps back. The creature circled around him, keeping at a distance, its arms raised to the chest with the long and slender fingers hanging.

Well, the more time you waste with me, the further away Adam will go. He didn't know where he was finding that courage, being the one who panicked when talking to the janitor. Somehow he believed that this being would not attack him.

The creature stood upright, blew air out and jumped onto the roof of the prefab. It produced its arrogant and sickening note again, this time in the direction of its prey, who tried to protect his ears as best he could.

With a rustle, two other creatures very similar to the first appeared on the open space. The one on the roof grinned, producing a sharp laugh that seemed to come through a wire mesh. Something had changed in the behaviour of these beings. They were surrounding him. Andrew began to lose his convictions, retreating. He didn't notice the branch behind him and stumbled, falling to the ground. He tried to get back on his feet, but something held him down. When he looked up, he saw the face of the man he had seen next to Agent Dawson that morning. A morning that now seemed a thousand years away.

"Stay there, Sleeper," the man ordered him, walking past.

The creatures seemed to go crazy. They began to jump up and down in anger, but they were no longer moving forward. On the contrary, they began to withdraw, unable to support the man's gaze.

Andrew was helped up and found himself face to face with Helena.

"Relax, everything will be fine," she said in her soothing voice. "He knows what to do."

Amin placed one foot in front of the other, knocking back the red-cloaked creeps. "Go away, mayaurli, there's nothing here for you. Prince Paneb Akenre exercised his will to take the boy with him. Go away and tell those you serve that there is no room for Belial's followers' plans." He raised his arm and something formed in his hand, shining purple, while a golden light exploded from his head.

Just like Adam! Andy thought.

Amin launched the *Orichalcum* spear against one of the creatures, which ended up impaled in a whirl of purple flashes. Seeing what had happened, the other two fled at great speed in the direction of the motorway, emitting their aberrant sobs. The stricken one struggled to the ground, croaking metal sounding hisses. The Hound approached it, looking into its tiny eyes.

"Tell the Translator of Light that I will find him and bring him before the judges. Whoever breaks the Code of the One must pay." He touched the spear with its amaranth reflections, which disappeared in a flash. The strong vibration faded, as did the glow on the man's forehead. With disdain, he threw the creature to the ground, who struggled before rising again, still alive. It ran away in the same direction of its companions.

There were no traces of blood.

"What were you doing here, Andrew?" Helena asked him.

"Nothing. Walking," the boy minimised, marvelling at the

promptness of his response.

"Tell us where Adam is. The mayaurli were only lookouts; there could be far more dangerous forces in ambush."

The boy remained silent.

"I understand that you're scared," Helena insisted. "What you've seen is strange and upsetting."

Actually, Andy was shaken, but he could not describe his feelings as fear. And the most curious thing of all was that even those beings did not seem so strange. It was as if he had fallen into a reality that anyone would have defined as impossible, but without batting an eyelid, without asking questions, almost with guilt at the presumption of having all the answers settled somewhere inside of him.

She'll know, he thought.

"Forget the Sleeper, Helena," Amin said.

She stared at the boy and he had the feeling that she was telling him to go home and forget everything. Then he saw her follow Amin, who was disappearing up the hill.

Helena didn't want to leave him there, but what else could she do? The more he stayed away from her and the Hound, the safer he would be.

Andrew waited for a few moments until they went out of sight. Then he hurried back towards home. He stepped through the net at the point where it had been opened and ran across the parking lot. He was almost by Emily's rust-coloured car, closer to his block, when he heard a whistle and he seemed to see something rise above the building, black and elongated.

Then a glow and a violent wave of hot air overwhelmed him, lifting him off the ground and hurling him backwards for several yards, making him bounce off the bonnet of a Mercedes. He stopped only when he met the soft flowerbeds that lined the street. He could only hear muffled sounds and couldn't quite feel his body. Beyond the mirror of the car, Andrew saw only a dense cloud of smoke illuminated by a dazzling orange glow. Lapilli rose to the sky with chaotic and elegant movements. The smell of burning was spreading in the air and he coughed. He rose from the ground, helping himself up with the symbol of the German car, which remained in his hands. With yet another effort, he clung to the bonnet and tried to move forward.

High flames roared angrily to illuminate the night sky. The tenants of the upper floors of the building looked out, stunned by the roar of the explosion, but drew back immediately because of the thick smoke coming in through the windows. Some were already fleeing through the emergency stairs on the side of the building, overcome by panic.

The atrium and the ground floor were overcome by flames and

only then did Andrew truly understand. He took a few steps towards that hell that until a few minutes ago was his home. The heat was so intense that it burned his face already over fifteen meters away. He had to stop, his hands protecting his eyes. Tears evaporated instantly.

He sobbed.

"Mum!" he shouted with all the breath he had, as if he wanted to put out the flames with it. He ran to the side of the building, surrounded by survivors who were screaming and looking for each other in a chaos of desperate voices and cries.

Even Adam's house was engulfed in flames. He looked for his mother among the frantic faces of his neighbours, still wrapped in dressing gowns and pyjamas. The cry of children acted as glue in that theatre of horror.

"Mum!" Andrew called again. But he couldn't see her.

Someone pulled him and a figure appeared before him, holding him by the shoulders. He stared into big feline eyes and myriads of luminous and sharp teeth. Yet he didn't even flinch.

"Boy, two choices," Yzenn growled, showing three long, tapered fingers. "You die and come with shivaks or stay in Oblivion always."

Part of the monstrous face of the creature was blackened and the hair on one of his long ears was burnt.

Andrew looked at the flames, hypnotized by the shock.

Another violent tug. "Emily who makes cakes back to Source. Nothing you can to on this," Yzenn continued. "Time for tears come later." And he drew a vertical line on his face with the long black claw.

What had awakened in Andrew since Adam had touched him on the forehead was not disturbed by the nightmare he was experiencing. And it kept talking to him.

It was telling him to trust those words. Everything would be just fine.

"Mum!" he shouted again, no longer resisting that creature. "Mother…" he repeated, almost whispering, while the being dragged him away and the burning image of light and destruction was imprinted forever.

27

"What the fuck just happened?" Helena cried, getting up from the mud she had instinctively thrown herself on after the blast.

"They got here before us," Amin replied.

"They killed him?"

"I do not know. If he was at home, probably. But I did not perceive any particular fluctuation in the living *keh*. Sleepers died, but not Woken ones."

Helena thought of Andrew and his mother. She hoped they were safe. She felt responsible for not helping the boy, but how could she have expected something like that? "I didn't think they would use an explosion, like terrorists! I imagined something much more... magical or esoteric."

"It was not Belial's followers. It was the Enlightened."

"Wait, those guys who attacked us at my house..." Helena didn't even finish her sentence. "You mean there's someone else chasing Adam? Wasn't this a war between your Atlantis and the people of Mu?"

The remains of burnt paper and lapilli began to fall everywhere like dark snow. Amin picked one up, which flaked between his fingers. "I said that they are the main forces involved. For the sake of simplifying."

"So we must also worry about the Enlightened, then?"

"It seems so. I thought they were after me. Maybe I was wrong."

Helena put her hand on the holster. It reassured her. "Can you figure out where Adam is right now?"

"No, but I think I know where the other kid is, the Sleeper. He is still alive." He pointed to the far north side of the building. Two people were moving away from the crowd of curious people and of survivors who were huddled near the fire. In the background, the flashing fire trucks rushing to the scene lit up the road that led to the group of buildings with the red bricks.

The policewoman and the Hound of Shadow came down the hill, throwing themselves in pursuit of the fleeing couple. Helena cried to the crowd about being police and to make way, but her voice wasn't easy to hear over the other noises. They headed for a pedestrian underpass, but before entering Amin stopped short.

"What's up?" Helena asked in a low voice.

The Hound looked into the passage, breathing slowly. "The boy has made the wrong friends. Stay here."

The sirens darted right above their heads. Amin approached the dark tunnel slowly, his eyes carefully studying every possible movement.

Helena remained about ten yards behind. She grabbed the gun, pointing it to the ground.

"Who are you?" Amin asked to the darkness.

"I am the one you were looking for, Shadow Hound," answered a baritone voice.

From the obscurity came a series of loud slaps, as when bodies clash against each other in wrestling matches, Helena thought.

"Come, son of Evenor. Come closer," the voice continued.

Helena reached Amin. "It's a trap; let's meet them in the light," she said.

He looked at her, assessing her statement. "It will not help. The shadow is more dangerous for them than it is for me. Come, don't you want to meet a giant?" he said without waiting for an answer.

The two entered the almost complete darkness of the underpass, Helena very close to Amin, gun ready to shoot. The voice, so close, made her jump with its potency.

"I'm Trummugan, of the Milesian line, and I'm here to talk to you." There was something enormous moving through the little light, but it was barely visible.

"You're coming late, Milesian. The non-aggression pact was to protect the boy you took away. Now it does not make sense for us to speak."

"On the contrary, it has even more meaning now. Because Adam is not with us or with you, rather than not."

Helena found that last expression odd.

"What do you have in mind, noble descendant of the Thuata de Danann?"

"I share what I think only with whom I know," Trummugan said.

"You do not need to know my name. It defines me neither with my people nor with yours."

"Well, then take it as a personal request. Let us leave the people alone."

The Hound snorted, knowing there was no way around a Milesian's dialectic skills. "I bring the birth name of Amin Setiana Akenre.""Setiana Akenre. Mmm…" the giant grumbled. "Are you perhaps of the lineage of the most Pure prince Setiana Paneb Akenre, of the Akenre dynasty, who reigned over the principality of Iunuat's Avalon before the last great war of the Sleepers? The same who died in mysterious circumstances still under investigation by your judges?"

For the first time, Helena saw Amin speechless.

But the giant gave him no respite. "If this is so, and it must be this way, you are the consort of Athena Annya Ayosmosi, of the Setiana, Akenre and Ayosmosi dynasties, a widow of the emperor. A Valkyrie."

"Are you married?" Helena asked in amazement.

"Trummugan, I am delighted about your knowledge of the destinies of the sons of Atlantis, but everything you talk about no longer has value for me. If you feel satisfied, I ask you to speak," replied the Hound, dark-faced.

"Ah, it was not my intention to offend you, Amin of the Pure Akenre dynasty. Between us, all your titles do not count, past or present. You come to us as a member of the Third People, and you are the same as everyone else. The non-aggression pact is based on mutual respect between the parties involved. I can still offer it to you, but you must see that the situation does not turn in your favour. Tell me where Adam is and I promise I shall make sure you can return where you came from."

"There is only one way in which I can go back, wise one. And it is with the boy. The provision that has been given to me is not debatable; you should know that. And I cannot say where he is."

"This does not allow me to help you."

"So what do we do?" cut in Helena, who did not like being treated as if she was not there. "Are we here talking politics while some monster takes Adam away?"

"Ah," said the giant, "I apologise for my rudeness, little Sleeper. I am so used to moving around without you seeing me that I did not remember you could see me. I am sorry; you must be very scared."

"Scared? I'm furious. The first twenty minutes after a kidnapping and the next forty-eight hours are critical to finding the victim. 90% of the possibilities vanish after this time frame. I decided to find Adam and I'll do it, damn it. And I don't give a damn about your intrigues. From now on I will shoot everything that seems dangerous to me… including giants!"

Trummugan was impressed. "I am very happy to know that the living keh still burns powerfully in the Third People."

"Now let's try to figure out how to collaborate," she continued, her hands shaking on the butt of the .357. "But first, tell me where Andrew Fawcett is. He has nothing to do with it; let him go."

"Oh yes, the young Sleeper. He can no longer live with you, my dear. Adam worked on him through the Four Forces, I believe. If I did what you asked, I would condemn him to suffering and death. It seems that this is not the will of the Mother."

"Whose will?" Helena turned to Amin.

Amin ignored her. "We are at an impasse then. I do not care about this Andrew, but the Sleeper is right. We want to save Adam and we should combine our efforts. If I do not find him again, Prince Setiana will position the Avalon on the borders of the Sleepers' cities. You do not need reminding what happened the last time such an event occurred."

"Of course, of course," Trummugan said. "But you see, Adam belongs to our people, and even Aeterna would oppose his delivery to the princes."

"Isn't it clear enough that you have no other choice? We risk an open conflict!"

"There is an alternative. When we meet the boy again, I will come with you and supervise your… examinations on him. If they give a negative result, I will bring it back with me."

"Are you kidding? A giant entering the Avalon? This is madness. Atlantis does not deal with the people of Mu."

"Oh, Amin, you are young. Atlantis has been dealing with Mu for a very long time. How else would you have managed to contain the Enlightened or the followers of Belial without the help of Aeterna?"

"Get over it. What you ask is impossible."

"Do you prefer a war? I am sure that even among our people there are those who are eagerly waiting for one. Convince your prince to take care of my requests and I will try to help you."

"It is useless. I cannot get in touch with the Avalon right now."

"You cannot, but I can," said the giant, leaving Amin speechless.

28

"You must be crazy!" said Shaun the bookseller, opening the garage door.

"It is a difficult time, my friend," replied Trummugan.

"We cannot compromise with Atlantis. They will never let you enter the Avalon!"

"The future is unknowable. We'll see if we need to enter the Avalon. Meanwhile, we act to find Adam."

"If he's still alive."

"I'm pretty sure he is. Whoever took him does not know what they did. Amin is what interests them. There are a lot of machinations in place, but have faith, Shaun. Bring them to Abriaros. I will stay here to monitor the situation and to understand where they brought the boy."

Shaun shook his head and greeted the funny guy dressed in a jacket several sizes larger and a scarf that was one with a huge hat.

A flicker of movement in the nearby trees caught his attention. He understood who caused it and gestured them with his hand. With a leap, the creatures descended silently on the asphalt and slipped into the backseats of a dated but well-kept pickup truck.

"Brother…" Yzenn and Ahiga greeted him.

"There are clothes on the seats," Shaun replied. "Leave the boy alone," he added in a low voice, pointing to the figure huddled in a corner.

The shivaks nodded, pulling their long hoods over their faces.

The headlights came on, producing a very clear and intense light. He drove through the garden and headed for the park, as Trummugan had told him. At the indicated entrance, he stopped the car and waited. After a minute or two, a blonde woman stepped over the gate and approached the car.

"Are you Shaun?" she asked.

"You must be Helena. Come in."

The policewoman took the seat next to the driver, and noticed that there were two hooded figures and a boy behind her.

"Andrew!" she called heartily. "How are you?"

He looked back, but Helena saw that he was exhausted.

"Later. Best," said one of the two figures with a wheezing voice and an Eastern European accent.

"Don't worry, I'll get you out of this," the woman promised.

Andrew said nothing and leaned his head against the glass, looking out.

"Where is our unwelcome guest?" Shaun asked sneeringly.

"I'm here, old man," Amin replied, just outside the car.

"We meet again. I would have preferred to know you were far away, but if this is the will of Trummugan…" He motioned for him to enter.

"Think about driving and do not ask yourself questions, nexus."

One of the two hooded figures leaned forward. Helena found herself five feet away from a constellation of sharp teeth. Locks of thick hair stood up in a cacophony of colours, barely visible under the hood. A scary, guttural growl invaded the car so that the mirror began to vibrate. The woman turned her head, looking forward almost without breathing.

"I see we want for nothing," Amin said, with sarcasm.

A tapered, palmate hand with long black claws leaned on his shoulder. It was its companion.

"Remember ghigas say. No attack this Atlantean, Ahiga."

"I have clean clothes," Amin joked, "I prefer to go in the back." So he jumped into the load compartment of the vehicle, resting his back against the bulkhead.

The heavy car slid silently into the night so that Helena at first thought that the old driver was taking advantage of the descent with the engine off. But when they began to face a steep climb, accelerating without producing any noise except for the noise of the wheels on the asphalt, she was amazed. It was too old a vehicle for it to be electric.

Shaun picked up on her stupor and adjusted the big square glasses on his nose seriously. "Are you a policewoman?"

Helena pulled herself away from that oddity. "Yeah. Or at least I was. I don't rightly know what I am right now. Are you also a…"

"Woken one, yes. Unlike a Roused one, I was born this way. My parents were such before I was born and I was lucky enough to grow up among my people."

"People… from Mu?"

Shaun looked at her from the corner of his eye. "Yes."

"Good," she replied, feeling stupid for the comment.

"What do you like?"

"Excuse me?"

"What do you like to do? What do you love?"

Helena certainly did not expect such a question. "I… I don't know. I'm not really up for chit-chat right now. I'm sorry."

"I see."

They spent a few minutes in silence. Andrew had fallen asleep, tears still wetting his youthful face. The two beings occasionally exchanged a few words under their breath in an unknown language. They looked very nervous, especially the one called Ahiga.

"You know," Shaun broke the silence, "I was born in Italy just before the Second World War. It was a difficult time; there was little food and life in the countryside was very hard, even without the bombs. There were no toys for the children so we would make do with what we had. We didn't understand war, as if someone could ever understand it. For us it was like an omen, a dark beast sifting through the world grabbing as many lives as possible without ever being satisfied. I had nightmares every night. I lived waiting for something I didn't even comprehend. My whole mind was focused on the hope of finding a way to save the people I loved, bringing them to a better world." He gave a long sigh. "One day, Trummugan visited us and saw my fear. Then he asked me what I loved and what I liked to do. I replied that I didn't know, that it didn't matter when the whole world lived the nightmare of war. He insisted, until, struggling, I remembered a day spent with my father in the mountains, the two of us alone. I may have been five years old. I remembered how much I had loved being there with him watching the clouds as we lay on the grass and imagined seeing the animals in them. For a moment, all the desperation and suffering of the war disappeared. I could almost feel the warmth of the sun on my skin. The giant explained to me that if you know what you love, you don't need to be afraid, because you are what you love. And from that moment on I took on the fear, accepting it."

Helena didn't say anything.

The bookseller went on. "Many things remain inexplicable if we don't undergo a profound change, a change that perhaps may never happen. The point is whether you will decide to live in the anxiety of what you don't know, or savour, in every instant of your life, what you really love."

She looked at him, trying to capture some signs of the different nature that distinguished him from her. But she saw none.

Instead, he reminded her of her grandfather, a gentle man who had endured everything in life with calmness and serenity. What made them different?

The shouting of the two creatures sitting behind them became more pronounced. "Shaun. Why we takin' tonkey to Abriaros?" Ahiga asked angrily while the other tried to calm him down. "No, Yzenn. We alreaty failet. Adam gone; we bat guartians; we let one to take boy away. Why son of Atlantis is with us to *Collegium?*"

Yzenn uttered a series of gurglings and notes in an unfamiliar, drawn language, but the disapproving tone was evident.

"If Adam has been able to live a good life all these years," said Shaun, "it was thanks to you, shivak brothers. You don't have to regret what happened. His abilities are increasing and this is possible because you protected him. The fact that he escaped to meet the young man sitting there saved his life."

"Who is Sleeper so interest in Atam? World full of Sleepersss!" replied the shivak.

"I don't know what Adam saw in Andrew, but it must have been something important enough to justify the risk he ran, don't you think?"

"Meh!" exclaimed Ahiga. "Ask everything, but no be with that," and pointed at Amin.

"You won't need to. Be patient; we only ask you this."

The trip lasted about an hour and a half. Shaun took secondary roads, turning sometimes without apparent reason and backtracking at least a couple of times. Suddenly, in the middle of the vine-covered countryside, they took a single-lane road that climbed through rocks and bushes. After a few minutes, it seemed that civilisation was light years away.

The pickup climbed across low hills. The animals seemed not to even see the vehicle and often flanked them closely.

Squirrels, wild boars and a deer walked just a palm away from the window.

At the top of a hill, some vast uncultivated fields came into view and a dark line on the horizon merged with the sky covered with myriads of stars. The barren cliffs descended towards the black sea and the foam created by the waves reflected like a ghost on the rocks. The road turned into a continuous series of curves close to the sea. Shaun brought the vehicle onto a dirt path that led them straight to a rocky bay, wet with water. A white cottage with a dark roof stood out against the very black and smooth stones, lit only by warm lights that shone through the windows. The house was built on a wooden structure, which ended to form a pier whose beams sank in the shallow sea floor. Somewhere in the middle of the sea, the flashing light of a lighthouse cut through the sky.

The car left the road and made for a wooden fence, stopping next to the house. Under the porch, a large tall man was waiting.

Yzenn picked Andrew up with such gentleness the boy barely made a noise before falling back to sleep. The others followed him, keeping a well-marked distance between Amin and the people of Mu. Helena closed the group and remained on the sidelines.

The place was enchanting, dusted with the classic underlying melancholy of sea cottages. But it also smelled of undeniable romanticism. The lanterns hanging from the eaves, the dream catchers tinkling in the light breeze, the sound of the sea restless and at the same time reassuring. Helena liked this place as a holiday home. Yet in some ways, it was disappointing. She had expected something more surprising, like an elven castle or a city suspended in the clouds.

The structure looked to be at least three hundred years old and showed them all, even though it had been restored with evident care and love. The only oddities that jumped out were the special symbolic engravings on the large beam above the door. They reminded her of the drawings of New Guinea, of Oceania or perhaps of the island of Bali. They were very beautiful and full of character, even if simple. She also noticed some swastikas in the corners and remembered reading somewhere that that symbol had been used for many millennia, with meanings quite different from the obscure ones that the Nazis had attributed to it.

The man by the door came up with a big smile. Over sixty, tall, he had a corpulent body and a reassuring face, embellished by long reddish hair and a thick beard faded with age. He wore a red and green checkered shirt and comfortable trousers. He had a beer in his hand. Shaun went to meet him and they hugged as if they had not seen each other for an eternity.

Then Shaun became serious. "This," he said, indicating Amin, "is the son of Evenor whom Trummugan spoke to you about, Enish."

Enish evaluated the Hound with severity. "I cannot say you're welcome, Atlantean. But I promise that I will try to make your short stay here as uncomplicated as possible."

"Do what you need to do and I'll leave as soon as possible," replied the other.

Enish then turned to the shivaks, welcoming them as he had done to Shaun and holding their webbed hands to his chest. "And this young man here must be Andrew," he said, looking at the boy in Yzenn's arms.

"Can we put him on a bed? He needs to rest," Helena suggested.

Enish looked at her with youthful, bright green eyes. "You must be Helena." He squeezed her hand firmly. "Sorry for all the trouble we've brought into your life."

She felt embarrassed and didn't answer, a child among adults who doesn't understand what they are talking about. *You can say that twice,* she thought.

Enish made them sit in the living room, which was furnished in a simple and rustic way. There were large old maps on the walls and a small table with a Steiner typewriter under the large window overlooking the sea. The lighthouse shone for a moment before starting its endless ride again.

Their guest led Yzenn through a corridor and into a cosy little bedroom, also overlooking the sea. The policeman followed them.

Andrew woke up as soon as they laid him down on the bed and he curled up, bringing his knees to his chest, emitting little sobs. Helena's heart tightened.

"I know what happened. We'll take care of you, boy," Enish told him, stroking him with his big strong hand. Andrew stopped crying and fell into a deep sleep.

In the living room, meanwhile, the situation had degenerated. They found Ahiga pacing back and forth, snarling in his tongue in the direction of Amin. He was leaning against the wall, his arms folded and his expression amused. Between them stood Shaun, who tried to mediate one in one language and one in the other. He didn't seem to be very successful, however. "Ahiga, please. Do not complicate an already complicated situation!" tried the bookseller.

The shivak pointed to Amin, admonishing the old man in an explicit if incomprehensible way.

As soon as they saw them, Yzenn grabbed his kin once again, trying to calm him down and Enish stepped in to help Shaun.

"It was a difficult day for everyone," said their host. "We lost Adam, we don't know who took him and we are all very worried. Yet in the other room we have a boy, just little older than a child, who's lost his mother." Then he turned to Helena and Amin. "And we've involved a Sleeper without taking any care to protect her from the truth of the world."

"He to that, us not!" Ahiga rebelled, pointing to Amin.

"Ahiga and Yzenn, you have done everything in your power. We placed the biggest weight on your shoulders and you made Mother proud, I'm sure. Now don't be overcome by pride and sorrow."

The shivaks looked down.

"And then there's Amin," he continued, turning to the Hound. "You represent everything we would like to keep away from us. You're a killer; we know that. And you are a son of Evenor, who is the one who allowed the world to fall into Oblivion."

"How dare you!" the Atlantean growled at him.

Enish showed the palm of his hands as a sign of peace. "We have a common goal. We must not ignore everything that has happened. It is everyone's duty, now, to remain calm and take all the necessary steps for the future to take on the form that can restore us to Adam."

"In any case, the boy will come with me, man of Mu," Amin said. Then, turning to everyone, he added, "Do not be under any false illusion: Atlantis rules the world. Do what you need to put me in touch with Avalon and maybe I will not order the complete eradication of this area."

Ahiga lunged forward with his huge jaw wide open. It was frightening. But Yzenn was ready.

"And you, animal, stay away from me or I will send you back to your Mother's arms without thinking twice. You have already proved your worthlessness by letting Adam escape you. If we were in Atlantis, you'd already be in the hands of the Translators of Light for the exploitation of your *keh*."

Ahiga calmed down and her feline pupils made a tight crack. "I look forwart meet with Telluric."

Amin shook his head.

"You cannot do anything until tomorrow night," Enish said. "I advise everyone to rest. Helena, you can sleep in Andrew's room. I'll bring you something hot to eat."

"What's the point of losing all this time?" Amin asked.

"We have to do things the right way," Shaun clarified.

The shivaks left the house, throwing their clothes on the patio. Their bodies were lean and powerful and they changed colour almost immediately, becoming invisible in the darkness.

"I'll stay here," Amin said, sitting down on the sofa and putting some items on the table.

"Won't you sleep?" Helena asked him.

"I'm busy," he dismissed her.

She was too exhausted to care about his answer. All that mattered was that she felt safe in that cottage by the sea. The promise of a hot meal and a bed appeared to her like the crowning of a dream.

"Are you hungry?" Enish asked the Hound.

"The *Orichalcum* in my body manages the resources I eat. I do not need to ingest food continuously. And anyway, I would not eat anything offered by you."

Enish gave a big laugh. "I'm not that bad a chef!" And he began to tinker with the soup.

Helena awoke at dawn after a deep and dreamless sleep. The sky over the sea cast pink and purple brushstrokes on the cliffs and pebbles. The water was a motionless silver slab and the lighthouse, also struck by the first rays of the sun, continued its incessant work.

She got up, freeing herself of a heavy woollen blanket and leaving the room. The smell of coffee reached her. She could barely hear the sounds of someone being busy in the kitchen trying to be quiet. In the living room, Amin was gone.

"Oh, good morning, Helena! I made a little breakfast," Enish greeted her, pointing to the table on which milk, coffee, homemade biscuits, honey, jams and a thousand other delicacies were laid out.

She sat down and smiled at him. He poured her coffee. "Amin?"

"He went out a few minutes ago. I don't think he's very happy here."

"I see," she nodded without understanding what could be so big to prevent these people, united by a single purpose, getting along. "And you, Enish, who are you?"

He sipped his coffee. "I'm just a fisherman, the son of fishermen who have been here for a long time," he smiled.

"Are you able to do what Amin does too? I mean… do you have special powers?"

"Powers? Ah!" grinned Enish. "No, no. Those things you saw are only possible for the Woken ones and the Roused ones. And not always."

"How? You mean that you…"

"Yes, Helena. I'm a Sleeper, just like you. I know many things, because I have lived with them for a long time, but it has never been possible to wake me up. It is a very dangerous process and in some cases it can kill. "

"I'm sorry… that you can't be awakened, I mean."

Enish covered her hand with his. "Just because your hand is covered by mine does not mean that you don't feel it or can't move it," he said.

"Don't you go crazy, living with this reality every day?"

Enish assumed an expression that made him look older. "For a long time I worked as an engineer. My wife and I moved here about twenty years ago, tired of the city life. We decided to spend my severance package to renovate this old cottage owned by my family for generations. About ten years ago, Eva fell ill with cancer. In a few weeks the disease transformed her inside and out; she had become transparent, she who had always been abundant." he laughed bitterly. "And her eyes were going, day after day."

"It's terrible."

"I loved Eva. She was my life, you know. We met as children and we never left each other. When she died, I wanted to die too. Life no longer made sense," he shrugged, surrendered to reality. "There was nothing to console me. One cannot live deprived of the meaning of life and pretend to survive. So, a few days later, I went up the cliff with the hope of finding peace in that extreme gesture. If God existed I would find her again. Otherwise, the unbearable pain would finally disappear. Together with me."

Helena didn't dare interrupt Enish's account. She listened to it almost without breathing.

"I did it. I threw myself off the cliff. But for some reason, I didn't hit any of the rocks. The impact of the icy water made me lose consciousness and, when I woke up, I was on a boat. Someone had saved me. I knew that man, but I didn't know who he really was for his people. He returned my life to me and helped me to make sense of it all, understand what had happened. He took a great risk in deciding to take care of me and I will never be grateful enough. So few of us can *really* live. Life is an extraordinary thing, Helena. Everything makes sense. And I'm happy you're here."

"Unfortunately I don't get anything about what's going on."

"The answers will come."

"Enish, how can the Woken ones, like Amin, do… those things?"

"I'll try to explain it from a Sleeper to another, okay? You need to understand something first, however: it is not them to be different. It is us Sleepers who lack something, not the opposite."

"Sure, OK. We are the losers on duty. And there's plenty of us."

"You can say that, yes." Enish grinned. "The Woken ones live an existence different from ours. They perceive their place in what they call 'All that is'."

"Amin told me about it. But I don't understand. You mean the Universe or something like that?"

"They are immersed in a… flow that encompasses everything. Science would say that they consciously perceive the energy in which we are all immersed."

"That's why they're called Woken ones?"

"That is a term coined a long time ago. For millennia there was no need for it, since there were no Sleepers. We are talking about a period that history would define as ancient, prior to the known civilisations."

"Go on," Helena said, grabbing another cookie, happy that someone would explain things to her in more understandable terms.

"A part of universal energy finds its home in living creatures and dwells in them, taking an identity that lasts for only a moment. That instant is the whole life of a person, or a giant or a cat, if you prefer. The Woken ones call this spark of energy keh, which comes from *kin*, the ancient term used in Mu for the Sun."

"The brightest light…"

"It's like that. The *keh* is able to interact with the energy flow, which we call *lumina*. It's like the sea," Enish said, pointing out the window. "And we're all in there."

"Why can't I see it?"

"Because you were prevented from seeing it. In this consists the Oblivion and the dormancy. They left us the senses, the taste, the sight, and so on; but they have deprived us of Awareness. And we cannot interact with the *lumina*."

Helena brought a hand to her chest. The sense of anguish that had oppressed her since she had met Amin had lightened, and somehow she knew that what Enish was telling her were not lies. She felt a shiver run down her back and a sense of euphoria seized her for a moment.

"Do you feel it? It's alive inside your body."

She smiled, shy as a teenager on a first date.

"The Woken ones are able to influence their *keh* and the *lumina*. And this is possible thanks to the Four Forces."

"The giant, Trummugan, used those words last night."

"Yes, my dear. Many civilizations have given them different names: the Four Columns, the Big Four, the Four Angels. Even modern science has come to hypothesise their possible existence."

"You're talking about the laws of physics!"

The man nodded. Enish got up and, followed by Helena, he approached the window. The sun had turned the sky into its brilliant blue. There were no clouds, only a low mist was rising from the cliffs. "By connecting with the Four Forces, a Woken person can intervene in the energy and consequently on reality. And not just on Physics, but also on space and time in the most exceptional cases."

"Are you saying that a Woken one is like a god?"

"No. I don't think gods pay for their mistakes."

"What do you mean?"

"Drawing on the Four Forces means changing reality, changing the energy flow. Every time a Woken one makes a request of this type, they expose themselves, and sometimes even other people; there is the risk that what they ask for is turned against them, destroying them. It is called Nemesis."

"With each action, there is an equal and opposite reaction," Helena commented, with the expression of one who has just made an astonishing discovery. "So, whenever Amin does one of his… things, he risks his life?"

"His life and much more. It takes talent, exercise and a huge balance."

The woman was speechless. It wasn't such a superhero world after all. There were rules and laws, same as in her world. Everything assumed a more regular aspect, from a certain point of view, if nothing else. "How do you influence the Four Forces?" she urged him on, overcome by curiosity.

"Well, everything you see is shaped by the Four Forces through laws called 'Orders'. There are Seven Orders, each of which defines reality. For a Woken one, it is possible to reverse the process and use the Seven Orders, according to what he or she decides to do."

"I wonder… how is it possible that all the things you speak of so naturally have happened, and continue to happen, without any trace of them in history?"

"It's more a political issue, I'm afraid. There was a catastrophic event many millennia ago called the Great Gorann. After that catastrophe, the world was devastated and men were reduced to living in small groups, scattered here and there on the land that emerged. It was at this point that Atlantis issued the Code of the One, a system of laws that provided for the isolation of the Woken ones and the construction of a new world order based on unconsciousness and control. For millennia, the Atlantean princes ruled alongside the Sleepers who worshipped them. There are many traces of this in history. But after of a series of bloody events, they became convinced that living completely separate lives was a safer and more effective way to exercise full control on humanity in their rebirth. Every aspect of human evolution became supervised and, if necessary, Atlantis intervened."

"Absurd. It's like scientists experimenting with lab rats. "

"Do you know what amazes me the most? The way in which, generation after generation, Atlantis knows how to anticipate and adapt itself to the random events that an immense mass like the human one is able to generate. They always know which strings to pull. They manage to predict the results of each movement over time. It's impressive, I have to admit."

"And what happened to Mu? And the Enlightened, where do they come from?"

"All in good time, my dear," Enish concluded firmly. "Now we have to take care of the boy."

After a few seconds, Helena heard footsteps in the corridor and Andrew appeared.

"Are you hungry, young man?" asked the man, pouring hot tea into a cup.

Andrew nodded and sat down silently. He began to eat, at first calmly, then with enthusiasm and by the end he had finished an abundant breakfast that left him well satisfied. They did not say a word until he who broke the silence. "Adam. They got him, didn't they?"

Helena looked at Enish.

"Yes, but don't worry, we'll find him again," the man replied.

"I can help you…" the boy whispered.

The two looked at him, perplexed.

"Adam did something to me before that creature found us. He told me that whatever happened, I would always be able to find him again. I don't know how to do it, but I'm sure it's possible."

"Good," Enish said. "Now listen to me, though. I have to tell you some things."

Andrew listened.

"This evening we will go to a very important place for us, for a family reunion. Decisions will be made and one of these will be up to you. You will have to decide whether to stay with us or return to the world you know. You can tell the world that you died in that terrible fire and start a new life with the people of Mu, your people; or you can let them find you safe and sound, you'll reconcile with your relatives and forget all this story." Then the face of the fisherman became pained. "My heart is broken for you, son. I know what it means to lose someone important and I cannot tell you that there is a cure for that kind of pain."

Andrew turned to the side, holding back his tears. Enish put a hand on his shoulder. "But I can assure you that your mother still exists. She still exists!" he asserted, staring into his eyes.

That force within him knew that the man was telling the truth. Unfortunately, nostalgia overtook him and was unbearable. "I have nothing out there," he said with a trembling lip. "My mother was all I had. I treated her badly, you know. She did so much for me and I only knew how to think ill of her. If I had known, I…"

At that point Helena hugged him tightly.

"You'll never be alone here, Andrew," Enish said. "Mother Earth has countless children and they will all be your brothers and sisters. I for one, if you wish."

The boy extended the hug to the fisherman too, and they stayed like that for a few seconds. Then he pulled away, wiped his face and said, "If my Mum still exists, I can't cry. I promised her I wouldn't cry anymore."

They knocked on the door. Enish stared at Andrew and they understood each other. There were things to do.

Shaun came in, looking suspiciously for Amin.

The fisherman reassured his friend. "He's around here. I don't think he's strayed far."

After greeting Helena and Andrew, the old bookseller sat down for a coffee but refused the cookies, which were excellent, in Helena's opinion.

Outside the window, Andrew noticed one of the shivaks standing on a cliff. He had assumed the form of a human being and was unrecognisable, yet he knew it was Ahiga.

Amin threw open the door without knocking but stood there startled, perhaps because he didn't expect to see everyone up already so early. "Any news?" he asked annoyed.

"We start tonight at sunset. We must be at the long pier when the sun goes down. It will take a while. I suggest everyone to get ready as soon as possible."

"Do you want to leave now?" The policewoman asked surprised. "How far is this pier?"

"Two hours on foot," Enish answered. "And we must take the path of the mountain."

Shaun finished the coffee quietly, while Helena shook her head, frowning. She had no idea what the man meant, but it would certainly not be a walk in the park.

30

The long pier was nothing more than a small harbour protected by a semicircle of artificial rocks, perhaps dating back to the beginning of the last century. Fishing boats were tied with sturdy ropes to rusty metal pegs off shorter wooden piers. The trees of small boats swayed, lulled by the light currents of the harbour.

Two low buildings were resting against the rocks, crooked houses with beams worn by extended exposure to the saltiness of the air and so discoloured as to make it hard to guess their original colour. They showed no sign of architectural design, more akin to huts like those seen in pictures of the Greek islands.

The furthest one sported the faded sign of a fishing emporium. It was dark and silent. The closest, however, was enlivened by the lights coming through the windows. A hammock hung on the porch, swaying in the light sea breeze.

Again, Helena noticed, just above the door, similar symbols to those carved on the beam of Enish's house, though this time more crudely and less visibly.

The sun was setting and the temperature, which had been pleasant if not hot during the day, was beginning to lower. The walk had been exhausting, dotted with inexplicable stops, waits in the middle of rocky nothings and brisk walks along grazing trails. They had even passed the same spots more than once, without a doubt.

The door of the house swung open and a woman in her forties, with Indian features, emerged, adjusting her sheriff's hat over her ruffled hair.

"Good evening, Swan," Enish greeted her.

"Hi," she said.

"All good in there?"

"Yes. Dubois pulled one of his stunts. He hit the bottle, but nothing serious. Greta has offered to take him back home." She looked at the group behind the man, pausing on Amin.

"I brought some friends for a drink at Boe's," Enish explained.

"Sure," the sheriff smiled nervously. "Have a nice evening. Any problems, I'm five minutes away, OK?" She passed them by, greeting Shaun by tipping her hat.

Inside, the room had some open spaces, none of which were on the same level. The planks were arched and the columns all swerved and creaking. Light music came out of an old radio tucked between the bottles behind the counter, and with oil lamps lighting the surroundings, they seemed to have travelled back a hundred years.

There were few patrons already, who didn't seem to pay much attention to the arrival of the group.

Enish invited everyone to sit around a table and wait for him there, then approached the bartender, asking for a round of drinks.

At the side of the counter was a man with a long ponytail of greying hair falling on his back and wearing a heavy cape. Enish came up to him, shaking his hand. They exchanged a few words.

At the table, meanwhile, jugs of a golden coloured, foamy beer had arrived. Amin didn't touch anything.

"It's probably the best beer I've ever had," ventured Helena as a way to break the ice, while guessing the reactions of the patrons to their presence. Above all, she was trying to figure out how was it possible that the shivaks now looked so human. Some signs betrayed their strangeness, like the flaps of skin gathered at the sides of the mouth or the lack of firmness of their epidermis. But these details could have been mistaken with signs of age, even if their movements and body proportions told a different story. Still, they stood there with their hoods on and did not seem to be arousing interest.

Helena had the feeling of being in a dream sometimes. She thought back to the many times she had found herself staring at some strange character during her patrols at campsites or subways. How many of those faces hid a reality that no one would have guessed or could penetrate? How many of those eyes and bodies that she had observed, moved by doubt and intuition, were creatures and protagonists of a millennial struggle? It was enough to give a headache. She thought of her parents, child-like, with their rules, their teachings of good and evil, their attention to social ascent. That world appeared to her as an unthinkable and ill-acted soap opera.

"Everyone knows who we are here," Amin told her, as if he had read her mind.

"How?"

"From the police to the fishermen, the postmen and the teachers. Most of them are Sleepers, of course, but they have lived with the people of Mu for generations and follow their traditions, even if they do not understand their meaning. Like Enish here. Atlantis invites them to distance themselves because it's dangerous to live with the conscripts, but they do not yield. On the contrary, they consider themselves Sons of Mu."

"The light that shines in the Sleepers shows them the way," cut in

Shaun, annoyed. At the same time," continued Amin, unperturbed, "they provide cover for the Woken ones, integrate them among the Sleepers and sometimes take care of them, and vice versa. There are thousands of these mixed settlements."

"Who are the conscripts?"

"All the Woken, the Roused and the Sleeper ones who live according to the ancient customs of Mu must be recorded and controlled. They are forbidden to gather in the *Collegium*, to try awakening the Sleepers, to exploit the Ancient Knowledge and, above all, they cannot support the *Arkanum*. Unfortunately, they rarely comply with these simple rules and pay the consequences."

"Basically we are prisoners on the land of our own Mother," Shaun said.

"Do not complain, old man. You enjoy many freedoms."

"*Arkanum?*" Helena asked.

"Subversives," Amin explained.

"Fighters," Shaun corrected him. "They have chosen the path of violence to confront Atlantis. But this is not the thought of Mu, only a small part of it."

"I already told you in your fairytale shop, Shaun. Keep them in their place."

"You have your pact of non-aggression, son of Evenor. The word of a giant is sacred."

Amin stared at him. "Tonight we shall see what your word is worth."

Helena looked first at one, then at the other. Those exchanges often came across to her as the rantings of lunatics, so convinced were they when talking about primordial wars, mysterious, subversive factions, giants and forgotten continents. Yet she had to surrender to the reality of what she had witnessed for herself. And in fact, the least probable reality was her own. The one in which she had lived for over thirty years.

"Wait," she cut in, "are you saying that the *Arkanum* will also be there, tonight?"

"The *Collegium* makes sense only if everyone can talk, otherwise it loses all meaning. The *Arkanum* is not always present, but I imagine it will be there today," explained Shaun with a thin veil of threat to Amin.

Enish returned to the table. "Our passage is ready," he said. The man he spoke to was standing behind him. Him and Andrew stared at each other, and the boy thought that his age-old face was smiling at him, though he didn't move a muscle.

When they left, it was dark and quite cold. The sky was clear and starry, and a light breeze rippled the dark sea.

They headed to one of the piers, where the white-haired old man began fumbling with a tall-sided fishing vessel no more than a dozen yards long. Quietly, the man helped those who wanted to get on the swaying deck. Once on board, he entered the square cockpit, lit by a green light reflected off the wide Poff balance. He grabbed the rudder and the water behind the boat rippled with a noise similar to that of a large washing machine.

For the second time, Helena was stunned; there was no sound of an engine, yet the boat moved and the propellers turned.

"It does what it was built for," Andrew said, not knowing where those words came from.

Shaun and Enish studied him for a moment, without the boy noticing them.

The boat came out of the marina and ventured into the sea, cutting nose waves with a slow swinging motion. Soon the coast and the lights of the pier were behind and to the left, a sign that the captain had turned to proceed along the coast. Now the bow was directed toward the illumination of the lighthouse, which appeared from time to time like a ghost in the night.

Nobody spoke. They were all immersed in their own inscrutable thoughts.

Every now and then Andrew realised what had happened and the sorrow overwhelmed him. He seemed to sink into a black hole in his soul, creeping into an unspecified point of his body.

Staggering from the boat's swaying, he approached the person who was accompanying them.

"You were right about the boat," the old man told him.

"I don't even know what I'm saying."

"It's simple. This object was built with the intention that it would sail the seas. It has been equipped with useful tools for this purpose, and lacks nothing." He pointed to the rudder, the speedometer and the drive cabinet.

"But the engine is off."

"There is no engine. No need. It's enough that the propeller turns so that the boat moves, is it not?"

"And what makes the propeller move?" Andrew asked, though he knew he had the answer somewhere inside.

"The boat has been branded with symbols of Ancient Knowledge. These contain the Essence of human beings that free the boat from the constraint of having to have an engine. They say *do what you were built for*. And she does it, my Betty."

Andrew looked through the moon-bathed Plexiglas. He touched the control panel, the tools, the wood. He detected a slight and distant vibration. He felt it in his chest, guiding his hands and eyes.

"Would you take the helm for a while?" the man asked him. "I could do with a rest." He left him in charge and sat down next to him on a foldaway seat, hands on his knees.

Andrew grabbed the large wooden wheel and immediately the vibration expanded, overflowing within him. He had the feeling that the space occupied by his body had extended to the whole boat. He could feel the sea sliding under the hull with a fluid and pleasant massage and the fresh wind slipping into the shady corners of the cabin, snatching a smile as they tickled him.

Helena realised that Amin was staring at the scene, very serious.

"Straight to the lighthouse, now," the old man was saying to the boy. And he lit his pipe. "Very good."

It took about an hour to reach the island. The captain resumed commands only at the time of circumventing the reefs when they were close to the great rock on which the lighthouse had been built.

"Next time I'll show you how my Betty knows where to dock," he said to Andrew.

Near the cliff, the sea became insidious and the currents very strong. The boat now swayed in all directions, and the spray of the waves bathed the passengers, forced to hold fast to each other and to the ropes.

The captain smoked his pipe, giving vigorous strokes at the helm, one to one side, one to the other. He didn't seem worried about those acrobatics.

Passing very close to the sharp rocks, the boat slipped into a short, frightening series of ups and downs between narrow passages and between shoals of fish, until it was sheltered in a bay that prevented the currents from entering. They sailed to a small pebble beach with big logs sticking out of the water and Enish helped the captain secure the boat. They disembarked, not without wetting their feet, and Shaun led the way through a very narrow staircase carved into the rock which brought them up just below the red and white structure of the lighthouse. The light twirled silently over their heads, forty yards above. Droplets of moisture trickled on their head and shoulders, slipping from the crags above.

They crossed a megalithic stone arch, perhaps natural, perhaps manmade, at least from the time of Stonehenge, on which large torches shone, lighting the street with vivid yellow colours. Andrew wondered if they were battery operated.

They came out on a dirt road and walked along it for a short distance. Turning a corner, they found themselves a hundred yards from a red-painted wooden structure, built into the white lime column of the lighthouse. It was a modest home, but well-maintained considering its position in the elements.

Andy felt his legs hurt from the long climb. However, it was nothing in the face of the growing excitement that gripped him with every further step.

Enish knocked on the painted wooden door, rubbing his hands against the cold.

No one answered.

Enish knocked again.

Amin stepped forward and grabbed the handle, impatiently. The door did not move.

"We're early," Shaun said, looking at his pocket watch.

"Maybe the warden went to the local disco," Helena said.

"Now we're on time," said the bookseller.

And Enish knocked.

Andrew perceived a very intense, rapid and very high vibration, which disappeared almost immediately. Amin grimaced with a slight hint of disgust.

The door opened inward.

*

"It is a difficult time for the Mother Earth," said the giant Trummugan, his aquiline nose-features and elongated skull facing the people. A long, pitch-black and tidy goatee, threaded with golden laces, embellished his face, with its ivory radiant skin and large pupilless eyes.

Helena looked around, dazed. Next to her, seated on worn-out benches, sculpted into the golden rock that made up the vast cave in which they stood, were the rest of her group. And there were more. Other benches were filled by people they didn't know and had never seen, from those of Andrew's age to older ones. Everyone listened in silence to the words of the three giants. Sitting on three immense stools, with very high stalagmite backrests that joined with the ceiling, they were in a more prominent position.

They wore splendid dresses, decorated by a multitude of extraordinary hues and chromatic combinations that formed bright geometries. They were adorned with soft veils, thin as wind, and rough stones that shone in the warm light. They had a thin chest, but their legs looked mighty through the slits of their robes. The feet, adorned with rings of red gold at the ankles, expressed perhaps the most extraordinary detail: they were at least as long as the torso of an adult man. Helena guessed that the giants would reach, or even exceed, ten feet from seated. They were living flesh, vibrant and present, occupying a space within reality, a large space. And they were real.

"Goodness," she whispered.

"It is very rare that a descendant of Evenor is allowed at a *Collegium* under the protection of a Milesian pact of non-aggression," another giant continued. "Last time, it involved a Ghenos Knight, Prince Ediazi Syul Acpasia XXV, during the subaltern kingdom of Shiva Faide Kirce. It is a desirable event, in a way, and it reminds us all of what matters most. Union. Now, we must all agree on the next steps to be taken together, brothers of Mu."

A man sat between two others, right under the feet of the giants, spoke up. He was dressed in simple clothes but adorned with huge necklaces of black stones that covered his chest. He must have been in his seventies, his shoulders straight and a cold stare that inspired respect.

"Nyutal, son of Liria and Naacal of the *Arkanum*, here to represent him. Together, you will tell us, Milesian brothers." He got up and took a few steps towards the centre of the room. "We should first be sure that this is not all a ruse, a game of the telluric ones to find our people and do what they started twelve thousand years ago: destroy us. A trick created to grab everything, the boy, and finally get their hands on the *Arkanum*, overwhelm it and launch the decisive blow. Together, you will tell us, Milesian brothers. Today is a day of sorrow for us. In addition to having suffered the kidnapping of a young brother, we must now welcome the Enemy in the most sacred of our *Collegium*. It is time to decide whether Mu should surrender to the brutality of Atlantis and to the disciples of Belial and condemn our communities, erasing a partnership that cannot and should not be broken. No, there are no choices, brothers. There are no alternatives to Life. There is only the end. And it isn't us human beings, or the Sikal brothers, nor the wise men who can make decisions about it."

Helena listened to those words, still wrapped in a feeling of scepticism mixed with confusion. In fact, she couldn't remember at all how that sort of great family reunion had begun, or how or when they had arrived in that magical place.

"Since Life always finds its way, it will also show us how to follow it," said another man, sitting at the giants' feet.

Helena recognised him; it was the fisherman who had taken them across the sea with his Betty.

Another giant took the floor. "Yes, Abriaros, Life finds its way. Your words are also wise, Nyutal. No living creature can decide the fate of 'All that is'. Perhaps it is not necessary to go so far as to take positions today. The *Collegium* was gathered to determine what to do to bring

Adam home, among his people."

"It seems to me that we are talking about delivering him into the arms of the Atlanteans' Translators of Light," Nyutal said.

"This word is banned by the *Collegium*," one of the attendees pointed out.

"Forgive me, brothers," the man continued, "but I cannot understand. You say we're here to save Adam, but you've let in a Shadow Hound with the promise to give the boy to him and then taken his word as an Atlantean to return him to us, after they've performed every atrocious experiment we can think of." He turned to Amin. "Besides, the word of a Shadow Hound has no value. He has no honour, as we all know."

The Atlantean remained impassive. He knew the rules of the game well and expected that the *Arkanum* would try to make him react. He stood up and many whispered to each other. "I am very satisfied that at least the Pacts between Giants are still considered and respected," he began. "But do not talk to me about honour, Naacal. Let me explain how things are. Atlantis reigns, guides and establishes the destinies of living creatures. Atlantis decides how the masses should be directed, what wars must be unleashed, what tools to use to push humanity in the right direction. And it decides on life and death, including yours, Nyutal of the *Arknum*."

"Do you hear that?" Nyutal replied, sorrowful. "He is invited and welcomed here among us in peace, yet he dares threaten us all."

Two thin and dark figures came to stand by his side. Andrew became immediately uncomfortable at the sight of them. They were perhaps a man and a woman, but hardly distinguishable from one another. Dressed in dark leather capes, they glistened with the large amount of metal they wore: rings, necklaces, bracelets on legs and feet, piercings jingling at their every step. They were hairless. The skin had a pale colour and their lips were blue, like the nails of their bare hands and feet. Tribal tattoos and designs covered all visible parts of the skin and the veins on their slim muscles were bulging.

PART FIVE

THE RIVER RUNS

*"So long as thou feelest the stars as an 'above thee', thou lackest the eye of
the discerning one."*

Friedrich Nietzsche

31

The clock was old and had been broken for perhaps a hundred years. Andrew stared at it from time to time, as if to see whether it decided to start by itself. He had slept well and had woken up early. Amin had left them, Enish explained, but he would be back. After talking to Cornelius, he announced that he would leave immediately to pursue the new information he had acquired to identify those responsible for the kidnapping of Adam and the attack. Enish had then taken Helena for a walk around the village, since Abriaros had asked to remain alone with Andrew.

So, early in the morning, they found themselves in the room next to the bar on the long pier, a wooden cottage with a high, pointed ceiling, not much better than the adjacent structure. The store was empty. There were many old chairs piled up beside several tables. A dust-covered service counter stood on the opposite side of the hall. An empty candy container rested on it. And above, that curious broken clock.

Andrew didn't speak, but the situation was making him uncomfortable. All those eyes on him made him blush. From the ground or from chairs or the counter, sceptical eyes looked at the city boy with curiosity.

"So," said Abriaros, as he tortured his irregular, thick, white-striped goatee, "what do you think?"

"Difficult to say," said Trummugan, who was bent over holding his huge face with his hands.

"Maybe nexus?" Aigha asked before taking a slap from Yzenn.

"He's not a nexus," Shaun said. "He doesn't have the traits. Nor the talent. He's impulsive, even if he hides this tension well with disciplined behaviour. It's an act, not his character."

Andrew felt the humiliation grow. He blushed, but soldiered on; he didn't want to give in to them.

"In fact, he does not show any peculiar trait at first sight," Abriaros commented.

"All the time he spent as a Sleeper does not help us, sure and rather than not," said the giant.

They returned to look at him in silence for several minutes.

"So," Abriaros began again. "Andrew will tell us. Boy, approach."

He took some hesitant steps towards the Naacal fisherman, who got up from his chair and crouched down on his legs to look at him from below, his eyes steady as steel and deep as the sea.

"Tell me what Adam did on the night he was kidnapped."

"He told me he would not leave me. Then he put a hand on my forehead. At that point I felt like… like…" he could not describe what had happened to him.

"I understand. Relax. And before? What happened before?"

"He told me about the trees. He said that a fallen tree still lives for a long time. And I wanted to leave, but then I accidentally touched one of those trees and I felt… I felt like I was a tree. I can't explain it better."

"Did this happen before Adam touched your forehead?" Trummugan asked.

"Yes, I think so."

"Adam must have perceived Andrew's *keh*," Abriaros clarified.

"Possible, but complicated. How could he perceive a Sleeper's *keh* without interacting with it?"

Abriaros concentrated elsewhere for a moment. "Don't forget who Adam is."

"We do not know if he is what we think," the giant admonished him.

The Naacal sighed, then turned to the boy. "What changed since you were touched?"

Andrew frowned thoughtfully, trying to find the right words. "I don't know. Adam told me that nothing had changed and in a sense it is true. I don't feel different. That is if we exclude the fact that I now know things and I don't even know where they come from, at least," he said softly, then his face lit up. "Actually, there is something different. When the mayaurli reached us, something inside me… convinced me that I had to get away, save Adam. I knew I was risking my life. I was terrified. Yet I did it. I took a decision, knowing the risk. It was the right thing to do, I can't explain it differently, to risk my life to save his."

"As if Adam's life were more important than yours?" asked Trummugan.

"No, I don't think so," said Andrew. "Rather it was my job. And Adam had another one. Like in a movie in which the character does something dangerous because it's his duty, because he must. Because it's his nature. I don't know if I've explained myself…"

Abiraros smiled. "Very clearly," he said, throwing a satisfied look at the giant. "Last night you said many things concerning the Woken ones. How did it happen?"

Andrew took a few steps, searching for words. "It happens. I seem to have a divider in the head and one in the stomach. At some point, when they both open, the information flows so fast inside me that I have to hurry up to stop it, otherwise they return from where they came. I can't control this thing. When Nyutal provoked me, the dividers opened up and I tried to grab everything that came out. At the end I felt empty, destroyed."

The Naacal got up. "It seems that Adam has awakened only the unconscious part of his sleeping *keh*."

"You can't half-awaken a living being!" said Shaun.

"It is possible," Trummugan answered. "But this means that Adam was able to perceive Andrew's sleeping *keh* and was able to touch him with such lightness that he showed him the way without awakening him."

"What does that mean? Am I sick?" Andy was getting worried.

They all laughed heartily, much to his annoyance.

Abriaros put his hands on his shoulders, staring at him with a magnificent smile that exploded from the wrinkles around his eyes. "You are not sick, young brother. You are great."

"So am I a… Roused one?"

"Is it so important to you?"

"I don't know. Is it?"

"What you feel here," he said, pointing first at the head, then at the chest, "is what you really are."

"So I'm not?"

"No. Adam started something on you, a process to free your *keh*. In order not to hurt you, he barely opened the door to the cage in which the *keh* is a prisoner, leaving you the freedom to decide your destiny. If it manages to find the passage, then you will experience awakening."

Andrew looked at him, then to the others. "I don't care about that. All that matters now is to find Adam again."

"Adam is very fortunate to have such a loyal friend in you."

"We are not friends, we are brothers!"

"Well said," the giant rejoiced. "Young *Andros*, who for the Greeks meant "man", I am sure you will give us a lot of satisfaction."

The door to the store was shaken by a series of incessant knocks, sudden and powerful. It opened and the sun shone through strongly into the dark wooden building. A girl of six or seven, dressed in white, peeked inside, still holding the door ajar. She had blonde curls, a delightful little face and wore a pair of red wellies. She seemed breathless.

"Hi!" she greeted them.

It was returned by everyone. In particular, Trummugan gave her a radiant smile.

"What is it, little Nouel?" asked Abriaros.

The girl had a cheeky expression. She tried to adjust her sight to the darkness of the store and, as soon as she saw better, she placed her big blue eyes on Andrew.

"Nouel?" insisted the Naacal.

She was shaken by her thoughts. "Is he Andrew?" she asked, studying him.

"They are all curious to meet him, Abriaros," the giant commented.

"Oh, you're right, Nouel. I didn't realise what time it was."

"Who's curious to meet me?" Andrew asked.

Abriaros approached the door and threw it open. The boy stood up, dazzled by the glare on the sand and the clear sky.

"Mu," said the elder. "Adam's family, your family."

Andy gasped, rooted to the spot. In front of the emporium, there were a hundred, perhaps two hundred people. Women, children, old people, men were all there in silence. There were the patrons of the bar, the sheriff, Enish and Helena and many others who he had never seen before. And he remembered Adam's words, *We have always known each other. We are brothers because we are children of the same Mother.*

"Go," urged Trummugan, "They're here for you." He gently pushed him with his huge hand.

Andrew took a few steps forward. He didn't know what to do or what to say. He bent his head, as if he could guess his feelings in the sand.

Nouel then approached him and put a hand under his chin, looking into his eyes. She stared at him with intensity, then hugged him tightly, crushing her pale face against his belly. "Welcome, little brother!" she said, squeezing him as tight as she could. Then she took his hand and approached the crowd. "This is Andrew!" she proclaimed, smiling.

The boy looked around in confusion, then raised a hand in a clumsy gesture of greeting. And he was overwhelmed by people. He was hugged, embraced, kissed and caressed enough times to cover the whole life of a human being. He was pampered with words, welcomed with smiles, condoled about his mother. He was enveloped in a whirlwind of humanity so pressing and extraordinary that, when he met Helena, he didn't even recognise her.

*

At the same time, a hundred miles east of the emporium, in the municipal city museum, the funeral of Emily and her son was taking place. In addition to the Christian priest, there was Carlyle and some other of Andrew's classmates, some of Emily's colleagues, and René Fawcett with his new wife and newborn son. The man felt sorry, of course, but at the same time relieved. A very unwanted part of his life had disappeared forever. It was a horrible thought, he admitted to himself, but in the end it was the truth. His ex-wife and son represented a failure for him, a man full of great expectations for himself and his career. Now that everything was just perfect, that he had an important and beautiful wife from whom he had had a perfect child, the disappearance of that chapter was the crowning conclusion of an era that no longer belonged to him, representing the earned freedom to live his existence as it should have been from the beginning.

The past is a book, the lawyer Fawcett pondered. Looking back, one could expand parts, modify others or, with a little imagination and little intellectual honesty, even rewrite some chapters to make them better match the present. It was a personal and fascinating choice that could be changed at any moment.

Yes, it was worth making some changes.

His wife looked at him with sympathy, holding him close and he did the same with his son, a delicate picture of family sorrow. Andrew's dad wiped his tears with a handkerchief carrying his initials, then carefully repositioned his Prada sunglasses over his moist eyes. "Rest in peace," he whispered.

32

The underground depot was in the centre of town, at the foot of a large building from the first half of the twentieth century, tinged with incessant smog in the current gunpowder colour. The traffic was intense, an endless queue of taxis and commercial vehicles progressing in fits and starts. Whole droves of professionals, freelancers, clerks and workers had poured out on the streets to find a corner to eat their packed lunch or to join some friends in the trendy bars of the moment.

The entrance to the depot was an old access for heavy vehicles, barred by a high net, full of warning signs and advertisements. A simple wire held the two halves of the net together and, from the smell of urine coming from the inside, it was evident that the place was frequented without the owners' knowledge.

Amin walked the short corridor that ended in the large, curved sliding door with a double mechanism that was the goods lift. He looked for a call button, but couldn't find it. What he did see were crumpled cans, broken bottles, newspapers and condoms scattered all over the place. He had to move a plank of wood stuck on a side post to finally locate the little circle of metal with the arrow pointing down. Below the button was the opening for a key. Amin brought his ring closer to the mechanism, and the pseudo-interface did the rest.

He went down, in darkness, for over two minutes, surrounded by the metallic sound of the lift. It stopped with a crash at the only scheduled stop and the door opened with difficulty. A worn sign stuck on the manual door, read:

-You are twenty-five yards below street level.
Always locate the escape routes closest to your vehicle.
Thank you for choosing our company-

Amin opened the second door made of net and perforated metal.

The room was huge. The timid light, coming from the only incandescent lamp above the freight elevator, was flickering, overcome by the oppressive darkness that was fighting it back as if it had a secret and inscrutable will. A few old cars had become enveloped with dust. Others had been left there covered by a cloth, silent, with the headlights like staring eyes fixed into space.

The Hound moved a few steps forward. He immediately felt a presence to his left, but didn't react. Then the same happened to his right and front. The moloch appeared with a slow, limping gait, right in front of Amin, announced by the dragging sound of one of his feet.

A long, light brown coat of worn leather covered the man's body, thin and hunchbacked. His hair was long and black, but grew only on the sides of his head. He wore an unkempt beard and a thicker goatee. He was leaning on a stick of black onyx, his eyes bright and crazy.

"It's an honour to have you here, Pure. A rare event around here. Welcome," he said, his voice trembling with amusement and excitement.

"And it will not happen again very soon, moloch."

"Oh, call me Kabot, please. I have a name. They gave it to me, you know how it is, at birth."

There were at least five people hidden in the shadows. Armed. *Perhaps Sleepers subjugated by the moloch*, Amin thought. In that condition, even twenty of them would have had no chance against a Shadow Hound trained in the dark. "I'm not interested in friendship, moloch. Let's get to the point."

"Yes, of course, lord. How can I serve you?" he added with an awkward bow.

"A trusted source told me that you have information about some mayaurli sent to hunt a Sleeper. The first question is: do you keep mayaurli?"

"Eh, let's see," Kabot said.

"I do not need to remind you that I am here as a court representative of the very Pure Prince Here XLIII. Your opposition to collaborating or your false testimony would break the Code of the One, condemning you on the spot. You had no choice in accepting this meeting, it is true. Maybe you need someone to remind you of the precariousness of your position."

"I want to cooperate, lord! If Mother was so cruel to me at birth, giving me the body and mind of a moloch. What fault do I have? What can I do, if not regret every moment of my misfortune and invoke the compassion of those men whom I would have liked to equal, like you? I want to cooperate, lord. I want to, yes. It is the only hope that still keeps me alive, that of favouring the very Pure and allowing my little contribution to… the good Reason!" He said enthusiastically with a theatrical movement of his arms. His eyes nervous, sharp with a restless light.

"I do not find you funny. I'll ask again. Do you have eugenic units or pseudo-technological conversions?" Amin insisted.

"Never!" Kabot answered, standing up straight. "Because these practices are forbidden outside the control of the Translators of Light and I, and I'm proud of it, know that."

"Have you received any requests for the supply of mayaurli, or have you heard anything about someone who owns them?"

The moloch became thoughtful. Or at least, he pretended to think. "A few days ago I heard from someone, a friend of another person who knew very well the cousin of a not so trustworthy type, a story about a load arrived at the dock of a nearby city. The guy made me understand that the load was dirty."

"What was it?"

"I don't know exactly. I tend to mind my own business. I don't want problems, you know."

"But?"

Kabot smiled. "Well, my personal advisor pointed out to me that the boat came from the port of Archangelsk in Russia."

Amin urged him to continue.

"Eh, it is common knowledge that it is a route often exploited for illegal trafficking of Sleepers. But not only that."

"Do you mean to say that Belial's disciples use Sleepers' transport to move clandestine pseudo-technological material? But this is madness!"

"Naa, this is business. On the other hand, the containers are full of stuff, and what is transported by the Woken ones is always of little matter, from the point of view of space."

"I do not have time for these matters. Go on".

"I have very little else to add," the moloch shrugged. "Except for the ship's name..." he added in a teasing tone, as if expecting something from Amin.

"I do not barter with Belial, you should know."

"I know, Pure one. I don't expect much! It's just that I have this little problem with a grim type that is ruining my business. I have a reputation to keep, you know?"

The Hound approached Kabot, continuing to focus also on his invisible companions, hidden among the concrete columns. "The name," he ordered.

"*Novosk*," Kabot answered immediately. "But be careful. As my personal advisor says, when pseudo-technology is involved, with what it is worth outside the Avalon, there is always someone who spends a lot to protect it."

"Is there anything else you're not telling me?"

"No, no. I just wanted to warn you, that's all. I could give you someone to help you. I have so many willing guys available."

"I don't want your thugs, moloch. And they should stay well away from you too."

"They love me," he protested mellifluously, adjusting his precarious position on his cane.

Amin turned to the darkness. "Go home, or this man will lead you to ruin. You have no idea with whom you are meddling."

The Hound knew that the ability to enmesh a moloch was able to exert on the Sleepers was strong, a glue made of charisma and talent which made them disciples and mind-slaves, subjects and martyrs of a cause they did not understand. Belial had created the molochs in ancient times and they had disappeared for a while. Alas, during the most recent centuries, these mysterious characters had returned, ready to satisfy their talent and primary impulse: war. Someone suspected that it had been the hand of a Translator of Light to whisper those mysteries that only Belial knew and allowed the transformation of a Woken one into a moloch. Only the heart of a human being was corrosive enough to accept so much darkness within himself. And only the mind of a human being was able to create in order to destroy.

"The second question is this," Amin continued. "Have you had or are you currently in contact with clans Fir Bolg who exploit the ancient ways of this kingdom?"

"Well, I have to say yes, here. Sometimes exchanges are made. But everything above board, nothing forbidden. We know that Fir Bolg often find, let's say, some little things down there. Ancient things maybe, or precious. It's always nice to have some memories of the old times, no?"

"You keep wandering away from my questions, moloch. What would I care of your petty tradings? That is stuff for the investigations of the eughenos or the tattling of the Onagros. I asked if you exchange favours, if you use them for some of your grim plans of conquest."

Kabot frowned. He did not seem to be interested in answering.

It only took a moment. The Hound was on him, holding him by the jaw against a column. A thick web of thin *Orichalcum* hair, bright and liquid, loomed from his face, pointing threateningly to Kabot's eyes.

Agitated steps all around.

"Don't worry, boys," the moloch said with all the voice he could muster.

"Speak!" shouted the Hound.

"If you allude to the Fir Bolg that took the life of that Sleeepr at the lake, no, I don't know anything about it."

"How do you know this story?"

The creature sneered, amused and in pain. "The rumour spread everywhere. Things like this don't happen often. Or rather, it does not happen that four Fir Bolg are taken out immediately after killing a Sleeper. I mean, Evenor's law is fine, but this seemed more like a cold-blooded execution than the judgment of the very Pure and revered princes. This aside, however, I don't know anything else."

"The Code of the One governs the world. Fir Bolg have forgotten and have paid the price of their amnesia." Amin let go and the moloch fell to the ground, breathless. "Keep yourself available," ordered the Shadow Hound, reaching the goods lift. Something moved in the darkness. It was time to leave that dirty and forgotten place.

"I'm not going anywhere," added the moloch, massaging his mouth. "Hey, what about that little problem I told you about?"

The door shut and the freight elevator began its excruciating ascent to the surface. Amin's eyes remained planted on those of Kabot until a concrete wall separated them.

The face of the creature changed. He was serious now, dark, determined. He struck his staff angrily against the column and the fragments flew off in the dark. "Dog!" he cursed.

From the darkness, a presence took shape next to the moloch. "Consider yourself lucky," said a mighty man, scars covering his face and surrounding glacial little eyes.

"What are you talking about, *brother?*"

"You're still alive," replied the other with equal contempt. "We have an imperative duty to kill any moloch we come in contact with. Amin has become a Shadow Hound without losing his Pure determination. He must be really in dire straits for letting you go."

"You were there to protect me."

Seven other individuals appeared from the shadows, approaching the first.

"Deactivate the *keh* suppressors," he ordered the men, tearing a patina of circular jelly from his forehead, which disintegrated immediately in his hands. He sighed. "Yours is a momentary fortune, Kabot. Take a wrong step and you will return to the Source by my hand."

The moloch advanced a couple of meters, the appropriate distance to be able to keep all eight Hounds of Shadow in his sight, squaring them with tight and cruel eyes. "You are not in a position to preach, Tutmos. Even I would have had more scruples than you, sending one of my disciples to be killed!"

"There are more important things than the life of the individual," said Tutmos quietly.

"Pathetic excuses. You are just like me. You betrayed your Great Intention. You acted against your prince. You broke your Code of the One," he counted on his fingers.

"If we have agreed to get our hands dirty with you and your father, it's only because there is a supreme good. We are aware of the risks we are running, but there is no other way for Atlantis to win the war."

"Ah! Perhaps you meant to say there is no other way to take back the power that has been taken from you. No, Tutmos, you are not different from me."

"There is nothing in you except hate and the will to destroy."

"And in you? What's in your minds, what in your actions that is so different?" the moloch shouted, hitting the concrete column with unpredictable fury. "You! You who are trying to kill a boy who could be the emperor you've been waiting for for 120 centuries? No, Atlantean. There is really no difference between my hatred for the world and yours!"

The hounds stared at him imperturbably, motionless as statues.

"You have your own profit, which is all that interests you. The rest is beyond what you are given to understand," Tutmos concluded.

Moloch's eyes became thin and his sneer of disgust turned into a tight smile, enigmatic and insane. *No, arrogant dog of a fallen. You have no idea what you've unleashed!*

33

Abriaros entered the room and sat next to Andrew, who was bent over a table, submerged in books. The boy couldn't remember ever working so hard in his life, even in the most prolific periods of school, motivated by satisfying his father's expectations.

History, English, Maths, Languages, Sciences, Philosophy. But above all History. History to infinity. He studied under the guidance of Professor Winchet, a despotic little Irish man who taught at the local high school about twenty miles from there and who swamped him with homework. The good thing is that he no longer had a specific study plan, but was touching on everything, without limits and for most of the day. In the morning, he studied in the staff room of the local elementary school, mentored by Winchet or Flou, a girl in her early twenties who was a programmer by trade, working from home with her boyfriend Hemmet, also a programmer. Flou was delightful and, unlike Winchet, she wasn't strict at all. He often wanted to chat and sometimes they spent hours talking about the most disparate topics, from music to cinema, to girls. Sometimes Hemmet would hang around too, and those were the days when Professor Winchet complained about Andrew's poor performance.

The boy rarely saw Abriaros, who, when not at sea, had to deal with numerous matters, even though Andrew didn't know what they were. *He's a Naacal*, he thought, *he'll need to do loads of... Naacal stuff.*

"Still on your books at this time?" the elder asked him.

Andy stretched. "Yup. Hemmet stopped by this morning and we haven't done much."

"I see. What were you studying? "

"Egypt. Third dynasty."

"Ah! An interesting period."

"Why do I have to keep studying this nonsense?" he protested.

"Because you must know what the Sleepers like you know. Otherwise, you risk to become isolated, unable to relate to this reality. The Sleepers would not recognise you and would push you away for fear of a diversity they cannot understand. You can't afford it, since you're not a Roused one. And, in any case, we also study the same as you."

"But if this world is fake, what's the point of being part of it?"

"Human history and its current condition are a falsehood. The reality that you are given to live. But whether you like it or not, you must learn to confront it. You're still too young to know how to separate truth from falsehood. There are many deceptions in which you can fall. You must study what you are facing in order to become able to know the difference. There will be a time for everything else. But that's not the point, is it, Andrew? There is something else that bothers you."

The boy nodded. "What's the point of me being here, studying crap and walking around, when Adam is in danger, and every moment could be a precious chance to save him? Don't get me wrong, Abriaros. I'm happy here and I would never go away. Just the thought of leaving breaks my heart. But deep inside, something shouts: *Move! Adam needs you! Don't waste time!* This is what bothers me."

The old man smiled, adjusting a book on the table. "Your concern is understandable. But your presumption is inadequate. We have alerted our Canvas since the day of Adam's abduction. Everybody knows. And everyone is making huge efforts to get information and find out where our young brother is. On Mu, knowledge moves swiftly. Much more than a single individual who throws himself from one side of the world to the other without any clue, driven only by impulse. Often doing is not doing at all."

"The Canvas?"

"Do you know what I mean? Try to explain it to me."

The boy inhaled, trying to let the energy that grew inside him find the road smoothed out from its starting point to the lungs, the vocal cords and the mouth. "Every person in Mu is bound to others. We are all connected in some way, some more, some less depending on the characteristics of your *keh*. Even if distant, the relations between the people of Mu are very tight, strong. It's a family spread all over the planet, tied through what appears to be a big spider web," Andrew gestured with his fingers as if trying to touch the invisible. "Communication takes place spontaneously and very quickly through these connections. In a very short time a name, a person, a problem can become collective domain. Everybody knows. The whole world knows," he said, stunned by his words.

"Now you understand. There is a limit to action that cannot be overcome by action. Beyond it there is no other action, but observation."

"And how long will we have to observe?"

"Don't be fooled by the great illusionist that is time. Everything that happens makes sense. Adam is alive, and he's fine."

"I'd love to share your belief…"

Abriaros rose from his chair and pushed aside the curtains. It was almost dark. "What do you see out there?"

The boy joined him. "Well, there's Ben's house, Druva's shop, McMillan's souvenir shop, and the florist, but I can't remember his name."

"Lerner. What else do you see?"

"The road with the lights stuck on orange, the road signs, the telephone poles… the beach, the rocks, the sea, the lighthouse, the sky. Nothing more, leaving details aside. But I don't think that's what you wanted to know."

"The light." Abriaros pointed outside. An unspecified point in the world. It was full of lights. The windows, the signs, the few cars, the bicycles.

"There are so many. Which one do you mean?"

"Tell me. Which one strikes you the most?"

"Easy. The lighthouse, without a doubt. Even if that horrendous neon shoe shop leaves his mark too!" Andrew joked.

"Why the lighthouse?" the Naacal asked seriously.

Andrew concentrated. "Because it's a strong flashing light. And because it's suspended in the dark, and…" then he understood.

"You see it. You see Adam's *keh* shining!"

Abriaros laid his hands on the disciple's shoulders. "Like the sun, brother. Like the sun. Adam is fine. And we will find him again."

"Let's go then!"

"We cannot. In the Essence there is no space and time. It is only my human limitation that allows me to see with my eyes. But I know it's an illusion. In fact, I don't know where he is, unfortunately. I cannot know that."

They looked at the lighthouse together, in silence. "Now go back to your Egyptians," said Abriaros.

Andrew nodded, following that intermittent dot as he sat down, obedient and somewhat relieved.

"History is the most important of the subjects you are studying. Without knowing the past, you will have no future. And without knowing the past invented for the Sleepers, you will not understand the present," said the Naacal, heading for the door.

"Abriaros… Can you see even the dead?"

The elder expected that sooner or later Andrew would ask that question. "Death is the first of the Seven Orders. Everything that begins must end. The dead have only returned to where they were before birth."

"I can't see them. I don't understand."

"It is the most powerful aspect of the Awareness."

Andrew stepped forward, the shadows of the windows on his face, painting dark lines. "Where are we when we don't live, Ab?"

The Naacal seemed reticent, then his face grew softer. He also walked into the cone of light and shadows generated by the pale moonlight. "We are inside time. Those who return to the Source lose their individuality as we know it when we live in reality."

"Enish told me that Mum is still alive!"

"Enish has tried to explain something that you have to experience to understand. See, Andrew, Life has no boundaries. It takes shape continuously as much as it loses it. It is not a single entity. Everything merges in it. What your mother was, here with you, is now part of 'All that is'. Before she wasn't, but now she is."

"I miss her so much," the boy confessed, fiddling with the eraser, a lump in his throat.

"Maybe one day you'll understand. When you will be able to see your mother in every other living being born after her return to the Source. Already at this moment thousands of human beings are born. In them, there is a part of the Essence of all those who have returned to the Source. And when you return there, everything will become simple and clear. If you experience awakening in the course of your existence, you will no longer care for these topics, because you will know. You will know that death is a passageway, just as birth is."

Andrew nodded. He knew that Abriaros was not lying. Suddenly, he conceived a thought. *Perhaps, once awake, I can find a way to get my mother back...* and the idea kept him awake all night.

34

Bob Wilson had been working on shipyard cranes for thirty years. He had manoeuvred all kinds and sizes. A job that seemed easy, from below; he knew that. Slow movements of a big slow machine. But it was not the case at all. The thinly stretched structure, suspended in midair, was supported by a precarious equilibrium and the margin of error was minimal. The taller the crane was, and the more its arm extended, the more these margins were reduced. For a month or so, after an intense training course, he had been entrusted with the only MTC 78000 Liebherr in the entire port area, a giant of over 600 tons, equipped with a 300-foot extendable arm.

Bob loved his job. He thought it relaxing, despite the great responsibilities. The long moments of pause during the anchorage phases of the ships or those waiting for new cargo even allowed him to doze or read. Even at that time of the year, when it was starting to get quite cold and the wind at that height made itself feel sharply, he always kept the roof opened at least a couple of notches. The cloud from his cigar, which he wasn't allowed to smoke, rose in curls as relaxed as Bob was.

From that height, he could see the lights of the already sleeping city. They vibrated just beyond the immense drainage basins of the port, beyond the cargo hangar barely illuminated by the lights mounted on pylons, which rose like bright mushrooms in that forest of metal. In the shipyard, hundreds of boats lay still, anchored to the wharves, while immediately beyond the two long concrete arms marked by the beacons stretched the boundless sea, fused to the night sky.

Bob took a long drag of his cigar. The bitter taste filled his mouth. Right then a knock shook the bolted door.

He almost swallowed the cigar, which fell between his legs; he burned his fingers as he tried to recover the stub. He looked at the radio, but it gave no signs.

"I am looking for a ship by the name of *Novosk*," a male voice began, outside the door.

There was someone there, but the small porthole and the reflection of the spotlights illuminating the ship they were loading prevented him from seeing well. Bob stood up to unlock the opening mechanism, but it seemed to be jammed. He went on the radio. It was silent. All the channels crackled. There was still a good ten minutes to go before the new cargo arrived, and the guys below were no doubt at Maxine's kiosk eating a sandwich. He was trapped.

"I am not going to hurt you. I just want to know where the *Novosk* is. It should have been here, but it is not," the man said through the glass.

"You can't be here without permission," Bob protested nervously. "Get down, or I'll call the port guard."

"You cannot call anyone."

The driver grabbed the phone, dialled the number and put it to his ear. A shrill whirring forced him to push it away. The phone ended up on the linoleum floor of the control room.

"I am in a hurry," the man continued. The tone of his voice was getting irritated.

Bob felt a strong sense of nausea and an inexplicable panic was taking hold of him. He had tachycardia and was breaking into a cold sweat. He felt confused. He thought about that time in church in the South of France, where he had gone on vacation with his wife, where he saw a person affected by Stendhal's syndrome. He was afraid.

"The *Novosk* left twenty minutes ago. It was anchored at the next dock," he indicated as if the other could see. Then he stretched out over the controls, looking over the giant arm of white trusses and big flat bolts. "You can still see it, just outside the port entrance. The red lights…" he stammered. "You can read the name of the ship from here if you have good eyes." And he made the sign of the cross.

It was still strange, for a Woken one, to see how desperately Sleepers relied on the gods. Men who lost contact with their *keh* were won by that absolute, unbridgeable absence. They were lost to such an extent as to create in their minds an image of what was missing, to which they had given the most varied and bizarre forms. Since the early days of Oblivion, the Sleepers had struggled to affirm these images, nurture them according to cultural, spiritual and social differences. Wars had been unleashed, and were still being fought, even outside Atlantis' will, to assert one or the other. The Woken ones and the Enlightened had enormous responsibilities in exploiting or directing this powerful energy. Sometimes the intention had been spontaneous and positive, but everything had always fallen into chaos. And religion had become an instrument of power.

Unfortunately, there was nothing to be done; what man was could have been restrained, but the power of the vital spark would still struggle to get out of that prison in which it had been held. There was something more and more conscious in Amin's mind. Living in the Avalon and learning the history of the Sleepers was one thing, being with them and assessing their despair, their loneliness and their confusion, was another. Anyone would have faltered in the face of this.

"You did your duty, citizen," he said to console him.

Amin jumped onto the cabin, climbing onto the upper truss and then on one of the supporting beams suspended in space, just above the quay. Bob saw him take speed on that precarious tubular support, a little wider than a can of beer, until he became small, near the head pulley at the end of the loading arm. He followed him in disbelief when suddenly all the lights in the cabin came on. The horns began to trill and the gigantic electric motor reached operating speed.

"What the…" Bob whispered, trying to understand how was it that the system had started in spite of the security key being still in his pocket. "It's not possible!" he cried, grasping at the card with his name on it.

The tower began to rotate, first slowly, then faster and faster in the direction of the port entrance. If the crane reached peak speed, an immediate stop would cause structural damage, breaking the tree and dropping a hundred ton steel boulder onto the wharf. Bob could not risk a disaster like that. There were dozens of people working under him, not counting the ship's crew. He raised the security flap and pressed the big "forced recovery" button, hoping it was not too late.

But the crane didn't react.

He could not react. Because it was responding to the command of a Lord of Matter, docile as a bunny, obedient as a sheepdog.

When the gigantic arm, sixty feet longer than a Boeing 747, was aligned with the port's spotlights, the crane slowed to a halt. The control parameters in the cabin came on again and the strident lamentation of the titan filled the harbour area. Bob sensed the structural cell deforming beneath him. The twist had lifted one side of the floor, tilting the armrest to the right. But as the elastic resistance of the metal accumulated, the centre of rotation unloaded an increasingly more powerful energy on the column, warping it. When he reached the point of return, the cabin, with Bob inside, tilted to such an extent that the Plexiglas exploded and vapour clouds screamed out of the pressurised pipes. The operator remained silent, kneeling on the linoleum, praying with his hands over his head.

Amin released his grip on the pylons of the front pulley and rose to observe the green light at the entrance of the port. He was seized by a spasm, a painful slap as large as his spirit. He risked falling but managed to keep himself balanced. His eyes bathed in shimmering tears. He looked at the *Novosk*, silently moving away in the dark night. He understood that something serious had happened, but he could not put the pieces together. What he had perceived did not seem to make sense. The release of *keh* exploded in the silent air that had washed over him, too vast and too dense to be real. And in that cascade of light there was something incomprehensible yet familiar, which distressed him. Woken ones had died. Getting on the *Novosk*, now, had become an imperative.

He estimated that the distance was over 3000 feet. Many. Too many. But he had no choice. He would not get another chance. "So be it!" he said to the night. Raising his arms, the Shadow Hound gathered up the Universe in himself. His dark eyes became stars and his forehead shone with golden light.

A low vibration shook the air. The metal cables resonated with the vibration, like the strings of a giant harp, and a mournful note, keyed by some divinity of ancient times, manifested itself, turbulent and overbearing. *The Seventh Order of Creation is "Crasis". In 'All that is' nothing prevails and everything changes, thought the Hound. May the Nemesis hit me, if my actions betray Atlantis.*

"I'm Amin Setiana Akenre!" he shouted to 'All that is'. "Atlantis is my land, my creation, my creed. Only you can stop the perfection born of the mind of man. You have your chance!" he cried to the clouds, knowing that these could be his last words. "I fear nothing."

The sky was charged with electric discharges that snaked at low altitude, and then stormed the metal structure of the crane. Lightning growled at Amin, ducking near him.

The eyes of the fallen prince became white and an aura of multicoloured lights emanated from his body, forming rings that enveloped him, taking the form of hundreds of eyes dense as smoke.

The vibration shattered the lights and the spotlights of the area below. The large ship that Bob was loading tilted on its side, crashing and crumbling the concrete quay. The gulls fled rushing in all directions, screeching in terror. "Now!" cried Amin.

Bob stood up and glass fragments slipped down from him. Shaking, he peered in the direction of the arm, where the man had risen above the commotion had started. He saw a strong light appearing in front of him. He didn't have time to realise what he was looking at before the crane gave a violent jolt. Bob's sleeping *keh* would have kept him from remembering, but what he saw filled him with wonder, amazement and fear. A mad, incomprehensible, irrational fear.

When the light disappeared, the end part of the arm froze, yet it had swayed until a moment before. It was as if someone had paused the world at that precise spot where the crane pulley stood. Everything was motionless. The sparks and vapours generated by the torsion of the arm were still, immortalised in a 3D photo. The light emanating from the man's head did not vibrate, and his clothes were motionless in the position impressed by the wind from the east.

But this lasted for the blink of an eye. Then the universe reacted to the Order "Crasis" and the Four Forces changed reality.

The mechanical arm that Bob had used so many times to lift two-hundred-ton heavy mechanical components twisted upward, bending like heated wax. Fragments of the quay were fired into the sky and so did some pieces of the ship.

The mysterious man rose quickly and silently, attracted by the clouds of lightning that had accumulated over the harbour, disappearing through it.

If there was a definition of God, thought Bob, that vision was the closest he would ever witness. Slow and warm tears ran along the Sleeper's face.

The note generated by the cables rose again and again until the vibration became unbearable. When the cabin broke off its base by one or two feet, so as to blow off all the bolts and welds before re-settling with a thud, Bob fell unconscious, overcome by the power of the Oblivion overwhelming his sleeping *keh*. Within a radius of over 100 miles, everyone was struck by the shock wave of that crazy, unnatural and devastating gesture that Amin had generated.

Old Mrs Dinberry, on the other hand, whose decadent apartment overlooked the shipyard, noticed the glow of thunder and got up to pull the few clothes hanging out back inside the house. Huffing at the noise, she turned up the volume of the television.

35

They strolled on the beach, their footprints stretching back toward Stapleton's bar. The evening was a perfect time to walk barefoot. The air was a bit cold, but the sand was still warm. They sat by the water's edge, next to an extension of rocks that kept the slow motion of the waves at bay. For a while, they said nothing.

"I went to town yesterday," Helena broke the silence. "I asked for some time off for health reasons, and they gave it to me. I don't know if it was the right thing to do, but what else was there?"

"You did well," Andrew said.

"I think so too. After all, I can't go back to my everyday life after what I saw… after what I discovered."

"Are you afraid of all this? I mean, of this new… vision of things?"

"I'm afraid of losing control. I feel like a teenager who doesn't know what's up or down." She immediately regretted those words.

The boy understood her embarrassment. "It doesn't matter," he reassured her.

"I'm sorry. I'm not good with young people."

"As a policewoman, you're not bad, though."

Helena smiled.

The wind subsided a bit.

"I'm stunned, as if someone stuffed me into a bag and beat me with sticks."

"Interesting metaphor," he said. "Sometimes I feel like that too. But not as much as if I had heard a story like ours told by someone else. From the outside, it all seems so surreal. But from the inside, it's normal. It's clear how things are going. Mu and Atlantis, the great war. I remember watching an animated movie as a child, *Atlantis*. That was the image I had about it. You know? Half-Greek cities sunk into the sea, monsters of the abyss, petty mythology."

Helena nodded, not that she had seen the movie, but she had shared the youthful vision of the Atlantis myth.

"Now that understanding seems a hundred years away from me," Andrew continued. "The now is real to me; the life I had before, however, appears inconsistent, empty, senseless."

"I guess the only confused teenager here is me, then," said Helena. Andrew Fawcett was much more mature than his age; she had noticed that since their first meeting. Still, his maturity had appeared different, on another track from that of his peers.

"I have no certainties, unfortunately," Andrew was saying. "In front of me sometimes I only see a big black wall. If I stare at it for too long, I feel like it's trying to suck me in. Finding Adam is all that matters. I thought I would have known how by now. Instead the days pass and nothing happens; no signal. I'm starting to think that I can't really help in any way."

"You don't have to take care of everything. It doesn't all depend on you," Helena comforted him.

"I can't tell you why, but I believe it does depends on me. I'm the key, but I don't know where to find the lock," he replied dejectedly.

It was difficult for Helena to tell whether Andrew had introjected Adam's disappearance as a way of making up for his mother's death, or if there were other unfathomable reasons which belonged to the world of the Woken and the Roused ones. The boy was straddling two worlds and she had no access to either of them. "Listen," she said, "I can't tell you what's right and wrong, if I'm honest. I don't feel like it and I don't think we can reduce everything to one or the other. However, I have the highest average of the entire police department when it comes to solving cases."

"Is this a way of telling me that you'll help me?"

"There's no Mu or Atlantis to hold us back. He's still a missing boy. It is my job to find him again and we are a team. We'll do it together."

He looked at her, serious.

She read in those eyes all of Andrew's need to have a certainty, a confirmation of solidity, something "normal" to hold onto. A hope, a help, a participation. "You have my word," she whispered, adjusting his windbreaker's collar.

"Whatever I will decide?"

Why do you speak in the first person? What's on your mind, Andrew? "I won't leave you alone," she commented aloud. "I trust you and I know you can find Adam. Of course, you will have to put up with me. I don't have superpowers!" She joked, giving him her hand, which he took gratefully.

"Do you know they call Saint Paul the 'cursinorme' school now?" the boy changed the subject.

Helena was taken aback for a moment. "And what nonsense is that?"

"I read an article in the paper at Hemmet's house in which they wrote that it is normal for schools like that, full of troubled kids, to have deaths or disappearances. I'm another one of their stats now. Well, the journalist insisted on the need to close such institutions, because they were useless. I think it's wrong to write things like that. There are a lot of people who work hard every day in there. Instead, it's enough for a journalist to write his truth, which then becomes the truth of all. It's too easy to make people believe what you want."

"Journalists are assholes."

Andrew looked at Helena, amazed and amused.

"It's getting cold. What do you say we go back?" she suggested.

He stood up, dusting the sands off his trousers. After walking for about thirty yards in silence, Helena began to whistle. It was a song that Andrew knew, *Over the Rainbow* by Judy Garland. Then she began to sing softly, with a sweet and graceful voice.

"I know this song. My Mum use to listen to this kind of music in the morning, in the car," he recalled with a bitter smile. "It was a real torture. I begged her, but she wouldn't budge."

"I can imagine. Some songs are immortal though, don't you find?"

Andrew thought about it. "You know, I think this was what Mum wanted to tell me. That there are things that last forever."

"I believe that too."

They walked on in silence.

"You look rather young to listen to that music."

"I am young!" Helena pointed out. "Anyway, in my small way I'm a big fan of jazz and blues. In college, I sang in a small group, the GangStar, and we often did covers like *Over the Rainbow*. Would you have guessed?"

He evaluated the policewoman. "Maybe," he replied.

They looked at each other then burst out laughing. Neither had done that since Helena had met Amin on the shores of the lake and Emily had signed the lease of the house on the ground floor of a suburban building.

They reached the only road that crossed the small town.

"Enish asked me to cook something tonight, so I have to go home."

"You like it there?"

"There is a great sense of peace. Enish is very sweet to me and he's a good man. I just hope not to poison him. I'm not great in the kitchen, except for microwave dishes."

After a quick farewell, Helena went to the upper part of the village, from where the dirt path began, which would lead her to the bay where Enish's house stood. Andrew stayed on the street, unsure of what to do. The village was almost deserted. After dinner, someone would likely go to the tavern on the beach, next to the store, to have a drink. Overall, life here was not unlike that of many seaside resorts.

And yet, to the young Fawcett it seemed as if those people lived with a curfew, as if all their existence was in danger and a shadow appeared at nightfall, ready to make that niche of Woken ones and Sleepers disappear.

"Hey, Andy!" he heard someone calling from a window just above the florist.

Lerner Cohen, a short man with thick curly hair, leaned forward from the windowsill, gesturing in his direction. He was wearing a tan coloured jumper with the collar of a white shirt sticking out.

"Hello, Mr Cohen," he answered.

"Have you eaten yet?"

"I haven't thought about it. Got a lot to study. Maybe I'll stop by the tavern."

"Why don't you come here to grab some food? Anna has made a delicious stew. Come on!" he exhorted him.

Andrew entered through the little door of the store and climbed the narrow stairs, guided by the light that spread from an open door on the first floor. The smell of plants was strong and gave the environment a certain flair of serenity.

The house of Lerner and Anna, his wife, was small but tastefully decorated. She was carrying a large steaming pot to the table. Already laid out were durum wheat bread, raw vegetables and wine. Lerner had already sat down and pointed with a smile to the chair next to his.

"Start, I'll be right there," Anna said. She was a round woman, slightly dishevelled but pleasant, always caught up in household chores.

"Thanks," Andrew answered, sitting down.

They began to eat. The stew was really delicious.

"So," the man asked, "how are you?"

"Good, thank you, Mr Cohen."

"A well-mannered boy, I see! You can call us Lerner and Anna," she said, taking a seat. "It makes us feel less old."

"I'm sorry. I'm too formal sometimes."

"Perfectly alright," she laughed, her cheeks full and red from the warmth of the kitchen.

"You are not Woken ones, right?"

The couple looked at each other surprised. "No," they said almost in chorus.

"Then it's true," said Lerner, "that you are able to understand certain things, even if you have not been awakened. How do you do it?"

"Don't be pedantic," Anna said, serving another big ladle of meat to the boy.

"It's no problem. I don't know how I do it. Maybe, in this case, it was just luck."

"No," said Lerner, "I'm convinced you have a special talent."

Andrew shrugged. "When I come into contact with things that have to do with the Woken ones, the answers jump out on their own. It doesn't always happen. Only sometimes."

The two stared at him, then the man began: "Shall we try?"

"To do what?"

"To see what happens."

Andrew felt uncomfortable. The Cohens were nice and kind, but he knew that Abriaros wouldn't like that kind of experiment. "I... I don't think my guide would agree..."

They smiled, a little saddened. "Abriaros is always very cautious. If this place has remained safe for all of us, it is only because of his sound and judicious guidance."

"We owe him a lot. Everything," added Anna.

"And yet," the man said, leaning back, "sometimes I just don't understand him."

"He's a Woken one and a Naacal. I think it's normal not to understand him," said Andrew.

"It happens to you too, right?" Lerner asked.

"Yes..." the boy admitted, more to himself than to the couple.

"I'm sure if Abriaros has advised Andrew not to use his skills, it's only for his own good," Anna said, returning to her food.

Andrew took a sip of wine.

"However," the man continued, "if I had your skills I would be curious to understand them, to probe them. Especially if it is the only chance to find Adam."

The boy stared at him, amazed. "You know Adam?"

The couple looked at him, then smiled uneasily. "Anna and I are his aunt and uncle, dear. To be precise, Anna was Shore's cousin, Adam's mother. We are the only relatives he has left."

Andrew gasped. "But you are not Woken ones. How is this possible?"

"Shore herself was a Sleeper," Lerner explained. "She fell in love with Finn, Adam's father, not knowing what world that immense love would open to her. They were made for each other. When he was born, Adam was a Woken one. Thus says Abriaros. It's not often that a Woken child is born from a mixed couple; it's very rare. But sometimes it happens. And it's a great blessing."

"What happened to Shore and Finn?"

The faces of his guests became gloomy. "I'm sorry, but we'd rather not talk about that."

"Are they dead?" Andrew encouraged them.

Anna sighed, nodding. "Their death is shrouded in mystery and is linked to events that everyone here prefers not to remember."

Andrew wanted to know. He needed to know. But the expression on the faces of Lerner and Anna convinced him there would be no way to get more details at this time. "You must be really upset by Adam's abduction."

Anna looked to the side, her eyes moist, pretending it was the fault of something that had ended up in one eye.

"Very much," said the Lerner. "See, Andrew, when Shore and Finn returned to the Source, we accepted Trummugan's advice to let Adam grow far from here, protected by shivaks, rather than with us. It was a painful choice, but the truth is that we would not have been able to protect him." The man rubbed his hands. "Anna and I could not have children and we loved our nephew. After the tragic event that struck his parents, we became even more attached to him. He was... he's more than a child for us."

"I can't even imagine how you feel. I complain because I would like to do more to find him, because I know I could do more, but I can't understand how. If only I could do something!"

Anna stepped forward. "We know what happened to you, your mother, and we're very sorry for your loss. When we learned of the special bond that exists between you and our nephew, hope returned to us. Adam has always known what he was doing, ever since he was a child. He's very special, you know? But I can't hide from you that even the subtle hope you represent and to which we have gathered all our strength around is waning in anguish. Time passes and we have no news of any kind."

"But there is the Canvas. Everyone knows and will help us," Andrew replied, although he was overcome by the sensation of saying something naive. The two looked at him with an expression that made him uncomfortable.

Lerner took his wife's hand. "The Canvas existed once. Today it is fragmented, so much so that it has become inconsistent. Woken ones and Sleepers live in a desperate condition. Atlantis has created a world in which space for Mu is reduced to a minimum and continues to shrink. Locations like this may appear peaceful to you, but remain places constricted by the Lords of Matter and controlled by the hammer of the Great Intention. We are not free."

Andrew didn't feel like eating anymore.

"The Woken ones who belong to the ancient tradition of Mu live separate from each other," Lerner continued, "except in exceptional cases. There are many who disregard what happens in the world and I don't even feel to judge them for this. You have no idea how powerful the Atlantean machine is. You didn't see what we saw. Non-human peoples are reduced to the brink of extinction. Sikal like Yzenn and Ahiga survive only thanks to their great adaptability, or where they manage to mix with the populations that this world has bound to a state of extreme poverty, in places where neither control nor civil rights exist. Not to mention the giants."

"Except for the Milesians who preside over the *Collegium*, we have not seen others for more than thirty years," added Anna, worried.

"And yet I know that the Canvas exists. I sensed it," Andrew said.

"It exists, it's true," replied Lerner, "but it's too weak and is composed mostly of individuals locked in themselves. It is only an echo of what it was at the beginning. In these conditions, we doubt that it could be useful to bring our nephew home. Many would pull back rather than help us. There is too much fear. This is the real victory of Atlantis."

Andrew felt disconsolate, frustrated and confused. "What kind of war is this, then, if there's only one front? If Mu doesn't fight, how will we manage to find Adam?"

"Only the *Arkanum* can face Atlantis," said Lerner. "At least directly."

"Mu has its own way of dealing with war," Anna added, as if that statement contained larger truths.

The man rubbed his temples, agitated. "You must know that the thought of the Naacal is linked to that of the Mother in a symbiotic way. Try to look at the existence of an individual through the eyes of Life. It has no weight. For Her, millennia are but moments, the creatures all identical, Her very Essence so immense as to be inconceivable to creatures like us. The Naacal filters this immensity and risks getting lost in observation and waits, convinced that one day everything will return to balance. For them, all that needs to be done is to fight to prevent that the damage inflicted on the Mother is so serious as to defeat Her."

"Adam can't wait for millennia!" Andrew protested, heartfelt. "Not even one day, perhaps!"

"Andrew, you bring a blessing with you. There's a special bond between you and Adam. Please help us find our nephew!" Lerner asked with prayerful hands.

"Help us," Anna whispered, taking the boy's hands in hers.

Andrew looked first at one, then at the other. "Tell me what you want me to do."

Lerner's eyes lit up with joy. "You must access Almath, the key to Life."

When he uttered that word, his face was enveloped in white flames and became blurred, while his mouth opened wide, vomiting light. An immense cascade of pure energy crashed into the helpless boy, overwhelming him. Or so it seemed to Andrew.

36

The black sea grew wild and long waves made the *Novosk* swing like a pendulum, ever more dangerously. From above, the big cargo ship appeared in total darkness like a tape, dotted with intermittent and fixed lights. A nullity suspended over endless oceans.

The thick rain accompanied the Shadow Hound in that vertiginous fall, as he tried to fly parallel to the sea, unable to keep his eyes open for the force of the wind slamming in his face at 270 miles per hour. He could hardly breathe and his legs were aching. It was only thanks to the *Orichalcum* that flowed in his veins that he had survived the frost and lack of oxygen due to the high altitude. Pseudo-technology was what raised man above the limits impressed by the Mother, there were no doubts.

By altering the Order "Crasis", Amin had triggered an explosion in reality, inducing the Four Forces to suspend the necessary gravity to allow him to reach a height useful enough to precipitate on the *Novosk*, with a unique and formidable leap. But he couldn't chance anything further, not without running the risk of being noticed or kidnapped by the Nemesis.

He took a breath as best he could and, at 3000 feet, he triggered the pseudo-interface. The first activation level was initialized. At 2000 feet he entered the deep state of consciousness that allowed him to separate the liquid *Orichalcum* from his own blood. The second activation level waited greedily for the Shadow Hound's *keh*. At 1000 feet he impressed on the living metal of Atlantis the idea of the form he had imagined. The third activation level began to drain Amin's vital spark. At 950 feet bands of fluid, purple and reflective metal, thin as hair, extruded from the back of his body, bringing the speed of fall to less than 20 miles per hour in three seconds.

With an imperceptible thud, the feet of the fallen touched the ship, just above the control room. Amin swerved, knocked down by the *Orichalcum*, and his hand found a thick antenna that had bent to give him support.

The control tower was located at the rear end of the *Novosk*, and from there it was possible to observe the whole bridge in its majesty, up to the bow, tucked away between the waves. Hundreds of containers arranged in regular groups formed a rusty metal labyrinth, whose map was only in the hands of the crew. The ship appeared deserted.

The Hound went down and peered through the windows that covered three out of four walls of the cabin. Large wipers tried to free them from seawater and heavy rain without much success. Inside, he saw five people, men and women, stationed at the various control systems. A sixth man was sitting on a large brown leather armchair. He had to be the captain. He wore a hat and had a thick white beard; he seemed to be drinking from a steaming cup, but Amin immediately noticed that he was not carrying it to his mouth. In fact, he was not making any gesture. After a few moments, he realised that none of those present moved at all. Their eyes were open, but they were rigid, immobile.

They seem struck by a glow. Is there a Translator of Light on this ship? he thought.

He slid downstairs while hushing his *keh* until it became a thin line barely audible. He reached the bridge and hid behind some giant cylindrical winches. Nothing seemed to happen and there was no trace of the rest of the crew. The *Novosk* was proceeding in the open sea, adrift. If, as it was almost certainly the case, that condition was induced by Woken ones, the probability that it was the result of a direct order from the prince increased. That kind of interference in the Sleepers' world was considered very dangerous and had to be limited to cases of extreme necessity.

He advanced, shielding himself with the lifeboats anchored to the bridge, up to the first container, and from there he looked at the front of the deck, where the Russian name of the ship stood out. A little further down, just near the only free area of the *Novosk*, he noticed something. It looked like a bunch of clothes huddled against the wall. Amin went through the first row of containers to examine that pile of rags. When the moon broke through for a few seconds to illuminate the deck, the eyes of the hound widened.

"No!" he cried. Even though he knew he was exposing himself, he began to run.

They were not clothes. They were people.

Amin lifted the still warm body contained in the candied robe and stroked the corpse's forehead. "Cornelius!" he called, without expecting an answer.

Everywhere lay bodies of elderly women and men, dressed in a manner similar to the Hound's old mentor. They were Nephilim. Five, six, seven.

The Atlantean took Cornelius' hand and looked at it. Then he studied the other bodies. They had no obvious wounds and there was no trace of blood. Their faces were relaxed, without any sign of suffering. Amran nervàl, *the Death that has no face. Only the Shadow Hounds can kill like this*, he thought.

Immediately afterwards he found what he was looking for. On the ground, scattered without an order, lay seven large rings of gold and *Orichalcum*, broken. And he understood what had caused that wave of Essence that had overwhelmed him on the crane at the shipyard.

The Nephilim pierced their *keh* through those objects, forged in ancient times not by Atlantis but by the giant Thuata de Danann through the Ancient Knowledge of Mu. Killing a Nephilim and then breaking their key to life was equivalent to dispelling the *keh*, condemning them to become reflections of the *lumina*, ghosts unable to return to 'All that is'. The most terrible end for a living being and the most feared by the Woken ones.

But there was a much worse thing. Now that the ancient and wise Nephilim were no longer next to the seven princes of Atlantis, the Translators of Light would acquire enormous power and the Avalons would rely even more on pseudo-technology. Amin grabbed the rings to study them. He could have recognised Cornelius' among a thousand if it had been necessary. It presented a peculiarity, a chip linked to the day when he had been expelled from the Avalon. He had caused it as they tore him away from his life as Atlantean.

He turned Cornelius' ring between his fingers. It was in bad shape, but not destroyed. Maybe something could be done. Perhaps Trummugan would be able to use the Ancient Knowledge to probe the ring in search of Cornelius' *keh*. Perhaps they could save him from becoming a reflection.

"He must do it and he will!" he promised the ring.

Amin became aware of another presence only when he recognised the click of a screaming spear of Evenor opening. The Hound jumped to the side, rolling, and then got back on his feet by leaning on his arms.

The figure, wrapped in a black cloak adorned with *Orichalcum* and covered with a wide hood in raven's feathers, snapped forward, brandishing the spear like a huge scissor. On one of the two blades, the name of Evenor was engraved. The weapon swirled in the air, forming *gorann*'s whirlwinds, scraping sparks from the metal floor of the ship hit by the rain. The duel was about to begin when the hooded figure stopped. The spear closed again.

"Amin?" a female voice called.

It's not possible! He thought.

The figure pulled the hood back and the sad, beautiful face of Athena appeared from that dark dress.

Athena, Widow of the only emperor of Atlantis. Athena, Amin's consort when still he lived among the purest human beings who had ever existed.

They stood looking at each other, unable to utter a single word. Unable to look away. Their *keh*, their Essences, had already locked in a knot made of spirit and there were no words that could replace that mutual belonging. To love, for a Woken one, meant to tie one's destiny to that of one's companion for eternity. Although they had lost their lives as children of Mother Earth, Athena and Amin kept the curse as they were Woken ones.

But something interrupted that inner dialogue. A note of suspicion which Amin sensed.

"What have you done?" she asked, looking at the corpses of the Nephilim.

He wanted to approach her, touch her, breathe in her scent, fill the immense emptiness that had gripped him every day for ten years. But he could not. Between them stood the imperishable and insurmountable Atlantis and the role they both played there.

"I could never hurt Cornelius!"

Athena hesitated. "Who, then?"

"Nobody except for the Brotherhood of Shadow could do this. Someone wants to frame me. And it seems they have succeeded."

She looked at him, pervaded by a thousand different sensations that she could not bear or contain.

"Believe me," he said with his eyes steady, as if from that request depended a sentence of life or death.

That's what you said when they took you away from me. Believe me. And I believed you, my love. "Amin, I am a widow of the emperor. I can believe you, but I still have to take you to the Avalon with me. Atlantis comes before my feelings for you."

"Athena, think, I beg you. Who would gain from destroying the Nephilim? I certainly won't. Someone has made a pact with the slaves of Belial on one side and the Shadow Hounds on the other to find and kill that little boy from Mu. When they realised that I had discovered something, they made sure to stop me from communicating with the Avalon or the House of Time, and they ordered this trap to eliminate me. Only I know what is happening and, if I disappear, these rebel traitors will attack Atlantis from within."

"It's impossible. Atlantis is perfect."

"You must know why the Nephilim gathered on this Sleeper ship."

Athena hesitated. "No. Nobody knows. It was a secret meeting. I followed Cornelius because I perceived that something was wrong, but I do not know the reason for the meeting."

"Perhaps Cornelius suspected something and wanted to share it with the other sages."

"What are you planning, Amin? Oppose Atlantis?"

"I intend to do my duty and fight for Atlantis, not against it. First of all, I have to understand what happened to Cornelius. Look! His passing ring is still recoverable. I will get help and I will return him on this plane of existence. With Cornelius, I am sure, we can unveil what is happening."

"Mu will never help you."

"They will, because only in this way will I be able to bring the boy back to them."

"Know this. The interest of Atlantis is now focused on the other boy, the Sleeper, who seems to be able to return the disappeared son of Mu."

"Andrew? How does Atlantis know of him?"

Athena shook her head. "Atlantis reigns, Amin."

The Hound was incredulous. "Is there a traitor in Mu?"

"They will send a huge force to get him. The eight army of the Kaiser Daimantis Aidele has been mobilised."

"Are you serious?"

"The strategists know about the presence of the *Arkanum* and don't want to waste time. The Ghenos Knights have already received the baptism of war from the Translators of Light. And the Onagros are in motion to contain the event in the world of the Sleepers."

"Do they intend to raze the whole town to the ground?"

"This will depend on Mu."

"No. The strategists know that the *Arkanum* will react to the provocation. I have to stop this madness. If Andrew were also killed there would be no way to find Adam again, and this would be equal to a conviction for him, as well as the victory of those who plot against Atlantis."

"Come back with me to the Avalon," she said, trying to speak over the sound of the rain that had begun to pour. "We will explain everything. I'm sure—"

"If I returned to the Avalon, now that Cornelius is gone, I would be executed. Athena, you must let me go."

The Widow stared at him. For the first time, she realised how much Amin had changed. While maintaining his splendour, he was clouded by a veil of suffering that crossed his Essence and his body. Something in him had disappeared forever, taken away by an unjust accusation, a machination against him. She had no proof, it was true. But she didn't need any; her heart knew the truth. Amin would never betray Atlantis, at the cost of his life. At any cost. He was Atlantis and there was no distinction between the man and the idea. They were one.

Suddenly, a strong vibration in the Essence surprised them both.

The Valkyrie looked up at the thundering sky.

"The Brotherhood," Amin said. "It has come to claim my life, with the blessing of the Translators of Light." He activated the pseudo-interface, feeding it with the "Structure" Order. *In everything that is, everything is unique, unrepeatable and nothing but itself*, he thought.

The *Orichalcum* galvanised itself with that amazing concentration of Essence and Amin directed it to become something that it had not evoked for a long time. Cycles of living metal wrapped around the vital organs of the Hound, taking the form of a complex armour with golden and purple reflections, sculpted by Essence, forged by pseudo-technology, as thin as a garment. A mask protected his head. Pure light emerged from the forehead and, from the empty sockets of the mask, the eyes of the fallen man became doors to the Universe.

Athena saw what Amin had been reduced to. A shadow bent on the defeat from the failure of one's existence. "No!" she begged.

The Hound's voice had changed, low and vibrant, a threat soaked with living metal that came from the depths of its dark *keh*. "I will not let them touch you. I can take half of them with me to the Source before I succumb. You must return to the Avalon and convince the prince to defend Atlantis from the threat looming over it."

Athena ran to meet him, taking his face in her hands.

Time seemed to slow down. "My love, my husband," she called. "Look at me." Their eyes drew from each other, closer again.

"Do not be afraid for my life," Athena assured him. "I'm not at risk. But you are. If you ask me to believe you, I will. But if you stay here, you will be killed and I would rather think of you lost in that absurd world of Sleepers than to look at yet another injustice perpetrated on you. You will not go back to the Source today. It is not yet time. Go now and do what you believe must be done. I will stall them, try and understand what's happening. Do not worry for me. Please."

The rumble of thunder turned them away. The spirals of *Orichalcum* retracted into Amin's body in a moment. "Athena," he whispered, full of shame as he walked away.

The sad eyes of the Widow followed him as he reached the parapet of the *Novosk*. Once again they separated; then he jumped into the stormy sea.

She returned to examine the corpses, heart galloping. Athena tried to analyse the scene of the crime, knowing she had only a fraction of a second available. The rings of the Nephilim had been broken. It was not an easy feat. To do this, an extraordinary energy was needed. She took them and put them in a safe container.

"My lady," Tutmos greeted her from the shadows.

She didn't even turn. "Hound," she returned coldly. "What is the Brotherhood of Shadow doing here?"

"We were on the trail of Amin and we followed him here."

"Really?"

"The road he has taken is unbecoming, don't you find?"

Athena did not answer.

"It is a big disappointment to me," Tutmos continued. "You, who know him well, what do you think is going through his mind?"

All around appeared numerous other hounds, in combat gear.

"I don't like this conversation."

"We are only following the commands of your prince. Don't you want to collaborate?"

"I doubt that the most Pure prince, my brother, has given such a command. Now step aside, I must arrange the return of the bodies and report to the Avalon."

Some of the hounds approached, tightening the circle around the Widow.

"As far as we know, Amin has exterminated the Nephilim, attracting them here with the excuse of possessing false information about a conspiracy within the prince's Avalon."

"I'm missing something. Your inquiries do not concern me. And anyway, I do not see Amin here."

"No, but he was. And you let him go."

"Your accusations are impertinent. If you have suspicions about my conduct, you can express them to the judges. As long as you do not perish on the journey and that they welcome a fallen like you in the Chamber of Time."

Tutmos touched one of the corpses, thoughtful. "I will. But since Amin has been responsible for such an intolerable act, letting you go, I would risk going against my orders. For the Brotherhood, you are his accomplice. You represent a danger to Atlantis." He gestured towards the other hounds. "Take her," he ordered. Athena pulled back, covering herself with the hood. Her spear hissed, opening. "How dare you to accuse a Pure one? You, who don't even have the right to place your gaze on me, Tutmos? You must have forgotten who you are. And above all, you've made the grave mistake of forgetting who I am."

"The good of Atlantis is more important than its laws."

"Atlantis is its laws." Athena's eyes blazed and a circle of golden light radiated from the back of her neck.

"Don't do it. You're alone against us," threatened Tutmos.

She carried the screaming spear behind her back and assumed the position of a twelve-thousand-year-old fighting technique. "Is that what you believe?" she answered.

The floor of the ship shook under the feet of the hounds. Heels of metal beating on containers. Hisses of dozens of screaming spears echoed across the *Novosk*. And a whole legion of widows aimed their weapons in the direction of the traitor, facing them.

"We only respond to our emperor. He is our only reason for existence," they proclaimed in one voice. "We are bound to secrecy, one to the other. Whatever happens, until Evenor returns!" thundered the Valkyries, while lightning skimmed the skies.

Athena gave a growl of pure *keh*. "Now, Tutmos, tell me, do you really want to face Evenor's chosen guard on Mother Earth?"

37

The compact and powerful mass slid swiftly into the depth of the ocean, fluid, as if the water refused to adhere to it, five times deeper than what new Sleepers' submarines could reach. Still, the most extraordinary difference that ran between the two was something else entirely. A submarine needed continuous maintenance and could hope for a thirty-year service period. The great pseudo-technological machine that sailed through the ocean had been working for ten thousand years and could do it again without ever being serviced. Silent, invisible and lethal.

Keizer Daimantis Aidele entered the great hall of marble and shining *Orichalcum*, announced by its commanders, the red cloak touching the ground. His perfect and radiant face was exposed to the radius of the navigation sphere of the sub, which struck him with its purple and pulsating glow. Inside it, immersed in the caustic light, three men floated. They wore thin, semitransparent suits adorned with gold filaments. A cord of precious metals connected them, suspended in the marine liquid held in that bubble by the unnatural forces generated by the pseudo-atlantean technology.

The crew waited for their Keizer, kneeling on one leg to salute their leader. Low vibration was felt everywhere, propagated by the pseudo-technological engine located in the centre of the machine.

"Atlantis reigns!" was the chorus that greeted Aidele with one voice, in a forgotten language.

"And the Great Intention will be fulfilled," replied the Keizer, following the ritual greeting, pleased and at the same time detached. Then he turned to his commanders: "Give me the details."

One of them waved and the crew rose, returning to their stations.

"We have entered a cycle in the reign of Prince Neime Resilien XXIV, with his approval, very pure Keizer. The Sleepers' activities have been redirected without obstacles and there was no violent reaction from the lower peoples of the Mother. They are under our control."

Daimantis remained impassive. "Learn that the Mother is not and will never be under our control, at least until the Great Intention is fulfilled, Septen."

"Your word is pure, Keiser."

"The wild Mother watches us, always. And is always waiting for the moment when we are weak to crush us. Even now I feel it, as She follows us with the unconscious eyes of the creatures creeping in the seas," he said in a low voice. "The inferior peoples can't fight against pseudo-technology, but She can do things you wouldn't even imagine."

"Forgive me, Keiser."

"The Ghenos Knights?" he asked another commander.

"Immersed in the addictive liquid. The synchronisation of the echo-tympanum is almost finalised and the resonance systems of the *keh* have all been delivered by the Translators of Light."

"Excellent. I don't expect strong resistance, so we will not use Ghenos Knights to begin with. When we are in position, send the messenger. We will give those who once we called brothers the chance to deliver us the Sleeper without facing an unequal fight."

"Keizer, oh very Pure!"

"Speak, commander."

"There is a real possibility of active resistance from members of the *Arkanum*. It could be a trap."

"It would be crazy. Still, if that was the case, it would prove a wonderful opportunity to remind Mu why Atlantis reigns over the world, Gaimnes," Daimantis replied, approaching the sphere of control. "However, we have no interest in engaging the Sleepers in a clash against the *Arkanum*. We'll leave them the first move and the responsibility to decide their destiny. Atlantis must defend those who dwell in Oblivion, as long as it is possible. Nevertheless, I welcome your perplexity; send with the messenger a support unit. Ghenos Knights, with murmodna exoskeletons. But they shall remain on the sidelines until further orders."

"Keizer," a third commander intervened, older than the other two.

Daimantis nodded.

"Information about the presence of a Shadow Hound has also been confirmed. It seems that he, for obscure reasons, might decide to try to defend the people of Mu and the *Arkanum*. The fallen is called..."

"Amin," said Daimantis, thoughtfully. "I know."

The three commanders looked at each other.

Aidele would not have liked to say what he was about to say, but there was no choice. Those who endangered Atlantis had to face the consequences. "If he were to attack our forces," he said, "do not hesitate to destroy him."

"Your order is perfect, Keizer," the commanders answered.

Daimantis shook himself from the reflective state that had slowed his momentum for an instant. He tapped his fist on the palm of his hand. "Warn the Translators of Light to arm the constrictor. I want that Sleeper on this *schugan* before dawn," he ordered. He turned away, leaving the navigation sphere, the red cloak grazing the polished marble of the floor.

*

The wind quieted down. The stars were clouded by dense clouds full of promises of lightning and soft rumbles that sprang from the belly of the skies.

Trummugan was furious; with every step he covered the length of a small car. Arriving at the only intersection of the city, he was welcomed by Abriaros. The two exchanged glances, continuing towards the flower shop. From the dark roof of one of the white houses that faced the street, Yzenn and Ahiga jumped down with agility, in their natural form and prone on their four limbs, the thick fur on their back raised by tension. The giant rushed against the window of Lerner and Anna, spreading it open with a hand and pulling the hinges apart as if they were paper.

"Where is he?" he thundered into the first-floor parlour while the Sikals went in.

The man and woman were cowering in the opposite corner of the room, an expression of bewilderment and fear painted on their faces. Their eyes were fixed on a specific point to the left of the giant. Yzenn and Ahiga entered the hall, clutching the ceiling, which gave way under the strong grip of their long claws.

Andrew lay right next to the radiator that stood under the window. He was shaking, his face contracted in a grimace of pain.

"What have you done?" the giant roared again.

Anna mumbled incomprehensible, shocked words. Lerner tried to defend himself. "Nothing, Trummugan. Nothing!"

"We have felt the scream of pain of his Essence from the beach, you fools!"

"We just wanted to help Adam!"

"Reckless fools!" the giant barked at them as he laid Andrew in Abriaros' arms.

"We only talked to Andrew about Almath. We thought that in this way he could help Adam," Lerner mumbled, his voice broken by tears. "But as soon as we uttered the word, he turned from his chair and began to beat himself and throw himself against the walls. Then he collapsed and started to moan. Streaks of light came out of his forehead as he called his mother. Oh God! Oh my God!"

"You just talked to Andrew of Almath, Sleeper? What are you hiding?" Abriaros asked in a voice so loud as to knock the plates off from the table still set for dinner. People began to appear at the windows of neighbouring houses.

"They said that if we handed them the boy, they would return Adam home!" Anna replied, trying to calm her husband.

"You'd sell us to enemy?" asked Yzenn in amazement.

"You've done worse than that!" cut in the giant. "You have signposted Andrew to who knows what force that waits to unleash its destructive power over the whole town! With whom did you bargain, wicked Sleepers?"

The two wavered. "Hounds," they answered.

Ahiga destroyed the table with a mighty bite, smashing the four inches of thick wood with a deafening pop. "Amin betray us. I never trust Hount!" he shouted, full of rancour.

Trummugan stared at the Sleepers with white, thin eyes full of contempt. "Have you made arrangements with the Hound bearing the name Amin?"

"No!" Anna protested.

"They approached us this morning while we were travelling to the city to refuel. I'm sorry!" said her husband in despair. "The big Canvas is so weak…"

"Who approach?" Yzenn growled.

"The same ones who want to eliminate Amin," intervened Abriaros, without letting them answer, his voice calm and flat. He looked outside, towards the dark sea, marked only by the subdued sound of waves on the nearby rocks. Nothing seemed to move. "Now that they have marked his *keh*, they can spot Andrew easily. They're getting ready to take him," he said to Abriaros.

"Yzenn, Ahiga!" called the Naacal. The two Sikal jumped out of the window. "Take a quick patrol around the village and on the coast. And be prudent, brothers."

They nodded, disappearing in a moment up the outer walls of the store.

"We need the *Arkanum*! Let's call them and they will defend us," Anna said.

"No," the giant answered sharply. "A reaction is what they want. We must not provide them with an excuse to attack. From now on, you two will stay at home, whatever happens. Understood?"

"Forgive us," the traitors whispered.

Trummugan abandoned Lerner and Anna alone with their desperation and crouched beside the Naacal. "How is he?" he asked kindly.

"I cannot say it. He's struggling between the *lumina* and reality, crushed by the Four Forces. Except for Adam, nobody knows the secrets of this boy. Who knows what Almath's vision has triggered in him, at what depth of his being it has opened the doors of awakening? Andrew is not like other Sleepers. Even one word can trigger unpredictable reactions in him. Perhaps even induce awakening… or bring him to death," replied Abriaros gloomily.

"Can you do something for him?"

"He's so fragile right now that I'm afraid to even touch him," he said, brushing his face. Then he lowered his voice, while a vibration invaded the air, electrifying it. "Mother," said the Naacal, "you alone know the heart of 'All that is'. There are no privileges in your womb, but you hear the song of your son Abriaros asking you to turn your gaze on this boy, Andrew. He is an extraordinary young man whose willingness to be near You exceeds the barriers of Oblivion. Look at him with Your infinite love, Mother. Raise him from his weakness!"

The vibration grew louder. Trummugan leaned against the wall so as not to fall. It was not the world that trembled, but the living *keh* of the Mother Earth.

Abriaros narrowed his eyes, listening intently. His body shone with symbols, written around his limbs, like blue fire tattoos imprinted in the physical and mental world of the Naacal. A solar crown blazed on his head and his eyes dilated with golden light.

A wind of Essence upset the *keh* of the giant and the Naacal and a powerful breath shook them, almost ripping them from the physical body.

"It's not time to go back to the Source, brother," the old man told the boy. Some filaments that extruded from the symbols on Abriaros' arms pierced the skin down to the hands, then continued onto Andrew's face.

The young man's eyes widened, filled with endless stars. Then they went out.

The Naacal kept looking at the boy. "Recognise him, Mother. He is Your son. Do not let the works of human beings who are against You distract You from Your universal wisdom. Do not let them blind You, preventing You from seeing how much there is in him… This creature is special and You must, must give him the chance to prove it!"

The sounds emitted by his words seemed to be fluidising in the symbols that shone on his body and then slipped away, volatilising in the ether. "Mother!" he cried. "Recognise Your son!" Andrew convulsed and coughed violently. The air entered his lungs like burning gas and he emitted a suffocating rattle that made him bend over himself. All the accumulated energy was dispersed in a ring of white fog.

Trummugan smiled and nodded.

Abriaros sat down, supporting the boy in his arms, exhausted.

"Wherever he went, Andrew was still very close to the Mother. But I cannot perceive his *keh*."

"The boy has not woken up," the giant confirmed.

"Maybe that's why he'll be able to save himself."

Suddenly, the headlights of a car from the hinterland illuminated the road and a light sedan slipped into the main street of town, slowing down to approach the Naacal and the giant. A man in his late twenties peeked out of the electric window. His wife, sitting next to him, was protesting with a map in her hands. On the backseat, a child of perhaps two years began to mumble excited words, however incomprehensible, to Trummugan.

"Excuse me," said the man, impatiently. "We have lost our way to the motorway. Can you help us?"

The Naacal struggled to follow the question, then answered calmly. "You have to go back and turn left at the intersection with the traffic light. Then continue straight up to the petrol station and turn right there. Continue and you will find the motorway."

"Thank you," the man replied. Then he noticed Andrew. "Everything alright?"

Abriaros didn't flinch. "Everything's fine. He suffers from epilepsy, unfortunately, but it is nothing serious. He will recover soon."

The man didn't seem convinced, but preferred not to meddle – the country was a strange place and it was better to mind one's own business. As he closed the window, they heard him scolding his wife, perhaps for not listening to him. The child continued to stare at the giant while his father manoeuvred.

"The sacred symbols guarding the town are still intact," said Abriaros as he watched the car disappear into the night. "For the moment everything is silent."

"We need to take Andrew off the road," suggested the giant.

"Trummugan, if Atlantis intends to attack the town, we must evacuate everyone."

"I know. I have already instructed Shaun to warn our brothers and prepare to leave, for safety."

"Good. Go with them; I will stay here. I'm sure I can find a diplomatic solution."

Trummugan smiled. "Thank you for your availability, rather than not, Naacal, but you don't believe to be better than me in terms of diplomatic abilities, do you?"

"No, brother," Abriaros replied, loading Andrew on his shoulders.

"Alas, Mu needs more giants than men. We are still many, you are few."

"Thank you for reminding me," Trummguan joked, scratching his bristly beard. "Still, I will not miss this meeting with Atlantis. I want to be able to greet some old acquaintances."

Abriaros shook his head. The giant released him from the weight of Andrew and walked towards the studio where the boy had spent his endless afternoons bent over the books.

"We must prevent them from taking him at all costs," said the Naacal. "There is much more to him than we can even imagine."

"I agree with you," replied Trummugan, looking at Andrew, who now seemed to sleep. The symbols impressed by Abriaros still burned on his boyish feature. And, in the soul of this living creature, Mother had impressed Her image.

PART SIX

ENDLESS LIFE

"To reach dawn, there's no other way than night."

Kahlil Gibran

38

"Andrew, honey. Wake up!"

Andy opened his eyes, a little at first. Then wide.

"Mum!" he said, throwing his arms around Emily's neck. He stroked her face and hair and kissed her a thousand times, clasping her face in his hands.

She smiled at him. "It's late. You must get up."

The boy hugged his mother tearfully, feeling her hair caressing his face and plunging into the scent of sandalwood it gave off. "I missed you so much!" he told her with infinite sweetness. "I'm sorry if I wasn't good to you. I didn't understand. But now… yes, now I understand, Mum."

Emily looked at him with a smile full of love, a love that enveloped Andrew, making him feel light and safe. "I missed you too, my darling," she said. "But now listen to me; there's someone who wants to talk to you."

He sat up on the bed and realised he was dressed. He thought he was dreaming, but he didn't care. He was back with his mother. Obediently, he got out of bed and, just to be sure, hugged Emily again.

They left the room together and reached the living room. It was nighttime. The warm lights brought him back to a simple life full of reassuring innocence. It was a pleasant sensation, at the same time uncomfortable and narrow.

"There's no one here," the boy said.

With an agile leap, a tiny figure jumped first on the hand, then onto Emily's shoulder.

"Mamuk?" Andrew called. The little monkey stared at him with deep and mysterious amber eyes. "Does it want to talk to me?"

"Yes, honey."

"Now I know I'm dreaming."

"You're not dreaming, love."

"Mum, you would never let a monkey sit on your shoulder. And Mamuk certainly can't talk," Andy said with the kind of sarcasm possible only in the allegorical version of dreams, where everything mixes without needing a logical thread. Then a flash of uneasiness surprised him and reality fell on him, banal and unexpected. "Also," he continued with the pain surfacing in his heart, "this house no longer exists."

Mamuk looked at the woman. "You're not dreaming," she continued. "This house exists because you have lived here, because in it are your memories, your dreams and your emotions. And mine."

"If this is not a dream, then what is it?" he asked, touching the sofa, perceiving with his fingers the imperfections as he remembered them.

Mamuk stared at him.

"'All that is'," Emily replied. "You are immersed in 'All that is', according to your ability to perceive it."

Andrew looked first at the animal, then at his mother. "Am I dead?"

"No, Andy."

"Who are you?"

"I'm your mother, as you remember me. There is no place yet in you to see me for what I have been, in my entirety, as a human being. This does not stop me from loving you, my darling. But it's not the time to talk about us, trust me."

Andrew nodded. Somehow his mind was prepared for that unexpected event. "Why am I here?"

Emily caressed her son's face. "You have to find out for yourself, honey."

The monkey nodded her agreement.

"I don't understand."

"Mamuk believes there's something here that you think you've forgotten, something essential to find Adam."

Adam! thought Andy, looking around. He was tempted to go open the door to see what was on the other side, but he was sure he would only find the landing, perhaps with the janitor swiping the floor. No, it didn't seem like a dream. The presence of his mother no longer focused all of his attention, so strong was the feeling that she was not really dead and that he could see her as often as he wished. The awareness of her loss in the explosion was a fact, like the rising of the sun or the tides, no longer a conveyor of emptiness and loss. In him grew the idea that the woman had never really belonged to him, that before being "his" she was a living being born from 'All that was' then returned to it.

Almath, Andrew thought fearlessly, letting what he knew came to the surface. *A word pronounced by the Ancient Knowledge. The breath of the Mother. Yes. The key to life is none other than the Essence of Mother Earth, giver of life, the will of existence that attracts the vital spark from the Source.*

He smiled, looking at his Mum. She was different, but this didn't scare him. She was still his beloved mother, who had carried him in her womb, protected him and looked after him for fourteen years; who had focused on him all the frustrations for an unrequited love and a life that had not gone the way she had wanted. But she was also a shining living being of the *keh*, attracted to Almath, to the Source, the same to which she had later returned when her physical structure had been destroyed. "I love you, Mum, and I will always love you," he told her.

Emily smiled in a way Andrew had not seen for a long time, perhaps as she had never smiled during her life.

"I know, honey, and I love you too," she replied, "infinitely."

There was nothing else to say.

Mamuk jumped on the boy's shoulder. "Let's find Adam," he said to it then, and began to think, walking around the room. *Something I forgot*, he thought.

He went around the living room first, then into the other rooms. He looked out of the window, where he could see the net between the gardens and the intricate plants tangled on Adam's side. At first, memories of his everyday life came to mind: the move, the boxes. Then he remembered the first meeting with the boy who would change his life forever and that time when he understood that Mamuk was going back and forth between their houses, stealing the cereals. He thought of Helena and her visit in search of information, and the rainy day when, shut in the bathroom, he had cried for the anguish he had felt in hearing the words spoken by Kyle in front of the hospital.

What was he missing?

He fell onto the sofa and leaned back, closing his eyes for a moment. The television. A movie by Fincher. The nightmare in which he had dreamed of the grave, a hand that dragged him down and the light that brought him back until he woke up. The fruit juice drank in the living room one night that he had woken up. And still the boxes. Then he sprang up and went to his room, and Mamuk made a shrill sound of triumph, jumping on his shoulder.

They got to the shelf with the DVDs. "Here it is!" Andrew cried. He grabbed the box set of a series that his father had refused to watch with him, in the name of the superior quality of the first version – the same one that had so mysteriously fallen to the floor, in the middle of the night – and opened it. He took out the discs, throwing them on the ground with all their booklets. Then he saw it.

He let go of the case, holding a piece of paper in his hands. On it were a series of symbols, quite similar to those that Adam had left when he had shown him how to reach him on the hill behind the buildings.

They were incomprehensible symbols, but not for Andrew.

His friend, his brother Adam, had somehow foreseen everything that would happen and had left him a map of the place where he would be taken. He had hidden it in a memory, which was alive and pliable in the universal mind of 'All that is'.

Andy went back to the living room. "You put it in the box, didn't you, Mamuk?" he said. "It was you who made it fall."

The monkey bared its teeth enthusiastically.

"Mum?" Andrew called.

"Yes, my darling?"

"How do I get back to the other side?"

Emily smiled.

39

When the door swung open, Abriaros did not even turn, but kept looking at the lighthouse that shone in the darkness beyond the reassuring lights of the town's main street.

"Naacal," Amin called him. "You must leave immediately. An army of Prince Here is approaching. They came to take the boy."

"We know," answered the old man. "Wasn't that what you wanted?"

The Hound, soaked from head to toe, hesitated. "What I want does not matter. My job is to find Adam and bring him to the Avalon. Dark forces threaten Atlantis from within. They've convinced my prince that Andrew is a necessary player."

"Even so you, will accomplish your plans. What do you worry about?"

Amin stepped forward and noticed the boy lying on the bed, unconscious. "Abriaros, if this young man is taken, he will not reach the Avalon alive. The Brotherhood of Shadow has made a pact with one or more Translators of Light. Perhaps even with Belial. I do not know why and I can hardly fathom the reasons, but it is their goal to prevent the finding of Adam. Or delay it, so as to get to him first and kill him."

The Naacal looked at him. "Atlantis and Mu await an event that has not happened since the Great Gorann, both in their own way. Us, the advent of a new Ra Mu, the creature that can bring back the ancient dialogue between the Mother and her children. You, the return of Evenor, the emperor philosopher from whom the thought of Atlantis originated. Adam could be the answer to both of these expectations. We are not so different, you see? On the other hand, we cannot say for certain whether he really is the ra and you haven't had the chance to know if he represents a new guide for your people. However, he is a single living thing. Therefore, one of us is wrong."

"What are you saying, Naacal? Evenor cannot be born in Mu. It must come from the heart of Atlantis, from the pure who are its legitimate descendants!"

Abriaros snorted, "So why so much clamour for a boy born in a remote town?"

"You try to pull the wool over my eyes!" Amin was furious.

"I say what I think. And I think that the word *Atlantean* is only the definition that you have tried to impose on a category which ultimately is always part of the Third People, that of human beings. As far as I'm concerned, even before ra or emperor, Adam is a living being who must be able to choose his destiny. Just like Andrew."

"Why do you waste time then? You must take him away immediately."

"It's useless. Someone made sure that his *keh* was marked. Moving him would not make sense; they'd find him anyway."

"Do you want to stop Atlantean combat units? The time of the Great Gorann is long gone, if you hadn't noticed. The Mother cannot protect you."

"We will try diplomacy. Trummugan is a Milesian; they will listen to him."

Amin turned around, agitated. "No. They will not. You will be returned to the Source, all of you. Mu will perish in the Oblivion, as it always was."

"This should not be a problem for you, Hound," said Abriaros.

"It is not, but I have to fulfil the prince's orders. And if you all get killed, I will not be able to find Adam before the Brotherhood of Shadow or Belial's followers. Where is the giant?"

"You'll find him at the dock. He's organising the evacuation of our Sleeper brothers along with the others."

Amin took one last look at Andrew and went out into the corridor, leaving the study.

In the street, many people were already busy loading their belongings in their cars and vans, silently marked by worry and anguish. The Hound remembered a winter of seventy years ago, in a different country. The same expression painted on the faces of men, women and children strung like animals in long convoys destined for extermination camps, factories that transformed human beings into shoes and soap. These were the fragments of a price that sleeping humanity had always paid whenever Belial's followers had succeeded in taking the lead, circumventing the princes or with their approval, to resolve the conflicts in Atlantis. It had happened endless times since the time of the Great Gorann, and it would happen again.

The Sleepers have no memory, he thought. *They live their existence as if they had no responsibility or legacy to be left to later generations. Where does such inhuman behaviour come from? This is not Atlantis…*

When he reached the pier, he had to make way between the people who came to meet him. In front of the emporium some groups had formed, which stopped just long enough to listen to the giant's few words, then returned in a hurry to their homes. There was tension in the air. Shaun, Enish and Helena helped Trummugan.

When she saw him, the policewoman went to him. "Amin, thank

God you're here. Do something to stop this madness!"

"I cannot do anything."

"But how? It's your people who want to attack us."

"Helena, I suggest you leave. There's still time. What do you care about these strangers? Soon there will be only rubble here."

She looked at him, unbelieving. "Is there a heart beating in there, Atlantean? Or did you replace it with some fucking pseudo-something?" she attacked him.

"This is my advice," he said simply.

Helena pushed him, but Amin did not move.

"What the fuck are you saying? Even I can understand that being here is the right thing to do. Even not knowing what's happening to me! These people need all the help they can get, as they are suffering a horrible injustice. And you, very Pure son of your damn Atlantis, you can't even understand why we have to stay? Andrew almost died to find a link that would lead him to Adam, out of friendship! Because of a human feeling!" She rubbed her hand under her nose, dripping from the cold, to calm down. "No. You have no feelings, Amin. You and all the Atlanteans are machines. You have rejected the most basic characteristics that make human beings such. I don't know anything about your war, it's true. And I can't understand what is it that makes you fight for ten thousand years at the expense of all of us Sleepers. But I still get why staying now is the right choice!" She turned her back on him and return to help the villagers.

Amin stood there, brushed by the people who came and went that didn't know who he really was. Helena's speech was childish and naive, though full of energy and pride; he would give her that. But the state of affairs didn't change. He had lived through similar situations a thousand times and knew how it would end. Atlantis would crush everything.

Someone shouted, pointing to the sea.

Beneath the surface, no more than 300 yards away, greenish glows stretched and neared slowly. The inhabitants began to leave in a panic, though the people of Mu were still trying to maintain some order. Yzenn and Ahiga emerged from the crowd, approaching the Hound. Ahiga was carrying something between his huge jaws.

"Happy you see family?" Yzenn whispered, pointing to the iridescent waters.

Ahiga threw a flimsy corpse to the floor, covered with a purplish liquid that gushed from deep wounds. Amin leaned over the little body. "Mayaurli."

"Belial invitet to party, huh?" Ahiga said, showing teeth dirty of *Orichalcum*.

"Sikal, there may be bad blood between us, but the followers of Belial will try to take advantage of Keizer Aidele's attack to get Andrew. We cannot allow it."

"Since you care for Sleeper?"

"I warned you."

The Sikals turned to Trummugan, who watched the scene. The giant nodded, casting a murderous glance at Amin, and the two snapped in the direction of the study, galloping among the fleeing people. The Milesian took a few steps towards the shore. Behind him were Shaun, Enish and Helena.

The greenish glow had just disappeared when the water rippled. At first, a dark shadow spilt onto the beach. Thousands of crabs fled to the mainland, slipping through the few people who remained to wait for the arrival of Atlantis. Then a sort of spherical machine with an irregular surface, bronze-coloured and no larger than a minivan, rose from the shimmering sea, releasing waves of faint purple light. A long vibration, similar to the one emitted by a chorus of didgeridoos, invaded the air and the sand began to slither under that impulse.

Enish held Helena, who was shaking.

With a metallic clang, the front part of the pseudo-technological machine shook itself, separating into several components according to a twisted and incomprehensible system. From the inside appeared a bent figure, wearing a long dark dress, rich in metallic ornaments woven like silk. A high biconical hat concealed part of the face, which was covered by a perforated veil and showed only the lower part of the mouth. It was a thin mouth of an unnatural indigo colour.

The figure came forward, but didn't step onto the beach. He seemed suffering, strained in his effort to hold on to a long, burnished metal rod.

Amin moved to meet him. He had to expect it. Without the Nephilim, the task of messengers passed to the Translators of Light. Especially when there was little to discuss.

"Fidias," he said, disgusted and surprised.

Shaun took a step back.

A metallic rattle came out at once from the tumorous purple mouth of the telluric, who dried it with a silk bundle woven into complex weave. "I offer myself as a messenger from Prince Here Paneb Akenre XLVI and by order of his Keizer, Daimantis Aidele. I carry with me the perfect word of the Purest. He wishes to thank the people of Mu for supporting Atlantis in his search of and for guaranteeing the protection of the young Sleeper, Andrew Fawcett."

Trummugan inhaled with a twist of his nose.

"I'm here to take the boy. Just as I'm here to take the Shadow

Hound, Amin the fallen," he added, without even looking at him.

There were no reactions.

Fidias continued in a shrill voice: "Accept these conditions and there will be no consequences. The prince, in his Pure benevolence, has indeed disposed to take better care of this community of Mu, favouring its liberties."

At that point, the giant spoke. "Messenger of the prince, I am Trummugan Ammun of the race of the Milesians, descendants of the wise Thuata De Danann. To say that we are honoured by your presence would be a lie you'd not believe. We expected to have a peaceful meeting, but your presence here insults the very earth on which, with wisdom, you refuse to set your foot upon. Mu's peaceful people are willing to dialogue with you, but only with an interlocutor who can understand our reasons and will bring us the exact thought of his prince. It cannot be a telluric to do that. Organise for us a meeting with a Nephilim and Atlantis will find us ready to reason. Mu does not speak with tellurics. We will not accept this provocation and I am certain that your Prince would not suffer it either. Decide wisely, Translator of Light." And he turned his back to the Atlantean messenger.

Amin kept staring at Fidias sternly. He deserved death, but there was nothing he could about it.

"There are no Nephilim to talk to," replied the Translator of Light with false displeasure. "But you, don't you dare turn your back on me, abominable deformity!" he croaked, spitting out purple liquid.

Helena watched the giant, who, undaunted, continued on his way.

A rose petal had touched her face, making a pirouette right in front of her. But it was not immediately clear to her that there was something unnatural in that movement. The thin leaf, in fact, proceeded against the wind.

"Fidias," Amin was saying. "Whatever you have in that mind of yours, obscured by the *gorann*, know that I will not allow you to act against Atlantis."

The other swelled with wrath. "You! You are only a stain. You are nothing, fallen! You will end like your friends of Mu and I will get rid of you once and for all. You're finished," the words came out of the mouth of the Translator of Light with twisted and overlapping sounds, the *Orichalcum* sullying his metallic teeth.

From a handful of yards away, Helena watched the seesaw swaying of the innocuous red petal, moving closer to the machine of Atlantis.

"I could not get rid of you once, but now the judgment of the judges hangs over you. And I won't wait for the verdict to see you burn in the sacred fire of Father Gorann!" he shouted.

Suddenly the petal took speed, driven by a strong and sudden gust of wind, and slipped with surgical precision in the throat of the Translator of Light, who had not even noticed it. The slim body of the telluric was shaken by a brutal attack of a hoarse and metallic cough, which immediately transformed into a subtle and aphonic whistle. Helena called Trummugan's attention.

Amin, suspicious, looked behind him, toward the rock spur that stood at the back of the emporium, listening to the barely perceptible vibration, hidden by the most imposing one produced by the Atlantean machine.

Sitting on the rock, overlooking the beach, Amin saw the Veined. Almost as invisible as he was dark, the warrior of the *Arkanum* looked like the statue of a gothic cathedral. From his pale hand, pushed by a breath, rose petals flew.

"The Death Dance..." the Hound muttered.

The Translator of the Light could not ingest anything that came from Mother Earth, and the Venatus knew this. They were able to kill every living thing with a single, precise attack.

Fidias collapsed on his knees, suffocating.

A glow darted over the beach and then plunged into a blaze of phosphorescent symbols over the Atlantean machine. With a single stroke, charged with a fall of twenty yards, a second Venatus sliced off the snout of the pseudo-technological object and beheaded the Translator of Light. The vehicle collapsed into the water, releasing iridescent fluids. The body of Fidias and his head sank separately into the black sea.

The Venatus made a further, extraordinary leap, breaking the Seven Orders in a blaze of waves of *keh* that shook the Essence of the Woken ones.

Amin rushed to Trummugan, hurriedly handing him Cornelius' ring. Then he activated the pseudo-interface. The *Orichalcum* armour of the Shadow Hounds enveloped him and two thundering blades of electric *gorann* appeared in his hands. "Use the Ancient Knowledge. Only Cornelius can save your people," he told the giant, preparing for the attack. The vibrations of the *keh* superimposed, forming a harmony that was the prelude to a clash between the Woken.

Two powerful beams of light exploded from the sea, petrifying the waves, then breaking them like they were ice. A dull rumble, followed by a low and jarring note, pierced the night sky just as Trummugan pushed Helena, Shaun and Enish into the hinterland.

All the artificial lights of the town went off.

"Get out of here," the giant ordered them. "Ghenos Knights!" But a compressed wave of icy water, launched at very high speed, overwhelmed them, throwing them into the wet sand.

It had begun.

Amin barely avoided the first blow of the Venatus, carried with an ancient eastern sword, and at the same time engaged the other *Arkanum* warrior that had attacked him, generating a sand vortex thanks to the "Moto" Order. Knowing that he couldn't face two such enemies, he immediately called the shadows to him, disappearing and then reappearing the next moment on the edge of the rock that overlooked the beach, about twenty yards higher.

A hoarse, hissing sound made the grains of sand jump. From the sea came a whistle, followed by a deafening pop. A fuzzy ball of air, so compressed as to become solid, carved the water surface separating it in two jagged flaps. One of the Venatus was hit and his legs were torn away, making him spin in midair like a rag doll.

The other performed a rotation and mysterious symbols blazed on his arms. The edge of the rock on which Amin stood shivered and shattered, but the Hound exploited his agility to move on the still solid parts. From above, he could see the blaze coming from Helena's Magnum .357 in the direction of the beach. The claws of four imposing armours, humped and harmonious, had sunk in the soft sand. Their complex and disjointed structure sent shimmering reflections sparkling and their appearance, limping yet fluid, was barely distinguishable. The policewoman pulled out the cartridge and reloaded. She didn't really believe she could make a difference, but couldn't just stand there either.

One of those strange armours, partly anthropomorphic, seemed to move back a step, then the face faded and long rows of crystalline teeth revealed a sort of mouth opened in a silent cry. Helena felt a sudden sadness, and her mind conjured the image of a tiger, caged, pacing back and forth with his vacant eyes.

Like a runaway horse being tamed, the creature-armour was dominated by his own knight, who managed to regain control of the Essence trapped in the pseudo-crystal, the marvellous object shone in the centre of the Ghenos' chest.

The Venatus took advantage of that moment of uncertainty, charging with his sword, the mighty Atlantean armour three times his size. Sand turbines rose up behind the hunter as his speed increased, driven by the Moto Order. When he stopped suddenly, the particles hid him from the sight of his opponents and, just at the moment in which a second Ghenos spun one of his clawed arms against him, the Venatus jumped high above his target.

Helena followed the hunter rising elegantly into the cloud, then falling back with an impossible movement against his goal.

"The dance of Death…" Shaun said softly. Then his eyes widened. "He wants to break the pseudo-crystal!" An acute cry shook the world.

The Venatus had pierced the Ghenos at the exact moment in which the dazzling crystal was exposed. The atmospheric pressure decreased and a luminous circle expanded from the armour.

A white light of unimaginable intensity dazzled the night. They all tried to shield their eyes and, in that storm of sounds, light and vibrations, Helena thought she had seen the outline of an immense and winged creature dissolving in the sky like a stain. On the ground lay the corpse of a woman dressed in a dark suit, bathed in a steaming liquid.

The tiger broke free, thought the woman.

The Venatus dodged a new clawed slash, which ripped the air with a grim sound, while another Ghenos Knight stretched forward one of his disjointed arms. The forearm gave way to a triangular mouth of fire, from which luminous particles formed a sphere as big as a cannonball. It was made up by the folding of the Seven Orders through pseudo-technology, and was shot at the Venatus, but missed, throwing into the air tonnes of sand and creating a crater of sufficient size to hold a small car.

Amin jumped off the rock and was greeted on the counterattack by the other soldier of the *Arkanum*.

How is it possible? thought Helena, half-covered with sand, dragged back by Enish. They were now sheltered under the rock. *I saw him fall to the ground, halved!*

On his legs, and against every physical law, the hunter had run vertically on the rock face, then leapt to intercept the Shadow Hound in flight. The two had fallen to the ground and were now getting up. Amin seemed to have felt the impact and was shaking his head, dazed. The Venatus, however, had not even collided with the ground that his limbs were getting ready to throw him against his hated enemy. When Amin's pure *gorann* blades stopped the two half-moons, their steel bodies blazed with symbols. The Venatus screamed in fury and began to alternate powerful blows on Amin, who had received his opponent still on his knees. The Hound was succumbing.

If this was not enough, bursts of lightning of an unnatural green precipitated from the sky, piercing everything they hit like huge drops of acid rain. The first structures to be destroyed were the bar and the pier with some of the boats, including Abriaros' Betty.

Dark shadows hovered over the town, darting those blinding destroyers everywhere. The gas pipelines, cars and everything containing explosive substances exploded, transforming the peaceful provincial town into a hell. Other armours, different from those that had come out from the sea, rained from the sky, landing with a crash on the road not far from the beach. They were black and thin. The screams of those who had not yet managed to escape rose up, torn and desperate. The situation was failing.

Only then did Helena realise that Trummugan was heading for the store while iridescent blows and explosions of light darted all around him.

"Let's take Andrew away!" she screamed at Enish.

The man gestured to Shaun. They rushed out in a desperate race, passing behind the engulfed bar and up towards a side alley, avoiding the main road. There were no lights apart from those of the screaming fires.

Meanwhile, the Venatus who had attacked the Ghenos Knights continued to engage the three mighty opponents, dodging their attacks with impossible movements and slashing with the sword, a weapon in appearance completely unsuitable against such titans. And all the while, he laughed.

The other Venatus sought an opening in Amin's guard until their weapons got stuck into the other. Their faces were close, only a few inches between them. The wrinkles in the skin of the immortal branched into an expression of hatred that challenged the perfect face of the struggling Atlantean.

"The Source awaits you, son of Evenor," he whispered.

Amin saw the two rounded blades moving closer and closer to his neck. "You are fighting your ally, hunter," he replied, knowing that his words would be broken against a wall of contempt that had lasted for one hundred and twenty centuries.

"The Mother will rejoice with us tonight for the disappearance of so many Atlanteans!" The eyes of the Venatus shone and an aura of light exploded on his face. The force he impressed on the blades increased to excess, becoming irrepressible. Amin could not oppose him. So he decided to disarm the pseudo-interface instead. The Hound's armour dissolved and the two shining blades of gorann disappeared. At the same time this happened, he used the weight of his body to fall backwards, and the half-moons of the Venatus closed themselves like shears, marking his jaw with two deep cuts instead of cutting off his head. The Venatus fell on him and Amin grabbed him, holding on. Then he reactivated the pseudo-interface, ordering the *Orichalcum* to extrude itself, impaling the Venatus repeatedly. The hunter groaned and his eyes widened. The Hound rolled, moving the enemy's body in his place. Anyone would have died, but it took much more to kill a Venatus. To defeat him, Amin had to hit the symbiotic creature that made him immortal, the ancient sacred worm Hirshammag.

So he redirected all the *Orichalcum* he possessed to form a single pulsing, purple energy spear and invoked the "Structure" Order so that the living metal flowed into every corner of the body of his enemy. Then he hit him in the centre of his chest with all his strength. The hunter's body flushed with iridescent fire, writhing, held on the ground by the weight of the Shadow Hound.

When the *Orichalcum* went out, Amin saw that the body was that of a young boy. This made no difference to the eyes of Atlantean: a Venatus was only partially human. And he had killed a Venatus.

He couldn't have known that burned and blackened body, now devoid of Essence, had belonged to a boy just a little older than a child, impetuous and full of rage. A passionate boy who had tried to protect his friend Adam. A young man who had sacrificed his life to enter the Venatus clan and avenge his Mother Earth. He was called Kyle.

Amin stood up, staggering.

All around the battle raged.

40

Everything was in ruins, consumed in the flames of destruction. The building Abriaros had taken Andrew to still resisted; the symbols on its door that recalled most of the Seven Orders of creation blazed with a rainbow of lights, preventing the besieging forces from entering and attacks to cause extensive damage. The wood of the building had absorbed their supernatural properties. The doors were impenetrable for anyone with evil intentions, and even the glass could resist the devastating blows. But they would not hold up indefinitely.

Abriaros leaned over Andrew, taking his hand, hoping to see his sad face come back to life. He had imagined that the *Arkanum* had intervened to stir up the millenarian hatred that ran between Mu and Atlantis, but there was nothing he could do about it just now. In its Woken mind he had full awareness that there was a sense in everything, and he hoped that the suffering would be the beginning of a new path. He also wanted to recall the Order "Mystery" to have access to future events, but preferred to focus only on Andrew.

Who was this Sleeper who had become the centre of the millennial war between the forces of Mother Earth and those of selfish and rebellious men? There were too many elements circling around him. A complex branching of wills, expectations and destiny, unmistakable signs of the power of Existence that converged towards that helpless Sleeper, unlike anyone else born in the Oblivion after the Great Gorann.

Adam had seen something in Andrew that was foreclosed even to the giants or the Naacals themselves. *We must save this boy and allow him to fulfil his destiny, he thought. Their link will reveal the will of the Mother.*

A strong impact hit the window, the same one which only the day before they had looked at the lighthouse that shone in the calm night. The beastly face of Ahiga appeared there, worn-out. Blood dripped from where one of his ears had been cut off and the hair was burned.

"Brother!" said the Naacal approaching.

"Relax. We goot here," the Sikal sighed in pain. "But no too long."

Abriaros put his hand on the glass and Ahiga placed over his own. "Stand strong. Trummugan will find a solution."

Suddenly, the Sikal dodged to the side and a greenish bolt hit the glass in a hot crash, loaded with green electricity. Then Ahiga reappeared. "Yzenn say Shaun and others come from back way."

"Trummugan will find a solution," Abriaros repeated.

Ahiga ran his tongue over his bleeding nose. "No matter. Think of boy. We think way reteem us for Adam no protecting. Andriu we save," he said, and then jumped off the window.

Frantic steps behind the door. Enish, Helena and Shaun, came in out of breath.

"They are destroying everything," Helena said. "We can't oppose an army."

"It's the end!" cried Shaun.

"The end is only the beginning," replied old Abriaros.

Another wave reached the building, penetrating the wall of the studio and the corridor, throwing crazy wood splinters everywhere. One of the Ghenos armour capable of flying rushed inside. An oblong head slipped into the opening, his four disarticulating limbs tearing at the scaffolding as if it was cardboard. When he had created a gap of a couple of feet, he found his targets. His belly split into parts, revealing a hexagonal mouth of fire, which began to shine with a powerful green light. Enish hugged Helena to protect her, but the fireball that emerged from the Ghenos passed over their heads with a vibrating hiss.

Yzenn had jumped onto the back of the exoskeleton, causing him to lose balance. The Sikal grabbed the head of the armour between his clawed hands and began to bite at the joint of the neck, his teeth screeching on the pseudo-technological material.

"In the study!" Abriaros shouted.

"He'll get himself killed!" Helena replied.

The Ghenos Knight reared up his armoured mount and Yzenn took advantage of that movement to slip on his chest, hanging from his head with his jaws. The weight of the shivak made the Atlantean lose his already precarious balance and both fell, breaking through the now arched floorboards all the way to the foundation of the house. Shaun fell into the chasm with a scream.

Enish shoved Helena into the study and threw himself into the void that was once the stairs.

"Enish!" she cried. The structure of the building began to tremble, shaken by powerful vibrations. "We need to do something!" she then said to the Naacal.

"Everything has a reason, sister."

Helena looked into Abriaros' eyes, seeing in him a fatalism, a faith, an awareness she could not name. "You called me sister…"

"You are here with us. As a sister would be."

Helena nodded.

The structure of the building was yielding. The windows in the room exploded into a million pieces and a giant air bubble poured into the living room. A large portion of the outer wall crumbled, leaving the room exposed. White and opalescent small hands climbed up the building, appearing in the cracks caused by the explosion. Numerous faces, pale and vitreous looking, searched the room for Andrew. The first mayaurlo to spot him gave a cry. He took only two steps when his head exploded, like a crushed orange.

"Good," Helena said, covered in soot and glass splinters, holding her gun firmly in her hands. "I found someone who likes it."

Tens and dozens of mayaurli opened their circular mouths and gave a choral bark, launching an attack. The policewoman fired again and again, breaking down the strange child-like creatures, even piercing two or three at a time so delicate was their skin, until the gun gave the unmistakable click. She was out of bullets.

The mayaurli continued to increase in number. They were now on her. Abriaros was on the ground, unconscious. Or dead. *It's over*, thought Helena.

She saw two of them jumping at her, eyes bulging. She got ready to receive them with her bare hands, but just when they were a few inches away, the creatures of Belial bounced backwards. As more came in, they trampled on the bodies indifferently, cramming on each other in a pile of writhing albino meat, moaning with anger. They could not overcome what looked like an invisible wall.

Helena fell, scampering back towards the bed.

"There is no wall," mumbled Andrew, "if not in their mind. As it is for the Sleepers, for the creatures plagued by Belial's thirst for power, there are insurmountable obstacles, created by their own minds." The boy had a vague look, as if he was immersed in thoughts that held him far from that place. From his chest radiated a multicoloured, intense and crackling glow which seemed to support him, almost lifting him off the bed.

Somehow, Helena left the amazement aside and reloaded her Magnum. She began to shoot. The mayaurli fell on each other, spraying green blood. The screaming creatures shuddered, fleeing like a compact and fluid mass.

"Andy, are you okay?" she asked, turning to him.

The boy fell back on the bed, confused. When he saw the Naacal, however, he rushed to his side. "Abriaros?" he called, trying to remove the rubble that had collapsed on him. The man coughed.

There was an explosion outside. The flower shop and the house of Lerner and Anna no longer existed.

"Let's get out of here!" Helena said, helping Andrew lift the old man.

Abriaros looked at the boy. "You finally woke up!" he said, catching his breath.

Andrew hugged him. "You're too old for these things."

"Mother doesn't think so…"

Andy grinned.

When they reached the chasm in the corridor, they had to lower themselves down through the stairwell void, burdened the weight of the Naacal, who was struggling to keep up with them. Of the ground floor, only the battered outer walls remained. There was no sign of the Ghenos Knight, Yzenn or Enish. Under a pile of rubble, though, they found a lifeless body.

"Oh God!" Helena cried.

Abriaros approached, caressing the bookseller's hair. "Shaun, my brother… Now that you are back to the Source of all life, shine in it. Now that you're one with 'All that is', let the awareness of what you have been fill the creatures that still have to be. In them I will see you again and the fruit of what has generated you. You lived a unique and unrepeatable existence and I was lucky to share my life with yours. In the endless life, I see you."

They didn't speak further. They left from the back of the building, using the secondary roads — now also prey to the destruction of Atlantis — to avoid being seen.

There were corpses everywhere, charred and torn apart. Some of them were the same citizens who had welcomed Andrew just a few weeks ago. But there were others too. Without a doubt, the mayaurli had fallen in great numbers during the clash. There was no trace of the other Sikal.

They crossed the primary school garden, a dismal museum of molten games from which rose black burnt plastic smoke. The smell was unbearable. Arriving at the top of a staircase descending between two battered buildings, Abriaros stopped.

"Once down, we have to cross the street and the square in front of the church," he said, pointing to an open space dotted with the wreckage of burning cars. "We have to run, as we will be exposed. If I linger, don't slow down but reach the wall at the bottom. Behind it, there is an uncultivated land that slopes down to the beach, below the rocky ridge. Trummugan will be there."

"Don't even think about it!" Helena replied. "We'll not leave you here."

"We cannot afford to risk everyone's life because of me."

"In that case, we will follow the rules of the Sleepers. The first to start is the slowest one. You will go first, then Andrew and I will follow you, all right?"

"Good idea," agreed the boy.

The Naacal sighed. "Agreed."

They made it to the last step, watchful. In front of them, on the opposite side of the road, a woman and her child walked on quietly, through the silent rubble. In the little boy's eyes were only fear and confusion.

There was nothing they could do for them. Helena motioned for Abriaros to cross the street, which he did, leaning against a small wall to catch his breath. He passed it, crossed the square and reached the opposite side, almost disappearing from view.

Following the footsteps of the Naacal, the other two quickly crossed the road and, without stopping, zigzagged among the car, in the direction of the church.

Suddenly, the armour rained down from the sky with a thud, crushing a car in a cloud of a thousand sparks. The opalescent and black material of which it was made reflected the fire that burned all around, giving it a diabolical appearance. Two thin, featherless wings vibrated like the strings of a guitar, drawing a haunting halo on his back. The Ghenos Knight got off the flattened car, the short frontal limbs gathering near the chest. Circling them with his head down, as if it were an animal rather than a machine, he studied the two targets.

Helena went for her gun but Andrew stopped her. "It won't work," he told her, as he followed the ten foot tall giant.

The armour performed a quarter of a turn around them before making a dull and metallic ticking noise. Then he raised his oblong head, as if listening to the sky.

Helena and Andrew saw numerous Ghenos rising in the air to disappear in the direction of the sea with incredible agility and speed. The one before them returned to watch them. They had barely time to see that his long limbs had increased the velocity of their vibration when the vortex generated swept them away. The armour leapt, froze in the air for a moment then followed the others, propelled at very low altitude. It passed right over Abriaros and disappeared into the darkness.

"What happened?" Helena asked.

"Looks like they've been recalled," Andrew said.

Abriaros seemed confused. "Something happened in the living keh. The return of someone who they thought had been erased. I don't understand, but it is clear that the Keizer has ordered the retreat of the Ghenos Knights. Perhaps there is still hope. Let's reach Trummugan, now."

Climbing over the wall, they slid into the wide unkept land that sloped down toward the beach.

41

The Venatus still alive was dripping blood. The holy worm Hirshammag held him up, despite having suffered injuries that no ordinary man could have borne. He spat on the sand a mixture of bluish mucus, surrounded by the three remaining armours that stood on top of him with their terrible weapons.

"Ah! Three murmodna for only one hunter. Our war is already won!" he smirked.

The Ghenos loaded their mounts and the triangular fire mouths blazed with compressed air. The hunter prepared for the counter-attack when suddenly they stopped. The explosive energy flaked like smoke, and the titans remained motionless. The Venatus turn on himself, observing his enemies, ready to take advantage of the distraction.

"Enough!" cried Amin. "It is over. Atlantis withdraws."

Kill the Atlantean! The order arrived peremptorily into the mind of the Venatus.

Streaks of a green glow darted toward the sea. It was the retreating Ghenos. Just before blocking the armours thanks his superior Purity, Amin had perceived a precise order of the Keizer, as all Atlanteans with pseudo-technological systems would have. Immediate withdrawal. He hoped the reason had something to do with Trummugan.

The Venatus approached the Hound, cleaning the sword on his thigh. *Kill the Atlantean. Avenge the Mother.* The voice was strong in his head.

"This battle is over, hunter," Amin said, hoping to breach the human side of his opponent. He couldn't fight anymore and the *Orichalcum* was draining him of his living *keh*. "Atlantis has been misled," he continued.

The Venatus answered by pulling out a shorter blade that he kept in his own body, as if it were a sheath. "I see only three targets at a disadvantage. As for you, filthy fallen, you're losing your strength with every passing moment, I can feel it. While I regain them." A golden aura appeared behind the hunter's head and his eyes gleamed.

"Who do you think stopped the Ghenos, if not me?" said the Hound, gathering from the ground one of the half moons that Kyle had used to attack him. "You are controlled by a lower creature who uses you as the Atlanteans use the living *keh* to generate their armour. Take control of yourself again; be human!"

The Venatus slashed forward, but Amin blocked it. Laughing, he parried another single hit. Then came the third one. The Hound was playing with him.

"It does not matter to me if you live," Amin insisted. "But let me warn you. The moment I should distract myself from the *gorann*, the armours will come back into operation and for you it will be the end."

Avenge the Mother, the voice insisted.

Fast and terrifying, the Venatus slipped under the guard of the Hound, avoiding the half moon with his short blade and sinking the sword into the opponent's chest. The centenarian tip pierced the skin, but stopped, producing a vibration that almost pulled his weapon from the hunter's hands. The *Orichalcum*'s shield concentrated around Amin's heart had held, the hit blocked.

Long purple striations ran through the hands and neck of the Shadow Hound. With a sidestep, Amin broke the blade, which shattered, then hit his enemy on the breastbone, recalling the Order 'Death' at the limit of its capabilities. The Venatus crashed to the ground.

It was true that nobody wanted to clash with a hunter, just as it was true one should be ready for such an unfortunate eventuality. So Amin had exploited the 'Death' Order to dilate the effect of his stroke in time, which continued to inflict pain on his adversary, depriving him of his strength for the time necessary to finish it. Because 'Death' meant 'Time'. And time was all he needed right now.

As soon as his attention wavered, the armours shook from their stillness, emitting a guttural sound similar to that of whales, but hoarse and out of tune. "Knights!" Amin called the powerful armours. "You have received an order. Do not make me fight against you. When Atlantis fights against itself, we break the Code of the One. When we pour our pure blood, or we take action against the Great Intention, we break it. And without code, we are like the people of Mu, deprived of humanity."

One of the armour stepped toward him, assuming an even more hunched appearance. The snout disarranged into parts, revealing a first row of teeth from which condensation escaped, as if the armour itself breathed. Then the teeth also moved backward, and between the folds of metal as soft as flesh, the face of a dark-skinned man appeared, embellished by golden decorations. Between his lips he had a bite endowed with silver fins, the echo-tympanum with which he governed the *keh* of the creature contained in the pseudo-crystal.

"Demitrion!" said Amin, surprised.

"Commander Setiana," he greeted him.

A shiver ran through him as he heard the greeting. Remembering that he was now a fallen, ostracised without rights, the Hound looked down. "Noble knight, I am grateful to you for executing the commands of your Kaizer and defending Atlantis once again. Now I beg you to bring your phalanx back into the shugan, as you have been ordered."

The Ghenos exchanged vibrations mixed with whipping moans. One of the murmodna moved, lifting the corpse of the woman torn by the Venatus, and went back into the water. The other grabbed with the long skeletal claws the strange machine that had led Fidias to the beach, dragging it back into the sea.

Demitrion's armour rose up. "Even if you're a fallen and you'll never come back to lead us," he said, "for me and for our phalanx you are still a commander of Atlantis. If we had to attack you, know that we would have done it with heartfelt sadness."

The Hound dared return the Ghenos Knight's gaze, nodding in silence.

"Atlantis reigns," added Demitrion.

"Atlantis reigns," Amin replied, looking at the snout of the armour recomposing and the knight leading it among the dark waves.

Silence fell.

The Venatus was still on the ground, but it was already giving signs of movement. And he would strike again. The Atlantean moved to finish him.

"Amin, no!" Trummugan stopped him, approaching him from behind. "There's no need."

The Hound, exhausted, formed a spear of *Orichalcum* charged with Essence, which glowed in his hands. "There's no way to stop a Venatus," he replied.

"There wasn't a way to stop the battle either," replied the giant. With a firm gesture, he turned the Atlantean away, who didn't even have the strength to react, and bent over the Venatus, still trying to get up. By mixing a transparent substance between the fingers, he spread it on the forehead and on the chest of the hunter who looking at him, dazed. "Mother is proud of you. Now you can go back to rest," he whispered. A blue haze lifted from the substance and the boy's eyes took on an innocent expression. The fearsome warrior returned to lay on the sand and curled up, falling asleep. "The *Arkanum* will get you soon."

Amin collapsed, sitting on the ground. "You understood what I meant when I gave you the ring, then."

"I am a Milesian," answered the giant. "We built those rings."

They heard footsteps approaching.

"Are you okay?" Helena asked, panting.

"Yes. The town?" Trummugan asked worriedly.

Abriaros shook his head. "A disaster. The Sleepers have paid a very high price." He took a moment. "Shaun has returned to the Source, brother."

The giant shook his head. "All this could have been avoided."

Andrew pointed to the mainland, his tired eyes looking more alive. Enish and Yzenn were helping Ahiga to walk, and proceeded towards them. They met a few yards from the store, one of the few buildings left intact.

Helena hugged Enish. And, after a moment of uncertainty, she also hugged the Sikals.

"Are you alright?" Andrew asked Ahiga, covered in bleeding wounds and purple bruises. The Sikal grunted something in a strange language, then added, "Suffer I. Good for me have sugar."

"What happened?" asked Enish, clearly in pain from his deep head wound. "At one point they stopped attacking and just… left."

"Difficult to say and rather than not," the giant replied. "When Atlantis attacked, Amin gave me a seal of Life. Every Nephilim passes from life to life through a sacred object, since the time of the Great Gorann. The ring contained the living *keh* of Cornelius, who sits to the right of Prince Here."

"I found that ring on a Sleeper ship," Amin added. "A secret Nephilim council had gathered there, but a trap had been set against them and against me. They were all killed and their seals broken. They accused me of being the executioner and the court trusted the Translators of Light. That's why Fidias was sent as a messenger."

Enish intervened. "You mean that there are no more Nephilim? Atlantis is in the hands of the tellurics?"

"One of them still exists," Trummugan answered. "Cornelius' seal was scratched, but still intact. Despite being worked through the *gorann*, those seals are in fact the work of the Thuata de Danann. Through a forgotten ritual of Ancient Knowledge, I tried to free the Essence of Cornelius. Shortly thereafter, Atlantis withdrew."

"I know what happened," the Hound said. "Cornelius' *keh* was attracted to the first pseudo-technological apparatus it found, the engine of the shugan. The Essence of a Nephilim is linked to the *gorann*. Taking advantage of the energy field created by the machine to bind reality, he has prevented the call to return to the Source."

"Incredible!" said Enish.

"It's terrible," added Abriaros. "But it doesn't explain why the Keizer has withdrawn his troops."

"It makes sense, actually," Amin continued. "The complex system that powers the shugan by exploiting Essence, the constrictor, acted as a sounding board, expanding the *keh* of Cornelius throughout the machine. This phenomenon is well known among our people and is called 'solo'. In the mind of the crew, and therefore also in that of the Keizer, the Awareness, or part of it, of what Cornelius knew and knows."

"My head is spinning," Helena said.

"At that point," concluded the Atlantean, "there were no longer any conditions for the Keizer to understand what was right or wrong, so he decided to stop the attack. Furthermore, perceiving the powerful essence of the Nephilim, Daimantis could not help but follow the Code of the One: Cornelius has a level of Purity a thousand times greater than a Keizer, and his commands become like those of the prince, in his absence."

"So it was Cornelius that halted the attack," Abriaros said. "And why should he do it?"

"Because he knows more than we do," replied Trummugan thoughtfully. "Because he wants to grant Amin his rightful redemption. And because he wants the dark forces that are threatening Atlantis to be stopped. If necessary, with the help of Mu."

"Are you saying that Cornelius is willing to support Adam's search by defending whoever wants him found, whether it be the people of Mu or Atlantis?" suggested Abriaros.

"This seems his plan," the giant commented.

The Hound nodded. "Cornelius is wise. It will give us enough time to find the boy again, whoever he is."

"What do we do now?" Helena asked.

"We need to choose the path to follow, taking advantage of the confusion of those plotting against Adam and beating them by being quicker. We play on equal terms. It will be a contest between Woken ones, in a world of Sleepers. And this is only the beginning."

"First of all, let's take care of the people of this town," added Abriaros. "Let's give them hope for the future."

"It is right," said the Milesian, supported by the others.

"I have to tell you something important," Andrew cut in.

They all turned to him. A gust of wind blew into the sky, thinning the frayed clouds and revealing the stars, giving them once again the memory of the immensity of the Universe.

The boy breathed deeply, carefully considering his words. Then he decided that the best solution was simplicity. "I think I know how to find Adam."

42

Light.

For the first time in days, they pulled the black hood off his head. Around his neck, arms and ankles were dozens of ropes and chains, from which all kinds of fetishes, amulets and effigies of the strangest forms hung. He was sure those unfamiliar symbols, written in a language he didn't know, had been painted on his body, even on his private parts. Everywhere. He knew he had to stay calm, removing negative thoughts and fears; relying on what he knew of the world of those Sleepers who called themselves Enlightened.

The thick scent of wood which had filled him since he had been thrown roughly into the hall came from the large chimney built into the opposite wall, in which a fireplace crackled. The boy rubbed his eyes, tired of the darkness. High windows let in snow reflections produced outside the room of this great Nordic mansion. Frescoes and tapestries showed off their beauty on the walls. The environment was built with stone and wood, with colossal wooded beams supporting the ceiling at least fifty feet high. A balustrade ran through the entire room, where about twenty armed individuals controlled the prisoner.

When his eyes were able to focus again, Adam rubbed his wrists marked by handcuffs. A very long table stretched right in front of his chair, with a dozen people sitting around it. Men, women, old people. Only the crackling of the fire made up the soundtrack to that scene full of people who silently, stared at him.

On the opposite side of the table was an austere-looking man with white frizzy hair tastefully combed and dressed in an elegant dark blue suit. "Welcome, young man," he greeted him ambiguously.

"Where am I?" Adam asked, his mouth thick. "I want to go home."

The man didn't flinch. "Your house no longer exists. It has been destroyed by demons, by the enemy," he explained. "Your new home is here with us."

The boy looked around but said nothing.

"We saved you from those who wanted to kill you; you know that, don't you?"

"Why would anyone want to do something like that?"

"A naive response. Some of us think that the enemy is hunting you because you have qualities they fear, and which could destroy them."

"Who are you?" Adam asked, trying to imitate the cold tone of his interlocutor.

He made a large gesture with his arms. "Ours is a story that begins a long time ago. Since ancient times, man has suffered at the will and the whims of a host of dark creatures, dictators and ruthless demons that affect the fate of the world. These beings appear similar to us, in some cases, but they are not the same as us. They even have superhuman powers and miraculous and terrible technologies, which they have no modesty in using for heinous and sinister purposes, deciding on the life and death of every single creature." The man pointed to some of the oil portraits on the walls, depicting men and women of older times. "One day, a long time ago, exceptional individuals, enlightened by Awareness, rose against this line of monsters. They were our ancestors, able to see beyond appearances, to perceive the dark nature of the enemy through the light. Thus the Enlightened were born, capable to find and fight Evil on its own level, to identify it among the people, to pursue it and destroy it."

The man stopped, and Adam tried to get up and stretch his legs.

The other then got up and put his hands on the shoulders of a young man dressed shabbily, with dishevelled hair and a captivating smile. Then he resumed. "From the secret union of the first Enlightened, the twelve patriarchs were born, our families, each of whom is presided over by three consuls. Each family is divided into suborders and groups, each with an ultra-millennial history. Each with specific skills rooted in society, from where we monitor the activities of the enemy."

The man ran his hands over the shoulders of an elderly woman, covered with jewels and furs, her gaze cold. "In front of you, today, are the representatives of all the families of the Enlightened, who together form the two empires of the Sword and the Compass. The first, military force. The second, knowledge. United together, they become one body, one *unicum*, the light that sweeps away the demonic world. The only one who can bring the enemy to the final battle."

Adam listened in silence, scared. He didn't know if anyone there was able to perceive his *keh*, kept dormant as he did in dangerous situations. But as long as this Enlightened continued that apparent game of cat and mouse, he decided he would not provide him any foothold. So he silently held the gaze of that table of human beings self-referenced and full of pride, convinced to possess the key to all knowledge.

"Have I answered your question, young man?"

"I'm not sure I understood everything. I am confused."

"It's natural. You yourself ignore the reason as to why they have rallied against you and it is indeed for this reason that we decided to risk so much in taking you before the irreparable damage happened. From now on we will protect you and take care of you. But you must help us."

"I don't know how…"

"You will only have to answer the questions we will ask you, with sincerity. We will draw conclusions."

The others nodded.

Adam didn't have much choice. "All right," he said softly.

The large, studded door behind him opened and a squat man came in, dressed in a jacket laden with snow and a black turtleneck sweater. He had a disproportionate jaw, his face parched from frost and a taurine neck. Two other individuals followed him, sharing with the first the clothing and a certain absent look. "*Semper in fulgore sed nihil fulgore timenti*," he said entering.

Everyone present stood up from their tall chairs.

"This is Captain Marcus," the man explained to the prisoner. "He and his Karman warriors will be your personal guard and they will follow you at all times." Then he approached the boy, staring at him. "I understand how you must feel, Adam. There will also be a time to answer your numerous questions, don't worry. But not now. If the enemy hunts you down as we believe, we will use every means in our possession to trap the demons in such a way they will not be able to escape, thus fulfilling the Armageddon prophecy. You maybe be the means by which humanity will be freed from obscurity. Be proud. Today a new hope is born!" he said to the room, shaking the chair where Adam was seated.

Mu's young man looked around, confused, trying to take on an expression as naive as possible.

Marcus helped him up.

"Now go," said the white-haired man with the elegant dress. "Maybe we'll meet again one day, or maybe not. But always remember the fundamental principle of the Enlightened and make it yours: the sacrifice of a few, for the salvation of all."

The Karman warriors accompanied Adam out of the hall, and the doors closed behind them.

The dishevelled-looking young man hoisted himself up and lit a cigarette, adjusting his puffed-up hair. "Impressive," he said.

The man gave him a condescending look. "What do you mean, consul Faust of the family Elanduck?"

"Nothing. I really hope the plan of the revered Elmuth family doesn't take us to the brink of a new catastrophe," he said, spitting a piece of tobacco.

"The consuls voted for this plan unanimously, may I remind you."

Faust smiled, sarcastically. "Not everybody."

"The Elanduck must abide by the law of empires, like other families. It is useless to sow further controversy. Everything is established."

"We are not against the plan. We just think that bringing the kid here was not a good idea."

"Do what you must. Or remain silent."

"Consul Edgard," Faust replied, mockingly, "remember the saying: no one moves a leaf that Elanduck does not want to!" And he burst out laughing.

The other sighed, inflexible. "This meeting is adjourned. Return to your strongholds and let's get ready to act. The enemy will not wait."

*

The swirling helicopter blades raised icy clouds of snow from the grey landing square. All around the gigantic northern mansion, there was nothing but trees as far as the eye could see. High mountains loomed on the horizon, far away.

Marcus invited Adam to get onto the vehicle and helped him fasten his seatbelts. One of his two companions closed the hatch and the sound of the rotors became a swollen and muffled whirlwind that enveloped the large cabin.

A man covered with a long, dark fur coat approached from the outside. Adam had noticed him standing there, so much so he had thought he was going to climb too. But he didn't. Squinting, the man bent his head for a few seconds. Then he broke a sort of stick he had in his hands and placed the stumps on the car body, moving the lips as if in prayer.

A slight vibration struck the boy's Essence. That strange guy was working through the Four Forces in a way that was unknown to him. Yet he was not a Woken or a Roused one, of this he was certain.

When he was gone, walking backwards, Marcus nodded to the pilot.

The blades turned faster and the helicopter lifted gracefully from the ground.

Who were the Enlightened really? Adam was amazed. He had discovered a completely different world of Sleepers, beyond his expectations. He knew he didn't have much time, and sooner or later they would know who he was. Abriaros' teachings returned vividly to his mind as he watched the tundra slide past him below.

There was a meaning for everything.

A meaning he should not need to understand. Not as much as a guy with curly hair and a long nose, gentle and with a big heart. A saviour of lizards.

Andrew, Adam thought. *I'm waiting for you.*

Epilogue

Being fourteen years old is difficult for everyone.

Not for the problems of growth, or the new neuronal connections that bloom like mushrooms in a wood inside the head of a teenager. And not even for the hormonal upheaval that causes so many incredible transformations in body and mind.

For Andrew Fawcett, the most difficult reality to deal with had been the inability to express his thoughts, too big and uncertain, like musical scores with blurry edges, forced to be played by cans of canned beans; unsuitable instruments to convey a song as supreme as the one he had inside him.

Every fourteen year old would have liked to have this faculty of expression, but there was always a feeling of not having enough time to travel a long and unknown way. That a whole life, seen from the bottom of his fourteen years, was too short if conceived as a repetition of duties towards parents or the boss, towards a wife, or towards unborn children.

In one thing, however, Andrew Fawcett differed from most of his peers. To him, one chance of escape had been given.

Now the Mother looked at him and a part of Her immense focus was dedicated to that single, bright dot that walked on Her face, tired but amused. And full of hope. Fatigued, she struggled to survive the continuous attacks against Her.

That moment of distraction She had allowed Herself, which contained the possibility of living a fulfilled, complex and extraordinary destiny, different from that of infinite other creatures, born then disappeared over billions of years. A destiny to be shared with a brother named Adam. A special destiny.

Discover New Fantasy

at

www.lunapresspublishing.com

www.ingramcontent.com/pod-product-compliance
Lightning Source LLC
Chambersburg PA
CBHW050839190726
48286CB00007B/2147